The Ice Margin

a novel by

MARCIA WOODRUFF DALTON

D1407573

Fleur-de-Lis Press   Louisville, Kentucky   *2010*

Author's Note

The epigraphs at the beginning of each chapter are taken from *These Fragile Outposts: A Geological Look at Cape Cod, Martha's Vineyard, and Nantucket,* by Barbara Blau Chamberlain, published in 1964 by the Natural History Press, Garden City, New York, and used by permission of the author.

Printed in the United States of America
First Edition

Library of Congress Cataloging-in-Publication Data
Dalton, Marcia Woodruff
The Ice Margin
1. Title
Library of Congress Control Number: 2010920892
ISBN: 978-0-9773861-5-4

Cover photo: "Summer Sunrise, Barnstable Harbor"
by Marcia Woodruff Dalton

Book design by Jonathan Weinert
Printing by Thomson-Shore of Michigan

Fleur-de-Lis Press of *The Louisville Review*
Spalding University
851 S. Fourth St.
Louisville, KY 40203

502.585.9911, ext. 2777
louisvillereview@spalding.edu
www.louisvillereview.org

To Ann Creelman Woodruff, who loved this place

Legacy

*Wherever the ice went it rearranged things on the earth
like a dissatisfied housewife.*

THE HOUSE IS right at the center of it. I want it, and Gregory doesn't.
Did Aunt Phoebe plan to set us at cross-purposes? There were
moments yesterday and today I would swear she was still there, that I
would find her at the scarred old kitchen table warming her hands around
a mug of tea, or hear the soft shuffle of her ancient lamb's wool slippers
in the hall overhead, as if her body were reluctant to relinquish its hold
on the place. And the house, in its turn, has a hold on me I can't explain,
having been there not more than—how many?—five or six times. I felt it
the first time I set foot on the glassed-in porch off the kitchen, cluttered
as it was with old newspapers and outdated magazines, motley collections
of shells and surf-rounded stones brought up from the beach. As if it were
my house. As if I lived there.

Greg doesn't feel that way at all. After the funeral he wouldn't even
sleep in it—it's too cold, he said, and too musty, the bed linen probably full
of mildew, bound to trigger his asthma. As usual I didn't object when he
opted instead for the new Victorian bed and breakfast just past the village,
the sort of place he normally hates, a sentimental fantasy with its sticky-
sweet aroma of scented candles and potpourri, lots of maddening little
pillows piled on the bed, everything covered in ruffles and coordinating
floral patterns. He slept badly in our chintz boudoir, whereas I sank into
unconsciousness and floated up in the morning feeling light, almost giddy,
as on the first day of vacation. It's not having the girls to worry about, not
having to sleep with one ear cocked for the thump or wail, attuned to the
needs of my big, my beloved, my always-to-be helpless daughter.

But Gregory is in a bad mood. Never overtly cranky, he shows his
irritation by making helpful little suggestions: "Anna, shouldn't you wear
a dress to the lawyer's office?" "Do you really want a second muffin when
you're trying so hard to lose ten pounds?" I'm used to these little digs by
now, interpreting them for what they are, a sort of nervous tic, and not, as
I sometimes thought early in our marriage, a puritanical attempt to spoil

all of life's small pleasures. Nevertheless, they sting. My mother was the same way. Sometimes even their words are the same.

It is a day of surprises. The first was finding that the three Boston cousins who showed up at the funeral were there again at the lawyer's office. They greeted Gregory with chilly graciousness, nodding vaguely in my direction. Do they expect to claim an interest in the house? It has come down through Uncle Dennis's family, and as his sister's child, Gregory is the nearest blood relative, the girls the closest thing Aunt Phoebe and Uncle Dennis had to grandchildren. But when the lawyer began reading the will I relaxed; it was just that Aunt Phoebe specified some of her Gardener family mementoes for them: the ancient flintlock rifle and powder horn hanging over the mantel in the parlor, a set of leather-bound medical books belonging to her grandfather, an engraving of the Boston Tea Party.

Demetrius Silva, Aunt Phoebe's handyman, was also there, wearing the same slightly old-fashioned suit he had on at the funeral yesterday. He came back to the house after the burial and stayed longer than anybody, spending most of his time talking quietly at the kitchen table with the neighbor woman with the garden, Mrs. Cole. Something about his manner, both deferential and proprietary, makes me curious, though it irritates Gregory. A dark, quiet man with the grace that comes from no wasted motion. Such an elegant name, Demetrius. Greek. Sounds odd with Silva. That's Portuguese. Practically a member of the family for years, since before Gregory's summers on the Cape, Greg's boss as a matter of fact, ran the cranberry operation for Uncle Dennis, though he couldn't have been very old when he started, in his early twenties at most.

He owns West Marsh now. The year after Uncle Dennis died Aunt Phoebe sold it to him, floating him a loan herself in exchange for work around the house and yard. And now, according to the terms of the will, the remainder of the loan has been forgiven and the bog is his free and clear. I glanced over at Gregory while the lawyer explained the terms. His mouth was set in a line. Calculating the value lost to the estate? Or thinking about the way Aunt Phoebe died? By rights Demetrius should have been the one up on the ladder that day.

But the real surprise was that Aunt Phoebe's house is not going to Gregory after all. It is going into a trust, with the two of us named as trustees, to benefit our elder daughter Dorothea, seventeen years old, beautiful, and for the past five years profoundly brain injured, paralyzed, and mute.

Ah, Aunt Phoebe, Gregory is not pleased. He feels it adds needless complexity. Afterwards, Mr. Flannery gave Gregory a copy of the will and two sealed letters, one for him and one for me, written out in a neat small hand and dated two years ago.

Gregory hands his letter over to me as we pull out of the parking lot. *"Dear Gregory,"* it reads. *"Forgive the whim of an old lady. I know something about wanting to provide for one who needs care and may outlive you. I trust you to find the best way for Dorothea to benefit from the property. And may this in some way settle the past for you."*

"Settle the past—what does that mean?" I ask. He doesn't answer.

I don't offer to read my letter aloud. It is a lot longer and more detailed. *"Dear Anna,"* it says, *"Gregory will want to sell the house and you may agree with him. But before you do, think about summers with the girls here. Wouldn't Dorothea feel happy and safe? However, if the house is to go as I suppose it must, I ask you to sort through my little upstairs office and look over my papers. Anything of historical interest the family doesn't want can go to the Sturgis Library in Barnstable. Not the journal, which I entrust to you. After you have read it I would like it to go to my friend Daphne Ault. And please invite my neighbor Harriet Cole to take anything from the garden she likes. You too, of course. The Siberian iris are a deep indigo and perfectly lovely in late May, and the globe thistles astonish everybody in midsummer if you dare take on anything so prickly.*

Such a magpie I have been! Forgive me for the time and work it will cost you. I ask this because I believe had our lives allowed we would have become fast friends."

All the way back to Needham I am conscious of Aunt Phoebe's letter like a small living animal inside my purse. "What's all that about?" Gregory asks, taking his eyes off the road to glance over as I unfold and read it again for the third or fourth time. I tell him about Aunt Phoebe's wanting me to sort her papers, and about the flowers in the garden, but not about the journal. "She's imposing on you," Gregory says. "You barely knew her. I thought we could just hire someone to hold a sale. The house is so full of stuff. Nothing's been got rid of in forty years. You haven't seen the attic."

I turn to look at his profile, trying to gauge his mood. As always he looks immaculate, his shirt unrumpled, every black hair in place as if just combed. But his eyes are tired, his mouth pressed into a line more grim than exasperated. So often his words and his body language seem at odds with each other. It must have dredged up the past, Aunt Phoebe's funeral, those sad years. And now his last meaningful link to his mother's family is broken.

"Don't you even want to look through and see what's up there?" I ask. "There must be some family things, some furniture or pictures from the Turnstone side. Maybe Lesley would want them someday."

"Don't expect me to spend my weekends driving to Cummaquid and going through it all."

"And there are her papers," I say, feeling defensive, as though she were my aunt and not his. "She asked me to go through them. I wouldn't feel right not doing it. I could take time this spring when it warms up a little." Greg is silent; I know he wants to argue with me but this isn't the time.

Aunt Phoebe's words keep echoing in my head: "*Had our lives allowed we would have become fast friends,*" she wrote. "*Think about summers with the girls here.*" Somewhere inside me a warm knot of eagerness is forming. Summers in Cummaquid, mornings on the porch with a view of the garden, the field on the bay side of the house dappled with sun and shade, the company of rabbits and innumerable songbirds, the easy walk down to the quiet little beach, just a small uphill slope, not too much for the wheelchair, and then down to the bay with the broad view of the water and the marshes opening out in three directions. "*Wouldn't Dorothea feel happy and safe?*" Wouldn't I feel happy and safe, away for a few weeks at least from my life in Needham, the disaster of five years ago like a thick plate of impenetrable glass through which I can see but never reach that time when we were a typical well-off suburban family, sociable and busy and blessed with two beautiful normal daughters?

Gregory is looking straight ahead, concentrating on his driving. He has never liked to talk in the car. Or talk about his childhood at all, so much of it shadowed by his mother's long struggle with cancer. She was Uncle Dennis's little sister. There's a picture of the two of them in Aunt Phoebe's parlor, taken when they were ten and fifteen or thereabouts, both of them with fine fair hair and mischievous expressions. Those summers Gregory spent on the Cape were a painful time. He was only fourteen when his mother died, and after that he was hardly ever at home in Dover. During the winter he was away at St. Paul's, and in the summer his father sent him to work for Uncle Dennis in Cummaquid. He has never talked about those summers, even on our few trips back and forth to the Cape to visit. I wish I knew more about that part of his life. If he could remember some happy times there, maybe I could suggest holding onto the house, at least for this summer, at least to give it a try.

"What was it like, those summers you stayed on the Cape?" I ask.

"I don't know. Just a summer job. It was a long time ago."

"Did you make any friends?" I ask, knowing perfectly well he's never mentioned any.

"Not really."

"How about the people you worked with?"

"We didn't mix after work." I wait for him to say more but he doesn't.

"So what did you do in your time off?"

"I didn't have a lot of that. I worked six days. And I did things around the yard for Aunt Phoebe. Sometimes I went swimming after supper, and one summer there was a boy down the street who had a motorboat we'd go out in, but it broke down a lot. It was mostly in pieces in his driveway."

"Did you ever spend time with Uncle Dennis, go fishing or anything?"

Gregory makes a little noise that isn't quite a laugh. "Uncle Dennis wasn't much for palling around. He liked to drink, even back then. He'd disappear right after dinner into the parlor and stay there until after we'd gone to bed. Sometimes he got pretty nasty. I learned to stay out of his way."

"How about Aunt Phoebe?"

"Oh, she was all right. I'd help her with the dishes and sometimes we'd listen to the radio. They had a little black and white TV, but we never watched it because it was in the parlor with Uncle Dennis. And I read a lot. She had hundreds of books, lots of nature books about birds and plants and such. And if the bugs weren't too bad we'd walk down to the harbor."

It doesn't sound like much of a life for a teenage boy, especially a boy whose family had been split apart, whose father retreated from the horrors of his mother's long, slow, painful dying by burying himself in work. I reach over and rub Gregory's shoulder, wanting to comfort the boy he was, to make up for that long-ago pain and loneliness. And for the first time I think about how his father must have felt, a sliver of ice lodged in his heart, refusing to acknowledge his own child's grief because that would mean confronting his own.

THE NEEDHAM HOUSE has its own smell, and its own feel, something I only notice when I first come in after being away. A not unpleasant smell, though a little closed in, emanating perhaps from the secondhand Orientals we've collected over the years. It's a formal house, built during the last boom years of the twenties, with a gracious and space-wasting front hall and chair rails in the dining room. I glance into the living room, remembering my delight and pride in the beautifully crafted mantelpiece framed by bookshelves, the time and care I took in furnishing and decorating. It seems a long time ago. I avert my eyes from the Steinway baby grand that takes up the whole front corner.

She hums. "Umm, umm," a sort of incantation. For a moment there in the hall I see her as strangers must, a big girl sitting off-center in a wheelchair, raising her left arm spasmodically, the light of recognition on the left side of her face clashing with the sag of paralysis on the right. As always, her hair is beautiful. Cutting it short was the right thing to do, though I cried when we had it done. It shapes itself to her skull in a close-fitting cap, thick and shining and nearly black, like Gregory's, the only neat, organized thing about her.

Jeannine greets us. She's getting a degree in physical therapy at Sargent and living in, helping with Dorothea, committed until she graduates two years from June. She's only been with us for six weeks and still has a lot to learn. But how quickly she's settled in.

"How did everything go?" I ask, as always a knot of apprehension in the pit of my stomach.

"Pretty good. She had a screaming fit last night when you weren't here to put her to bed. But today went fine. We played a lot of tapes, the ones that were out on the top of the cabinet there." Jeannine keeps moving past me to go out to the car where Gregory is unloading the suitcases. How young she looks with her open Irish face, her guileless blue eyes, her skin white as milk between the freckles. She would be pretty if it weren't for her thin brown hair and her lack of color. She has the sure instincts of a good nurse, sensing when to help and when to leave well enough alone. Like right now. Is she conscious of how glad I am to have a moment alone with my daughter, to reconnect?

"Hey, Sweetheart, I'm home," I say, squatting down eye-level between Dorothea and the door she's looking at, the door through which Jeannine has just disappeared.

"Umm," she says again. She's happy to see me. Her good eye is squinting with the effort of her half-smile. But she's not agitated as she sometimes is when I leave her in the care of someone else and things have gone badly. Maybe this arrangement will work out. How many people have we hired in the past five years, live-in people, people by the day, the hour? The first year and a half, a nightmare time when we looked every day for signs of progress, there was Mrs. Greer, a practical nurse in her sixties who lived in Mondays to Fridays. She'd taken care of innumerable stroke patients, most of them elderly, and she loved Dorothea like a granddaughter. It was she who made me face, finally, that Dorothea was not going to get better, sitting me down in the kitchen one day over a year after the operation and telling me flat out that after so many months the chances were slender or nonexistent. I hated her that day, but now I'm grateful. It wasn't until then that I agreed to leave Dorothea overnight for an occasional weekend away with Gregory and finally begin the counseling that started to prepare me for the way things are, the way they are going to be, the essential fact of my life now and forever that I have a paralyzed and brain-injured child who needs full-time care.

But then a miracle happened to Mrs. Greer. A high school classmate, a widower she hadn't seen in over forty years, looked her up and fell in love and married her and took her off to his retirement home in Florida. I tried to be happy for her, but it felt like a death in the family. How could she leave? How could we cope without her?

After that we went through a succession of people, so many I lost count, the incompetent, the rigid and insensitive, the slovenly, the overly possessive who wanted me out of the way, even the sadistic young nursing graduate I caught pinching Dorothea when she "misbehaved." What attracts some people to the helping professions? How frustrated it makes me feel knowing I can't manage my own life, my own family, without prevailing upon the reliability and good sense of another human being, someone who is there not out of love or even family obligation but because she's being paid.

Jeannine might work out, though. Already Dorothea has attached herself to her and has come to enjoy her morning exercise sessions which Jeannine seasons with jokes and banter, singing along with the latest pop tunes on the radio in her off-key soprano, talking to her constantly, showing her colorful ads from the expensive fashion magazines she's so incongruously fond of, keeping a constant buzz of stimulation going whenever they're together. And in between, off to classes in Boston, to clinics, to the library. Where does she get the energy? And how will we get along without her? She'll graduate in two years and then go heaven knows where. And if romance can spirit off Mrs. Greer, surely it will find Jeannine, who is just the kind of young woman so many men dream of marrying, easy-going and generous, destined to raise a houseful of noisy, freckled, good-natured children.

Jeannine is back in the hall with my overnight bag, my funeral dress over her arm. I can't help noticing how Dorothea shifts her attention from me to her, graces her with the same welcoming half-smile. "Here I am, Dor. Don't worry, I'm not going anyplace. Want music? You really go off into the music, don't you, Dor?"

I wish she wouldn't call her Dor, but I don't say anything. It's important, Jeannine says, to reinforce her identity, to encourage whatever sense of self remains locked in her mind, destined to wither away if it isn't nourished. "She used to play the piano; did I tell you that?" I say to Jeannine. "She was very, very good. That year she had the surgery she'd been chosen . . ." My voice trails off; I remember I've already told Jeannine this, in the very same words, that first day when she came for her interview. And I promised myself I was going to stop thinking about Dorothea's music. If nothing else, two years of therapy have taught me the futility of dwelling in the past. I shift gears. "Where's Lesley? Not home yet?"

"Yes, she is. Upstairs, I think. She came in right after school, said she was tired."

Lesley these days is always tired and more often than not in her room with the door shut. Three months ago she would have been with Katy Shields, her best friend, but something has gone amiss since Christmas. Katy has acquired a boyfriend of sorts with whom she has endless conversations on the phone. And Lesley feels displaced.

"Where's Lesley?" Greg asks, coming in the door with his suit bag and heading straight for the stairs without waiting for an answer. "I'm going in to the office and see about the mail. I've got that seven o'clock flight in the morning, remember. I'll grab something on the way home." It's nearly six o'clock; couldn't he wait and go after dinner? I want him there at the table for Lesley; now she won't see him until Saturday. I start to protest, but it will just lead to words. And where is Lesley? Didn't she hear us arrive? Is she asleep? I relieve Jeannine of my suitcase and dress and climb the stairs.

Lesley doesn't answer my knock right away. Her voice is cranky and faint. "You woke me, Mom. I'll see you at dinner."

"It's almost time for dinner now. May I come in?" I open the door a crack and peek in. Lesley is lying on her bed still wearing her ski jacket from school. Once again I am amazed at her long legs; already she is taller than I am. "Are you okay?" I ask doubtfully.

"I'm fine. Just tired."

"Don't you want to hear about Aunt Phoebe?"

"Not really. Funerals are so depressing."

I can feel my irritation growing. Lesley rolls over on her side away from me, flipping her long light red hair out of the way. So far she hasn't looked at me or even said hello. Why is it she can make me feel unwelcome in my own house? Her manners, as Greg keeps reminding me lately, are inexcusable.

"I made up a big pot of vegetable soup," Jeannine says when I get back down to the kitchen to see about dinner. "There's no meat in it, but I saw you had that dry mix, and I added a big can of tomatoes and whatever I could find in the crisper—there're some carrots and celery and that half a squash that was left, and onions. And the cabbage left over from the cole slaw we made the other night. Mommy says the secret of good vegetable soup is cabbage."

Jeannine sounds like a child sometimes, like now, calling her mother Mommy. But she's so agreeable, so willing to go beyond her designated duties. I smile at her, grateful that I don't have to contend with dinner. I don't mention that we had vegetable soup at Aunt Phoebe's last night. It's companionable, having Jeannine in the kitchen with me, setting the table while I mix up some corn bread to go with the soup. When the girls were younger, I imagined them with me like this, laughing and chatting about the day's events while we chopped onions for salad and cleaned up the dishes afterwards. But Dorothea is already pushed up against the table in her wheelchair, lost in some inner world, humming to herself, and Lesley is dozing upstairs on her bed, her sulky face turned to the wall.

I sit propped up against the headboard watching Greg pack for his trip to Washington, thinking how much our way of going about small tasks reveals about us. Greg likes to pack for himself. He says it's because that way he can find everything, but the truth is he's better at it than I am. He takes two shirts, one for Thursday evening, one for Friday, and lays them face down on the bed, deftly folding them into thirds lengthwise, arranging the sleeves just so, turning up the bottom a few inches, folding them once more, and laying them, perfectly centered, in his overnight case. My mother was astonished the first time she saw him do that; in her opinion no man was competent to do anything with clothing except get it wrinkled and dirty. Greg's father taught him to fold his shirts, the fall after his mother died and he was getting ready to go to St. Paul's. It occurs to me that for that steely, remote man it was an act of love.

I have things to discuss with Greg this evening. Ever since supper I've been thinking about Aunt Phoebe, about the house. "What should we tell Lesley about Aunt Phoebe's will?" I say.

Greg has his back to me, holding up two socks, trying to discern whether they are blue or black. "Why not just tell her what it says?"

"I'm worried about Lesley. She's not herself at all these days. I don't want her to feel left out, with the house going to Dorothea."

"The house isn't going to Dorothea, the money from it is. Surely that's what Phoebe wanted. If you think it will bother Lesley, why discuss it with her at all?"

"So you're determined to sell the house?"

"Ye Gods, Anna, be realistic. What else are we going to do with it? We could clear it out and rent it, I suppose, but do you have any idea what fixing it up would cost, and what a pain it is to be a landlord, running down there to fix things, getting it cleaned between tenants, making sure they don't wreck it or rob us blind? I don't want to get into all that."

I hadn't wanted the conversation to go this way. There's no way to lead up to it—I have to come out and say it. "Have you thought about keeping it for us, using it summers, maybe?"

Greg turns to look at me, surprised. "How could we do that, with Dorothea?"

"She's the one I'm thinking of. Do you know what Aunt Phoebe said in her letter to me? She said, 'Think about summers here. Wouldn't Dorothea feel happy and safe?' It would be nice for her down there, that big yard, the beach. And for me. I'd be away from Needham for a few weeks." Away from everybody who knew us before, I'm thinking. "And it's only an hour and a half. You could come every weekend and even during the week sometimes, go for a swim after supper."

Greg's face is impassive. He has finished packing; he lifts the overnight bag off the bed and sets it carefully on the floor over by his closet, still open so the clothes won't get crushed and so he can add his Dopp kit in the morning. "It's where you used to spend summers," I go on, "and the Cape—it's where all your mother's people are from. It's part of your past."

He laughs, a quiet, bitter-sounding laugh. "Well, you're the one who feels nostalgic about it, not me. As far as I'm concerned, the past is just that, over. Can we talk about this later? I've got a long day tomorrow."

In bed Greg lies turned away from me. I touch his shoulder, run my fingers lightly down his arm, cup his elbow in my hand. It's a familiar signal between us, but he doesn't respond. I knows he's not asleep from the tenseness in his body. "Just let me hold onto you," I finally say, wishing he would turn over and look at me, take me in his arms.

"It's going to be a long day tomorrow," he says, shifting a little so I can curl up behind him. How little he needs me, I think sadly. How seldom he is the one who reaches out in the night with that light touch, that small gesture that says come to me, make love to me, I need you. How many nights have I lain here, afraid to touch him, afraid to ask? I want so much more from him than he wants from me. Sex, yes, but more than that, comfort, connection, tonight above all nights protection from the cold, the dark, the horror of dying alone in a drafty house like Aunt Phoebe, being laid under the winter earth by people who pay their last respects with a mixture of resignation and relief.

We are growing middle-aged. In the past year we have lost two friends, one to cancer, one to a heart attack that came without warning. Aunt Phoebe is the last of our parents' generation; now there is no one ahead of us. Forty-four, I will be in November. Halfway, probably more than halfway. And from here on, the path grows narrower, the losses greater, the possible dreams fewer and fewer. Hold me, Greg, I want to say. Make love to me. Touch my body, electric and alive, make me forget about the darkness all around us. But Greg's breathing has deepened and evened out; he has fallen asleep.

The Drift Boulder

The term drift boulder *dates from the time when geologists believed that some phenomena were caused by the currents of the Biblical flood.*

I CAN'T SLEEP. IMAGES of the funeral and the odd little reception afterwards keep coming into my head. The service was all wrong for Aunt Phoebe, for one thing. I wish I could conjure her up and apologize to her. If it hadn't been February and so cold, I would have been tempted to go out across the field and climb the big rock she showed me the day we met and stand straight up on top of it without holding on the way she used to, looking out across miles of salt marsh and harbor. That's how I want to remember her.

We buried her in the little cemetery off Mary Dunn's Road, the coldest day so far of a cold winter. Cold and windy, not more than a clutch of people there, all huddled together, the minister hurrying through the briefest of ceremonies, "I am the Resurrection and the Life," the wind snatching his words away. He tried his best, but then he's only been on the Cape for five years and doesn't know anything about Aunt Phoebe other than that she was somehow related to the Turnstones who donated the stained glass window on the north side of the church back in the 1880s. He used words like *selfless* that had little to do with the woman I remember.

The earth felt like iron under our feet. I stood with my back to the machine they used to thaw the ground and dig the grave, but I couldn't block it out of my mind. It was parked in plain sight not more than a hundred feet away, a large, yellow crustacean-like presence with a tractor cab and two metal arms leaning forward and resting on the ground. Some things are better off done by hand, Aunt Phoebe used to say.

I stood next to Gregory, trying to stay in the lee of his body. The wind was fierce. Greg's face was unreadable. Not sad. Remote. Uncomfortable, the way he looks when I launch into a discussion he would rather avoid. I noticed the youngest Boston cousin—Joan or Jane Gardener, wasn't it?—watching him, sizing him up. Gregory would catch any woman's eye still, with his lanky, dark, slightly old-fashioned good looks reeking of character and integrity. I used to call him Gregory Peck to tease him. He's weathered well, kept most of his hair, developed only a trace of the stoop common to very tall men who look as if they've ducked under too many lintels.

I always feel plain next to Gregory despite my good figure, too short and ordinary-looking. And the years have added some pounds I realized lately, after Nan, my maddeningly slender Needham friend tried to reassure me by calling me *softig. Softig*—wasn't that a polite term for women too old to be called buxom? And my hair, whipping uncontrollably in the inexorable wind, escaping from under my wool hat.

It wasn't Gregory's looks I noticed first. I was in the middle of my junior year, suffering through a painful weekend in Cambridge on a blind date with a law student, a friend's cousin. We were at a crowded party in someone's tiny Somerville apartment, and I had stepped outside to escape the smoke and noise. I was sitting alone on the front steps of the old duplex when Gregory sat down beside me. "It's better out here, isn't it?" was the first thing he said. His voice and manner impressed me, a sort of calm rare in young men, especially the ambitious, aggressive sort who get into Harvard Law School. It was years before I realized that he sounded like my father.

"I don't know anyone here," I responded. "It feels less lonely out here than in there with all those people."

"Yes," is all he said. I liked that he was willing to sit there quietly beside me, that he didn't need to fill up the empty spaces with glib chatter. And I liked his hands, resting on his long thighs, the neat square nails, clean as a surgeon's.

There are lots of Turnstone markers in the cemetery; the family has been on the Cape forever. Back in the early days they would have buried Aunt Phoebe within sight of her own house, the men at least having a chance to warm themselves and work off their grief with pickaxe and shovel, the job slowed by having to wedge out the ubiquitous stones, the women busy inside with the cooking and the laying out. But who in that thin gathering of nephews and cousins and a few neighbors was grieving? Not Greg, certainly, who worried about her and resented her in about equal portions. Not the cousins from Harwich, who never accepted her because she came from off-Cape and who wrote off alcoholic Dennis years ago. Nor the three cousins on her side down from Boston, only one of whom we've met before. Nor I, who in spite of all my curiosity never took the time to get to know her. So it's regret, not grief, I was feeling.

It's a nice cemetery, except for the wind. It was opened by the town when Cobb's Hill ran out of space in the middle of the nineteenth century. Jack pines and scrub oaks shade the graves in summer, and roses and rhododendron grow rampant around the older ones, simple granite headstones bearing the old family names: Thatcher with two t's and Thacher with one, Higgins, Phinney, Crowell, along with all the Turnstones. In the oldest sections there are family plots, many of them with two or three little marble headstones carved in the shape of lambs, babies' graves. So many babies lost, and wives, young women eighteen or twenty years old, dying in childbirth or from the terrible fever that came afterwards. One large square monument for a man in his fifties lists three wives, all dead before thirty. If you own property in the town you can reserve yourself a space in the cemetery. There is something heart-warming about that.

I remembered being there before, eight years ago when Uncle Dennis died. It was Indian summer that time, a soft, breezy day, the wind sighing gently in the pines. Dorothea and Lesley were little girls then, just nine and four, and kept squatting down searching the mossy ground for acorns.

Back at the house after Aunt Phoebe's burial, the parlor was freezing with the wind coming straight across the marsh and rattling all the north-facing windows. Gregory got a fire started, but everyone retreated to the kitchen anyway. From the looks of things it was the only downstairs room Aunt Phoebe used in winter. It faces south and west, out of the wind, and can be closed off and heated with the stove, a large black contraption, half gas and half wood, that probably dates from the thirties. We had plenty of food to serve everybody—the women from the church saw to that: a ham, three cakes, a loaf of whole wheat bread, a platter of sandwiches, and a pot of vegetable soup we heated up again for supper.

Not many people came back to the house. The church was only quarter full, and only a few braved the wind for the burial; other than the family and the three women who had brought the food, there were only the local lawyer Gregory had finally talked Phoebe into hiring to write a will, a handful of neighbors, five or six of the cranberry workers who remembered Uncle Dennis, and Demetrius of course. Perhaps we should have brought the girls, or at least Lesley. A few people remembered them from Uncle Dennis's funeral and asked about them. But I don't know how we would have managed Dorothea in that cold house.

Aunt Phoebe—how strange to sit at her scarred old kitchen table, full of rings from her endless cups of tea, listening to the house where she lived and died whine and creak in the cold February wind, half expecting to see her there across the table in Uncle Dennis's old brown sweater with the leather arm patches. Who was she? Certainly not the self-effacing, self-sacrificing woman the minister described. How could he possibly know? She was never a church-goer, hadn't set foot inside the place since Uncle Dennis died. The arrival of a contingent from the Ladies' Circle with all that food was out of respect for the Turnstone name, not Aunt Phoebe.

What I remember is how she was when I first met her twenty years ago, infused with energy, looking at me with restless blue eyes that kept darting beyond me, skittery as a sparrow poised to fly off any minute. Abrupt, innocent of the social graces, so different from the women in my family. Her one piece of correspondence directed specifically to me, as opposed to Greg, to whom she reported two or three times a year about expenses or taxes, was a cryptic note that arrived a few months after Dorothea's operation, shortly after she finally came home from the rehab center. "*I am sorry about your lovely Dorothea,*" the note read, "*but don't fall into despair. She has gifts for you yet.*"

I was relieved when the minister left—poor fellow, he was out of his depth. And the Ladies' Circle ladies annoyed me by cleaning up energetically, assiduously polishing the stove that had been untouched in many a moon, carefully transferring the leftovers onto Aunt Phoebe's cracked and mismatched plates so I wouldn't have to worry about returning any dishes, dear, they said. Mr. Flannery, the lawyer, was nicer. He changed his schedule around so that he could read the will early the next morning after Gregory told him he needed to be in Washington at the end of the week and was anxious to get back.

I thought everyone had left except Mr. Flannery and Demetrius, and I had just gone upstairs to change into wool slacks and socks when I ran into that tall woman from down the lane in the upstairs hall—looking for a bathroom, she said. Or maybe just nosing around, I thought. Daphne somebody. She asked what we planned to do about the house, making me wonder if she was in the real estate business. Such vultures they can be.

Demetrius stayed around longer than we expected. He talked a lot about the house, which he knows inside and out because he's been taking care of things since before Uncle Dennis died. Uncle Dennis was sick a long time, and even though he had an engineering degree he never was the practical sort who would actually get around to thawing a pipe or replacing a cracked window pane. Up close I could see Demetrius was older than I thought, one of those men who seem ageless. Greg remembers Demetrius from when he was working the cranberry bog in the fifties, so he must be sixty, at least, but fit from all the outdoor work he does, lithe and graceful, quiet when he moves. The kind of man who would be good around animals.

He seemed amazingly well-spoken, but not forthcoming. I sensed there were things he wanted to say, or ask, but didn't. Like the neighbor, Daphne, he must want to know what's going to happen to the house. After he left, we discovered he had filled the wood box on the porch with cut and split logs from the back of his truck. And of all the people at the burial, he was the only one I saw with tears in his eyes.

I still can't sleep. Greg is on his back now, snoring softly, lying diagonally across the bed so I have to curl up in the triangular space he has left me. It feels hot in the room, claustrophobic. I keep seeing images of Aunt Phoebe, not the gnarled old woman spending her first nights under the bitter hard earth on Mary Dunn's Road, her slippery unkempt hair uncharacteristically crimped and dull-looking after the mortician's attentions. (How can an old lady have such shiny hair, Dorothea asked the last time she saw her, at Uncle Dennis's funeral.) No, I see the Aunt Phoebe I first met when Greg brought me down to meet his Cape Cod relatives when I was his brand new fiancée, shy and Midwestern and anxious to please.

Uncle Dennis was all right back then, drinking all day but functional. I found him charming and interesting to talk to. He took me on a tour of the cranberry operation. Gregory wouldn't go and we had words about it. I thought he was being ungracious, but he said he'd seen enough of the place those summers he had to work there. His manner with Uncle Dennis was sullen. I was so innocent in those days I missed the signs of drinking and mistook Uncle Dennis's effusiveness for natural volubility and charm. He knew everything about the history of the cranberry industry and talked on and on about it.

And Aunt Phoebe—what was I to make of her? So unlike my own family, where cleanliness and good manners were elevated to a religion, where excesses of emotion—anger, joy, or sorrow—were pointedly ignored, where the avoidance of unpleasantness was carried to such extremes that I sometimes used to feel that if I were to fall to the floor unconscious everyone would just step over me and go on about their business. Sitting in that old wicker rocker on the porch facing the garden, taking in Aunt Phoebe's faded house dress and bare feet (how old was she then? Fifty-four?), trailing after her to the garden when she abruptly got up and went outside in the middle of a sentence, trying to hunt for clues about Greg in what she was saying about the Cape, the real Cape, winter people who live backwards, she said, hibernating in tourist season, moving to beach shacks on Sandy Neck or staying home and sticking to the back roads in July and August. "Gregory is a Cape Codder," she said that first day. "He just doesn't know it yet. Things got in the way. It'll come to him."

She kept on talking, bent over the garden, pulling out clumps of crabgrass, brushing aside my compliments about the flowers tumbling over the edges of her perennial beds ("Black-eyed Susans. Volunteers. But who am I to quarrel if nature wants to improve on my design?") or the perfect dry breezy weather. ("Weather? This isn't weather. This is something the Chamber of Commerce puts out. Come back in January if you want weather.") Somehow I was never put off by her peculiar old clothes or eccentric manners, her incongruous Beacon Hill accent surfacing when she asked if I would like some *tomahtoes*—for she was true blue old Boston; it's her ancestor, not Uncle Dennis's, third from the left in the engraving of the Boston Tea Party that hung in the parlor.

Later that first afternoon she took me up through the field above the house, skirting a grove of leggy black locusts with slender gnarled trunks and a lacy canopy of leaves. On top of the hill at the back corner of the property was a little stand of pine trees that showed the effects of the winter storms, leaning down the hill, their north sides discolored with rusty needles and dead branches. We followed the low stone wall marking the boundary back towards the road, stopping halfway along where an enormous boulder, ten or twelve feet high, lay in our path. Aunt Phoebe disappeared behind it and seconds later called out from over my head. "Come on up. There's a place on the back side. Just put your foot into that crack and haul yourself up. You can see the whole harbor from here." I managed to clamber up with some difficulty, following her instructions about where to grab hold and where to place my feet, and marveling that the older woman was able to climb up so quickly, stand so easily in that narrow space with the rough granite pitching away steeply on all sides. And then I was up, crouched down because I didn't dare stand, and there was the bay spread out before us, a great broad expanse of blue, and beyond it, a narrow spit of land with a row of weatherbeaten cottages and what looked like an abandoned lighthouse at the end.

"Well, there you are," Aunt Phoebe said. "That's Barnstable Harbor. And that's Sandy Neck over there. The only way to get there is by boat or beach buggy."

"Oh, what a beautiful view. And with just this little hill between you and it. Why didn't they build the house up here?"

She chuckled. "You'd know why if you were here six months from now. See those pine trees? The way they lean, and are all brown on one side? The wind did that, and the salt. We don't get a lot of snow here, but when we do, it's apt to blow horizontally. And it was a farmhouse originally, remember, not a summer cottage. This field around us was all cow pasture when Dennis was a boy. Besides, I like that the view isn't there right in front of my eyes all day, that I have to walk a ways to get to it. Otherwise I might forget to see it."

I was entranced by the view, even though I felt as though I could tumble to the ground any minute. "Is that a lighthouse?" I asked. "It's so far from the point."

"It wasn't when they built it; it was right on the end. The dunes have walked away from it. It's twice as far from the point as it was when Dennis and I first moved in here. That's what happens along the coast here. The barrier beaches keep moving all the time. People build houses on them, and docks and jetties, and think they own what's described on their deed, but the sand keeps on drifting and piling, pushed along by the wind and the water, and sooner or later a storm comes along and they find what they own is a piece of the Atlantic. Sandy Neck will break someday and those houses will wash away, not in my lifetime but maybe in yours."

"It's a big harbor."

"It is. But we'll come back after supper if you can stay that long, and you'll be surprised. We have a big tide here, more than eleven feet sometimes. At low tide during a full moon we can walk halfway across without getting our feet wet."

"This is such a wonderful view. And what an amazing rock."

"Yes. I'm very fond of it. It's a drift boulder, a glacial erratic. You know, we live right on the ice margin here, where the glacier stopped. Cape Cod is mostly terminal moraine, a big pile of gravel left when it melted.

"Glacial erratic—a wandering rock?"

"Yes, isn't that a wonderful name? It's because it was dragged here from somewhere else. Sort of like me." I looked at her quizzically, but she had already started down, nimbly placing hands and feet with a grace born of long practice. "And now let's go down and look at the beach."

I followed her along the old stone wall to the lane and down to the beach, entranced by the brightness, the way the water seemed to contain every shade of blue and green. Aunt Phoebe chattered on about the harbor, what it was like when she first came to Cummaquid as a bride, how back then the fishermen still dried their nets on the salt meadows called Common Fields, all dotted with summer cottages now, and how long before that there were salt works. It was as if she wanted me to see it the way she did, through all the layers of years and changing seasons.

How happy I was, driving back to Boston that night, thinking about the family I was about to become part of. But what did I ever really know about it, I ask myself, pressing my feet insistently against Greg's leg until he shifts over and gives me space to stretch out. No doubt I romanticized it all, comparing it to my own unhistorical Midwestern past, so lacking in adventure and icons and with nothing to compare to Uncle Dennis's colorful dinnertime stories about his forebears. How eagerly I drank them in, tales of sea voyages and whaling, laced with Aunt Phoebe's irreverent correctives. "Did I ever tell you about Greg's great-great grandfather," he would start in, "the time he came back from four years at sea with a Tahitian girl and tried to pass her off as a servant? Of course she died of homesickness six months later."

"Or poison, maybe," Aunt Phoebe muttered under her breath.

And how ready I was to imagine summer vacations a few years hence, walking down to the little inlet beach on the bay with my own children, a slender dark duplicate of Greg, a little girl with the curly fair Turnstone hair, named like generations of Cape women for one of the quiet, sturdy New England virtues—Faith or Prudence or Mercy.

But that scene never materialized. By the time Dorothea and Lesley had come along Uncle Dennis's drinking was out of hand and his liver was beginning to go. We spent just one weekend in Cummaquid while the children were small, listening to him apologize for sleeping through dinner, saying he hadn't felt right all day, watching Greg's mouth tighten into a line, waking in the night to Uncle Dennis's shouting and Aunt Phoebe's faint answering monosyllables, both of them appearing the next morning at breakfast as if nothing were the matter. Gregory was the one who looked white around the mouth and ill, Gregory who had the car packed up right after lunch in spite of the perfect beach weather, saying he wanted to beat the traffic. After that he visited Cummaquid by himself, in the off season.

Northeaster

Each ice advance across New England announced its
coming by turbulent and unpleasant conditions fringing
its borders . . .

WHAT SEEMS LIKE an ordinary gusty rainstorm in Needham is a full-blown northeaster by the time we get to Cummaquid. It is the Saturday after Easter. For over a week it has been damp and rainy; there are few enough signs of spring in Needham, and nearly none here. The forsythia whose yellow flags are unfurled all around the Boston suburbs are still tightly closed in the shrub border behind Aunt Phoebe's garden.

There seems to be no one in residence on the lane. The house feels sepulchrally cold and smells of mildew and wet plaster. Gregory gets a fire going in the parlor in hopes that some of the heat will penetrate to the room above. He has an appointment with Mr. Flannery, the lawyer, and I plan to get started on my task of sorting through Aunt Phoebe's papers.

As soon as Gregory drives out of the yard I feel utterly alone. It's so cold in the house. And the water is drained from the pipes; why didn't we think to bring along a thermos of coffee? Is this what it was like for Aunt Phoebe, being here in the off season, no living soul within hailing distance?

I have an unaccountable urge to walk down to the harbor. The exercise will warm me, I rationalize, and in spite of the spitting rain and the wind, the air seems warmer outside than it does in the house. The parlor door is sealed shut for the winter, so I go through the kitchen and porch, making sure I haven't locked myself out. I cut across the yard through the rough, wet winter grass and follow the lane, which rises gently before sloping down again towards the beach. At the top of the hill the wind hits me like a solid object. I stop to catch my breath; I have to lean into it to avoid being blown backwards. The tide is halfway in, or out, the channel full of whitecaps and the shallows marked with swiftly moving stripes of lighter and darker gray as great sheets of wind whip across them straight from the mouth of the harbor. Sandy Neck with its little row of houses is a faint outline of gray against gray. There is no sign of life, not a boat, not a bird, nothing but the fast-moving patterns of air on water and the incessant whine of the wind. Intimidated, I turn and make my way back to the house.

An air vent in the floor of Aunt Phoebe's little upstairs room lets in a little heat from the parlor, but it will be a long time before the room warms up. I am going to have to work in my coat. How to get started? As far as I know, no one has been in here since my brief visit the day after Aunt Phoebe's funeral. The bed is neatly made—did she fold the sheet down over the blankets, tuck them carefully in, that last day before she decided to climb a ladder and clear the gutters, all by herself on a February morning? They were iced up and causing a leak in the parlor, she told Demetrius when she called him after somehow dragging herself all the way around the house and up the porch steps to the phone in the kitchen. She had broken her hip. We heard the news in a succession of phone calls from Demetrius: Aunt Phoebe had been taken by ambulance to the hospital, she had thrown a blood clot that lodged in her head and was in a coma, she was gone. How long would she have lived if not for that senseless accident? How would she have lived—what would we have done—if she had survived, crippled and unable to walk? Like Dorothea. Can people will their own deaths? I am beginning to think that sometimes they can.

I sit down on the bed for a moment. It is narrow and sags in the middle, nothing more than a metal cot with old-fashioned springs, no headboard. The spread is tufted white chenille, the kind I remember from childhood visits to my grandmother's house in Knoxville. Aunt Phoebe has placed the bed opposite the north-facing dormer window. The first thing she would see when she sat up in the morning would be a faint glimpse of the harbor, invisible now through the rain and the film of salt left on the glass by winter storms. I remember Greg saying he liked the view from this window; this was his room when he stayed here those summers. The wall all around the window is fitted with homemade bookshelves. The only other furniture in the room is a small nightstand with an old-fashioned mirror over it, a battered Hitchcock chair, and a simple kneehole desk, its entire surface piled with books, notebooks, stacks of mail, and papers. There is no closet in the room, and no bureau. Aunt Phoebe must have left her clothes in the master bedroom when she decided to sleep in here.

I need to devise a plan. First I should look for Phoebe's tax returns to give to Gregory. We found her checkbook in her purse, and an address book and all the recent mail and bills stacked in a corner of the kitchen counter, but her older financial records must be up here. What I really want, though, is to find the journal. What would it look like? Would it be a leather-bound volume, tucked into the bookshelves along with her bird and botanical guides, her worn copy of Thoreau? Or a stack of loose sheets in a box somewhere? How far back in time would it go? Why does Aunt Phoebe want to give it to Daphne Ault, the tall neighbor I ran into in the upstairs hall the day of the funeral? And why haven't I said anything about it to Gregory? *"The journal I entrust to you,"* Aunt Phoebe wrote. For my eyes only? Because she somehow saw me as a friend? Or simply as another woman, someone who would understand?

The rain rattles like pebbles thrown against the windowpanes. How narrow Aunt Phoebe's world has always seemed, small and cramped like this room, containing less than the bare essentials. How like her life this house seems, placed one hill away from the beach, so she would have to climb the stairs for even a glimpse of that broad expanse of ocean and sky, nearby and yet out of reach. I was amazed when Gregory told me that she had grown up on Beacon Hill and still had relatives there and on the North Shore, that she had gone to Smith and graduated with honors, that she had taught for two years at a private girls' school in Cambridge. There was a child, a daughter born when she was well into her thirties, who died when she was only three years old, during the polio epidemic in 1957.

To my knowledge Aunt Phoebe never crossed the canal in all the years I knew her. She seldom even went off the lane except for her weekly trip to Hyannis to buy groceries. Dennis's illness lasted a long time, and for years he took all her attention. But he's been dead for eight years now. Did she have a social life, friends? Was there room in her narrow life for secrets?

I get up from the cot and walk over to the desk. It's time to stop daydreaming. Between walking down to the harbor and musing I've eaten up nearly an hour. Gregory will be back from the lawyer's and I will have made no progress. How to start? I pull out the chair and sit down. The entire surface of the desk is full of books and stacks of paper, making me think she must not have worked here lately. The cold probably drove her down to the kitchen in winter. To my left is a handmade pottery mug in shades of blue like the harbor in summer, full of pens and pencils. Aunt Phoebe was left-handed, like me. I open the top lefthand drawer; it contains no papers, only a jumble of pencils, paper clips, an odd-looking key, a battered pair of worn out dress shears, a stapler devoid of staples. In the drawer below a mixed stack of blank paper, plain bond for typing, a few lined yellow pads, a mix of envelopes and stationery. The deep file drawer on the right side is full almost to the top. Bundles of bills and receipts marked paid and held together with rubber bands, organized by the month, evidently. More bundles of bank statements. A thick green old-fashioned ledger book labeled *West Marsh*. And near the bottom, a stack of fat manilla envelopes marked *Tax Returns* and going back to 1982. Eureka. Not a neat drawer, but all her financial records together in one place. Gregory will be relieved.

The top of the desk is less logical and orderly. It seems to be mostly stacks of junk mail, fliers advertising coming events, catalogues for clothes, for seeds and garden tools, for Victorian light fixtures and old-fashioned hardware. A big packet with a questionnaire for her sixtieth Smith reunion. Newspaper clippings having to do with a harbor dredging project, with managing a compost pile, with a new sort of toilet that doesn't use water. A small stack of Christmas cards, some of them containing notes and the inevitable family photographs. A few handwritten letters. Nothing resembling a journal.

And books. What had Aunt Phoebe been reading that week she died? Peterson's bird guide, in paperback and looking newly bought. A beautifully bound, well-thumbed edition of John Donne's *Songs and Sonnets*. I open the cover and find an inscription on the title page: *They who one another keep alive, ne'er parted be. D.* Dennis. Was Uncle Dennis ever enough the romantic to read John Donne, to make a gift of him to Aunt Phoebe? How little we know, I marvel, how little we can guess about the lives of the people around us, these old ones with their aphorisms, their endlessly repeated anecdotes from the years before we were born, their string of misfortunes, their worn out bodies that make us want to avert our eyes.

I hear a car door slam in the yard. Gregory is back. I make my way downstairs and arrive in the kitchen just as he is coming through the porch door, balancing a large envelope and, bless his heart, two cups of take-out coffee. His hair is disarranged by the wind and rain, reminding me of how he looked when we first met in the late sixties, when he wore it much longer. It's still nearly black, without a sign of gray, whereas mine is turning white right on top in the front, where it shows most. He's starting to look younger than I do.

We sit at Aunt Phoebe's table. The coffee isn't as hot as I would like but strong and black. Gregory slides a pile of papers out of the envelope. "Things are pretty straightforward," he says. "She had more put away than I thought, money from her family, and a little more invested after she sold West Marsh to Silva. Evidently she handled it and not Dennis, with an account executive from the bank. Most of it's in mutual funds."

"Is that what she's been living on?"

"Pretty much. She used the income, but had to dip into the capital for about two thousand a year after Dennis died. She seems to have lived pretty much on air. I'd love to know what her household expenses were. Did you find any records?"

"They're all upstairs in her desk drawer tied into bundles. And her tax records for the past nine years. She was more organized than she looked."

"Great. I'll take those home and look them over. You want to do anything else today? It's colder than a witch's you know what in here."

"I'd like to take a look at the attic."

"Jesus, Anna, it'll be even colder up there. Couldn't it wait for a warmer day?"

"Just a look. I want to see what I've got in front of me." It occurs to me I'm using first person singular. Gregory is not going to sort through this house, make decisions about pieces of furniture which are not quite antique, old family photographs. Why does the prospect of doing it excite me? Why does Gregory's lack of interest not surprise me? Is it a uniquely female trait, this fascination with the remains of someone else's life, that drives so many of my friends to estate auctions, garage sales, some curiosity above and beyond the pleasure of finding a bargain?

The attic door opens off the small upstairs bedroom next to Aunt Phoebe's. It's locked with a small brass padlock, but the key is in plain sight on the window sill. The stairway is narrow, leading past a small window set in the gable facing east. There are cardboard boxes on several of the steps, full of papers. A narrow ledge beside the stairs holds a rolled-up flag and a faded striped canvas beach umbrella. I squeeze past the boxes ahead of Gregory, pausing at the angle of the stairs. The attic stretches before me down to another window in the opposite gable. Except for a narrow walkway, every available surface seems to be taken up with old-fashioned foot lockers, laundry baskets, cardboard boxes, and piles of clothes and linen. Three metal cots, also piled high, are pushed under the eaves, along with a battered cottage bureau. There isn't enough room to stand and it's bitterly cold. Gregory is right. This isn't a job to tackle today. But now I know there are boxes of papers up here. Maybe this is where I'll find the journal.

Two WEEKS LATER Jeannine comes into the kitchen while I am making dinner, so uncharacteristically quiet that she startles me when I turn around. Her face, usually so open, is unreadable. "Mrs. Dylan—" she begins.

"Call me Anna, remember? Otherwise I feel like an old lady."

"Yes, Mrs.—Anna. I'm so excited but I'm worried you'll be upset. I've been offered a research assistantship—it's at a clinic attached to Children's—it's really an honor, and I'm lucky to get it, but I know my first commitment is to you. It's just days and just for the summer."

"Oh, Jeannine, that's wonderful! Of course you must take it." I can hear the false enthusiasm in my voice; it feels like a replay of the day Mrs. Greer told me she was getting married. Just days? The whole summer? How will I manage?

It isn't until that night, in bed with Greg, that I think of Cummaquid. If Jeannine is going to be unavailable all summer, why not take the girls to the Cape? It's the dream I had the first day I read Aunt Phoebe's letter. To get away from Needham, from the daily reminders of the life we've lost, from running into Dorothea's classmates, high school seniors now, young women about to go off to college, from the pitying looks of friends, and the people I thought were friends who avoid me at all costs. Life would be simpler there; I could manage by myself; Lesley is twelve now, big enough to help with lifting Dorothea and stay with her while I run errands. Could I do it? Maybe we could put in a washer and dryer, a new stove, even. I could go in late May, take Dorothea with me and spend a week working on the house. Jeannine would be free to study for exams with Lesley still in school all day, and Greg doesn't have any trips planned that I know about. It would be a test run.

I broach the subject to Greg, knowing I'm taking unfair advantage. We have gone to bed early and made love; he is relaxed and sleepy enough to agree to anything. And I, as so often happens after lovemaking, feel energetic and full of plans. This time I will find Aunt Phoebe's journal.

What is it about the idea of the journal that fascinates me so? What of Aunt Phoebe's life would be of interest to me? What was it like, all those years of living with Uncle Dennis, his unforgiving family and hers, for that matter, all those steel-spined New Englanders who spawned my own silent husband? How much of his remoteness, his silence, is the response of a boy shaped by tragedy, and how much was there all along, bred in the bone?

I fit myself against Gregory's broad back, turned away from me but solid, warm. The warmth is comforting, but it isn't enough; it doesn't make up for the silence, the words that spin in my mind, hang in the air of the room, words of anger, of passion, humor and despair, rage against the fate that transformed our beautiful, gifted daughter into what she is now, locked into herself, silent. Talk to me, Gregory, I want to say, let me hear your rage, your sorrow, and I will hold you; it will be all right. But there is nowhere for these words to go. I am overwhelmed with loneliness. Did Aunt Phoebe feel this way when her little girl died, when Uncle Dennis shut himself off and slowly poisoned himself to death with alcohol? Is that what the journal was for, a place to write the words down?

The Gannets

*As the ice pushed forward . . . life zones moved outward
in front of it like a retreating army.*

Daphne reaches across to the back of the work table where she
stacked the mottled notebooks back in February. It's been two
months now, and she's done nothing with them except arrange them
chronologically. Two months: The thought still brings tears. But it's time.
She pulls the bottom notebook from the nearest pile and leafs through the
pages until she finds the last entry.

February 23: A week of ice stretching out nearly to the channel,
then 24 hours of thaw and a brisk west wind and it's gone. Nearly
to the second creek this morning, pleasant going but hard coming
back, teary-eyed and leaning against the wind. Wide bands of sea ice,
frozen foam, all along the beach like ruffles of lace. It's insubstantial,
makes a funny sound when stepped on, softer than the crunch and
squeak of boots in snow. Beach much wider-looking since the no-
name storm brought in all the sand, trust rugosa roses will make their
comeback (poison ivy too) to cover the sad collection of debris—
boards, window frames, even part of someone's back steps! And dead
birds. Counted three gannets between here and the creek, two pure
white except for wing tips and one darker immature one. Bodies here
all winter. They don't rot—is it the cold, or the salt?—but gradually
wither and dry out, slowly growing insubstantial under their beautiful
indestructible feathers. What's left of us in our lonely dark boxes
under the ground? Hair, of course, Donne's "bracelet of bright hair
against the bone." Death more palatable on the beach, the grounded
sea birds, even the sand sharks and skates in summer with their
shocking stench yield to dessication, crumble back into sand.
      D busy sanding cove bog today with the Canty boys. Ring on
parlor ceiling gotten bigger since yesterday. Ice dams in the gutters
out front.

Ironic that would be the last entry, Daphne thinks. Reading it, she can practically hear Phoebe's voice, matter-of-fact, the trace of Boston overlaid with flat Cape Cod *a*'s. They'd talked about the gannets last November, when they both first saw them on the beach. Storms drive them in, and they fly in circles around and around Cape Cod bay, trying to stay over water, until they die of exhaustion, Phoebe said.

And the business about the ice dams coming right after. Did Phoebe have a clue how the day would turn out? Careless! Stupid! No more sunsets on the deck with wine and meandering talk about the past, about books, about the plants encircling the pond below, the little creatures swimming in it or hovering over it that Phoebe knew so well, a walking botanical and zoological encyclopedia. The neat small script swims in front of Daphne's eyes. She closes the mottled black notebook, less than half full, and replaces it on the pile.

She shouldn't have taken them, of course, but who's to know what would have happened if she hadn't? The Dylan nephew, Gregory, was it? Only showed his face once or twice a year. Handsome, Dennis's nephew, but not looking like a Turnstone, who are all fair and red- or sandy-haired. Tall and dark, a cold fish. And the wife? Seemed gracious enough at the house, didn't suspect why she was upstairs, but quiet, obviously under his thumb. Distracted. The girl to contend with, who wouldn't be? They'll sell the house. Probably without a second look at anything in it. An auction with a stranger holding the hammer. She'll have to go and bid on something, something valueless except it was Phoebe's. That flat basket with the British name Phoebe carried out to the garden to lay flowers in. Trug. It can go on her mantel, filled with dried sea lavender and teasel. Like having her here.

Almost. The window glass sags in front of her eyes, distorting the trees beyond, like the glass in old houses. "Too soon for this," she says aloud, startling herself, and shifts the pile of notebooks to the back of her work table. She gropes with her foot for the switch on the surge protector, waits while the computer boots itself up, hits the keys that bring her new story collection onto the screen. She'd rather not look at them, but they're overdue. Her editor doesn't like the title story. Sprawling, she said it was. Cutting is the easiest thing to do when the creative juices won't flow. On a dry day, revise. Sometimes the muse arrives out of self-defense. Two hours, she promises herself, and then see about the new book. Priming the pump.

She shifts her bifocals to the top of her head for a moment, presses her fingers against her eyes, looks outside. The window glass has evened out; beyond it the tracery of bare locust branches looks ink-black in the cool early spring sunlight. Hardest part of writing is getting to it, sitting down, turning on that switch. The work itself easier with every hour, once she sinks into it. Phoebe marveled at that, said she should thank her stars for it, nothing in her own life to compare except her garden, and nobody paid her for that. She's right, Daphne thinks, work is the one constant, more faithful than husband or lover. The saving grace.

One of these days she'll write about Phoebe. How to get at her, the drama of her mind, her life without a plot? People felt sorry for her, stuck in that drafty old house with Dennis, ne'er-do-well, a dreamer going through the family money, first his and then hers, trembling and querulous those last years, yellowing and shrinking everywhere except that horrifying distended belly as his liver gave out. Cranberrying the only thing he stuck to, and even that thanks to Demetrius who pretty much ran the operation himself.

But Phoebe grieved when he died, in spite of all the time and work he took. They had something together, something no one saw or understood. Phoebe wasn't the sacrificing type. She'd snort at the thought. When people felt sorry for her, she thought it was funny. The life she gave up, the Beacon Hill mansion in the family for generations, the coming out ball at the Plaza to announce she was on the marriage market—she'd once shown Daphne a yellowed newspaper photograph of herself in a long white gown—deb parties a sort of rehearsal for the wedding, which was the real event, she'd said. Another picture of two slender young woman in light suits, gloves, elaborate hats with veils: "Gardener Sisters Attend Easter Services at Trinity Church." Marriage to the proper young man, a move to a suitable suburb like Chestnut Hill, nurses for the children, summers in Maine, charity balls and the garden club, ladies' nine-hole golf at the Country Club, her hair slowly silvering as week after week she makes her way to the excellent center section seats at Friday Symphony passed down through the family.

People—those inescapable commentators on our lives—can never forgive us for giving up the things they envy and can never have. Daphne can understand that much. The burden of being noticed, how it weighed one down, whatever the reason for it, wealth or notoriety or social position or accomplishment. She wishes she had said as much to Phoebe. She did understand, all too well. She was a runaway too, from the burden of early fame, the unreal world of book tours and Public Radio interviews, of agent lunches and editorial nagging, the disappointing second novel, anticipation gradually giving way to puzzlement, then impatience. Soon the last stage: indifference and unreturned phone calls.

This is pure procrastination. Time to work on her stories. But first a quick peek to see if Phoebe mentions her anywhere—how hungry we all are to know how others see us, Daphne thinks, smiling at herself. Often it's a total surprise, and not a pleasant one. She shuffles through the last ten or twelve notebooks until she finds the spring of 1979.

> March 24: Harriet Cole over from next door scolding me for turning over my garden so early; she thinks I've been addled by the warm weather. There's something to be learned from everyone—with Harriet it's gossip and perennials. Gossip is we're to have a new neighbor in the Carey cottage, a writer from New York, a woman, "tall and brusque" according to Helen Bowden, who showed her the house. Harriet happy at the thought of another year-rounder on the lane, but my guess is she won't last, the romantic fantasy of peace and quiet being so different from the reality. She'll want the comfort of neon lights and sirens in the night.

> June 8: The voice of the chain saw is heard in our land. Lots of activity over at the Carey cottage, too noisy to garden against so I strolled over to see, some contractor I've never heard of with a new white pickup and two workmen, clearing out the woods behind the house down to the pond, which is bigger than I remember. They'll go home with poison ivy, the Cape's revenge against those who won't leave well enough alone.

> June 17: First sighting of our new rara avis, *Ardea herodius gothamica*, tall and brusque indeed, giving directions to the workmen with great sweeping arm motions. Does she mean to cut down all her woods? Why are people so insistent on rearranging the landscape before they've settled in? How often they cut and bulldoze and build, and then in a year or two they are gone, leaving the destruction behind them. I write this and then laugh, thinking of the city girl who arrived forty years ago and who the neighbors predicted would ruin the place and not last the winter. Does old age start the moment we stop wanting to make changes and start grumbling about anything newfangled?

So Phoebe wasn't immune to stereotypes and resentment against change, Daphne thinks, chuckling. How amusing to be accused of just what she'd come here to escape. Well, Phoebe, we were both wrong about each other. Remarkable we got to be friends at all. Met each other over a ladder. Ironic, a ladder to begin it, and a ladder to end it. Mistress Quickly was responsible—in shock over the move and hesitant outdoors, a city cat who didn't know what to make of grass and trees, squirrels and beetles. Up to the top of one of the locust trees the second day here. And me wandering up and down the lane looking for someone with a ladder—remembering seeing Demetrius using one over at Phoebe's, though of course I didn't know his name yet, or hers either. She came along to brace it while I climbed up and grabbed Quickly and got scratched for my trouble. And I offered her tea or wine. She took the wine, and that's how it started. She should have called me, that last day. I would have talked her out of climbing up, or at least held the ladder. But she'd never disturb me during my working hours, and Demetrius was where?—sanding the bog.

Daphne closes the notebook, gets up and crosses to the kitchen to put on the kettle, then comes back to the work table. She feels restless and impatient with herself—all this musing over Phoebe, just a ruse to avoid working. She leafs through the last notebook again before replacing it on the bottom of the pile. Only a few pages filled, with a long gap lasting most of the summer and fall. She turns to the first entry.

March 8: Counted spare notebooks today. Two more after this one from the cache of ten I bought at Halley's. Halley's gone now, stationers going the way of creameries and soda fountains. Two left—then what? I must hunt up more. Cousin Libby called to invite me to ladies' lunch. A fencing-in sort of word, *lady*, putting me in mind of Pinckney Street. I decline.

March 12: Listening to weather forecasts isn't wise, storms promoted like adventure stories. This latest passed less than advertised, the drama leached away by too much anticipation. It was better the old way, to wake to the surprise, the change of light the eyes feel even before they are open. This one a windy and wettish snow from the southeast, stuccoing the house with white. How happy to be sealed in a small white ball of a world! D broke through to me and we measured the drift against the door—39 inches. A few feet away, bare ground.

April 7: Easter Day—a cold, raw one. Dirt too soggy to work and planting sweet peas was going to be my "church"—I'm with Emily Dickinson on that. Walked to the first creek instead—northeast wind stung my face with sleet on the way up, blew me back. D brought a lily with the groceries. Its scent fills the parlor, too sweet to bear, love with a hint of rot.

April 8: A good big coastal storm has brought in wet snow—flakes sailing by the window horizontally, big as polka dots. I'm happy to be shut in, even sorting papers. The daffodils look forbearing, like wives hearing the same bad joke one more time.

April 9: Sun and dead calm this morning between two snowstorms, if I can believe the forecast. Bulbs and daylilies shoving up everywhere, the Georges' big willow putting out pale serrated leaves, yesterday's snow mostly melted, more due tonight and tomorrow. Went out early to poke around. Climbed my rock first time since November. Thankful I can still do that! Houses on the neck reflected upside down in the water; it's that still, just a few eiders idling halfway across. Eiders idling—I like the sound of that. A cheering sort of morning smelling of spring.

The kettle is screaming for Daphne's attention. She closes the notebook, for real this time, she promises herself. She adds it to the pile and crosses into the kitchen to make herself a cup of tea.

The Ice Margin

*Like a mighty creature at bay before the warming air, the
ice lingered with its front against the Islands.*

SOMEONE IS SHINING a light in my eyes, a flashlight. I turn away on the
narrow cot. It is Maine, a cabin screened all around—this is not my
bedroom at home, the bed is too narrow, too hard, the light coming from
a different place. I'm back at camp, really here again at last, everything
that is going to happen will happen now, summer with all its possibilities
begins when I open my eyes.

I draw in my breath with excitement and wake myself, conscious
of something bothersome—light, a rainbow, but too bright, coming not
from the window but from another direction. Then I'm fully awake. It's
not summer yet but only May, not my girlhood camp in Maine but Aunt
Phoebe's house, the little square bedroom on the northeast corner. The sun,
filtering through the moving branches of the locust outside the window, is
hitting the beveled glass of the heavy oval Victorian mirror over the wash-
stand and reflecting into my eyes, more effective than any alarm clock. The
sky seems as light as mid-morning at home, but the color more tender,
watered-down, paler than it ever is in Needham. I will rise early here.

The hallway floor is cold under my bare feet—I must remember to
bring slippers next time. Looking through the window at the end, I notice
someone striding determinedly up the hill towards the bay, a woman with
a shock of short gray hair and long, stork-like legs. There is something
familiar about the hair, yes, she's the woman who came to the burial, the
neighbor I found in the upstairs hall. That could be me if I lived here,
starting my days with a walk in this milky air, going down to have a look at
the water. A writer, wasn't that what Demetrius said? There is something
elegant, citified about her, even in the colorless, shapeless man's sweater
she's wearing, the denim shorts, the long bare enviable legs—aren't they
cold? Taut and lean, not an ounce of extra flesh on them. And the woman
must be fifty.

My mind feels cloudy, confused, the dream still there, along with the
disorientation of waking in a strange bed, a strange room, the windows

in unexpected places. A walk to the beach seems like a good idea; it will clear my head for the long tedious task of sorting out Aunt Phoebe's life. And maybe I could strike up an acquaintance with this neighbor. It would be comforting to know someone on the lane. Could I leave Dorothea? I make my way downstairs and carefully open the door to my daughter's room and peek in. Dorothea is turned away from the door, curled up under her thin blankets. I must find a quilt for her. She's sleeping cold. But soundly. She'll keep until I get back. I climb the stairs again and throw on jeans and a sweatshirt and sneakers without socks.

It is colder outside than I expect, too cold for shorts, I think, remembering the neighbor. Does one's blood get thicker after living here for a while? But the air is wonderful, jolting as caffeine. I feel a wedge of adrenaline move through my body. Excitement—what is it that makes me feel this way? The air?

When I reach the top of the hill, the bay spreads out before me, silvery lavender and pink in the morning light, sky and water blending together imperceptibly, so the two motionless fishing boats east of the point could be floating in either element. The tide is near low, the only movement a few gulls settling themselves on the big bar and a single figure far down the beach beyond the creek, out at the tide line, moving away. The neighbor. I'm tempted to walk in the same direction; then we would meet after she turns back. But she could go on walking for a long time, and there is Dorothea. What will she do, waking in a strange house? I turn back up the lane, suddenly nervous about leaving her alone, and find, on the top step of the porch, leaning against the storm door so it will be noticed, the morning paper.

I needn't have worried about Dorothea. She sleeps until nearly nine as if drugged by the salt air. Blessing the unknown donor of the paper, I perk some coffee using a half-used can from the cupboard and sink into the wicker rocker in the corner of the porch, content as a cat with the morning sun warming my back. The garden is a tangle of weeds, but clumps of daffodils bloom undiscouraged. I rouse myself to go outside and take a closer look. Worn-out tulips with only a few spindly buds, lots of hardy perennials, narrow-leaved Siberian iris just sending up purple spears, big clumps of daylilies that should be divided, an old-fashioned bleeding heart big as a shrub and about to bloom, phlox and asters across the back for late summer. Mostly plants that take care of themselves. Behind them a border of mixed shrubs—forsythia, bridal wreath, butterfly bush—and another sturdy woody shrub that hasn't begun to leaf out. I'll have to look it up in Aunt Phoebe's shrub book later. Plenty of raw material here to start with, and with some delphiniums and flats of annuals to fill in, white cosmos and marigolds and blue salvia, I could have it in shape by summer. I laugh at myself. Who will be living here in a year? Someone who likes gardening, I hope. Me, I hope. Then I hear the thin wail from inside. Dorothea is awake and frightened. I must go in to her, ease her into her new surroundings, just as I have eased myself.

It is eleven before Dorothea is dressed and fed and exercised and settled in her wheelchair. I am about to go upstairs to Aunt Phoebe's little office when a truck, an old blue pickup, turns into the driveway. Demetrius, whom I called last week about turning on the water, explaining I'd be down for a few days with just Dorothea, that Jeannine was staying with Lesley, who still had school, has come to check up on us, just as he must have checked on Aunt Phoebe those last years. He gets out, walks towards the house, and stands at the bottom of the porch steps looking up at me, squinting in the sunlight. "You get your paper all right?"

"Oh, that was you," I say. "Thank you. I must have been on the beach when you came."

"Ah. An early riser. Thought you'd be sleeping."

"I'm not usually up so early, but the sun woke me. And it's nice to have time to myself before . . ." Demetrius follows my glance towards Dorothea, whose wheelchair I have positioned on the corner of the porch so the sun will shine on her. "Will you come in? I have coffee made."

"Wondered if I could do a grocery run for you. There's not much here except canned goods."

"That would be wonderful. But I need to do a big shopping."

"Well then. I'll drive you and help with the hauling. Take you up on that coffee if you want to make a list." He hesitates at the bottom of the steps until I motion him up. He moves lightly, quietly, his lean body showing its age only in the springy iron-gray curls and the veins standing out on his forearms and hands. From a distance, and with a hat covering his hair, he would look forty.

"Well, hello," he says to Dorothea, crossing the porch and squatting down on his haunches to put himself at her eye level. "What's this you've got here?" He reaches out towards the arm of her wheelchair, not quite touching it, not wanting to alarm her. Dorothea's good eye widens, her head shifts sideways to glance at me, then back to Demetrius, on whom she bestows her half-smile.

"Such a fancy steed you've got there. Does it have a name? Pegasus?

That's what you should call it. My mama always used to say we could use a little mythology."

Dorothea's smile grows wider, a little more crooked. "She doesn't speak," I say, wondering what sort of response Demetrius is expecting. "I'm not sure she understands you, but she likes you, that's plain." Practically no one I know speaks directly to Dorothea. Most people are careful not to look in her direction. The ones that bother me most speak about her as if she weren't in the room at all, as if she were an inanimate object. But Demetrius has walked right up to her and named her wheelchair Pegasus. And Dorothea, usually nervous around strangers, has taken to him right away.

Dorothea loves supermarkets. I don't take her food shopping often; it's such a huge physical effort, but when she's with me I sometimes can see the local Stop and Shop as she must, as an ever-changing panorama of light and color. Dorothea beams as best she can at the people we pass in the narrow aisles, not noticing their furtive glances, the way they turn their heads with a quick embarrassed motion and look away. And today Demetrius is there to manage the wheelchair, to wrestle it out of the back of the van and set it up and lift Dorothea deftly out of her seat and position her in it before she has a chance to be frightened. And to wheel her up and down the aisles while I handle the shopping cart. I'm too grateful to think it's odd for him to offer to come shopping. I usually dread it, but today it seems almost festive.

We spend a long time in the produce section. Demetrius has surprisingly strong opinions about vegetables. All the spring lettuce is in. We ponder the relative merits of romaine, its long deep green heads heavy and dense, a bargain at the price, and the looser, less substantial but beautifully ruffled ruby, its edges shading to deep red. I end up buying both. Should I splurge on anchovies and make a Caesar salad? Is Caesar a misnomer if I leave them out? We pause to discuss these matters in front of a display of flavored croutons, ignoring the irritated glares of other shoppers forced to detour around us. Despite the looks I'm enjoying myself.

As soon as I get out of the van back at the house I hear the phone ringing and make a dash into the kitchen for it. It's Gregory, sounding worried. "Where in blazes have you been? I've been calling for an hour. Is everything all right?"

"Everything's fine. We've just been to the grocery. It took a long time—you know how Dorothea loves to food shop."

"Anna, you think she knows where she is? One place is like another to her." Gregory thinks I'm being flip, and he can't bear it when I joke about Dorothea. The irony is I'm not joking. "I don't understand why you didn't take Jeannine down there with you so you could get out without her."

"She has exams, remember? Anyway, it was all right. Demetrius came with us and helped with the chair. We had a good time, actually. And I shouldn't need anything else for the week, except maybe milk from the store up town."

"What was he doing over there?"

"He came by and offered to do the shopping himself. He's just being neighborly. I think he feels responsible for us."

"If he'd been a little more responsible about the gutters, Aunt Phoebe might still be alive."

"Gregory, that's not fair." I drop the subject because Demetrius has appeared in the doorway carrying two brown bags. "I have to go now; I've got ice cream in the car," I say curtly. Somehow I don't want to tell him Demetrius is still here.

"You be careful," he says. "And call me in a couple of days."

I am on the edge of getting angry; my cheerful mood has evaporated. It feels good to get off the phone. I follow Demetrius back out to the car, glad to see Dorothea already in her wheelchair, relieved to let him take charge of her while I carry in the last bag of groceries.

The bitter aroma of overheated coffee fills the kitchen; I've left the percolator on. I offer the last cup to Demetrius apologetically. "Thick and strong," he says, "the way I like it. I make a pot in the morning for the whole day, so I'm used to old coffee."

"Sit and keep me company while I put the food away. You've done enough," I say, glad to be distracted from my irritation at Gregory. Demetrius pulls out a chair and sits down, looking momentarily uncomfortable, suddenly older, tired. Thinking of Aunt Phoebe? Does he blame himself for her accident? He looks at home here at her battered table. Did she invite him in like this, give him cups of coffee? He'd worked for Dennis, then for her, so many years, one of the few people she saw with any regularity.

I pour the last dregs of the coffee into the sink and get myself a glass of water to sip on while I unload the bags and arrange milk and orange juice and vegetables in Aunt Phoebe's ancient refrigerator. Only a thin metal wall marks off the freezer section. The ice cream probably wasn't a good idea.

"How long have you known Aunt Phoebe?" I ask, my back to Demetrius as I try to fit a cereal box sideways onto the narrow pantry shelves.

"Started working cranberries when I was fourteen, making bog," he says. "My papa worked for his cousin at a big operation in West Barnstable—that's where I started out. Guess you could say cranberries run in the family. A few years after Dennis bought West Marsh, I came over here. There was a lot of repair work to do, and one whole section we remade pretty much from scratch, had full-grown trees on it. I was fourteen."

"So you've been working at West Marsh since then?"

"'Cept for my time in the military. 'Course, there's not a lot to do in the summer, so I babysit houses for the summer folk, mow lawns, that sort of thing."

The groceries are all put away. I bring my water over to the table and sit down opposite Demetrius. Immediately I regret it. It's nearly one. I realize I'm very hungry. Dorothea will be hungry, too; it's well past her usual lunchtime, though she seems content out on the porch in the sun listening to the radio and humming softly to herself. Should I offer lunch to Demetrius? Probably not a good idea. "Never be alone with a strange man," I can hear my mother warning. Out of nowhere I feel nervous, sitting here at the table with this Portuguese man I barely know, a laborer, handyman, really, looking at him with my mother's eyes and hating myself for it. What sort of rules operate in his world? If I offered him a sandwich, would he interpret that as a signal? Of course he's not really a stranger, and Dorothea is here, I think, arguing mentally with my mother.

But there's something disconcertingly intimate about being here, in this kitchen, sitting together at Aunt Phoebe's table. I look at him surreptitiously. He's a small man, barely as tall as I am, but strong, wiry, with a kind of quiet energy radiating from him even now, though he's only looking pensive, sitting perfectly still. He's wearing workman's clothes, a blue-black wool sweater that looks like Navy issue, a pair of faded jeans, heavy leather high-top work boots. He speaks with the barest trace of Cape Cod accent, as if he were educated, as if he had lived elsewhere. I want to ask him questions about himself. But he makes me nervous. And feeding Dorothea is tedious and messy; I don't like to do it in front of people outside the family. I do not ask him to stay for lunch, though my stomach is growling and Dorothea is beginning to make faint complaining noises.

IT'S FOUR O'CLOCK before I get up into Aunt Phoebe's room. Dorothea has fallen asleep in her chair; the trip to the store has worn her out. I decide to let her nap there while I work upstairs. Aunt Phoebe must have moved into this room for the view; there's little else to recommend it. It's small and cramped and dark, now that it's late afternoon and the sun is on the other side of the house. Other than my open suitcase on the floor, it's pretty much as Aunt Phoebe left it. None of the papers on the cluttered desk have been touched since that day in late March when Greg and I were last here. I look at the narrow cot with its white spread, again overwhelmed with a sense of Aunt Phoebe's presence, waking that last morning in February, making up the bed—would she go downstairs and have coffee first? Would she lie for a while under the warm covers and plan out her day the way I do? Glad, maybe, that the weather has cleared, the sun is out, and now she can do something about those gutters on the north side? Why didn't she call Demetrius and ask him to clear them? Did she try and not find him home? Was she like me, impatient with any delay once she got a bee in her bonnet? Or tired of asking for help? Maybe she wanted to test herself, to see if she still had the gumption, the strength to climb a ladder and take care of things on her own.

I didn't get very far that day we were here in March, other than sorting some of the things on the top of Aunt Phoebe's desk and getting rid of the junk mail and catalogues and finding the tax records. I should attend to some of the letters, check them against the address book and make sure we notified everybody. But the journal is on my mind. Where is it? Not in or on the desk. There are four stacks of manilla folders and loose papers laid on the bookshelves; would it be there? Or in a bound book, like the leather travel diary my father gave me the summer I went to Europe?

I decide to check the bookshelves first. What insights our books reveal about our minds, not to mention our capacity for organization. Aunt Phoebe had a system, evidently, though there are many gaps in the rows. Nearly two shelves worth of books about Cape Cod, science books of varying complexity. A college geology text, looking as if it dated from the sixties—would it be Gregory's? Henry Beston's *The Outermost House*. Rachel Carson's *The Sea Around Us* and *The Edge of the Sea*. A geology book with the romantic title *These Fragile Outposts*. Thoreau's *Cape Cod* and *Walden*, both well-thumbed. A collection of Emerson's essays and poems. A leather-bound edition of Sir Thomas Browne's essays, equally worn. Darwin's *Origin of Species*. A falling-apart bird book she must have replaced with the new Peterson's on her desk, guides to trees, to New England wildflowers, to seashore plants. A whole shelf of poetry books looking as if it had once been organized alphabetically, but now somewhat askew, with Gerard Manley Hopkins set in sideways to the left of Emily Dickinson, two editions of Robert Frost, a paperback John Donne looking as well used as the leather-bound one on her desk. And some newer poets I've never read. Mary Oliver. Galway Kinnell. Aunt Phoebe was an English major. She taught at a private girls' school in Cambridge in the late thirties, before she and Dennis were married.

But nowhere on these shelves is there anything resembling a diary. Would she have kept it somewhere else? In the bureau, among her clothes? In the attic, even, hidden away where Uncle Dennis wouldn't find it? But he has been dead for eight years and never climbed the stairs for four years before that. Where could it be? It's supposed to go to that friend Aunt Phoebe mentioned in the letter, Daphne Ault, the tall neighbor I saw this morning. Would she know something about it? Wherever it is, I won't find it today. It's time to go downstairs, wake Dorothea so she'll sleep tonight, time to do something about dinner.

I'm sleepy after supper, so I decide to walk outside for some fresh air. It is still broad daylight—there is much more light here than in Needham what with the open sky, the reflection off the harbor. I don't dare go as far as the beach; Dorothea might get frightened. So I position the wheelchair in the parlor, turn on the TV to distract her, a noisy game show with rather snowy reception, and make my way out through the kitchen and porch to the garden. It's still too early in the season to be buggy, thank goodness. I crouch down and pull out a few bunches of crabgrass from around the fading daffodils. In a week or two the bleeding heart and iris will be in bloom, and one or two clumps of the earliest daylilies. I'm sorry I'll miss them.

On an impulse I walk around to the north side of the house and head up the hill towards Aunt Phoebe's rock. At least that's what it seems natural to call it. I decide to climb up so I can see the harbor. It's more difficult than I remember, but at last I find the crack where I can position my foot, grab hold of the projection above, and hoist myself up. The narrow space on top seems even more precarious than it did that day Aunt Phoebe first brought me here, but once I sit down I feel secure.

I picture Aunt Phoebe as she was that day, a barefoot middle-aged woman in a faded house dress and windblown hair, standing upright and surveying the landscape around her, naming its features. "We live right on the ice margin," she said, "where the glacier stopped." The harbor spreads out before me, silver in the dying light, quiet, not a breath of wind. How lonely it seems, and how beautiful. A glacial erratic, Aunt Phoebe called this boulder, caught up in the ice and dragged here, scarred with long striations on one side from scraping against bedrock. *Erratic*: wandering, far from home, and yet belonging here now, part of the landscape. A odd word for a rock, a word used for people who don't follow the rules, who might be dangerous.

What has brought me out here at this hour, I wonder, all alone when Dorothea waits for me back at the house? Aunt Phoebe. How much more real she seems after today. All day I've been following her tracks, down to the marshes, out to the porch and garden, into the kitchen, upstairs where she read and wrote and dreamed, up here on this perch where she escaped, perhaps, needing one last glimpse of water and sky. Is that why I already feel at home, safe, as if this were the place I've been looking for?

IT IS TWO more days before I finally speak to the tall woman. She overtakes me at the crest of the hill as she's heading back toward her house from the marshes before breakfast. She's wearing the same shorts and old sweater, swinging along at a good clip and not looking as though she wants to stop and chat. "Lovely morning," I say lamely.

"You're Phoebe Turnstone's niece, aren't you? I'm Daphne Ault. I was at the funeral; maybe you remember."

So this is the Daphne who is to receive the elusive journal. Does she know anything about it? I decide to search the house more thoroughly before I ask her. "Yes, I remember. I'm Anna. We talked in the upstairs hall."

"I've seen you on the beach, mornings," she says. "You like to get up early?"

"Yes, I wake so early here, earlier than at home, right after sunrise, and with so much energy, anticipation, I don't know, but I have to get up and out. It's as if every day were some special day I've been waiting months for."

"It's the negative ions. Ocean air. They're in the mountains, too. I was in Colorado once, staying at nine thousand feet, and felt the same way. Woke every morning thinking I was at the beach."

"It's wonderful. Does it wear off?"

"Hasn't yet. I'll let you know. It's why I'm here. And now I've got to get back. Nice meeting you." And she is off down the road with her long loping stride, leaving me staring after her, though she is walking in the same direction. I feel mildly slighted, but I learn later not to be surprised. In the middle of a conversation Daphne will begin leaning sideways, as if she were being drawn by some magnetic force, and with barely a word of apology abruptly head for home, her internal clock signaling that the time for casual socializing is over; she must get to work. How I envy her the ability to turn away from a friend and walk down the road like that! Time to me is endlessly malleable, adjustable to the needs of the people around me.

The Goldberg Variations

Many and varied and sometimes beautiful are the
patterns etched by all comers into these yielding sands.

I SHOULD HAVE KNOWN better than to call Daphne in the morning. Writers are supposed to be night people, but obviously this one isn't, with her walks down to the harbor at dawn every day. I debate calling her at all. Had Phoebe mentioned the journal to Daphne, and would she ask about it? Probably not, but I don't like the idea of being thought selfish or underhanded. And besides, Daphne knew Phoebe; she was a link.

When I do call, about ten o'clock, I get a recording: "Leave a message and I'll call you back." And then between the curt announcement and the signal, piano music, Bach, the *Goldberg Variations,* one of Dorothea's favorites. But almost as soon as I identify myself, Daphne is there on the line.

"I'm here, Anna. Is everything all right?"

"Oh, yes. I'm just calling about something Aunt Phoebe asked me to do."

"Well, I'm working now. I thought you might need help with your daughter or something. Call back after three, if you don't mind."

I'm still sitting there next to the phone, trying to decide whether to be hurt or angry, when the phone rings and it's Daphne again. "I'm sorry I was so abrupt. It's just that I have this rule, no phone calls while I'm working. I usually let the machine take them, but I thought you might be in some sort of trouble over there. You said something about Phoebe?"

"Yes. She left a letter about what to do with some things in the house. She mentioned a journal she wanted you to have, but I haven't found it anywhere. Did she perhaps give it to you before she died? She said she'd like me to read it."

There is a long silence on the other end of the line, long enough to seem peculiar. "I do know something about it," Daphne says carefully. "Why don't you come over here and we can talk about it? I'm through working at three. How about tea-time, around four or four-thirty?" Daphne annoys me, I decide. She's being deliberately mysterious.

"That would be nice," I say. "I'll have to bring my daughter with me, though. Can we get her wheelchair into the house?"

"Oh, I should think so." No hesitation, which makes me feel more kindly towards her.

And so at ten after four I transfer Dorothea onto the wicker armchair on the porch, fold the wheelchair and carry it down the porch steps and set it up on the grass and then go back up the steps onto the porch and hoist Dorothea up from the wicker rocker, supporting her under her arms while she bears some of her weight on her good leg, and we go bump, bump, backwards down the steps and into the yard where I settle her into her chair. It's difficult and awkward. I mustn't try it again by myself when I could use the parlor door on the other side of the house, wide enough to roll the chair through and with only one step, but still sealed up for the winter with tape and weatherstripping.

Daphne's house is two down on the other side of the lane, a low, nondescript shingled cottage nearly concealed from the road by large rhododendrons. The yard slopes down toward the house and is full of locust trees, bare still but beginning to put out tiny sprays of leaves. There's no driveway. A few daffodils are just past bloom on either side of the door amidst overgrown clumps of daylilies. Daphne is not a gardener, evidently. Unassuming surroundings for such a dramatic-seeming woman.

Then there she is at the door. Two cats streak out from behind her and dart into the yard. "Welcome, Anna," she is saying. "And Dorothea?" She reaches out and takes Dorothea's good hand briefly before steadying the front of the chair as I bump it up the two steps and into the house. Dorothea is wary but doesn't jerk her body away, as she so often does when strangers get too close.

Once we are inside I can see where the drama is, the wall opposite the door all glass, and beyond that a deck looking out through the trunks of locusts to a small pond. The room is long and full of light, some filtering from the sky through the tree branches, more reflecting up from the water. In front of the glass wall is a long cluttered table made from a door laid over two small filing cabinets, and to the left a large stone fireplace flanked on one side by a well-worn wing chair containing still another cat, an enormous gray one who's sound asleep, and on the other by a wooden rocker. To the right is an old pine table marked up by years of use; beyond that a galley kitchen with a pot rack over the stove and open shelves stacked with what looks like hand-thrown pottery the color of sand. A hall to the right of the door leads, presumably, to a bedroom and a bath.

Books are everywhere. The walls beside the fireplace and facing the road are lined with shelves filled to overflowing; more books are piled in front of them, on the mantel, and under the writing table. Somehow, even with the clutter, the effect is not claustrophobic. I'm aware of light and space and the subtle, subdued tones of the marshes in winter, the colors of the beach and dried grasses and the bleached bones of gulls.

I wheel Dorothea over to the glass wall so she can look out at the pond. She brightens and sits forward as a goldfinch and two house sparrows take turns at the feeder fastened to the balcony railing. "Do you have any music?" I ask Daphne, thinking about the Bach on the answering machine. "She loves listening to music."

"Of course. I have hundreds of tapes, a little jazz, but mostly classical. What does she like?"

"Am I right in thinking you have the *Goldberg Variations?*"

"Ah. The phone machine. She's got sophisticated taste. Would she prefer harpsichord or piano?"

"Piano, I think. It's one of my favorites, too." Was one of my favorites. Dorothea was just discovering Bach when everything changed. She wanted the music, even though much of it was beyond her—she was already working on the opening statement and some of the simpler variations.

Daphne rummages through several shoe boxes of tapes stacked under the bookshelves before she finds the Bach. As soon as the music begins Dorothea relaxes back in her chair, smiles her half-smile. I turn down Daphne's offer of a soft drink for her; it hasn't occurred to me to bring her drinking cup. But I don't turn down a glass of wine. I sit in the rocker facing the view and Daphne settles herself cross-legged on the floor next to the chair where the cat sleeps on, undisturbed.

"Did you build the house?" I ask, thinking that it doesn't have the right proportions to be historic.

"Oh, no. It was built in the sixties, just a two-room cabin. It was awfully dark and musty when I bought it, but it was the only thing this close to the harbor I could afford. I fixed up the bath and kitchen and added the glass and deck in the back and cleared out a lot of underbrush. When I bought it, you couldn't even see the pond in summer, it was so overgrown." She gestures toward the window, where the water below the house has broken the afternoon sun into shards of light. How peaceful it must be to live alone here, to face that view and write.

"Well it's wonderful now," I say. "The pond is so perfectly round, and it throws so much light into the house. It makes me think of Thoreau—what did he call Walden? A lower heaven."

"Oh yes, I treasure it. It's a kettle pond; that's why it's so round. It formed where a big chunk of ice was left when the glacier melted. The Cape is full of them."

"Is that why this is called Kettle Lane?" I look over at Daphne, who is reaching up absentmindedly to scratch the big gray cat behind the ears. Does he ever let her sit in the wing chair, I wonder.

"Some people think the kettle has to do with Iyanough," she is saying.

"The Indian chief?"

"Yes. His grave, or what they claim is his grave, was found in a marsh just east of here. Some farmer dug up a copper pot, and under it was the skeleton of an Indian, buried in a sitting position."

"That must have given the farmer quite a start," I say, laughing. "How long have you been in the house?"

"Eleven years, twelve next month. Gosh, that's hard to believe." Even as she says it I'm conscious of my envy—her having all that time to get to know Aunt Phoebe. Were they good friends? Of course they were. Otherwise why would Aunt Phoebe want her to have the journals? And Uncle Dennis, what does she know about him?

I pause. "Where were you before you came here?" I ask, the inevitable question.

"New York. Manhattan born and bred. And no, I don't miss it, except for the theater."

New York. That explains a lot. "Do you get up to Boston?"

"Sometimes. I have a friend I can stay with. But it gets harder and harder to make myself cross the bridge. Everybody who moves here jokes about that, but it's true."

Then I remember why Daphne's name seemed familiar. She was in the news and on the talk shows several years ago. Her first novel had made a splash, won some sort of prestigious award. I had even read it. It was about growing up during World War II on Staten Island, a child's-eye view of a semi-rural paradise on the brink of change, the war a kind of backdrop, a parade of troop ships passing by on their way back and forth across the Atlantic. "I read your first novel. Are you working on one now?"

Daphne sighs. "That's the one everybody remembers. I suffer from a fatal disease—early success. Everything else doesn't quite measure up. One reason I moved out of New York was so I wouldn't run into publishers in restaurants."

So Daphne has people she doesn't want to run into. We've got that in common, at least.

"Did you grow up on Staten Island?"

"So you really did read it. No, I lived in Manhattan, but I had cousins over there I spent a lot of time with, holidays and summers."

"And what are you writing now?"

"A conglomeration of stuff. Revamping a collection of short stories I've had lying around for years. And some articles. I write for *CapeNews* and do some freelancing. And there's a new novel in there somewhere, trying to get out. It's roiling around in my head sort of like chaos the day before the first day of creation."

"What's it about?"

"I'm afraid to talk about it; I don't want to put a form on it before it's ready."

"Talking about it puts a form on it?" I ask.

"Absolutely. Have you ever tried to explain one of your dreams to someone else? As soon as you put it into words, it changes."

I'm enjoying myself, I realize, listening to Daphne talk about her writing, even though I'm not quite sure what she means. Then all at once I do. That therapist I went to when I was trying to get over what happened to Dorothea would ask me about my dreams. Whenever I tried to explain them, I ended up feeling as though I were telling lies.

I look around the room, cluttered with books, dominated by the makeshift desk with its view of the pond. I wonder what it must feel like to sit at a desk all day spinning lives out of your head. I wanted to write when I was in junior high; that year I spent one whole hot Ohio summer working my way through my parents' leatherbound set of Dickens, one novel after another. I even started a story of my own, something about a foundling, a young girl of course. It was a year when I couldn't stand anything about my parents and would have welcomed finding out I'd been born to somebody else. But writing was hard, I discovered. And lonely. I spent a lot of time in the kitchen fixing snacks for myself. Does Daphne get lonely? She doesn't seem the type.

"You don't mind living here alone?" I ask.

"Not at all. I've always found my own mind more interesting than most of the people I know."

"Don't you need someone to talk to?"

"Not often. Sometimes. And I have my cats. They're a great comfort—so physical."

"I guess I'm more of a people person. It's talking to others that—I'm like that woman who didn't know what she thought until she could see what she said. When I'm with a friend, someone who knows me, and we're talking and laughing—it could be about cooking or the children or politics or anything—that's when I feel most real, most completely myself." As I say the words, I realize how long it's been since I've talked and laughed with a friend, or sat in someone else's house in the late afternoon drinking wine and enjoying the view.

Daphne smiles at me. "And I feel most real when no one and nothing is pulling at me, when I'm alone and truly within myself. Out on the flats in the early morning, say, I can feel everything, the wet on my feet and the breeze ruffling the hairs on my arms and that low tide smell, of brine and fish and decay—"

"Oh, yes, that's one of the first things I noticed when I came here. It's so elemental."

"The bottom of the food chain. Life. I get immersed in it. That's when I'm really myself."

"Yes, I know," feeling an odd rush of emotion, as if this woman, nearly a stranger, had reached inside my head and found words for my feelings. "That's why I love it here. Out there on the flats, I feel connected, as if I belonged there with the seaweed and the hermit crabs. I want both, I guess. To have people I'm connected to, and freedom to be alone when I want."

Daphne sighs. "Easier said than done," she says. "Live alone and you're lonely, some of the time, at least. It's the price you pay for independence, like the real estate tax on prime shore front property. If you have to ask how much it is, you can't afford it."

The first side of Daphne's tape of the *Goldberg Variations* has ended; she unfolds her long legs and stands up in one swift graceful motion and crosses the room to turn it over. Dorothea is sitting quietly in her chair, still lost in the music, humming something that sounds like the first line of the theme. Daphne stops on her way back across the room and stares at her. "Hear that?"

"Yes. She has an ear. She used to be—she is—very musical. She played the piano wonderfully. And that part of her brain, where the music is, wasn't so badly damaged."

"Oh my." Daphne looks at her sadly, looks away, a maneuver I am familiar with from long experience. I'm grateful she doesn't say any more. It's Daphne who remembers where we were in our conversation. "Living alone—it's hard sometimes. But how many people do you know who can really talk to the ones they're living with? Husbands, children?" So true, I am thinking, surprised to feel my eyes tearing up. Did Daphne have a husband, ever? Children?

"When you have one of those truly satisfying conversations, who is it likely to be with?" Daphne asks. "A woman friend, I bet."

I set the rocker in motion, thinking that this is one of those conversations. Will we get to be friends? "Yes, that's true," I say. "But I don't get to do it much any more, since Dorothea. My friends have been wonderfully supportive, but they don't know what to say. It's as if we've had a death in the family that's gone on and on and on. We're not normal anymore; we're special—those poor Dylans who had that lovely girl who—you know. It's one of the reasons I'm here. I'd give anything for a conversation that wasn't tinged with sympathy."

"Well, you're having one now," Daphne says curtly, getting up again to fetch the bottle of wine. "There are lots of Dorotheas around; most of them just aren't so easy to spot. Think of Phoebe."

Yes, Phoebe. I have thought of little else since I arrived at her house. Who did she confide in, all those years, those long gray raw winters when no one was around but Dennis, and he more apt to keep company with a gin bottle. There's no way to know how much they shared. My thoughts shift to Gregory and the many unsaid things between us. Why haven't we ever learned to confide in each other? We never had heart-to-heart talks long into the night, even in the beginning. He grew up in a silent house, and I was trained early not to make demands, to keep my feelings to myself. Was that why Gregory sought me out all those years ago on those front steps in Somerville? Because I didn't mind being alone, because I could tolerate, even welcome his silences?

Now maybe Daphne will bring up the subject of the journal—isn't that why she invited me over here? But she doesn't. And I don't dare. There's a little space of silence, which I feel obliged to fill. "You've lived here twelve years, you say? You must have made some friends."

"Not many. Phoebe was, of course, and I miss her. My editor at *CapeNews*, and she throws these literary-artsy soirées in the summer I get invited to. The cats' vet, believe it or not, who likes music, and we go to concerts and movies sometimes. She moved here about the same time I did. She's young; early thirties, and not the sort to attract men. There aren't many people her age around in the winter, at least not with her kind of education. And she works all the time and doesn't have time for much else."

Might the two of us go to a concert, a movie? How long since I've been to a concert? Five years. At first even hearing piano music on the radio was enough to undo me. And Gregory isn't really musical; if we got symphony tickets, it was for Dorrie's sake.

I want to ask Daphne if there are any men in her life, but I don't. Perhaps she likes women, or is simply asexual. I don't know how to tell. Despite her thinness, her big frame, her hair cropped short and shaved at the back of her neck, there's something intensely female about her. She is unquestionably womanly, not yielding and soft, but lean, spare, pared down to essentials, keen and alert with quick responses, attuned to everything around her. Brusque and off-putting, yes. I think about the phone call this morning. But she picked up the phone; she thought we might be in trouble, might need her. She would have been there if we had.

Daphne gets up again with the same economical motion and crosses the room to the long table pushed against the glass facing the pond, her writing table, every space not taken up by her computer filled with books and papers piled in heaps. She comes back with a tall stack of twenty or so notebooks, the kind I remember from grammar school, with black and white mottled covers. She collapses back into her cross-legged position and sets the notebooks between us.

"Here they are. Phoebe's journals. I have a confession to make. I stole them out of the house. Do you remember, the day of the funeral, finding me in the upstairs hall? That's what I was doing. I took my big travel bag to the funeral because they'd all fit inside. I don't know what to say, except Phoebe told me she wanted me to have them, and I didn't know but you might just burn all her papers or sell the house as is, and they'd be lost. I'm sorry. But here they are, and you should read them. You're in them in places. She thought a lot about you, especially after your daughter—"

I'm startled by the distress on Daphne's face, and by what she is telling me, but not angry. Not even surprised, really. I think of Gregory. If he'd had his way we would have done just that, sold the house as is. "I understand," I say. "And I'm grateful you told me. I'll return them."

"Phoebe was a manipulator, in her way," Daphne says. "A kind of witch, I sometimes thought. How I miss her! I think she wanted me to put her in a novel, and maybe I will—it would be a way of keeping her around."

"Did you know she left the house to Dorothea? In trust, of course, with Greg and me as trustees. I was surprised she included me; I'm not her kin."

"*Kin*. Such a Southern word. Are you Southern? You don't sound it."

"Ohio. But with Tennessee relatives. Or kin, I should say."

Daphne stretches her legs out in front of her and leans back, laughing. "She leaves the house to Dorothea and makes you trustee. Oh, that's just like her. She knows Greg could care less about the house. But you might. It's a plot. And all this business about the journal—it's to go to me, but you're to read it? We'd have to meet and talk about it, wouldn't we? A gambit if I ever saw one. So like Phoebe." She leans back on her hands, looking into the fireplace and smiling, remembering something Phoebe said, maybe, or is she planning how all this might fit into a novel?

Daphne lends me her same big black nylon bag to carry all the journals home. I'm wild with impatience to get Dorothea fed and settled for the night and start reading. It seems to take forever to get the wheelchair out through Daphne's door, up the lane, into the house. I haul Dorothea backwards up the steps more roughly than I mean to, worrying about bruising her heels. Even with her wasted muscles she seems unbelievably heavy. I should not have declined Daphne's offer to help. I must unseal the parlor door tomorrow.

What an amazing afternoon, what a surprise to find a *simpatica* friend in this offputting woman. But isn't friendship often like that, something we fall into unexpectedly, like love?

Snow White and Rose Red

In a glacier we see the snows of many yesteryears.

LESLEY ROLLS OVER and squints at the clock beside the bed. Nearly one. She could sleep all day, all week with Mom and Dorrie gone, no one here but Jeannine to bother her. Her head aches still from the fall yesterday. She and Sally bicycled to Dover to see Deb somebody, Sally's camp friend, and they'd all tried to ride her mother's old mare. Lesley was in back and got bounced off when the mare shied at a white plastic bag on the path. Moon-blind in one eye, Deb said, something that happens to horses sometimes, no one knows why.

It all happened too fast to scare her. It was weird how much time she had to think before the back of her head hit the ground. What she thought about was Dorrie. She was twelve too, when it happened. Some things just happen. People go crazy if the moon shines on them while they're sleeping, Dorrie told her once, to scare her, back when she was so little she'd believe anything.

It's supposed to be spring but it doesn't feel like it. The river banks look awful, junk everywhere, stuff washed down by the rain, shredded diapers caught in the overhanging branches, those gross plastic tampon things on the edge of the path. "Needham girl dies tragically; plastic bag blamed," Lesley imagines reading. "Mother vacationing on Cape Cod." Not really fair. A week down there in that junky house with Dorrie the Lump wouldn't be a vacation.

Anyway, the headache has got her a day off from school. She didn't dare tell Jeannine about the horse so she's all concerned. Shouldn't be having headaches at her age. Getting her period? Not yet, though it's making her nervous; she keeps checking. Get out of my face, Lesley wants to tell her. I don't need a sitter. Go study for exams. But she just says she gets them sometimes, the headaches, and no, don't worry Mom about it; it would bring her back for no reason, and isn't it lucky to have Dorrie gone just before exams? No way to stretch it out to another school day, though. She better get up and think about last night's homework.

Sally will be home by three; maybe they can go down by the river.

She'll tell Jeannine she needs to get out to clear her head. Mom's always saying that. Sally is who Lesley spends time with these days, now that her best friend Katie's "in love" and can't talk about anything else but Jackie Jackie Jackie. Sally is Judy Nissen's older sister. The Nissens are handy, right up the street, three years apart in age, Lesley falling right in between. She started hanging around with them two years ago when Judy appeared in her back yard with a butterfly net. Judy knows everything about butterflies, and for a few weeks they stalked *Papilio gloucus* and *Danaus plexippus*, giving up their plan for a collection when they realized it meant asphyxiating and stabbing their beautiful specimens through the thorax.

Judy's smarter than Sally even if she is younger, but Sally's more of a daredevil. She likes to play with matches for one thing, and she's always making up words. She's the one who started the name game. First it was fairy tales. The Dylans were the seven dwarfs, except there were only five, counting Jeannine. Dad was Grumpy and Mom was Happy, not that she is, but she's good at putting it on. Dorrie the Lump was Dopey and Jeannine was Doc because she had advice about everything. Lesley was Sleepy. Now it's initials. Sally's Mom is W.I.B.F.T. for "Wouldn't it be fun to—" the phrase that seems to start every sentence she directs at the girls. Lesley's Dad is G.G. for Galloping Ghost because of his habit of running in the evening after dark, and her mother is O.O., for the Oblivious One.

Lesley swings her long legs out of bed and shuffles down the hall to the bathroom. The bump on the back of her head is still tender. It hurts as she brushes the tangles out of her long hair. It hangs down, straight and lank. Should she get it cut short, shaved in the back like Sally's? People are always exclaiming about her hair, the color. Strawberry, a stupid name for something more like apricot. If she cut it she wouldn't have to think about it. But Sally's haircut doesn't look all that great, especially in the back where it's all bristly. Really short hair is fine if you're beautiful, but sometimes Lesley's grateful to let hers hang forward the way her Dad hates, a curtain to hide behind. She heads to the kitchen and fixes herself a bowl of Cheerios.

There's a note on the table from Jeannine. She's gone in to school to the library. No one home. Lesley smiles, feels herself expand in the empty house. She fetches the milk from the refrigerator, pours it over her cereal and carries the bowl through the house to the sunroom and switches on MTV. Not allowed any time, let alone mornings, and no "wet snacks" in the sunroom, either. But there's no one to boss her, make her follow the rules. That hardly ever happens.

She gets to see MTV anyway at her friends' houses. It's surprising the same videos are on on a weekday morning. Well, early afternoon. A rap song with a quick hypnotic beat, the staccato patter of words like a snare drum overlaying the rhythm. She can only understand a few of the words. Lots of artsy videos done in black and white like old forties movies, like that one her Mom rented and made her watch last summer—*Casablanca*. She's still in front of the TV in her nightshirt when Sally arrives at the door in her school clothes, not dressed for the river. She's almost fourteen, in eighth grade, a stocky girl with chubby legs, not any taller than Lesley and not pretty, her severe haircut unflattering with her glasses and round face.

"Let's go snooping," Sally says, checking out Lesley's earrings while she pulls on jeans and a sweatshirt. "Ever go through Jeannine's stuff?"

Lesley stiffens a little at the idea, then thinks why not? Jeannine's room is on the third floor behind the girls' playroom, still stocked with their outgrown toys. Lesley used to read up there but hasn't since Jeannine arrived. She still feels funny around her. She's there to help take care of Dorrie so Mom won't go crazy, to dress and feed her and move her arms and legs so she won't freeze up. Jeannine keeps trying to make friends with Lesley but mostly she talks to Mom, the two of them in the kitchen getting dinner together, it's like they don't notice if she's there or not.

"Come on. Maybe she's got a diary." Lesley follows Sally up the attic stairs, through the playroom where a row of dolls waits patiently, a few tucked into beds, the rest propped against the bottom drawer of the toy cabinet. Lesley didn't arrange them like that, leaning toward each other as if they were carrying on a conversation. Did Jeannine do it? Or Mom? Lesley was never a doll lover anyway; her passion was her stuffed animals, piled now in a heap in the cradle Mom said is going to be hers someday, bought the afternoon she found out she was pregnant.

Jeannine's door is closed but not locked. Lesley is secretly sorry. She feels jumpy as a housebreaker in her own house. The bed is made, the room neat except for a pile of clothes on the little armchair, the top bureau drawer hanging open, underwear and a jumble of jewelry clearly visible.

"Come on. Help me look," Sally insists. She's rummaging around in the top drawer under Jeannine's bras and panties, surprisingly colorful considering what she wears on top of them. Sally systematically works her way through all the drawers, remembering to leave the top one open. She looks like she's done this before. "Try the desk," she says. "I'll get the closet. Shoe boxes. That's where Judy keeps hers."

So Sally's been through her own little sister's room? Has she been through Lesley's? Lesley tries to remember if she's ever left her alone in there. Not that there would be anything to find. Except her drawings, the private ones. She'd have to think of a better place to hide them. If Sally can snoop, so can her mother.

Lesley sits down at the desk, covered with textbooks and different colored notebooks. Physiology notes for Jeannine's first exam, her hardest one she's been saying, are arranged in little piles. Lesley picks up the other notebooks one by one, opening them to the first page. Tidy round handwriting, the kind the nuns teach in Catholic schools. A neat title page in the beginning of each one, the name of the course centered on the top line, Jeannine's name and home phone number under it, the Dylans' added below since she's living here now. *Clinical Practice*, the blue one reads. As she picks it up a paper falls out from inside the back cover, typed and folded lengthwise the way Lesley's sixth grade teacher makes them do. She opens it and sees her own sister's name on the title page. "Dorothea Dylan: Initial Report." Underneath, a grade scrawled in red ink: A minus.

"Hey, look at this," Sally is calling from the closet. She's opening a brown paper bag, folded over and tightly closed. "Oh, gross! Want to look?" She reaches gingerly into the bag and pulls out a small shapeless object, something soft and squarish wrapped over and over in white tissue. Toilet paper, Lesley realizes. "Her old Kotex! What's she saving them for? Want to see?" Sally has had her period for a year now; Lesley has seen her used sanitary napkins in the wastebasket at their house, hastily folded and haphazardly wrapped, not neatly swaddled like this. Before she has a chance to say anything Sally is unrolling the little package, gingerly unfolding the napkin to reveal a long rusty brown stain. A sharp fishy odor fills the room, just as Lesley hears the downstairs door slam, Jeannine's voice calling to her. Sally hastily dumps the napkin in the bag without re-wrapping it, replaces the bag on the closet shelf as Lesley answers.

"Up in the attic. Sally's here." By the time Jeannine is halfway up the stairs they are sitting cross-legged in the playroom, pretending to play dolls.

"BLUEFIN TUNA, WHAT'S that?" Sally is asking. "Tuna with blue fins? I used to call tuna lumpfish because it came in those lumpy chunks." Sally's mother has commandeered them into putting her groceries away. *Lump* is what Lesley calls her sister, Sally has just remembered; Lesley can tell she's embarrassed. They start in on one of their word routines. "Bluefin lumpfish; lumpfin bluefish. Lumpyfin tuna."

"Lumpy tuner."

"Looney tunes!"

"Toonalumpy."

"Yeah! A big fat musical seagoing elephant." They collapse out of their chairs onto the cool hard Mexican tile floor in the Nissen's newly redecorated kitchen, rolling over and tickling each other, giggling until they are completely out of breath. The noise brings Sally's mother into the kitchen. It's dinnertime, she says, mindful that Lesley has taken the day off from school while her mother is out of town. Time to get home.

Dorrie used to tickle her like that, Lesley thinks as she cuts through the yards back to her house, tickle her until she panicked and thought she might die; Dorrie was so much bigger, sitting on her, making her squeal. Hated it, hated and loved it. Dorrie the Lump, lumpfish, tuna, tuner, hummer of tunes.

JEANNINE IS STILL in at school when Lesley gets home on Tuesday afternoon. She's supposed to call Sally, but there's something she wants to do first. She climbs the attic stairs and enters Jeannine's room. The desk looks different, neater, a couple of the notebooks gone. But the blue one is still there, second one down, with the report still inside the back cover. Lesley unfolds it, turns to the Table of Contents and begins to read. "Introduction." "Clinical symptoms." "Prognosis." "Remarks." She doesn't know the word *prognosis*, but she can tell what it means. She carefully folds the paper and puts it back where she found it.

It's a half mile down to the stone bridge where Lesley can step over the low metal barrier and drop down onto the path along the river. She's not supposed to be down here by herself or walk along this secluded part of River Street where there are no sidewalks and the cars tend to go faster than the speed limit. She hasn't called Sally. She just wants to be out of the house and by the river. The sun has come out and the wind has died down. After a gray beginning the day is starting to feel like summer.

A few hundred yards away from the road, the path cuts across a series of sloping yards backing on the river. The canoe she and Sally spotted on Saturday is still there, pulled up on the bank in a brushy area between two yards and loosely tied by one of the thwarts to a tree. To float down the river, let it decide where to take her, that would be nice.

Lesley grabs the near gunwale and drags the canoe into the water, the rope just long enough to allow it to float near shore, swinging back and forth slowly in response to the current. She steps into the water, totally soaking one shoe, places the other foot in the center of the canoe and shifts her weight aboard the way she learned at camp, lowers herself to a sitting position, then lies down under the thwarts. No one can see her now. She looks up at the mild May sky. The sun feels good on her face, nothing between her and it except a few narrow willow branches, still pale yellow-green. So warm and peaceful, she'd like to lie here forever. The canoe swings quietly beneath her, out into the current, back when the rope goes taut, like a rocking chair, a cradle.

"YOU'VE GOTTEN YOURSELF some color," Lesley's mother says Saturday at supper, really looking at her for the first time since she got home. "It looks nice. It reminds me of what Gram used to call you girls that summer we went to Knoxville and it was so hot. Remember?"

"I was just a baby."

"You're right; of course you can't remember. You'd just learned to walk. Not that you toddled; you ran. Dorothea stayed inside and played Gram's old piano all day long and you ran around the yard so much you were flushed all the time. Snow White and Rose Red. That's what Gram called you."

Under a spell, sleeping all alone in a dazzling white room—that's how Lesley's seven-year-old mind had imagined Dorrie when she was gone for so long, when Mom tried to explain to her what a coma was. Dorrie isn't Dopey, Lesley realizes. She's Snow White. But fairy tales are lies. There isn't any prince coming with a key to the glass box, to kiss her awake.

In the Wilds

Many of the shelled species of creatures found as fossils in
the pre-Pleistocene sands . . . are living on the flats today.

A T LAST DOROTHEA is settled and I can tackle the journals. So many!
What made me think there would be only one book to record all the
years of Phoebe's life? I pull them out of Daphne's voluminous nylon bag
and set them on top of the desk upstairs. Then I settle myself on the little
cot with the oldest one and begin to read.

> June 6: Here I am, Phoebe Turnstone, with a new name and a new
> life and a new black notebook to record it in. Part of my favorite
> wedding gift, from Selena, a lovely old lap desk of beautifully
> grained walnut with brass fittings, clever little drawers and a secret
> compartment where, of course, she hid her note. I imagine her eyes
> crinkling with mischief as she slipped it in. "This shows some wear,"
> she wrote, "like old people who have had interesting lives. Don't you
> dare put it on display! It is for your inner life, dearest Phoebe, which
> ever has been and will be interesting! Place it amidst the clutter on
> your desk and carry it to some sheltered leafy corner there in the
> wilds where you live now and write 1) your memoirs as a frontier wife
> and 2) long juicy letters to ME!" In a separate package, wrapped in
> the same silvery paper, a box of creamy stationery with a narrow red
> edge and a stack of five notebooks with mottled black covers. Will it
> take me five years to fill them? By the time I get to the last one will
> we still be here? Will we still be two, or three? Or four?
>
> I miss Selena—all those long sleepy talks late into the night,
> from our narrow beds in Washburn House. Her sly wit, her running
> commentary on everyone who intimidated us. How quickly we found
> each other, the shy misfit from Beacon Hill and a less shy but equally
> odd Southern girl lacking, as I did, all the social graces that seemed
> handed down genetically to our classmates, inevitable as curly hair or
> green eyes. I once introduced her, with thoughtless Yankee smugness,
> as from "darkest Alabama." "And you, Phoebe," she retorted, "are a

hillbilly from the hills of Boston." "Darkest Alabama" and the "hills of Boston" became our standard response when boys at mixers asked us where we were from, and when I wrote Selena about marrying Dennis and moving to the Cape, she sent back a long list of essential items for a covered wagon trip to the wilds of Cape Cod.

The old Turnstone farmhouse is not a covered wagon, surely, but primitive enough to make me grateful Mother won't see it for a while! Dennis has been camping here for the past two months, trying to make it livable. No one but mice has lived here since the twenties! Dennis washed down the walls and swept, but it still looks grimy—smoke and watermarks on the walls, and all the floors need sanding and a coat of varnish. He's put a gas water heater in the kitchen—if only I could remember I have to light it and wait an hour for it to heat up, and most importantly, turn it off! I have nightmares about it exploding. But it beats heating kettles to pour into the tub. Next will be a Frigidaire, but for this year we make do with the old icebox. Dennis's mother says we can use her washer and mangle, but I'll try to get along for the summer, at least, with the scrub board and washtub. I do feel so WIFELY hanging out our clothes, all mixed together, shirts and blouses, nightgowns and undershorts, on the line. And in this weather they smell like heaven when I gather them in.

June 10: Back door cold front is what the locals call it. After two days of humidity that kept me limply reading old books on the parlor sofa, a moist, foggy wind from the northeast, drizzly and damp, and now a shining June day that keeps tempting me outside, then sends me back in for a sweater and kerchief. How my hair whips around in this wind! I must find someone who knows what a feather cut is.

A day for pacing around the yard and dreaming. A garden I MUST have right away! The vegetable garden needs to be reclaimed now if we want any tomatoes and beans this summer, but it's flowers I imagine. MY garden, perennials! Blooms from March until frost cuts them down! But where, how large, what colors? This place, so windswept and wild, so different from Mother's orderly enclosed haven on Pinckney Street, with its old brick wall and square of immaculate lawn, the perfectly pruned roses and patriotic edging of red, blue and white: geraniums, ageratum, alyssum. Every year the same. And dear old Armando appearing magically two mornings a week to tend it.

I think about Professor Golden in studio art freshman year at
Smith, his disapproval more terrible than the terror of the blank
canvas. "Stop trying to plan everything ahead of time. Pick up
your brush, draw a line; take it from there." With every line we
set boundaries, define the game. "No rules, no creation!" he would
thunder at us. "The moderns weren't against rules, just old rules. They
made new ones up as they went along."

So I pace through the yard and plan my garden. By the parlor
door seems the natural place, but that is north, shaded by the house
and too full of trees. Out back, to see from the kitchen window, or in
the ell the kitchen makes with the old part of the house? Or both?
The front sunny and protected but not private, facing the lane. The
back exposed to the wind, more open, a boundary in front of the back
pasture. Which first? And what? The summer wildflowers here so
beautiful and hardy—couldn't I just transplant them? Queen Anne's
lace nodding in the pasture behind us, black-eyed Susans, tiger lilies,
that sky-blue shaggy flower that grows all along the roads—chicory.

How much I've written! Do I want to plant, or write about
planting? To be honest, it's the writing I love, a form of dreaming. No
storms, no bugs, no drought, no sore muscles. I can have exactly what
I want.

June 12: Just finished a long missive to Selena and picked up my
journal—and realized I'm still writing to Selena! Don't we ever and
always write *to* somebody? I thought I was doing it for myself—to
reread when I'm older, wiser, and *know how things turned out*. But it
isn't me, it's Selena: friend, soulmate, gadfly! Who somehow sees me
as wise and gallant and brave, and so I become those things, as best
I can, to please her. Isn't that the best part of friendship? To be seen,
not as we are, but as we *might be*? How I miss her!!

And now I miss Dennis! Gone all day, for the first time. I've
been mooning around like—a honeymooner, such happy lassitude (so
little sleep!), reliving last night, all the talk, the sweetness of waking
skin to skin. Sleeping so we always touch somewhere, a knee, a foot,
his hand in my hair. Will we outgrow all this? Everybody says so, but
I think not anytime soon. A day with nothing accomplished except
daydreams, two letters (a short one to Mother), and now I think a
nap. I will sleep, and then bathe (lighting the dragon, as I've come to
think of the gas heater) and pick some tiger lilies for our table, make
supper for my sweet love. The rest of the chicken, peas, and mashed

potatoes. Fresh cherries for dessert. Tomorrow I'll attempt a pie—there is rhubarb in the corner of the garden.

June 13: Still lovely weather, but getting muggier. Let it not heat up like last week. Lessons for a new bride: 1) Tiger lilies only last one day and wither when the sun goes down. Good for luncheons but not for dinner. 2) Pie dough looks simple but isn't. I've been struggling with my rhubarb pie, had to roll it out twice. The second time it held together but it's too thick and I bet tough. In the oven at last, and beginning to smell delicious, also a little burnt because it's bubbling over. I guess one puts the pie on a baking sheet or some such. Why didn't I learn more about cooking? (Answer: because Mother assumed I would HAVE a cook!) She is sure I will be miserable in the wilds of Cape Cod. But I'm not, I'm not!

June 16: I lack the discipline for daily writing; weather too fine all weekend anyway. I've started an herb garden out front, in the angle the porch and kitchen make with the old part of the house. Sunny all afternoon and protected from the wind. Borrowed Dennis's truck Saturday to drive to Hallet's, and on the way found the little shed near the golf club open for business, selling all manner of plants, flowers and herbs. Proprietress named Betsy, enthusiastic blonde woman about my age. She said dig first, then buy plants, so I did, all Saturday, back in the late afternoon to purchase chives, parsley, basil, a big rosemary plant like a miniature shrub, tarragon, and a lovely plant with blue flowers called hyssop. And oregano and silver thyme. Aren't the names wonderful? And a flat of yellow marigolds to put in front. Used half of this week's grocery money. Things look rather puny and bare, but Betsy assures me they will thrive and spread and that I will be back for more next year.

Real news from yesterday is that we are owners of a cranberry bog! That's where Dennis was all Thursday and Friday! It's about two miles from here, in Yarmouth Port, called West Marsh (west of East Marsh, I guess!), needs reclaiming because has lain fallow for years. Dennis drove me over there Sunday afternoon. Hard to tell exactly what it was, it's so overgrown with young scrub oaks and brush—and poison ivy! But you can see the outline of it—perfectly level with a sort of raised road around the edge, and places where ditches are, or were. And a small rectangular building they call the bog house for storing stuff and sorting berries. Needs a new roof but basically

sound, Dennis says. He is afire with plans! We celebrated last night
with martinis—I am paying this morning with a headache. Should
I write that last night was the first night we "didn't"? (The martinis.)
But made up for it in the morning.

June 19: Talked with Mother today about the bog and Grandmother's
money. She called the idea "harebrained," is concerned about the
cost of reclaiming, machinery, hiring people, etc. Should *not* have
told her—I am grown up (legally, anyway) and do not need her
permission, except for my need to please the unpleasable. Also should
not have mentioned what she said to Dennis, who's touchy enough
about money matters as it is. Disappeared into the parlor for a long
time after supper, emerged at ten o'clock anxious for bed. I was
grumpy but persuadable. Major difference between men and women:
We like—need!—talk. It's hard for me to summon warmth when I
am feeling disconnected.

June 20: Woke happy again this morning, with a solution to our bog/
money problems—I will work with Dennis! Broached the subject
over a special breakfast of bacon and pancakes. He grumbled he does
not want me working, but what else am I going to be doing, at least
while there are only two of us, except reclaim this old house. Why
can't we cut down trees and clear brush *together* and then sand and
paint here *together*? Next Tuesday, to Boston to sign papers, then we
pass papers on Friday and are in business!

June 28: To Boston yesterday by train. Felt so strange to go out of
South Station and enter the bustle. Met Mother at Schrafft's for
lunch. Felt underdressed despite the hat and gloves—had on the
wrong shoes, as she pointed out. After all the signing of documents
we had an hour—took Dennis on a swan boat for a lark. He had
never been! Nice to wander in my beloved Public Garden on such
a clear blue day. I thought about my flower garden out by the fence
and what might go in. No cannas! Too big and artificial. No glads.
No geraniums, even. Everything wild, perhaps, a sturdy, tousled,
windblown sort of garden, not like the even rows we see here.

Not back home until after seven. Dennis impatient on the train,
and I too hungry to be patient, so we sniped, quietly. All better at
home; we drank a toast to the big check we had carried back and I
was grateful for the leftover lamb, too tired to think about cooking
supper from scratch.

June 30: We are now official owners of West Marsh. Tomorrow we
start with the clearing! Dennis came home with champagne, so again
we celebrate.

July 2: Welcome, oh innocent one, to manual labor! We worked all
day yesterday on West Marsh. Hot, damp, and buggy. I lopped with
loppers and Dennis sawed. We only cleared about one-tenth of it, and
the hard part is getting all the roots and stumps out. Dennis will have
to hire someone with a tractor to help with that. I am all burned on
the arms and back of neck (must write Selena I am now an official
redneck), bug-bit, and scratched on the legs. But better off than
Dennis, who is blooming this morning with poison ivy. I sent him off
painted with calamine.

July 15: A long hiatus in my journal—physical labor not conducive
to writing. We have been working and working on West Marsh,
knowing Dennis will start back at his uncle's shop on Monday. It will
be three years or maybe four before any cranberries will be ready for
harvest, and lots of hard work between now and then. In two weeks
we have cleared away all the brush—both of us now itchy messes
with poison ivy all over—limits the hugging. We have worked every
day until dark, even in the rain, with an hour or two off for lunch
and a swim when the tide is right—the salt water helps cool off the
poison ivy. Skin on my arms is blistered and peeling at the same time;
Mother would faint dead away if she saw me. Went to the barber in
Barnstable last Saturday for something resembling a feather cut. At
least it's short, and in this humidity very curly. Dennis likes it well
enough now that he's used to it, calls it my Shirley Temple look.

Dennis is at West Marsh supervising stump removal, so today I
have off to tend my own gardens—vegetable plot full of weeds, and
my baby herbs in need of water. Started so late we'll be lucky to have
tomatoes by Labor Day. Hope to start digging the perennial bed this
afternoon. How strong I've become in two weeks! I like the way it
feels, even the sweat and the dirt under my nails. I could be a farmer.

July 16: We rode over to inspect the bog this morning—a sad sight!
All torn up and tracked, raw dirt drying in the sun, an enormous
heap of stumps and roots over to the side. Now we need to hire more
machinery to grade and level it, then there are ditches to clear—
that has to be done by hand—and the irrigation system to set up. I
imagine months and months of dollars flying out of our West Marsh

account, with nothing coming back. Tomorrow Dennis starts back to work full time, so we will need to hire help. Our honeymoon—the month of idleness and drinking mead—officially over, marred only a little by poison ivy. We drank our share of mead but were hardly idle!

July 17: Dennis exhausted last night after his first day in the shop, and out of sorts—Uncle Otis grates on him, tends to give him the humdrum jobs and save the creative metalworking for himself. I've been musing about what makes work satisfying—Dennis went into engineering out of a love for tinkering—it's the hands on part of the work he loves, not the theory. My Rube Goldberg. His talents will stand us in good stead when it's time to set up the irrigation at West Marsh. But for now he's frustrated. Me too. He disappears into the parlor with the gin—I want him to talk to me. He needs to be his own boss! We must hang on in the meantime.

July 20: For the first time in a long time I am "late." Four days of terror/anticipation followed today by relief/disappointment. What am I thinking? Now is not the right time; we're barely underway here. And yet, and yet . . . I did not share this with Dennis.

August 15: A long silence in my journal. Life is settling down to a routine; Dennis at work every day and I am chipping away at home, like a good hausfrau. Amazed at the time just daily living takes—meals, scrubbing and hanging out laundry, cleaning up after ourselves, since we are both "strewers" of clothes and papers. Then the yard and garden. I have taken over mowing the grass as well as weeding, will start painting inside when (if!) it ever gets a little cooler. I have made a little vow to walk down to the beach every day no matter what. Now that it's August the pesky greenheads are gone. At low tide I go out to the sand bar and take a dip in the channel—cold water and cooler air than on the beach or up here at the house. So many odd creatures to ponder. Will I ever learn all their names? I must find a book about them.

Dennis has hired two high school boys to work on the ditches in the evenings so he can supervise them after work. Necessary, but it makes me glad the days are growing shorter.

August 16: I have a friend! A neighbor! Her name is Peg and she's here for two weeks with her little daughter, staying with her mother in the cottage just over the crest of the hill on the left. Mother lives here all year but I've never laid eyes on her. Peg lives in Dedham, has been coming here since she was a little girl and knows *everything* about the flora and fauna—was a botany major (can't remember where) and determined to teach her little girl all about nature. The little girl is Shirley, has shoebutton eyes and a mop of light brown curls and really does look like Shirley Temple. An assertive little miss with that disconcerting self-confidence common in only children. At age six she knows the names of all the shells and doesn't mind telling me what they are. Peg I know I will enjoy, a sunny sort of person who exults in her surroundings. I realize how lonely I've been.

August 20: Have been out on the flats with Peg and Shirley, learning about two odd things I've wondered about: sand collars, all made of sand grains held together by a sort of glue extruded by moon snails to protect their eggs. Take one home and let it dry out and it disintegrates into a little heap of sand. Also mermaids' purses (isn't the name delicious?), little black pouches with long points on the four corners, made by skates to hold their eggs. These are more durable; they would make an interesting addition to a driftwood collage.

After our walk (a delight, except for Shirley's constant interruptions), back to Peg's to meet her mother, whose name is Marge. She is lame from childhood polio, which explains why she is never at the beach. Has a glorious screened porch with a view of the harbor (how I wish we had a view!) and a garden tucked in back, out of sight of the street. Told her about my dream of a wildflower garden. She didn't laugh, even said she would help me with starts of things! Said I should include "escapees," her name for things planted long ago which have taken off on their own and multiplied. The ubiquitous tiger lilies are a good example, she says, and the pink phlox that blooms in spring along the marshes, and the purple loosestrife that is blooming now, though she says watch out for that; it will take over.

August 21: Sad to think Peg will only be here one more week. I've been musing about friends, new and old, Peg and Selena, whom I miss and who *hasn't written*! How essential they are to our happiness. Even as a newlywed I can see that Dennis can't be all and everything to me. I love his dreamy imagination! Our plans for our life together! His jokes, the whimsical games he likes to play with language. (Oh, and my body loves his body—how could I survive without him?) But his mind (and heart!) go places I can't follow, and mine do the same. I must find a friend who will not go home in six days. I am sad already.

August 24: Weather has reverted to the thick warm haze we had too much of in July. But by midday a good breeze cleared things out. ·
How different the light seems once August begins, as if someone had changed the filter. Sky and water paler, clearer, the heat gone out of the sun. The rest of the summer will drain out fast like the last grains of sand in an hourglass.

PHOEBE'S JOURNAL IS not what I expected, but what did I expect? Not
to feel this way, like a voyeur, even though there's nothing particularly private or startling. Phoebe as a bride! A young girl from Beacon Hill who wore a hat and gloves on the train to Boston, who was afraid of the water heater and didn't know how to roll out pie pastry! Who was lonely, who missed her friends. Selena—who was Selena? Someone from college no one in the family has ever mentioned but who was central to her life, at least for a while. Phoebe's feelings about the house, the garden—so similar to mine it feels spooky. And how ominously the journal hints at what will happen later. Dennis already disappearing into the parlor after dinner to drink, emerging to charm her into bed regardless. How odd to imagine our elders feeling passion. They must have been happy, at least for a while. Enough for tonight—I'll decide tomorrow how I'll read the journals. Chronologically, or starting with the last one and working backwards? Dipping in, here and there, in the middle? What's the best way to plumb the mystery of another life?

Independence Day

The more carefully we look, the more we shall see.

JULY FOURTH ALREADY; I wake with my mother's words echoing in my head, "Summer's over on the Fourth of July," words I'm finally beginning to understand as the years roll by faster and faster. I wake with the sound of my mother's voice in my ear, verging on the edge of irritation. I used to think I irritated her, but it wasn't me; it was her life; I was just the nearest object to focus on.

It's going to be hot—if I'm going to get any work done I'd better do it early. The Fourth of July. Will Lesley expect to celebrate? I remember the flag rolled up on the ledge beside the attic stairs. Everyone on the Cape flies the flag, and not just on the Fourth, either. I want to fly it too, to see it fluttering from the corner of the porch when I turn into the yard. The thought propels me out of bed and sets me tiptoeing into Lesley's room where she sleeps the heavy sleep of the young. I have to struggle with the sticky catch of the attic door before it finally comes free with a loud click (a sigh from Lesley, an unreadable murmur as she ingests the sound and fits it into the plot of her dream)—how innocent she looks with her damp reddish hair, one cheek pink and creased, an enlarged version of the exquisitely colored baby I could never get enough of watching, that I would drag Gregory protesting up the stairs from his newspaper to see.

Back in my room I unroll the flag, faded but intact, a few threads given way around the grommets, a strip near the outer end lightened to pink where the sun has been hitting it as it has wheeled across the attic all these years. Wooden pole. Cords still there and only mildly frayed. Forty-eight stars, six by eight, set foursquare like the nation they used to stand for, before the Sixties, before Vietnam or the gunshots in Dallas or Watergate or AIDS. I can see Aunt Phoebe in her chenille robe and slippers wet from the morning dew putting it up, or would it have been Uncle Dennis's job? Put the flag up, take it down. Something to give shape to his otherwise formless day.

The brass flagpole holder is still there on the corner of the porch, green from years of weather and loose at the lower end where the wood holding the screw has softened, but it will do, it will hold. The flag is not large but heavy for its size, coarsely woven cotton, the stars not printed but sewn on, a set for each side, the edges painstakingly stitched, proudly made, the kind of flag bought to honor our boys over there and handled according to the rules I remember dimly from Girl Scouts and summer camp, raised and lowered with ceremony, protected from rain and the night and the dark defiling earth, and in the end given a proper disposal by burning.

I have just cleated the flag in place when I hear him call. "Anna? Ah, good. You're up." It's Demetrius, calling to me from his pickup as he turns into the driveway. "And the girls? Get them going. There's a parade—starts at nine. I'll take you. Dorothea will love it."

A wave of fatigue washes over me; I'm not ready for the daily struggle. I want coffee, and quiet, an hour to sit on the porch in the sun and look at the garden. "Oh, Demetrius, I don't think so. They're both dead asleep, and I . . ."

"Come on. They'll love it. I'll help you. Where's Pegasus? I'll load him up."

And riding on the wave of his enthusiasm I wake Dorothea, cranky and hot, and hoist her up by the armpits for the trek to the bathroom and wrestle on her flowered calico slacks to protect her flaccid legs from the stares of passersby. Lesley won't get up, won't come, turns her back crossly. I know how she hates these public excursions and don't insist. Demetrius sets his mouth in a line as I tell her to go back to sleep. "You shouldn't let her do that," he says under his breath and then drops it.

Demetrius parks up by the Unitarian church, a steep heart-stopping hill above the village. He maneuvers Dorothea's wheelchair down the narrow sidewalk as I walk in front in deference to my fantasy that if the chair gets away it will run into me and I will be able to stop it, fighting my old phobia of lurching forward, tipping out into space that comes over me whenever I'm descending in a crowd. People hop nimbly into the street to let us by. A few of them smile and speak to Demetrius, nod graciously to me, as if it weren't at all queer for him to be wheeling a large strange paralyzed girl down the steepest hill in Barnstable.

The smallest children stare, as they always do, but it's all right, so much is going on, and Demetrius is right, Dorothea is loving it, smiling her half-smile and crooning her I love music croon. Then we hear it too, the faint rattle of drums and the wail first of sirens and then bagpipes, and I forget to be on the lookout for sidelong pitying stares, oh that poor woman, mother to that girl what do you suppose is wrong with her, retarded or what, and enter the loudness and bigness of firetrucks, the 1939 hook and ladder with its brass bell, the latest fluorescent yellow pumper bought with the town's outrageous tax rates and the last windfall of Federal matching funds, and the keen and skirl of bagpipes played by a dozen men in kilts and full regalia. And then old cars, restored beyond newness, some of them, and a model A Ford pickup with wooden sides, not restored, with Floyd's Fish Market printed on the door, and a half-dozen homemade floats, a bedroom complete with four-poster and a Washington slept here sign, and a tractor pulling a big flat farm wagon with a group of women and girls around a quilting frame at one end and a boy watching a man hammering at an anvil at the other. "Pride in American workmanship. Pass it on," says the sign. I think about Aunt Phoebe's flag and wonder where flags are made now. Taiwan?

Then there are children in costume, children riding decorated bicycles and walking, very small children dressed up as firecrackers and Betsy Ross and astronauts being cajoled or dragged or carried by weary parents in red, white, and blue T-shirts, a solemn bald baby girl in a ruffled white dress with a red, white, and blue ribbon scotch-taped to her scalp, a set of triplets dressed as an American flag, one in a blue T-shirt with stars, two with red and white stripes, a pair of giggling ten-year-olds on roller blades who cling to each other and come a cropper in front of the firehouse, whose inmates show off their EMT training by gathering up the fallen girls, bleeding but still giggling, and administering disinfectant and band-aids and warnings about proper headgear.

And a clown handing out candy to children in the crowd. He comes right up, bless him, to Dorothea, her mouth wavering between astonished lopsided O and delighted lopsided smile, and produces a lollipop, which Demetrius unwraps and holds for her to lick before she has time to decide she is frightened. Why has it never occurred to me to give her a lollipop? The ease with which he handles her, the tenderness and humor. I think of the young orderly who shifted Dorothea into bed that day six years ago when she finally left transitional care for an ordinary semi-private room, lifting her as if she were light as air, precious, beautiful. As if there were nothing at all the matter with her. I smile at Demetrius, or at the back of his head. He is squatting down beside Dorothea, talking to her, his head at her eye level. The lollipop delights her; her smile is back, her good eye shining. If I didn't know better, I would swear she was flirting with him.

When we turn into the yard there is the flag fluttering at the corner of the house. I am feeling festive—I want to continue the holiday mood, share some of it with Lesley. "Will you stay for lunch?" I ask Demetrius. "I thought we might eat out in the yard."

"If it's not too much trouble. You might want to go up on the hill, it's so hot. There'll be a breeze up there under the pines. Do you need help carrying things, or should I take charge of Pegasus here?"

I consider. No doubt Dorothea needs changing, or at least a visit to the bathroom. Demetrius understands the pause. "Probably needs a trip inside, doesn't she. You get the door."

And he wheels her around to the parlor door and waits just outside while I take her down the hall and then back to him. Then he steers her across the yard and up the slope towards the pine grove while I go through to the kitchen, where I find Lesley at the table eating a bowl of Rice Krispies, her hair tousled, wearing a T-shirt and a pair of Gregory's plaid boxer shorts, the ones she'd given him for Christmas and stolen back. Her face is still flushed from sleep.

"Don't fill yourself up. We're going to have a picnic outside."

"Mom, I just woke up."

"It's the Fourth of July; where's your holiday spirit? Besides, Demetrius is here, the man who used to work for Uncle Dennis and Aunt Phoebe. He wants to see you; he remembers you from Uncle Dennis's funeral. Come on out and visit with him, at least."

"Mom."

I choke back the impulse to say "Mind your manners, young lady," hearing my mother's voice again in my head. Instead I say, "I made chicken salad. Would you get that old quilt from the parlor, the one with the blue designs? And some forks and napkins for all of us? What would you like to drink, Coke or that fruit punch? Or should I make iced tea?"

It's twenty minutes later by the time Lesley and I get to the top of the hill with the makings of a picnic. I wish I had something more elegant than plain whole wheat bread and seedless grapes to serve with the salad, that I had made a pie or some cookies for dessert. Demetrius is right about the pine grove; there is a lovely breeze, carrying a rich salty scent. The tide must be out. I feel a little self-conscious feeding Dorothea in front of him, but he doesn't seem to mind. She is smiling; eating outside under the trees like this seems to amuse her.

Demetrius concentrates his attention on Lesley, who has managed to eat half a chicken salad sandwich in spite of herself. He is telling her about working the cranberry bogs when he was her age. Does he know instinctively how much she hates to be asked about herself? "We loved fall," he is saying, "'cause we got off school for a couple weeks. With the war—most of the able-bodied men were gone. We'd get to scoop—that meant more money. But mostly the children got to pick along the ditch banks. It was cold wet work, but you know how kids are—nothing like a little money jingling in your pocket."

I lie back on the quilt, looking at the pale hazy sky through the pine branches. I have an overwhelming desire to sleep, but Demetrius's story interests me. Gregory worked Uncle Dennis's bog, those summers he was a teenager. "The summer I was fourteen we had some German prisoners in the work crew," Demetrius is saying. "We had a Finnish foreman—he hated those Germans all right. One time he caught one of them calling me a name and he let him have it."

"What did he call you?" Lesley is interested in spite of herself. She is forgetting her cranky mood. I lie still on the quilt and close my eyes.

"Something in German I couldn't understand. And the Finn wouldn't translate. But that prisoner got a cracked tooth from it. Mostly, though, they were friendly. Grateful they could be outdoors and working and no one was torturing them."

I try to imagine Demetrius at fourteen. His hair would be darker, of course, but otherwise how would he look different? Thinner, slighter, maybe. And then the image mixes itself with Gregory a few years later, taller and less mature at that age, probably, reserved and shy, still numb from his mother's death, his sadness forming a shell keeping him apart from the rest of the crew.

WHEN I WAKE, the sun has moved towards the road and I am no longer in the shade. I feel hot; the breeze has died away. It is silent here on the hill—where is Dorothea? I open my eyes and sees Demetrius standing a little way down the hill, looking at me. How long has he been there? Why is he just standing there like that? I sit up quickly, flushing with embarrassment. It makes me feel exposed, being watched by this man I barely know. "Where are the girls?" I ask, the fear in my voice surprising me. He's been so attentive to them both all day, Am I that much like my mother, that suspicious?

"We went for a walk down the beach. You fell asleep, so we let you lie. Lesley came along. She's grown up. I wouldn't ever know her except for that strawberry hair."

"She's changed a lot in the past year. She's maturing so fast; sometimes I don't know what to expect from one day to the next. How long have I been asleep? Last thing I remember was you talking about the Germans. And I was interested in hearing about the business. I don't know why I fell asleep."

"Not used to the air yet. Knocks everybody out for a few days. How long you been here, three days, four?"

Demetrius has approached the quilt where I am sitting. Having him stand over me like that makes me uncomfortable, so I start putting things back in the picnic basket. "Since the night of the first. Where are the girls?"

"Lesley's watching her sister. I set her up on the porch, and Lesley said she'd keep an eye on her until you got back."

I hide my surprise. Lesley hates to sit for Dorothea. Was she trying to impress Demetrius? "I really was interested in hearing about the cranberrying. You know, Gregory worked for Uncle Dennis for three summers."

"I remember. I'd just been made foreman then, about in '59, wasn't it?"

"It was '58 and '59. He remembers you."

"Yes. Kind of a loner he was those summers. Phoebe worried about him, I remember."

"Aunt Phoebe talked to you about him?"

"She said to keep an eye on him. He was here in the slack season; we only had a small crew to work on the weeding and keeping the ditches clear. The pickers would arrive a couple weeks after he left. He missed the excitement."

"He doesn't like to talk about that time. He was pretty unhappy." I say the words and immediately feel disloyal. How Gregory would hate being talked about this way, having his boyhood wounds exposed, just as Lesley bristles whenever she suspects I have been discussing her with my friends. And how strange to be sitting here, now, with Demetrius, in his jeans and work boots, the skin on the back of his neck leathery from years of exposure to the weather, imagining him worrying about Gregory at fourteen, awkward and sad, sulky and withdrawn the way Lesley is now. And just as strange to think of Gregory, with his impeccable gray suits, his reputation for precise cross-examination, once having Demetrius for a boss, that the two of them knew each other long before either of them knew me. Funny how I got them mixed up in my dream. Demetrius is considerably older, of course. He would have been in his twenties that summer. Was he old enough to know how to be kind to Gregory, the way he's been kind to the girls today?

The conversation is starting to feel awkward. I've been too forthcoming, Gregory would think. I don't feel like talking anymore. I stand up so quickly that my head swims for a moment and bend down to finish repacking the picnic basket, gathering up Aunt Phoebe's blue and white quilt. "It's late. I need to see about the girls," I say, feeling ungracious. "It was a lovely day. Thanks for the parade."

"No trouble. Here, let me," Demetrius says, taking the basket and falling in beside me as we head down the hill toward the house.

Sand Grains

*Every time we watch the waves of the sea pounding
against a shore, we are watching a sand factory at work.*

L ESLEY LIES DOWN flat on the sand so she can feel its warmth soak into her. A cold front has come through, freshening the air and stirring up whitecaps on the bay. Too cold for swimming even though it's July already, but warm down here out of the wind. She likes being the only one on the beach. She sifts some of the sand through her fingers. White and coarse, none of the yellowish dust that clings to her feet at the freshwater ponds at home. So much to see when she looks at it close. Lots of white crystals, like sugar almost. A few tiny chips in other colors—yellow, slate gray, pink quartz almost as clear as glass. A weensy clamshell, both halves hinged together and perfectly shaped like the big ones at the fish market. Colored a faint purple. So small. The tide is pretty high, above the marsh grass, endless little waves driven in by the wind, curling over like miniature breakers. The sound soothes her.

A new sound, a crunching that seems to be coming from under her ear, prompts her to raise her head. Footsteps. Bare feet, long brown legs, the tall woman from down the street, the one with the sailboat. Now that Lesley's raised her head there is no way she can pretend to be asleep. She looks down, picks up a few sand grains with her fingers, studies them intently.

"Amazing, isn't it."

"Yeah," Lesley says. She's being rude. She's supposed to stand up when a grownup speaks to her. Does that include someone in a bathing suit? If Mom were here, she'd be glaring.

"I used to pretend I was so small I had to climb over the grains, like boulders," the woman says. "It helped me to see them better." And instead of waiting for Lesley to answer—what could she say anyway that wouldn't sound totally stupid?—the woman continues down toward the water, wades in despite the chilling wind, and swims straight out with a strong overhand crawl. She's headed for the little black-hulled boat moored about a hundred feet offshore. Going sailing in all this wind?

But when she reaches the boat, she just hangs on for a minute, pushes off, and swims back toward the beach, doing the backstroke this time. Lesley rests her head on her arms and shuts her eyes. The woman strides past her without stopping and disappears up the road.

Yesterday Lesley and Mom wheeled Dorrie down here. It was warmer, not so windy. Dorrie seemed to like it, got excited in the only way she can, moving her good arm up and down and making more noise than usual. What does she think when she looks at the water—all that space, so much blue, without things or people? Maybe that's what her mind is like, not gray and foggy the way Lesley always imagines it, but bright—bright and empty and blue with everything sad and confusing washed away. Are there any memories left in there? Maybe she remembers being little, the Sunday breakfasts in the dining room with French toast and maple syrup, how they used to dig holes in the soft yellow bread to make faces. But if she remembers anything, it's probably the piano. She still likes music, always humming. All those hours and hours practicing and practicing when Lesley wanted her to go outside and play. Probably her fingers, if she could move them better, still know where the notes are. It was okay, having Dorrie down here at the beach, with no one around to stare. She liked it and got excited, the way a baby would. It's like the wish Lesley used to make a long time ago when Dorrie teased her, that she could be the oldest and Dorrie the little sister. Now she will keep on getting older and older and Dorrie will always be the same, in her mind anyway. Someday an old lady, with wrinkles and those knobby hands old ladies have, but her mind still like a baby's, empty and clear like this water, this sky.

Lesley sits up and looks at the sailboat just offshore, where the tall woman swam. Lesley'd like to swim out there, except she'd freeze when she came back out. She strips off her T-shirt and walks down to test the water. Warmer than she thought. Why not? She wades out along the narrow path worn in the marsh grass. The water is up to her thighs where the grass ends and there is a big step down onto sand, the moment of truth when she has to plunge in or turn back. She hesitates, then takes a breath, swings her arms above her head and dives under, already doing a brisk crawl by the time her head breaks the surface, moving too fast to feel the cold. Out here the warm water lies over a much colder layer she can feel with her legs and feet. And the current is sweeping her rapidly to the right of the boat. It's a struggle to swim against it, upstream against this silent force, invisible but powerful. By the time she reaches the boat, she's

too winded to think about hauling herself up onto the deck. She hangs
onto the little square hole in the stern and catches her breath.

She glances back towards the beach, which looks farther away than
she thought it would. The tall woman is back, standing on the dry sand
above the marsh grass and looking at Lesley. Wondering if she brought
an axe to chop up the boat, or if she's going to climb aboard and sail away,
probably. She's going to get yelled at. Lesley turns on her back and kicks
herself back to shore, feeling the current shift her sideways as she goes. By
the time she can reach down and feel solid bottom beneath her feet she's
nowhere near the path, but over in the place where the grass is shoulder
high and prickly. She propels herself forward with her hands the way she
used to when she didn't know how to swim yet, the grass parting for her,
until the water is so shallow she has to stand up.

The tall woman is still there standing in the same place, watching
Lesley and not moving. She begins to shiver as soon as the cold air hits
her wet body. There's nothing to do but head for her towel.

"You must be Lesley," the woman says as she bends down to shake
the sand from her towel, then wraps it around her shoulders and sits
down. "I knew your Aunt Phoebe. Been swimming on this beach before?
This is the first time I've seen you."

"Just a couple times when I was little." Now she'll get the lecture
about the boat.

"You looked like the current surprised you. I was worried for a minute,
but you're a good swimmer."

"Yeah, I forgot about it. Mom used to tell us. But I could barely even
swim the last time I was here."

"I forget one season to the next. It's strongest at about half tide. The
trick is to gauge your angle. Head upstream so when you get even with the
boat you can just float down."

"Is that your boat? I'm sorry I . . ."

"That's okay. Swimming seems to make more sense when you have
someplace to head to. You can climb up and rest if you want. There used
to be a raft on this beach, but now there aren't usually any children, so
nobody puts it in. I'm Daphne, by the way, Daphne Ault. I live in that
house in front of the pond. I knew your Aunt Phoebe."

Lesley doesn't like being categorized as a child, and she doesn't want
to have to chat politely with this stranger, least of all about old Aunt
Phoebe who fell off a ladder and is dead now, dead and rotting and lying
in a box under the ground. Lesley sighs and lies down on her back to get

out of the wind. Maybe the woman will leave her alone. And the woman, Daphne whatever her name is, seems to take her cue. When Lesley opens her eyes again, she is far up the beach, striding along just above the tide line where the sand meets the marsh grass, her long shirttail blowing back in the wind.

Lesley rolls over onto her stomach and looks closely at the sand again, remembering what the woman, Daphne, said, imagining herself down to miniature size. Most of the grains are rough cubes or rectangles, hard to climb on. She remembers the Girl Scout trip to Mount Madison when she was in fifth grade, the rocks above the timber line, a tumbled heap of huge boulders, their upper surfaces at every angle, and how hard it was to jump from one to the next, tired as they were from the long climb and worried about slipping and getting a leg caught in the dark spaces in between. No one up there besides their little group, at least until they got close to the Madison Hut where they were spending the night, no signs of life except the amazing splotches of lichen on the rocks and one scrawny, confused rabbit who slipped into a crack ahead of them, looking like he was starving and had lost his way.

These boulders would be white, though, and hot, hard on the eyes and painful to touch, though some, the purple and pink quartz crystals, would be huge shining jewels. Blinding light, like the surface of the moon. Maybe she would need special equipment, dark goggles and gloves anyway, to protect herself from the light and heat and sharp edges. It would be hard, but beautiful. Glass is made of sand. That makes sense looking at it this way. She lays her head sideways on the edge of her towel, noticing the tiny dark shadows cast by the crystal boulders.

"You're getting red."

Lesley starts, confused for a moment, then raises her head. The neighbor, Daphne, is back. Lesley must have fallen asleep. The wind has died down to a steady breeze from the west.

"Want to go for a sail?"

Did she really say that? Lesley has been wanting a ride in the little black boat ever since she first laid eyes on it. "What time is it? Mom will—I'll have to go ask."

"About eleven-thirty, I'd say. I've got to go up and get the life jackets. I'll stop by your house and see what she says. It's still a bit breezy; I could use you for ballast. If she says yes bring a hat and some kind of windbreaker that you don't mind getting wet. It'll be chilly out there. We'll make it a short one. Can you eat lunch a little late?"

"Oh sure, thanks, I—thanks." Lesley gathers up her towel and heads back toward the road at a trot, feeling more wide awake than she has since she arrived.

Ten minutes later they are both back on the beach, Lesley in her mother's blue nylon windbreaker and an old crew hat of Aunt Phoebe's, Daphne in a bright yellow hooded sailing parka and carrying two orange flotation vests. The tide has gone out nearly halfway, so they can wade to the boat without swimming. Daphne hauls herself gracefully aboard and gives Lesley a hand up. The open cockpit is curved like the hull, painted gray, and slippery under Lesley's feet as the boat rocks up and down. It's straining taut against the mooring rope. To the rear the wake formed by the swift current makes them look as though they are already under way.

"Been sailing before?"

"No, never." Lesley feels apprehensive, unsteady on her feet in this rocking boat, her stomach a queasy little knot of apprehension.

"Don't worry. Just hang on and I'll tell you what to do. I'll be barking orders; I might even yell, but don't take it personally. There's always a chain of command on a boat and there's a reason for that. Sometimes things happen fast and you have to snap to. I'm captain; you're crew."

"Aye, aye, sir." Will Daphne think Lesley's too fresh? But the woman is smiling as she drags a heavy curved object out from under the deck.

"Okay now. This is the rudder. Watch how I attach it. It slips on over these two metal rings. Always put the rudder on first; then if you sail off unexpectedly you've got a way to steer." Daphne is leaning over the rear of the boat as she speaks, trying to attach the rudder as the boat bobs up and down. It takes several tries. "Now hand me the tiller—that long wooden thing. There's a little arrow pointing to one side—see? That side goes up. Here; you put it in." Lesley pushes the tiller through the open square hole—so that's what that hole is for—and inserts it through two metal keepers on the top of the rudder. "Give it a good shove so it's in tight," Daphne instructs. The tiller sways back and forth slowly in response to the movement of the rudder. "Okay, now you can undo the sheet." Daphne is pointing to a rope tautly wrapped in a figure eight around a cleat in the stern.

"I thought the sheet was the sail."

"I know; it's a silly name. Half of sailing, or anything, really, is learning the lingo. Once you get the sheet undone make sure it's free and not tangled up anywhere. Then you can help with the sail ties. You start in the back." Daphne is crouched on the small deck next to the mast, struggling to loosen the tight knot on one of the tapes fastening the neatly rolled sail. Lesley has bitten her nails down to the quick; loosening the knots seems impossible until Daphne shows her the trick of pulling one end of the tape up at an angle. Finally all the tapes are free, and Daphne begins to bark orders.

"There. We're about ready. Put these ties in the little bucket under the deck and just sit down and watch your head." With that Daphne uncleats two more ropes on the deck, stands up and begins hauling up the sail. For a moment it swings wildly back and forth. "Watch it! Keep your head down!" Daphne cries. She's nervous, too, Lesley can tell. She was right about the yelling. No matter where Lesley sits, she seems to be in the way as Daphne cleats the ropes she's been hauling on, coils them up, lies flat on the deck and reaches forward to release the mooring line, unpins the centerboard, and settles herself in the rear of the boat next to the tiller. All at once she is her calm self again. "Okay, we're under way. Here, sit in the front on this side where I am. There's a lot of scrambling around in a little boat like this. I hope you're ready."

All at once the bobbing up and down that has been making Lesley feel a little sick to her stomach is gone, as the round little boat cuts grace-fully through the water with a gentle slapping sound, talking its own language of creaks and rushes. It's like being on a living creature, wonderful, like riding a horse. Lesley had been worried about being frightened, had felt awkward and scared in the confusion of getting ready, but now she feels relaxed, and something else: free. She looks back toward the shore; it seems very far away. Already the lighthouse across the harbor is notice-ably bigger.

"How much do you know about boats?" Daphne asks her.

"I know about canoes. I've been to camp. But not about sailboats."

"Then you know about bow and stern and port and starboard?"

"Sure."

"Well, then we have the spars, the poles holding the sail. Mast you know. And this horizontal one is the boom. And that forked one at the top is the gaff."

"Gaff?"

"Yes. It means fork. But the important words are for the lines—the ropes—because when people give orders you need to know what they mean. Sheet you know. The important thing is never to let it get fouled—tangled up or caught on anything. Because if you get in trouble on the water all you have to do is let the sheet out and the boat will right itself.

Watch." As Daphne lets the taut rope slide through her hand, the sail swings out until it's flapping in the wind. The little boat stops leaning over and comes to what feels like a complete stop. "The closest thing we have to brakes. Then when you want to get underway again you haul the sail in and off you go. Unless—oh dear—we're in irons."

"In what?"

"Irons. It means the boat is stuck in the water, maybe even slipping backwards. If we're lucky we can use the current to swing us around." After what seems like several minutes of pushing and pulling on the tiller and hauling the sail in, Daphne settles the boat back into its forward motion.

"Want to give it a try?"

"I don't know—what if I—"

"Don't worry; nothing will happen. Just come sit where I am. Hold the tiller while we shift; I'll keep the sail." The boat wobbles as they trade places, swinging into the wind. "Just remember to push the tiller in the opposite direction from where you want to go," says Daphne. Lesley is surprised at the tiller's resistence, its constant motion. It takes a few minutes to get the hang of it, a sort of push and pull in response to the boat's rocking, the changing wind pressure, the waves and the current.

"This is neat," she says, relaxing again and smiling at Daphne. "It's like riding a horse, getting the feel of the reins."

"Exactly. Letting her have her head, but keeping contact, not fighting her unless she goes off course. Now. Find a spot on shore and line the mast up with it, and see if you can keep a straight heading."

By the time they are back on their own beach and the boat is put away the tide is well out, only knee-deep at the mooring. Lesley is sunburned and hungry, sleepy from all the light and air, but happy. Daphne has promised to take her sailing again next week. She only takes one day off a week, a weekday so not so many people are around. Which day depends on the weather. The other days she has to write. Coming into the kitchen Lesley smiles at Dorrie and remembers to thank her mother, who is getting a tuna sandwich out of the refrigerator for her. She doesn't even complain about the whole wheat bread.

Daughters

More than 4,000 acres of marsh grass ripple in the salt
winds like inland fields of grain.

DAPHNE DOESN'T LIKE to talk on the phone. If there's any way to conduct a conversation face to face, she'll do it. If she has something touchy to talk about or wants to ask a favor she'll maneuver to have the interview at her house. I challenged her on this once, accusing her of wanting to watch other people in case they did something she could use in her writing. Daphne's characters are always shifting their weight to the other foot, shrugging shoulders, turning away, making silent gestures.

"You think I set up dramatic scenes with my friends so I can write about them?" Daphne laughed. "I'm not that devious. It's just that nothing makes me more nervous than asking other people for help. And I hate to apologize; it's not in my nature. So I have to get my courage up, and that's easier to do on my own territory."

Daphne insecure? It's hard for me to imagine. But I'm learning that everyone I know is hard to imagine, unimaginably complex under the smooth surface turned outward to the world.

She appears at my door at six-thirty in the morning a week after the Fourth, while I'm sitting in the sagging wicker rocker drinking coffee and reading yesterday's *Cape Cod Times*. It startles me to look up and see her tall form filling the doorway behind the screen.

"Pretty day," she says, as if it were perfectly normal to be calling at that hour. Of course from her perspective it is practically the middle of the morning. "And now I've met both your girls."

"Lesley was thrilled to go sailing. Thank you for taking her."

"I have a book about sailing I want to lend her."

"Oh, she won't be up for hours. She sleeps till noon when she can get away with it."

"Ah, yes. The lassitude of the young. I didn't mean now, of course. This afternoon. Can you all come for tea around four?"

"That would be lovely," I say, happier than I expected to see her again, thinking how pleasant it would be to join her on her morning walks and knowing I could never ask for that—the hour on the flats was her private time to gather her thoughts for the day ahead.

"Good," says Daphne, turning and disappearing down the lane before I can invite her inside. But we'll see each other this afternoon, like that day in May when she gave me the journals. Demetrius is the only other adult I've spoken to here on the lane. It would be nice—and comforting—to have a woman friend.

Lesley will have none of it. It's almost eleven by the time she gets up. No way she's going to put on those yucky new shorts to go over to Daphne's house for tea, Lesley declares as she sits hunched over her cereal. She hates all the new summer clothes we bought, and the two pairs of cutoff jeans she wore last summer are indecently tight; she has grown six inches this year and her hips have broadened out. Any mention of clothes, of her body, and she flies into a rage or disappears. She sulked for days after Greg looked her up and down in those jean shorts and said, "You're not going out on the street in those. Not my daughter."

I remember my own puberty but it doesn't help me to be patient. Just getting through the day with Dorrie uses up all of my energy. Lesley, my fleet antelope of a girl, where did you go? To be replaced by this sulky young woman with hair falling over her face, covering the eyes she will never turn in my direction. She can't stand the sight of me, braces herself against every word I say. Sometimes—but who can I tell this to?—I hate her when I see the way she throws her ripening body carelessly into a chair and gives me that slow, contemptuous look, innocent and knowing all at once. It seems that every monosyllable, every gesture she makes is calculated to infuriate me. I swallow my anger, try to sound reasonable, though I want to slap her sulky face. The only thing I hate more is the sound of my own voice, edgy, sharp, filled with ill-concealed anger. My mother's voice, the mother I could never please.

"Lesley has two modes," Greg says, "asleep, and gone." They used to be close. Lesley as a toddler was her Daddy's girl. But now that she's maturing physically, he doesn't know what to make of her. He seems threatened, somehow. And since Dorothea's operation he's withdrawn from all of us, spending more and more hours at the office and lately, in Washington. It's his way of avoiding the tragedy we live with every day. Something else his father taught him along with how to fold a shirt.

I miscalculated about what staying in Cummaquid would be like for Lesley. Somehow I thought there would be young people around for her, but we live on the quiet side of the Cape. She'd be happier on one of the south-facing beaches, with their warm water and hoards of summer people. Did I even think about Lesley in my eagerness to escape Needham for the summer, marooning her here without anyone her own age? I've been so focused on Dorothea that I haven't seen what's happening to Lesley, how quickly she's growing up. I've neglected her. No wonder she's sullen. Here there are no friends for her to escape to, no place to go except the beach and the marshes, nothing for us but to coexist in this cluttered house in an uneasy truce between her ill-concealed contempt and my ill-concealed frustration.

Were things this bad between my mother and me? In all honesty, yes, I suppose they were. I barely spoke to her, was less than civil once I got into my teens. My mother was not someone I wanted to be like, and she had little interest in my friends, my life at school. She was absorbed by the small, sealed-in world she had created, the perfectly kept house, the deftly blended patterns of curtains, slipcovers, pillows, all things she had made herself. "You have such an eye for color," people used to exclaim as she showed them through the rooms. She lived as if nothing existed outside her walls, her family. Does Lesley see me that way? Someone whose range of vision doesn't extend beyond getting Dorothea through another day? Probably. Sometimes that's the way I see myself. Is it the terror of imagining herself living my life that appalls Lesley so? The inevitable anger between mothers and daughters—it can feel so ugly. The one thing we can never forgive our mothers for is not living the life we want.

I'm too tired to make an issue over Daphne's casual invitation. "All right, then, stay home," I tell Lesley crossly. "I'll leave Dorrie, since you'll be here to watch her."

"Mom," she begins, then thinks better of arguing any more. A mean little part of my mind gloats silently at the victory, feels cheered about an outing without lugging Dorothea along. Dorrie the Lump, Lesley calls her. Truth be told, sometimes she feels that way to me.

It's embarrassing to have to call Daphne to explain, but she doesn't pick up the phone. Working, of course. I leave a brief message and walk out to the porch where Dorothea is. "Want me to brush your hair?" I ask. She won't answer, but she'll like it; she always does. She always did. I fetch her brush from her bedroom and come back to stand behind her, smoothing her hair with slow, gentle strokes. Beautiful hair, nothing like my unruly brown wisps. Gregory's hair, black and shining. We kept it long until after the operation when it no longer seemed practical. She would sit at the piano practicing, and I would marvel at her concentration, and at the way her hair would fall all of a piece in a satin sheet down her back. She loved to have me brush it, even as a little girl, happy to sit still, happy for my touch, my attention. I taught her to count to a hundred brushing her hair. Not like Lesley, who never wanted to sit still for anything. Even as an infant she would squirm in my arms, turn away. Her hair is every bit as beautiful, equally straight and satiny, an extraordinary pale copper color everybody notices. Tigerlily, I used to call her when she was two and three, running all over the yard.

I'M ABOUT TO go out the door at four-fifteen when Daphne calls. "Bring a hat," she orders, "and comfortable shoes. There's a place I want to take you."

"I can't be gone for long with just Lesley here to sit."

"No more than an hour, I promise. You'll like it. Then we'll come back for tea. You can check on the girls in between."

It's a day of strange weather, muggy and hot but with great gusts of wind whipping the trees, turning up the undersides of their leaves. Daphne drives up route 6A into Yarmouth Port, turning down a narrow street I've never noticed before. Shingled cottages fill in the spaces between a few much older houses from the early nineteenth century. We pass an old cemetery, turn down another road lined with tangled wild grapes and rugosa roses, and pull into a small grassy parking lot, seemingly in the middle of nowhere. "Here's where I like to bring people who've never been on the Cape," Daphne says. "Follow me."

We cross the road and climb a few steps leading to an opening in a high privet hedge. A green corridor opens in front of us, completely enclosed by arching branches. After a few minutes the dense undergrowth gives way to trees, the scrubby pitch pines and oaks common all over the Cape. "Whose land is this?" I ask Daphne.

"It belongs to the town," she answers. "There's a whole series of trails, down here around the marshes and up in back of the post office. You can hike for miles."

We come to a fork in the path and turn left. Here the trees are taller, more oaks, some maples, and then a stand of enormous white pines. "I've never seen such big pine trees," I say. "Wonder how old they are."

"I wonder that they haven't ever blown down in a storm," Daphne answers. "Look how close to the marsh they are." She disappears around a corner. By the time I catch sight of her again, she is perched on a weathered bench by the side of the path. "Here, sit and look," she says, patting the space beside her. "Watch out for the poison ivy."

I sit and look at the view. We can see out across acres of salt marsh, all the way to a boatyard a quarter of a mile away, with tilting, ramshackle shed roofs and the masts of sailboats poking up, a rusty crane no doubt used for hauling out. Close to us, a red-winged blackbird flashes by and disappears into a stand of cattails. The whole scene is framed by the sturdy shrubs that line the path and a wild, glistening tangle of poison ivy. "How lovely," I say.

"I thought you'd like it. I'm sorry the girls didn't come, but we wouldn't be able to bring a wheelchair in here."

"I apologize for Lesley, and after you've been so nice to her. Teenage girls—there's no surviving them."

"I know, I remember."

Yes, I remember now what I was so surprised to read in Aunt Phoebe's journal—Daphne hasn't always been single. She had a husband, and a daughter. "That's right," I say. "You were married."

"Oh, yes, I was married—I had a life, as they say. Do you find that so hard to believe?"

I'm taken aback by the sharpness of Daphne's tone. Have I offended her? "Of course not," I say carefully. "It's just that you seem so self-contained. I always imagine you springing from the head of Zeus, like Minerva."

"Athena. You've got your Greeks and Romans mixed up, but I'll take it as a compliment."

"What happened?" I ask tentatively.

"To the marriage? That's always the question, isn't it?" Daphne gets up and starts walking down the path, which turns another corner and skirts the edge of the marsh. I have to hurry to catch up and hear what she's saying; she could be talking to herself. "As if a marriage ends because of some event we can assign a time to. Why do we always want to quantify everything? Anyway, my novel happened. All of a sudden I was a celebrity. Daniel is a trial lawyer, very competitive. He wanted a wifey. He liked that I wrote, at first. It kept me home and out of the Junior League, for one thing. And it added a sort of élan—you know, she has style, she can cook, she writes—"

"I would think the Chambers Award would add even more élan."

"But it was too much, you see. It wasn't his thing. And all those people in publishing, all those parties and book signings. He was out of his element. He never read fiction, and they didn't want to talk about the law. They kept quoting that line from Shakespeare to him: 'The first thing we do, let's kill all the lawyers.' He hates situations where he's not in control. It shifted the balance of power and he didn't like it."

"Balance of power? Is that how you see marriage?"

Daphne stops for a moment and turns to face me. "Don't kid yourself. It's all about power. Everything is about power. The biggest difference between men and women is most of them know it and most of us don't."

We've come to a muddy stretch along the marsh rim, but at least here we can walk two abreast. I'm thinking hard about what Daphne is saying, and harder still about what to say to her. "I never think about power, not in relation to Greg—or to anybody I care about. What does love have to do with power?"

"Everything. It's always there. I was raised in a world where women weren't supposed to have power. You're younger than I am, Anna—you don't remember the fifties. I went to Smith, you know, and Jack Kennedy was our graduation speaker. This was before he was President. He was just a senator, but oh, the charisma. He turned around and flashed that smile at all of us after the processional was over and all the women drew in their breaths and said 'Ah.' It was audible. We would have believed anything he told us. And what he told us was that we had been given the best education in the country and now it was our job to use it to support our husbands and raise our children and get involved in local government. Husbands, children, volunteer work—that's about the time they started calling it 'volunteerism' to make it sound more professional—that was our high calling. There were women in my class who went to medical school and law school, not many, but some. But they were considered mavericks. We were trained to marry young and have big families and do volunteer work, as long as we got home in time for dinner. And graciously do whatever we needed to further our husbands' careers, whether that meant throwing big parties every weekend or moving once a year. Period. And never toot our own horn."

It's a long speech and Daphne is walking fast, and I am getting a little breathless trying to keep up. The path has left the marsh and ended in a playground with swings and a slide and a pavilion with picnic tables. Beyond that is a parking lot half filled with cars, a small beach punctuated by a few bright umbrellas, a clutch of young mothers with toddlers splashing in the shallow water or exploring the fascinating array of pebbles and shells at the water's edge. The salt marsh with its network of creeks stretches out before us, its brilliant green grasses undulating in the stiff wind.

"Come on; this is the best part," Daphne says, leading me across the parking lot to a long wooden boardwalk built out over the marsh. It extends a long way in the direction of the bay beyond. Without the protection of bushes and trees, the wind is fierce. We lean into it, walking single file out to the end and settling ourselves on the wooden seat we find there. I realize that what we're looking at is Barnstable Harbor and Sandy Neck seen from an entirely new perspective.

"You surprise me," I say to Daphne, glad to have a chance to look at her instead of trotting along behind.

"For being so traditional?" she asks. "Remember the times, Anna. It was before N.O.W., before *The Feminine Mystique* even. When were you in college?"

"In the late Sixties. Class of 1969."

"Ah, all hell was breaking loose by then. Vietnam. All those assassinations."

"Marrying and having a family looked pretty good to me then," I say thoughtfully, the realization just now forming in my mind. "Nothing felt safe. I wanted a home, a stable life."

"A nest. Yes. More important than power. Women had to choose between the two. I think in spite of thirty years of rhetoric they still do. Men can have both, as long as they have a wifey to take care of the nest. My daughter has opted for the power."

"That's right; you have a daughter. Phoebe mentions her in the journal. Where is she?"

"She's in San Francisco. She's a lawyer, like her daddy. She's good, too."

"Does she ever visit?"

"Hasn't yet. Says she's too busy. But the truth is, she's never forgiven me for leaving her father."

"How old was she when you got divorced?"

"Twelve."

"Tough age. Lesley's twelve now. Sulky and contrary. Sometimes I want to smash her."

"Oh, but Lesley's fabulous. I loved watching her in the sailboat the other day. She didn't say much, but I could see her mind darting around. She reminds me of Phoebe."

I feel a stab of jealousy, thinking about Lesley at home, silent and morose. Will I ever get to hear about her flights of fancy? What is it about mothers and daughters, the wall that grows between them at puberty, that roiling mass of emotion that feels so much like hate? Like a tangle of briars we have to force ourselves through, seeing all around us examples of women who spend the rest of their lives caught in the middle, never making it through to the other side.

Loud footsteps on the boardwalk make us turn around to look. A small girl with a mop of pale blonde curls, not more than two and dressed only in a pink bikini bottom and tiny sandals, lets go of her mother's hand and comes running towards us full tilt. Her foot catches on an uneven board and she falls hard, begins to howl. Before we can stand up her mother is there, snatching her up and holding her close against her shoulder, comforting and scolding her at the same time. The howls subside suddenly as she pops her thumb into her mouth, looking at us accusingly as if we had somehow caused her to fall. How like Lesley at that age, I am thinking. All except for the curls.

"Do you remember being twelve?" Daphne is saying.

"All too well. Seventh grade. That was my first year in junior high. I got my period—I used to go home every afternoon and look—did you do that? And my best friend started having all these boyfriends and got herself a reputation." It's amazing how just talking about junior high brings back the way I felt then, the conviction that everyone was staring, my fear of being excluded.

As if on cue two young girls on bicycles wheel down the boardwalk and stop between us and the view, darting impatient glances at us for being there. I'm equally annoyed at them for invading our space and interrupting our conversation. They are coltish and pretty, one dark and one blonde. Junior high girls, Lesley's age or a little older. They stop for a moment without getting off their bikes. The blonde one gives us an exasperated stare, no doubt hoping we'll yield our ground to them. I'll be damned if I will. I turn to Daphne as if the girls weren't there. "So you grew up in Manhattan? That's where you were twelve?"

"Yes, and what I remember is losing the sense of freedom, of going and doing whatever I wanted. Instead there was this new body, with breasts, with bleeding, so messy and inconvenient, this body I had to watch out for all the time."

The two girls have given up by now and started back down the boardwalk. I wonder where they live. They didn't seem very nice, but maybe I'm projecting my feelings onto them.

"Do you think girls still feel that way?" I ask, remembering the stricken look on Lesley's face when Greg criticized her cutoffs. ·

"Yes, I do. Freer in their bodies, maybe. Susan was an athlete, tennis and hockey player, and did a lot of backpacking, that sort of thing. I raised her to think she could do anything. But she's very careful with her looks, thinks about her weight all the time, eats practically nothing. Always borderline anorexic."

I glance back down the boardwalk. The girls have disappeared. Pretty girls, neatly dressed, even with their hair whipping in the wind and their lack of manners. "I don't think Lesley thinks about her looks."

"I bet she does. Look at her. Pull the hair back out of her eyes and get her to stand up straight and she's a real beauty, a full-grown woman. She probably doesn't know what to make of it so she hides it. One of these days she'll give herself permission to be beautiful. But not until she's ready to handle what goes with it."

I don't want to think about what goes with it, not yet. Nevertheless it's a revelation to view Lesley through Daphne's eyes. Not burdened with past impressions or my present tangled emotions, she sees Lesley as she is now. And probably sees things Lesley takes care to hide from me. My daughter a beauty? I hadn't noticed. Dorothea at that age was fragile-looking and shy, a slender and graceful child-woman. Caught up in the intensity of her music, she was remote at times but never sulky or disrespectful. Lesley seems so big and clumsy by comparison, so unfocused and lazy, difficult and moody. And she's just the age, the exact age that Dorothea was when she went in for her appendectomy. Does Lesley ever think about that?

"It's a terrible age, twelve," I say.

"Yes. That's how old my character Carrie was in *One Way to Staten Island*. I was describing her grief for a lost place, but it was really grief for a lost self she was feeling. Her lost childhood."

"Do you think boys feel that way, coming into puberty, that it's a loss?" I'm thinking of Gregory at fourteen, his losses.

"I don't know. I would say generally no. We get less freedom and they get more. But they're scared they won't measure up. They have to prove themselves, show they're men."

It's hard for me to imagine Daphne not feeling free, or being twelve years old for that matter. "I'm not sure I see becoming a woman as all that negative," I say thoughtfully. "After all, look what we come into—the power of an attractive young girl, the power she has over men."

"That's true. I think some girls get absolutely drunk on it and do a lot of damage, to themselves and other people. But eventually we pair off and have children, and then what are we? People who exist for others, who have little or no lives of our own."

"That didn't happen to you."

"Yes it did, for a while anyway."

"What's wrong with loving someone, living for him and for your children? What could be more valuable than that?" As I say the words, I realize I'm not only justifying myself but passing judgment on Daphne—at least she might hear it that way.

"But it goes. They go. The children grow up, the men leave or die off, and then where are you? You can't count on other people to give meaning to your life." Daphne stands up and crosses over to the railing, leans out over the wide, swiftly moving creek below. "People leave. If not physically then emotionally. They betray you. You can't count on them. In the end there's just yourself."

Daphne's voice has risen; she's speaking out of more than conviction—out of anger and a very private sorrow. I feel guilty for having prompted this outburst and amazed at her frankness. We barely know each other. I don't believe her but her words frighten and sadden me. Could I do what she is doing, deliberately choose to live my life so utterly alone? I badly want to comfort her, but I don't know how.

I get up from the bench and together we turn and make our way back down the boardwalk toward the little beach. The clutch of mothers and small children has thinned out, driven away by the wind, probably. I'm beginning to worry about the time. Daphne follows the road past the playground and veers to the right onto a different path, not the way we came. "This will take us straight back to the car," she says. "Not as interesting but quicker. I'll have you back to your girls soon." She speaks briskly without hurt or irony, herself again. The moment has passed.

West Marsh

*. . . green cranberry plants are reaching down beneath the
sand, drawing their nourishment from the remains of the
plants which created the swamp.*

WE NEVER DO get to drink our tea. Back on the lane Daphne drops me
off in my driveway so I can check on the girls, and even before I get
out of the car I can hear Dorothea. She's making the keening sound that
means she's having one of her tantrums. Lesley has wheeled her into the
parlor and turned on the television, but the snowy cartoons aren't helping.

I telephone Daphne from the kitchen. "I'm sorry, but I've got to take
a rain check on the tea. Dorrie is having one of her upsets and it will take
me awhile to calm her down."

"Oh, I'm sorry. I can't tomorrow, but how about Thursday? This time
see if you can bring the girls. I have a favor to ask Lesley. She likes animals, doesn't she? I want to ask her to feed my cats while I'm in New York
next weekend."

I feel irrationally jealous—of what? My answering voice sounds cool
and polite. "She'd probably love it, but you should be the one to ask her. I'll
make sure she comes this time." With Lesley I pick my battles.

I hurry back to the parlor, where Dorrie is rocking from side to side
in her chair and moaning. "How long has she been like this?" I ask Lesley.

"Just a while. I didn't do anything, honest. We were just sitting on
the porch." She's on the defensive, ready to fend off the criticism she feels
sure is coming. For once she's wrong; I've dealt with these tantrums long
enough to know they can arrive for no reason.

"I know you didn't. You know how she gets sometimes. I'm sorry you
were here by yourself."

"It's okay. Oh, and what's-his-name, Demetrius came by in his truck.
He wondered if we wanted to go see the cranberry bog. He said his
number's on that list by the phone."

"Would you like to go?"

"Sure, I guess." Lesley is so relieved not to be blamed that she's feeling
agreeable.

Demetrius was here. I haven't seen him since the Fourth, and I've been wondering why. And now he wants me to call. I'm surprised at my feelings: anticipation, guilt. Silly; he's just being polite. I asked him questions about the bog on the Fourth.

Dorrie is red and sweating and nearly hysterical. It's obvious she has soiled herself. She needs cleaning up and soothing, a bath. I wheel her back to her room and start filling the tub, help her onto the bed so I can undress her and wipe her down. On top of the mess, her period has started. The room fills with her pungent odor. She hasn't had an accident in a long time and it distresses her, I can tell. Her naked body always surprises me; she's fully mature, heavy-breasted, a woman despite her wasted limbs. She bleeds, has moods like the rest of us. She's incredibly hard to lift, so much dead weight despite her efforts to help. I sit her on the edge of the tub, leaning her against my body as I swing her legs over and into the water, then lower her carefully down into her bath chair. She likes the feeling of being in water; it lightens her, probably makes her feel she has more control. She relaxes, moves her left arm back and forth, ruffling the water. Tears come to my eyes as they always seem to do when I bathe her. My beautiful lost daughter, my burden, my love.

I DON'T CALL Demetrius until after supper is over and Dorothea is settled down and Lesley is trying to peer through the snow on the little TV to watch some silly sitcom. I try to remember whether Aunt Phoebe mentions where Demetrius lives in her journal. He's a widower, I do know that. Aunt Phoebe wrote to Greg when his wife died four, maybe five years ago, and I remember ordering the flowers. I let his phone ring eight times, but no one picks up, not even an answering machine.

Feeling let down, I climb the stairs to Aunt Phoebe's little room, where her journal notebooks sit on top of her bookshelf. Back in May when Daphne gave them to me I read them all straight through. It took a good part of three days, fitted in around taking care of Dorothea and sorting stacks of bills, papers, and magazines. I want to go back and read parts of them again, now that I'm more familiar with the cast of characters, the parts about Daphne, and about Demetrius, though most of the entries about him have to do with cranberries. I arranged the notebooks chronologically as I read them in May. Maybe this time I'll work backwards.

They are arranged in four piles on the shelf under the window. I pick up the top notebook on the last pile. December 1985. Just a few months before everything changed for us. Aunt Phoebe's entries in these more recent years are less regular, her handwriting beginning to enlarge and show the shakiness of age. They lack the breathless effusiveness she had as a bride. There are some long lapses between entries, though none so long as that puzzling silence back in the fifties. Some names are rendered as initials. D for Dennis. No, that couldn't be right—he was dead by then. D for Daphne. Or maybe Demetrius.

> December 8: Today cold and full of wind, the bay dark as a pea jacket and heaving straight at us out of the north. Rafts of ducks everywhere, common eiders mostly, a few scoters mixed in, spotted a lone white-winged scoter, slighter and more graceful than the others. They bob unconcernedly up and down in the waves, then dive to the bottom to feed. One disappears, then another, then the whole group, as if it occurred to them all at once that it was a good idea. How showy the male eiders are, nothing like their mates, white backs and peculiar faces, like another breed entirely.

> December 25: Christmas over again, that day of ghosts. To Janet and Tom's, a kitschy Hallmark day with eggnog before dinner and infuriating little bells playing carols. The woman lacks artistic sense, not to mention her over-consciousness of charity to poor Phoebe. I am insufficiently grateful? Happy to get home to my own house with no plastic Santas, just real greens that smell of real woods. D left a box of cedar logs and an armload of holly by the porch door. Made a fire and lit the candles in the parlor and read until well past midnight. Only a few thoughts of Christmas past, the years with the cousins in Hamilton and the three precious ones with C. Some tears, and so to bed, safely past it again.

> December 31: Too gray and raw to be outside, a day for a fire and self-reflection, another year alone. They feel like gifts, these winter days of perfect solitude. A call from the Boston cousins. They can't imagine my life. I guess from their perspective it looks uneventful, wasted. But inside it's long stretches of calm disturbed by terrible upheavals. Inner storms nobody sees. Almost nobody. Reticence, crown of New England virtues—curse or saving grace? The denizens of Pinckney Street. Poor Phoebe they call me, as if Phoebe were my middle name. It used to make me angry, but now it amuses me. They pity me, and I pity them, all of us convinced we live on the right

side of the bridge. My people clucking because I married a swamp Yankee, the Turnstones looking down on me because I wasn't a first comer. The whole vast population out there never dream of such distinctions, just see the lot of us as worn out, bled white, sipping weak tea from cracked export china cups and making do with our great-grandparents' threadbare orientals.

January 1: A gift of a day, warmish and still, 50 degrees by the back door, early January thaw? I have resolved to walk two miles a day. Went west on 6A and circled around the salt marsh on Commerce Road; lots of sea ducks settled in there (do they sense a storm coming?) and my friend the great blue put on a show for me, reward for my noble intentions, skimming over the creek and settling down to take his immobile stand. How awkward he looks when he walks, with those long legs and neck. How graceful when he sails on those wide astonishing wings!

January 2: Woke this morning to a white silent world, not snow but frost, and a perfect stillness, the sun a weak yellowish presence through the mist. Back steps slick without looking frozen, treacherous. Walking up the hill I leave footprints, the grass crunches, I dare not climb my rock. Houses on the neck look close (mist not obscuring them; it's higher up in the air), water palest blue and mirror-clear. The word *rime* comes to mind; I'm driven to look it up. It means hoarfrost, *hoar* for aged, shaggy with white hairs, like an old man. Exactly. The magic lasts an hour only, the sun soon dissolving it away.

The phone is ringing and there's only one in this house; I have to hurry down the steep narrow staircase to catch it on the fourth ring. I'm surprised and happy to hear it's Demetrius.

"Anna? Not too late, I hope."

"Oh no. I was just all the way upstairs."

"Lesley tell you I came by?"

"Yes she did, and I tried to call you, but you weren't home. We'd love to see West Marsh."

"Tomorrow suit you?"

"That would be fine. Can we manage Dorrie's chair?"

"Sure. Can't take her everywhere, but there's a good solid dirt road up to the bog house. I'll help. We'll manage. Want me to come get you?"

"No, that doesn't make sense. I'll bring the van. I just need directions."
He explains. They're not complicated—east on 6A about a mile and a half
into Yarmouth Port, and then just two turns down side roads. I write them
down. "When do you want us?"

"It'll be hot. I've got some ditch work to do in the early morning—
maybe about eleven?"

"Fine. I'll bring some sodas. In fact, why don't I bring lunch?"

I stare at the phone for a while after hanging up, and then on an
impulse find Daphne's number on Aunt Phoebe's list and dial. She's
surprised to hear from me, but relieved I'm not canceling our tea date a
second time. I don't tell her I've surprised myself by calling her. "What can
you tell me about Demetrius?" I ask.

"I'm not sure what you are asking, Anna. Does he want some sort of
job reference?"

"No, no, nothing like that. It's just that he's over here every now and
then. He came and spoke to Lesley today while we were gone, though I
don't think he got out of his truck. He handles Dorothea really well, but I
just need to know—is he reliable?"

"Oh absolutely. You don't need to be afraid of him. He's worked for
the family ever since he was a teenager, and he and Phoebe—they were
more than just employer and employee—they were friends. He's—well,
still waters run deep."

That old cliché my mother used to use. I've never understood exactly
what it means. "I can see from the journals he took very good care of
her. What do you know about him? Does he have a family? Where does
he live?"

"He lives out on the marsh in Yarmouth Port, in a tiny little cottage
that was somebody's hunting shack. I've never been there, but Phoebe's
shown me where it is. You can see it from the boardwalk where we were
today. What's this about, Anna?"

"Just curious, that's all. He's almost a member of the family and I
don't know anything about him. Didn't his wife die a few years ago? Does
he have children?"

"No children. Lots of relatives, though—his family has been on
the Cape forever. His wife was an interesting woman. I knew her when
she had a store on 6A. She made beautiful driftwood collages and
arrangements of dried flowers. Amazing she could do it because she was
terribly crippled—rheumatoid arthritis, I think, had it since she was in her
teens. In a wheelchair by the time I knew her."

A wheelchair. No wonder Demetrius handles Dorrie with such ease. He's done it before.

THE NEXT DAY is indeed hot, as Demetrius predicted. It takes the entire morning to get Dorrie fed and exercised and ready and transferred to the van, to make sandwiches from the leftover ham and cheese, peanut butter and jelly. No time for homemade brownies; we'll have to settle for the few Oreos Lesley hasn't managed to devour. We stop at the little shop in Yarmouth Port to fill the picnic cooler with ice and cold cans of soda.

As we turn onto the dirt track leading to the bog house, I remember that I was here before, years ago with Uncle Dennis. Just the two of us; Greg hadn't wanted to come. Demetrius's battered blue truck is parked beside the shed, and he emerges as we drive up.

"Uncle Dennis brought me here once," I tell Demetrius, "just before Greg and I got married. But I can't remember much about what he told me."

"Come on inside," Demetrius says; "it's cooler in the shade." He deftly relieves me of the picnic cooler and sets it on the floor as I wheel Dorrie inside. "Now, miss," he says, turning to Lesley, "what do you know about cranberries?"

"Just that I like them, and we have them every Thanksgiving. When I was little, I called them red stuff. I always took seconds and thirds."

"Glad to hear that. We've had a surplus the last few years. Brings the price down. The more you eat the better."

The bog house is the simplest of structures, about 25 by 40 feet I would guess, with a shed room added in back, broad barn doors in front and two smaller doors on one side and the back, a few windows with overhanging storm shutters propped open. Inside it feels surprisingly cool, with a strong cross draft from the warm west wind. Demetrius has positioned Dorrie where she'll feel it, in the middle of the room opposite the door. It has the look of a small barn, built post and beam with a loft above. The space around the edges of the room is crowded with heaps of rough burlap bags, stacks of boxes, and a few odd mechanical devices not looking like anything I could name. The little shed room opening to the back has a small potbellied stove, an old mattress laid over an arrangement of boxes, and a kerosene lamp. A pair of fisherman's rubber waders hangs from a hook on the wall.

"You sleep here sometimes?" Lesley wants to know. I want to know too, but I would not have asked.

"Sometimes. Mostly in the fall when I'm worried about frost. I've rigged up an alarm connected to a thermometer outside. If the temperature goes below 30 degrees I turn on the sprinkler system."

"What good does that do?"

"It mists the vines; then they get covered with a coat of ice, and that protects them from freezing."

Lesley looks skeptical. "That doesn't make sense."

"I know; it seems crazy, but it works. The ice is like a little overcoat keeping the cold off the leaves. Think about Eskimos and their igloos. Same principle."

I look at Demetrius with interest. He explains things like a good teacher, I think. I did some teaching, back when Greg was in law school, English as a second language. So often explaining something clearly means finding the right analogy.

"What's this thing?" Lesley asks, pointing to a peculiar machine made of metal tubing and consisting of two handles and a small engine mounted behind a bicycle tire and connected with a series of belts to a cutting blade up front.

"That's a weed cutter. Your great uncle Dennis made that. It's like a mower, but the only thing that touches the ground is that thin tire, so it doesn't do much damage to the vines. Dennis loved inventing things— came up with a whole lot of rigs for this and that. Some worked better than others."

"Did he build that truck out there?" I ask.

"Sure did. That's a 1934 Ford truck chassis, stripped down with a flatbed added in the back. Classic bog buggy. Dennis thought to add another loading space in front of the engine, too."

Uncle Dennis—what was it Aunt Phoebe called him in her journal? "My Rube Goldberg." Happiest here, probably, tinkering, rigging up one-of-a-kind machines. His regular job, when he had one, was in a machine shop, but he could never get used to having a boss, especially when it was his uncle. Once the cranberries began to bear he got more and more erratic about showing up at work until finally even the family loyalty got strained too far and he was let go. It's easy to see why he was happiest here, in charge of his own operation, working at his own pace. With reliable Demetrius to take up the slack.

I think back to that day years ago when Uncle Dennis brought me here and took me out to show me the sluice gate he'd designed to flood the bog in winter, his enthusiasm as he described the difference between wet and dry harvesting, the hard hand work of scooping the ditches, the way things were in the old days when children were let out of school to help get in the crop. He loved this place. If only he could have made a go of it, without having to rely on Phoebe's family money. The bog belongs to Demetrius now. Is he making a go of it? Evidently, along with the odd jobs he does around town in his spare time.

"What kind of work do you do in the summer?" I ask.

"Mostly maintenance, but there's more to do here than you think. I use that weed cutter, for one thing, to clear the ditches. Keeps me busy part of most days. Come on, we'll take a walk around the perimeter and I'll show you." Demetrius leads us out the door and off to the right past his truck, where a high dirt track, wide enough to drive on and packed hard in this hot, dry weather, circles the bog. We pass two more small buildings, a pump house and a roughly put together shed sheltering Uncle Dennis's bog buggy, a tractor looking at least forty years old, and another smaller machine Demetrius says is used for harvesting. Lesley moves up beside him and I follow along, pushing Dorrie, who is leaning back and smiling, looking curiously at the wide bog to our right. It is rounded on this end and shaped to fit into the low wooded hillside rising on the other. The bog itself is perfectly flat, crisscrossed with a network of narrow ditches, and covered with a thick mat of fine, tangled green vines. It's rather like walking the perimeter of an enormous pie. I push Dorrie up closer to Demetrius so I can hear what he's saying.

"This was a kettle pond once," he's telling Lesley. Then it turned into a swamp, and after that a peat bog."

"They burn peat in Ireland," Lesley answers. She's enjoying this lecture more than she'd admit. I wish she could feel as easy with Gregory, but she doesn't. She always feels he's judging her.

"This peat's different—no good for burning," Demetrius goes on. "But wild cranberries grew in it. The Wampanoag ate them, used them for pemmican."

"What's that?"

"Dried meat mixed with suet and berries."

"Yuk."

"Depends how hungry you are," Demetrius says, smiling at her.

Dorrie is getting red; I forgot to bring a hat for her. I put my sunhat on her head but she knocks it to the ground. She hates hats, always did, even as a little girl. "I need to get Dorrie out of the sun," I say apologetically to Demetrius. I like hearing about what he does, what Greg might have done when he was here as a teenager.

Gregory—how little I have thought about him since I've been here. It's as if I've stepped out of his world into one of my own, as if Aunt Phoebe's house were mine, not ours, even though it's his family's place. Here—West Marsh—is where he worked, doing hard physical labor through the hot summer days. And Demetrius was his boss. It strains my mind to imagine it. Did they ever sit around and talk during their lunch breaks, like we're doing now?

We turn and head slowly back toward the bog house. It's a relief to get inside, to unpack the cans of soft drinks from the cooler and lay them against our necks to cool off. I offer Demetrius one of the ham and cheese sandwiches and take one myself. The girls are happier with peanut butter. Watching him eat, I'm a little embarrassed by the plainness of the lunch. Nothing homemade. My mother would turn up her nose at the store-bought cookies, the supermarket bread I bought under protest as a concession to Lesley. Plastic bread is what I call it. Picnics in Ohio meant platters of cold fried chicken, potato salad, deviled eggs, gallons of cold sweet tea, homemade brownies and at least two kinds of pie. An iced watermelon to top it all off, with a seed-spitting contest to go with it. And in recent years, back when Greg and I would tailgate with friends before the Harvard games, the women quietly competed with little gourmet touches—pickled shrimp with chunks of French bread and unsalted butter, washed down with some newly discovered Australian Chardonnay, inexpensive but amusing.

Lesley wants to walk all the way around the edge of the bog, she says after lunch. As she sets off, Demetrius helps me pack up the cooler. "Thanks for the picnic," he says. "No one has brought me lunch over here since—for a long time."

I resist the impulse to apologize for the food. I must remember one of my assignments back when I was in counseling: practice not being perfect. "My pleasure," I say simply. He is looking directly at me and smiling, white teeth and green eyes set off by his dark skin, ruddy brown from exposure to the sun. I feel myself blushing the way I did on the Fourth, when I woke up to find him watching me.

"Will you come again?" he asks. "Not necessarily with lunch," he adds, breaking again into that melting smile. "I want you to see what happens, how we go through the seasons here. The bogs are beautiful when they turn color in the fall, even all through the winter."

"We'll be back in Needham by fall, but I'll come again this summer, if you want." I'm happy he has asked; I look at him shyly and look away. That springy hair—would it feel wiry or soft? He wears it longer than I'm used to. I very much want to reach out and touch where it lies over his neck in curls. I stand up and release the brakes on Dorrie's chair. "Now I've got to get the girls home. Dorrie is hot, and I imagine you've got more work to do."

"No. Too hot. I'm done here for the day."

"Clearing ditches—is that the sort of thing Greg would do for you, those summers?"

"Sure, lots of digging and weeding. Usually we'd have our feet in water all day. By evening our toes would look like prunes and the top half of us would be burned to a crisp. And back then we did a lot of spraying. Dangerous stuff, some of it, though we didn't know it then. Greg didn't like the job one bit, but he was a good worker. Rest of the crew was on the rough side—they gave him a hard time. Maybe that's when he decided lawyering would be easier."

Just as we are about to go out to the van, Lesley bursts into the bog house, startling us. "Mom, guess what! I saw a huge bird—an osprey, maybe. He was in a tree and took off up the hill towards the woods."

"What color?" Demetrius asks. "Did you see what his tail looked like when he flew?"

"Not really, but he was big. Mostly brown all over, I think."

"Marsh hawk, most likely. Ospreys you'll see out by the harbor. Could have been a red tail, but they're more gray than brown."

"You sound like Aunt Phoebe," I say, laughing, as we finish loading the van and I turn on the engine. "She knew more than anybody about birds. Did she teach you?"

Demetrius smiles again, his eyes crinkling and looking as gold-green as the densely tangled vines carpeting the bog behind him. "Some," he says. "And some I taught her. It was mutual."

Gods and Goddesses

*...from an airplane, we see so many ponds riddling the
land surface that we are likely to wonder how some parts
of the Cape hold themselves together...*

LESLEY REALLY DOESN'T want to have tea at Daphne's, wants to stay right where she is, curled up in her damp bathing suit in the weathered old Adirondack chair next to the house. She's drawing nothing in particular on one of Aunt Phoebe's faded yellow legal pads—hawk-like faces of men who could be rock singers or serial killers with high cheekbones and prominent noses and ominous black shadows, triangles dissolving into curves, a study of the odd vine spilling out of the shrubbery next to her, with its stiff segmented stems ending in fine curling tendrils and funny pink flowers that look almost like butterflies. It's hot, too hot to get dressed and think about manners, and she doesn't even like tea. Tea is something old ladies do, people even older than her mother. But Daphne—Mrs. Ault she's supposed to call her—has been nice to her, Mom reminded her, took her sailing. She asked specifically for Lesley to come. And Mom needs her to help with Dorrie.

Lesley's sulkiness disappears as soon as she sees the cats. Two of them flank Daphne as she greets them at the door, and another is asleep on the chair by the fireplace. Lesley squats down and reaches out to the nearest one, entranced, forgetting to be self-conscious. "What's his name?" she asks, stroking the sleek gray one under the chin.

"That's Mercury," says Daphne, "and this is Juno," picking up the long-haired calico entwining herself around her legs and meowing. "She's temperamental—you've got to let her warm to you. She'll be very affectionate if she's in the mood. But she can be whiny or scratchy, even with me. Unpredictable. And most talkative, as you can hear."

"And who's this?" says Lesley, quietly approaching the big tabby curled up in the wing chair.

"That's Hephaestus. He's easy. A pussycat, as they say, and very lazy."

"Festus?"

"Hephaestus. The Greek god of fire. Like Vulcan, blacksmith to the gods. He was born lame and got thrown off Mount Olympus for knowing how to make fire. My Hephaestus isn't lame, but he has extra toes."

"He does?"

"Here, see? That makes him special. A cat of good fortune. Hephaestus was an artist, made beautiful armor and jewels and even a perfectly lifelike woman. I hold him when I need inspiration."

"They're all named after gods and goddesses?"

"All except Mistress Quickly. She comes from Shakespeare. I had her before I moved here. Your Aunt Phoebe inspired me to name the others. She always said we could use a little more mythology."

"Where is she? Mistress Quickly I mean," Lesley asks, looking around the room for her. She likes the room; it's big and open with glass all across the back and not a lot of furniture or stuff like at Aunt Phoebe's, just books and papers piled everywhere.

"Oh, you'll meet her when she's ready. She's probably back in the bedroom. She's getting old and cautious. She'll peek around when she thinks it's safe. I don't think she's forgiven me yet for moving her out of New York. A city cat. Hates the outdoors. Suspicious of strangers."

"What color is she?"

"She's white. You can't miss her."

"Daphne . . ." Lesley begins.

"Mrs. Ault," her mother prompts. Lesley flushes angrily. Why does Mom always spoil everything? Wanting her to babysit Dorrie and then treating her like a baby. Daphne told her to call her Daphne, didn't think she was being impolite. She likes talking about her cats—probably feels like they're her children.

Daphne in the meantime is fetching a big pitcher from the refrigerator. "I've made some lemonade. Would you like some?"

"Real lemonade?" Lesley asks, pretending not to see the sharp look her mother darts at her.

"Of course real, with real lemons and even real sugar. I don't believe in indulging halfway," Daphne laughs. Lesley can see the little swirls the dissolving sugar grains make as Daphne stirs the lemonade with a long spoon. The ice cubes clink against the glass, and layers of lemon slices float on top. Lesley's mouth begins to water. She can't remember when she last tasted real lemonade. A long time ago, when her grandmother from Knoxville came to visit. Before Dorrie's operation. Everything good that happened in their family seems a long time ago, before Dorrie. Daphne is filling a tall glass and offering it to her mother. It has a sprig of crisp dark green leaves on top. "I was going to make iced tea, but I always drink it for the lemon and sugar anyway, so I just left out the tea. I thought you girls might like it better."

It feels queer to Lesley to be lumped with Dorrie in that phrase, "you girls." Most people don't talk about Dorrie as if she were a real person. Mom will want Lesley to help Dorrie drink her lemonade; they'd talked about that. Mom hates anyone watching Dorrie eat, and Lesley doesn't like it either; Dorrie always tries hard, but she makes weird noises and usually makes a mess. She wears a bib at home and eats in the kitchen in case she spills stuff on the floor. Mom didn't bring her bib today, but she did bring one of her special drinking cups, a little round-bottomed plastic one with a removable top Dorrie can sort of suck out of, a training cup for babies. They always come in baby colors. This one is yellow.

Lesley is relieved when her mother suggests she could wheel Dorrie down by the pond and give her her lemonade there. She's been wanting to look at the pond, anyway. Of course Mom and Daphne have to supervise getting Dorrie's chair out the door and down the hill to a flat shady place under a tree, and Mom has to check the brake and warn Lesley not to go wheeling Dorrie into the mud. The mud is kind of bad, and there don't seem to be any frogs or fish or interesting animals to look at, other than a few amazing-colored dragonflies lazing around the cattails on the edge. Bright turquoise blue. Lesley's grateful she brought her legal pad along, stuck in the pocket in the back of Dorrie's chair. When Dorrie is finished slurping her lemonade, Lesley leaves her gazing at the pond and settles herself on a rock just above the muddy edge. There are lots of things to draw here. She wishes one of the dragonflies would come close and hold still for a few minutes. She settles for the cattails, nice and neat, pointing straight up like so many skinny brown cigars. Later they'll get fat and the stuffing will start leaking out.

Lesley doesn't look up when she hears the footsteps—she's intent upon studying the way the narrow cattail leaves bend over at an angle. It will be her mother coming to fetch Dorrie back up the hill and she'd like to get out of being the one to push.

"You've got a good eye for detail," Daphne says, pointing to the little sketch. Lesley, startled, turns the yellow pad over on her lap. She doesn't like other people looking at her drawings. But she doesn't resist when Daphne takes the pad out of her hands and turns back to the previous page, to the drawings she'd done earlier in her own yard. "Those are beach peas," Daphne says. "You really have their stems, kind of awkward and graceful at the same time. They remind me of praying mantises."

"Thank you," Lesley says, feeling embarrassed and putting her hand out for the pad. She doesn't want Daphne turning back to the weird faces on the previous page.

"Do you have art at school?"

"Sure." A stupid question. Lesley doesn't think of her drawings as art; they're just something she wants, has to do. The question reminds her of her teacher, who wants her to take an art class at the museum school in Boston, talks about developing her talent. Lesley doesn't think about her itch to draw as talent, doesn't want to take art lessons. She'd rather keep it private. Daphne is waiting for her to say more, but she doesn't. Instead she gets up and walks up the little slope to straighten out Dorrie, who has started listing to one side. Daphne follows her, watches while she brushes a mosquito away from Dorrie's face, adjusts her sun hat, lifts her dangling right hand and replaces it on her lap.

"I have a job offer for you," Daphne says. "Would you like to take care of my cats while I'm in New York next week? I'll be gone three days."

"I don't think Mom could deal with four cats."

Daphne smiles. "Oh, no, I didn't mean at your house—I meant here. You'd have to come over once a day and feed them. You don't even have to let them out. They've got a litter box they can use, and you wouldn't have to change that. Food and water is what I'm talking about. And maybe a little attention. They can get a bit squirrely when I'm gone, especially Juno."

"I guess I could do that. You'll tell me about the food?"

"Of course. I'll show you where everything is. And I'll show you where I keep the key. You just have to be careful to lock the house when you leave and put the key back. And make sure the cats have plenty of water. I can tell you'll get along with them. You didn't impose yourself on them the way some people do. I wanted them to meet you before I asked."

Lesley imagines the cats having a little discussion about her, taking a vote. So that was why she'd been invited to tea. The idea makes her smile. "I'll have to ask Mom."

"I already did. She thought you'd be pleased." Lesley is pleased, but the thought of the two women talking about her makes her cringe. Is that why they sent her down to the pond? How old do you have to be before people stop discussing you the minute you are out of the room? And how much will Daphne pay her? Would it be impolite to ask?

"Is four dollars a day okay? That's a dollar for each cat."

"Sure," Lesley answers, getting that familiar feeling she always has when adults talk to her, that her head is made of glass and they can see exactly what's inside.

LATE ON FRIDAY afternoon Lesley walks across the lane and retrieves the key from its hiding place under the rock near Daphne's lilac bush. It takes her a few minutes to get the door open because the lock is sticky. Finally it yields and she is inside. It feels very different with Daphne gone and the windows closed, like she shouldn't be here. The air is stuffy, with a faint catty smell. The gray cat—what's his name?—and Juno, the Calico, appear from the direction of the bedroom as soon as she shuts the door, followed by the big tabby, the lucky one. The artist cat. How will she ever remember their names? Mercury, that's the gray one. And where is the Shakespeare cat, Mrs. Quickly? No sooner does Lesley think of her than she appears, peeking around the doorway from the bedroom just as Daphne said she would. A little cat, slender and neat and all white. Lesley stops to see what she'll do. She doesn't come near but doesn't retreat, either, just regards Lesley with her large green eyes. A sweet cat, maybe her favorite. Juno's eyes are amber to match her yellow patches, and so are Mercury's. The big tabby has retreated hopefully to the kitchen. Lesley follows him and makes kissing sounds to get him to turn around. His eyes are green, but not as green as Mrs. Quickly's. On the kitchen table is a large bag of cat food, a smaller paper bag, and a note in Daphne's dramatic scrawly handwriting:

> *Here you are. Just make sure the two cat bowls and the water dish are full.*
> *A cup a day per cat is about right, but sometimes they eat more, sometimes*
> *less. Don't forget to lock up. And could you bring my mail in from the*
> *box and leave it on the table? I forgot to mention that. See you Monday.*
> *Thanks, Daphne.*
>   *P.S. Look in the bag—it's for you.*
>   *P.P.S. Cats' names are Mercury (gray), Hephaestus (tabby), Juno*
> *(calico), and Mistress Quickly (white). Thought you might not remember*
> *them all.*

The feeding bowls look full to Lesley, but she shakes a little more into each from the bag. Daphne probably filled them before she left this morning. All four cats are attracted by the sound and quickly align themselves two and two and begin to eat. Lesley resists an impulse to stroke the shy white one. Mistress Quickly, not Mrs. Tomorrow maybe they'll make friends. Then she opens the flat paper bag on the table. Two packages, one small and narrow, one larger and flat. A book, probably. Wrapped in dark red paper, shiny like enamel. A plain white card is taped to the larger one: "To Lesley, with thanks. Enjoy." Lesley opens the flat package, carefully loosening the tape. The red paper is beautiful; she'll use it later for something. A plain black notebook with large rings along the spine, "100 percent rag acid free" printed on the back. Lesley opens the cover. Blank pages inside. She runs her hand over the heavy paper, smooth and satisfyingly creamy. Beautiful. She opens the smaller box. Two calligraphy pens with removable nibs and a small bottle of black ink. Permanent ink, like real artists use. Never has she owned real artists' pens like these, such beautiful paper.

It's a temptation to try the pens right away, but she wants to experiment with them first on her yellow pad. And Mom will be wondering what took her so long. She packs her treasures in the bag along with the shiny red wrapping paper, says goodbye to the cats, addressing each of them by name, and tucks the bag under her arm as she carefully pushes in the lock button and shuts the front door behind her. She's halfway home before she remembers the key is still on the kitchen table.

Thank God her mother hasn't started supper. She's in the parlor reading. The house is silent—Dorrie must have fallen asleep. Lesley climbs the stairs as quietly as she can, quickly changes into her bathing suit, and doesn't call out to her mother until she's halfway out the door. "I'm going to take a quick swim."

"Not too long. We'll eat in about an hour."

An hour to figure out how to get back into Daphne's house. Otherwise Mom will know something's not right. Maybe the cold water will inspire her somehow. The tide is halfway out, meaning the water will be freezing. Lesley picks her way along the path through the marsh grass, wading out until the water is above her knees. It is freezing, just as she thought. A quick plunge to get herself wet; she's not tempted to stay in longer than that.

She'll have to get into the house somehow. The only neighbor Daphne ever talks about is Aunt Phoebe. She probably fed Daphne's cats when she was alive. Maybe there is a key in her house somewhere, in the jumble of hardware and tools she saw in the pantry drawer. If not, then what? Maybe Daphne left a window unlocked and she could climb in. Not likely. She's from New York. New Yorkers are really freaky about locking everything. She'll have to figure out a plan. Try the keys from the drawer first. If they don't work, check the windows. If they're all locked, then what? Break in?

Supper is agony, but Lesley has her chance when Mom is occupied with getting Dorrie settled for the night. She slips the pantry drawer open as silently as possible, picking through the jumble of screws, small tools, hooks, and small change, pocketing everything remotely resembling a house key. So many of them! She wishes she had paid more attention to the shape of Daphne's key. At eight o'clock she tells her mother she wants to check on the cats. It's still light but dusk will fall soon. If she's lucky no one will be out taking an after-dinner stroll.

Lesley empties the keys out of her pocket and lines them up on the step in front of Daphne's front door. Eleven of them, some single, some bunched on nondescript key rings, none of them labeled. She tries them, one at a time. Most won't even begin to enter the lock. Two fit snugly in, giving her a moment of wild hope. But they won't turn. She can hear one of the cats, probably Juno, meowing on the other side of the door. Now what?

She circles around to the back of the house. Maybe an open window? She doesn't dare test the windows facing the street; someone might come along and see her. And the side windows to the bedroom and bathroom are too high to reach without a ladder or at least a chair to stand on. The deck across the back is her best bet; big sliding doors open into the living room and the bedroom. In between, there's a small window above the kitchen counter. But how to get up to the deck?

There's an old-fashioned redwood picnic table with attached benches in the yard below the deck. Good and solid. With some effort, Lesley drags it toward the house until it is just under the deck railing. Standing on it, she can just reach the wooden supports of the railing. It takes several tries to pull herself up so she can kneel precariously on the lip of the deck outside the railing. Mustn't look down; just hold on. Finally she's able to hoist herself into a standing position and swing her leg over the rail.

The big sliders are both locked. Lesley can see Daphne has taken the added precaution of laying a long piece of wood in the tracks. The small kitchen window? It's too high to see, so Lesley carries one of the metal chairs on the deck over and stands on it. Yes! It's unlocked, but she'll have to remove the screen somehow. And she'll have to work with what she has; if she drops back down off the deck she may never be able to climb up again. She fishes in her pocket and pulls out one of her collection of keys. The screen is tougher than she thought, but eventually she's able to poke a hole in each lower corner and get her fingers inside. The catches holding the screen in place are sticky, and so is the track, but she's finally able to raise it up far enough to make room to climb inside. The window raises easily, leaving just enough room to boost herself inside. The uneven sill hurts. As she swings her legs onto the kitchen counter something crashes to the floor. A glass pitcher, the one Daphne used for the lemonade. But she's in, four pairs of cat eyes are regarding her curiously, and the house keys are there right where she left them on the kitchen table.

TELLING DAPHNE TURNS out to be less of a nightmare than she thought. In a way Daphne is relieved because arriving home Tuesday afternoon she'd noticed the damaged screen and thought there'd been a break-in. What she's mad about is that Lesley hadn't asked for help. Demetrius has a key to her house and most of the houses on the street. Of course her Mom might not know that. Lesley has to realize she owes Daphne for the screen and the pitcher. She can work it off by feeding the cats for free for the rest of the summer when Daphne goes away. And there isn't any reason to tell her Mom. She has enough on her mind already.

The Pronoun *I*

Water is not the only thing that wears back the land.

A S IT TURNS out Gregory doesn't make it to Cummaquid for the
weekend. He calls on Thursday to say he has to go back to Washington for another deposition—the case he's been working on for months is
finally winding down, but he'll be flat out for the next several weeks. He
works until late Friday evening and stays over, then his plane is delayed
and he doesn't get back to Boston until midafternoon on Saturday. I agree
it doesn't make sense to fight the traffic for a one-day visit. He promises
to get down early the following Friday, when we're having dinner guests,
Needham neighbors who have a cottage in Chatham.

I feel disappointed and relieved in equal measure. I miss Greg physically—even though we make love rarely these days, it's comforting to have
his warm body there next to me in bed. On the other hand, I'm tense and
anxious when he is here. It isn't just the unresolved issue of what we will
do with the house. It's his unhappiness here, as if he's being thrown back
into the grief of that first summer after his mother's death. I keep hoping
to replace those sad memories with newer, happier ones, but I don't know
how. It's hard to imagine him lounging on the beach, or fishing, or taking
on a boat with all the hassles and expenses that go with it.

Then there are my own feelings to think about. I'm starting to like
living according to my own rhythms. I still have Dorothea and all the
demands of getting her through the day, but for the first time in years
I can carve out some moments for myself. I've started to treasure those
early morning walks down to look at the harbor, the ease of not having
to fuss quite so much over dinner, the freedom of not having Gregory's
eyes judging me. Is it his fault or mine, the way my self-esteem crumbles
whenever he's around?

Saturday brings an east wind and a damp, muggy fog that hangs
around until Sunday afternoon. I turn my attention to clearing the clutter
out of the downstairs, hauling stacks of old newspapers and magazines
out to the garage. Lesley agrees to thin out and rearrange Aunt Phoebe's
vast collection of beach stones and shells. I scoop heaps of old ashes out of

the fireplace and scatter them in the garden, scrubbing the old bricks and storing the grimy screen and black iron fire dogs in the garage, replacing them with one of Aunt Phoebe's big baskets filled with dried yarrow and money plant. I find an absurd feather duster in the broom closet and show it to Lesley, who's so amused that she doesn't mind when I send her out to the porch to sweep the cobwebs out of the corners of the ceiling. She's been cheerful lately, spending a good deal of time with Daphne, out sailing and visiting the cats. I strike a bargain with her: If she'll help me clean, I'll fix anything she wants for supper, nutrition be damned. We send out for pizza on Saturday and make an entire meal on Sunday of tender new corn on the cob and French toast.

On an impulse I invite Daphne to the Friday dinner party. "Me and your suburban friends?" she asks quizzically.

"Why not? You'll be our celebrity guest. You can namedrop. Seriously, I want you to meet Gregory, and for him to meet you."

"With your friends as buffers? I'll try not to be too shocking."

Entertaining in this ramshackle house with no one to help is daunting, but the Coltons have known us for years; they'll understand. Their younger daughter was a close friend of Dorothea's, and for several years I've avoided them, not wanting to hear what Stephanie is doing— the contrast would be too painful. This invitation is a first attempt to mend fences, plus it's a chance for me to see how well I can cope on my own. I plan the simplest of menus: grilled swordfish, my tried and true baked vegetables, the tender local corn that is just now appearing in roadside vegetable stands, a huge green salad, a couple of baguettes from the new French bakery in Hyannis, and something light and tangy for dessert. A raspberry bombe surrounded by blueberries would be perfect, but ice cream melts in Aunt Phoebe's old refrigerator. I decide on lemon chiffon pie, my mother's recipe. Not simple, but something I can make ahead of time.

Greg is held up in traffic and arrives just minutes before the Coltons. He barely has time to shave and change and has no time to ask about my week or tell me about his.

Dinner turns out to be more painful than I thought. The Coltons haven't seen Dorothea for three or four years, and the shock is visible on Ginny's face when they encounter her on the porch. Lesley is feeding her supper, and she's making a mess as usual. Ginny's reaction is not lost on Lesley, who has cleaned Dorrie up and moved her out of sight into the parlor by the time we get back from our walk down the lane to look at the beach and Sandy Neck. We are settled on the porch for drinks, cheese and crackers—I had completely forgotten the obligatory fancy hors d'oeuvres—when Daphne shows up, looking elegant in a magenta silk shirt and white linen slacks. I wonder how she manages to keep the cat hair off those white pants. Her hair is as it always is, combed severely off her face, and a little eye liner and lip gloss seem to be her only makeup, but the effect is stunning. I have forgotten how intimidating she seemed the first time we met.

"This is my neighbor Daphne Ault," I announce to the group. "She's been teaching Lesley how to sail." I have no intention of bringing up the subject of her writing, but Ginny recognizes her name.

"Are you *the* Daphne Ault, the one who wrote that memoir about World War II? I saw you on the *Today* show, didn't I, a few years ago?"

"Fiction, not memoir," Daphne says.

"Well, yes, but isn't fiction just disguised memoir?" Stu interjects. It interests me that he would enter this conversation. He's an insurance actuary with an obsession for sailboats; I don't ever remember him talking about books. But then it dawns on me: It's the obligatory male display in the presence of an attractive woman.

"One could just as easily say that memoir is disguised fiction," Daphne says, beaming a smile at Stu and then glancing slyly in my direction.

I place Daphne between the men at dinner and put Ginny next to me. It's a mistake. She and her daughter have spent several weekends this past spring looking at colleges, and she can talk of nothing else. Stephanie's grades, Stephanie's soccer team, Stephanie's rank as a National Merit semifinalist. Every sentence feels like a knife turning in my gut. I wonder what possesses her. Maybe her nervousness over seeing Dorrie has made her go bananas. I leave the table several times to check on things in the kitchen. I drink more than my share of the wine, and halfway through dinner Greg has to open a bottle of the cheap generic stuff I drink during the week. In between the swordfish and the pie I excuse myself to put Dorrie to bed. After she's washed and changed and settled for the night, I lock myself in the bathroom and abandon myself to tears.

I must have been gone a long time because Greg sends Lesley to knock on the door. It's gotten dark while I've been in there. I turn on the light to be confronted with my own ravaged face, swollen, red, beyond repairing. Lesley looks at me curiously as I emerge. "You all right, Mom?" she asks softly.

"Yes, Honey. Just a fall-apart." Then I decide to go on. "It's hearing about Stephanie—she and Dorrie were friends, remember? She's getting ready to apply to college."

And then Lesley's there with her arms around me, giving me a hug, the first one in a long, long time. She's taller than I am. I cling to her, feeling stupid, more than a little drunk, my eyes filling again. Her hair smells like salt. "Hang in, Mom," she says, "and turn out a few lights. You look like hell."

GREG IS ALWAYS tired after we've had company or been out to a party. It's not that he's unsociable; most of my friends envy me because of his relaxed good manners. He never shows off or dominates the conversation; he doesn't spend the whole evening huddled with the men talking shop; he remembers to circulate, to chat with the women. But once we're in the car and on the way home, or the door is shut on the last guest, he's silent. My impulse is to talk about the people we've been with, rehash the evening, but he hates to do that. I think people exhaust him. Friendly and outgoing as he seems, it's an effort for him. It uses up his energy.

But tonight he has met my new friend, someone who is going to be important to me, and I want to know his reaction. I corner him in the bathroom where he is brushing his teeth. "Well, what did you think of her?"

"Daphne? She's very sharp. Very clever. But something of a ball-buster. I'm not surprised she's living alone over there."

"What makes you think she's a ball-buster?" I'm not being sarcastic; I'm truly curious. What is it about some women that a man like Gregory finds so threatening? I try to replay in my mind the snippets of conversation I overheard from his end of the table. Sailboats. Books. Living on the Cape in the winter. No politics. Nothing I would define as controversial.

"She's so caught up in her world. Her writing, her novel, her whatever-it-was award. Are you drunk?"

"Chambers. And she didn't bring it up, Ginny did. Writing is what she does; why wouldn't she be interested in talking about it? Did you expect her to talk about the law?"

"I can't explain. She just uses the pronoun *I* a lot."

She does, now that I think about it. Ginny, all my old friends in fact, invariably married, most with half-grown children, what did they talk to Gregory about at parties? Vacation trips, past and anticipated. The impossibility of Russian hotels, the high prices in London, the skiing at some as-yet-unspoiled corner of Utah. Additions to the house, planned and underway, the spiraling expenses, the elusiveness of contractors once the job is half finished, the primitive hardships of living for a month with the kitchen torn apart. Increasingly in recent years, strategies for maintaining health and fitness. Aerobics. The new power yoga versus kick boxing. The marvelous new artificial ice cream that tastes as if it were loaded with cholesterol. And the pronoun is never *I,* always *we.* Is that what a ball-buster is? A woman whose life does not include a man, who survives, thrives even, on her own money, her own work, her own wits?

We left the outside porch light on to light Daphne's way home, I realize as I turn off the bedside lamp. I go back downstairs to turn it off and take one more look at Dorothea. She's breathing quietly, looking beautiful, as she always does when she's asleep. By the time I am back upstairs Gregory is turned on his side away from me. I slip into bed. I'm too wound up to sleep—if wine and company exhaust Greg, they stimulate me. Part of me wants to reach for Gregory; I'm restless and edgy, my period is due, and as always at that time I'm keyed up, easily irritated, easily aroused. Sex is always best then, my impulse evenly divided between needing to lose myself in passionate lovemaking and wanting to pick a fight.

It saddens me that Gregory doesn't like Daphne; it means that our friendship will have to be limited to weekdays and daytimes when Greg isn't around. "She uses the pronoun *I* a lot," he said. Suddenly I have a flashback to a dinner party years ago, when we were newlyweds and Greg was in law school. I had just started teaching and was all excited about it; every day I was learning something new. I was talking about it to Greg and two of his classmates, when right in the middle of a sentence Greg interjected a joke about something that had happened in their contract law class that morning, and the three of them began to laugh. I remember my embarrassment, my flash of anger, but I was too new a bride to complain to Greg later about it. The lesson was clear. What you do isn't important. We don't want to hear about it.

That was the beginning of my education. There are topics appropriate to discuss with men. And there are topics that are only for the ears of other women. Anger flares in me; it feels exactly like the anger at that party years ago; I can feel it pulse through my body. Greg's wide, impassive back is turned away from me in the bed. I put my hand on his shoulder, not knowing what I want, what I am going to do. I have an impulse to hit, to scratch. Instead I pull him over until he turns to face me and kiss him full on the mouth.

I WAKE AT daybreak Saturday morning. My mouth is dry and my head is pounding from all that wine. I down two aspirins and a big glass of water and decide that a walk on the flats might clear my head. Just as I step off the path onto the soft sand at the top of the beach I encounter Daphne, on her way back from her morning constitutional. Just as I hoped.

"Interesting evening," she says to me wryly. "How's your head this morning?"

"Throbbing."

"That woman—Ginger? Somewhat lacking in tact, wouldn't you say? I'm sorry I couldn't figure a way to rescue you."

"Ginny. She's usually not so obtuse. I think seeing Dorrie really threw her, and she just started to babble."

"I'll put her in a story; that'll teach her."

Daphne has shed the glamour of last night; she's back in her faded shorts and long-tailed man's shirt, her face innocent of makeup. I think about what Greg said about her last night. It makes me curious about her impression. "Well, what do you think of my husband?" I ask.

"I was more interested in watching you. You're very different around him. Very wifely."

"What does that mean?"

"Deferential. You watch him a lot. And during cocktails he interrupted you two or three times when you were right in the middle of a story. It didn't seem to annoy you."

"Well, it does. I'm just used to it, that's all." I look at Daphne. It seems her reaction is as negative as Greg's.

"Daniel used to do that to me a lot and it would drive me crazy. I used to interrupt him right back, and that drove him crazy. It's one of the things that pops first into my mind when people ask me why we got divorced."

Daphne squats down on the soft sand, balancing on her haunches. I'm surprised; she's usually in such a hurry to get back to her computer. I sit down beside her, grateful she wants to continue the conversation. Last night has left me with more than a headache. I feel physically sore, my muscles stiff from the effort of holding myself together in front of the Coltons.

"I think most men interrupt when they're talking to women," I say, "especially if there's another man in on the conversation."

"You're right. I read about a study they did on it once, with college students. I think sometimes men don't hear women's conversation; it's a kind of buzz or static to them, background noise. They think it's all recipes and gossip, not about real things."

"Well, they put out a lot of static, too. At parties—sometimes I get so sick of all that competitive one-upmanship. Lawyers are the worst."

"I know all about it. I was married to a lawyer, too."

Again I'm reminded of that long-ago evening when Greg was in law school. What kept me from speaking up about how patronized I felt? It was because I agreed with the men. I wasn't important. My teaching job was temporary anyway, a means to support us while Greg was in school. We knew that once he passed the bar he'd be the breadwinner and I'd be— what did Daphne call me? Wifely. By the time the women's movement got rolling I was changing diapers.

The air this morning is thick and humid, not good for my headache, which shows no signs of going away. Daphne's going to want to get back, but she still hasn't told me how she feels about Greg. I try again. "Was Greg what you expected?"

"He's very attractive."

"That's no answer."

"He's"—Daphne hesitates—"someone who has himself very well in hand."

I laugh at that. "You're right there. And he's never quite sure he has me in hand."

"He does, I'd say, after watching you last night. Do you two ever have fights?"

The question gives me pause. Since Dorothea it's been as if we're walking on eggs. I wish my head didn't ache so much; it's hard to think. I'd like this conversation to be over. "Not for a long time. When we were first married, I used to get upset, cry a lot. But he'd just tell me to calm down and then he'd walk out of the room or turn his back if we were in bed. It's impossible to confront him. He's not going to have an argument no matter what I do, I finally figured out."

Daphne stands up and pauses a moment, looming over me. "Ye Gods, what do you do when you disagree about something? If somebody did that to me I'd hit him over the head with something, something heavy. Daniel had his faults, but at least he'd fight. We used to have these knockdown, drag out verbal battles. They'd leave us exhausted. But then we'd have great sex afterwards, sometimes at least."

"I guess Greg and I have felt so beset since Dorothea happened that we don't argue about little things. There isn't enough energy left."

"I should think there would be an awful lot of garbage accumulated between you. You're a better woman than I. Well, I'm off. Thanks for dinner, in any case."

I smile after her, imagining her settling down in front of her computer to turn last night's disastrous dinner party into a story, feeling a mean little twinge of satisfaction at how ridiculous Ginny Colton would seem. Then my mind slides back to a conversation Daphne and I had that afternoon she introduced Lesley to the cats. The girls were down by the pond, and we were inside by the fireplace drinking lemonade. I was asking her how she dreamed up her characters. "All my friends keep asking me that," Daphne said, "looking for themselves in what I write. But they're just there in fragments, a gesture, maybe, or one isolated physical detail. I had a lover once, in New York, who wanted me to write about how we made love, but what I used about him was the way one ear stuck out from his head more than the other. So endearing. He was obsessed by it—he used to flatten it against his head with his hand as if he could make it stay that way. It bothered him terribly. He was tremendously good-looking otherwise, and irritatingly conscious of that. But it was that ear I loved. I used to like kissing it. It's what made him human."

"Human as in imperfect?"

"Yes, I guess so. Isn't that what we love about the people we love? Their oddities? Their moles, their foibles, their peculiar ears? And I'm fascinated by the one telling detail that gives a glimpse of the inside of a person. Like Phoebe's stockings. Even when she was dressed up she wore them rolled and knotted under the knee. Rolled-down hose."

"'Flapper, yes sir, one of those.' Amazing to think Aunt Phoebe could have been a flapper. You can spin a whole character out of one detail like that? Phoebe may have been a witch, but you're a spider."

"You could say that. I feel like a spider sometimes, off here in my dusty corner spinning webs."

"To catch what? We all· know what webs are for."

Daphne laughed at that, stretching her legs out in front of her on the floor. "Oh Anna," she said, "how I love your metaphorical mind. Phoebe was right. We were meant to be friends."

And that was the moment I knew we would, and that Phoebe had a hand in it. That night as I was lying in bed, Daphne's image came back to me. Phoebe and her rolled-down hose. Suddenly I had a vision of her, not Phoebe Crowell but Phoebe Gardener, at eighteen maybe, her pale wavy hair bobbed to a shining cap, her skirt just skimming her knees, dancing wildly at some Boston speakeasy. Before she scandalized the family by marrying a ne'er-do-well dreamer and wasted her life away holed up on the Cape, watching her inheritance dwindle away and coping with Dennis's bouts of drinking. She should have been disillusioned, regretful, shouldn't she? But try as I might I could never imagine her as anything but happy.

I've been woolgathering. Daphne has disappeared up the lane, my head still aches, and I need to get back to the house. I think about that word Daphne used to describe me—wifely. It makes me uncomfortable. Is she finding fault with me because I won't fight with Greg? Most of our friends marvel at our marriage, the harmony, especially in the face of the past five years. How is it we settle things? What do we disagree about? Mainly, since Dorothea's operation, about time together, time for Greg to be with the girls, his helping me out on weekends when I have full responsibility for Dorothea's care, the exercise routine, getting her in and out of the bathtub, the car. And usually I defer, realizing how tired Greg is, how hard he works, how difficult it has been for him to face what has happened, something he couldn't protect us against, couldn't prevent. And now that Dorothea is full-grown, sexually mature, he doesn't feel right about taking her to the bathroom, seeing her body. So I do it. It's physically exhausting; she's a big girl, tall and big boned, built like Greg's father's family. If she were normally muscled she'd weigh more than I do. I get tired, I work hard, and who is there for me? It's a question I try not to ask myself—it makes me too angry. I'm just beginning to realize how angry.

I don't want to go up to the house just yet, so I stand up and head down toward the water. The tide is almost dead low, but it's a neap tide—the bar is minimal size. I'll have to hurry if I want to get out there before it disappears. The water is over my knees. I force myself to walk fast, feeling the drag of the water against my legs and the strain in my thighs. It's tiring, but the resistance feels good. It's a relief to have something to struggle against.

Squall Line

The tearing down of the land . . . is a product not only of the sudden orgies of tempests, but also of the slow nibbling of daily wind, rain and waves.

WHEN DOES BEING newlywed turn into simply being married? And when does disillusion replace those youthful hopes we all start out with? Does it happen all at once, or gradually, the way the brilliance of a sunset over the bay will darken and fade so slowly that we can never name the moment when the color is gone? How did it happen for Phoebe, I wonder. Her habitual frame of mind was optimistic; she woke every morning, it seemed, embracing a hope that the day would bring delight. And because even in old age she saw the world with the eyes of a child, more often than not it did.

I have days when my sadness overtakes me and I accomplish nothing, when I sit and stare at the same page of the book I am reading or lose track of time in the middle of folding laundry, when only the unavoidable physical chores of caring for Dorothea prevent me from sliding down into inertia and despair. Today is one of those bad days, the weather damp and oppressive, the promised rain stalled somewhere west of here, the flag hanging limp and discouraged in the morning stillness. I wake early with a headache, unable to breathe, unable to think. I dose myself with aspirin and coffee and retreat to Phoebe's room for an hour with her journals, tiptoeing so as not to wake the girls.

Did Phoebe have bad days like this? There had to be times when she could no longer avert her eyes, when her life overwhelmed her, the way mine does me.

> August 7: Dennis and I up late last night listening to the radio; news is we have dropped a huge bomb on Japan, so new and secret no one was sure it would work; it has laid a large city flat—Hiroshima— never heard of it, thousands of people dead, vaporized, the light from the explosion visible hundreds of miles away. Hard to comprehend, though Dennis says Japan will surrender now, many American lives

will be saved, the war will be over in a matter of days. Four years! Can
it be true? People talking about it up and down the lane and all over
the village when I walked up to the Post Office, with great pride and
cheer . . . but a part of me cries these were not soldiers, just ordinary
people like us—what have we done? How far away all that seems
to me here, at least until I remember my cousin Edward and now
Dennis's brother, lost in the Pacific.

August 20: Heat is oppressive as it has been for days now; I have
pulled a chair up the hill under the pines to get a breeze. Wanted to
write atop my rock but the sun beating down; walked down to the
beach for a dip but retreated quickly, the sand burning my feet and
air shimmering in the heat. Coolest here in the shade. Almost a week
since the war ended. Where has the time gone? Magical to hear the
news, Peg and her mother had the radio on and she came running
up the lane to tell me, invited us to an impromptu celebration at their
house for everyone on the lane, bring what you can, she said. We
drove over to Salten point for mackerel and clams in her Ford coupe
and then through the village, gas rationing be damned, everyone out
on the street or driving up and down honking horns, I riding back
in the rumble seat with little Shirley, everyone waving and hallooing
like crazy people. I picked all the corn and tomatoes I could find in
the garden and carried over both of Dennis's bottles of gin, everyone
brought pot luck and as usual the food was plenteous and delicious—
pot lucks always seem to work out like the miracle of the loaves and
the fishes. After dinner we built a fire on the beach and sat around
and told jokes and stories, the children called upon to recite poems
they had learned in school, and then we sang "Old Mill Stream" and
"Don't Fence Me In" and "Coming In on a Wing and a Prayer" and
then all the patriotic songs, ending with "God Bless America" that
brought most of us to tears. Dennis never showed up, though I had
left him a note, and not home when I got back after midnight. He'd
heard the news at West Marsh and gone out with the boys—they'd
been working on irrigation pipes all day. Woke me at two a.m. furious
the gin was gone.

August 22: Came to mind today that it's been a year since my visit
with Dr. Miller. All those weeks—months! of temperature taking,
the humiliating tests, nothing wrong, he says, "You must relax; tense
women have trouble conceiving"—why do people think "Relax" is

useful advice—useful as "Ignore that body on the floor"! And despite
my pleas Dennis refuses to see him. Angry when I mention it. It
seems unpatriotic to feel anything but euphoria these days. And so I
grieve, silently, and go out to pull weeds in the garden.

August 25: Dennis home early and bubbling with cheer, over his long
sulk; drove me back to West Marsh to show me the new sluice gate
he's designed. Pump is working again and piping back in order. My
Rube Goldberg, happiest when tinkering—why can't he always be
like this? Also says Demetrius's father will sell us his '34 Ford truck
when he buys a new one, which he will as soon as they come back
into production. Then Dennis can make our own bog buggy. These
things make me realize the war is really over—rationing over soon,
and then the factories will stop building bombers and start making
cars!

Reading the journal, I realize it was Uncle Dennis's generation
who fought in World War II. He was 4-F, Greg told me that day I met
him, a heart murmur or something. I wonder if being left out of it had
something to do with the drinking. And there's Aunt Phoebe grieving
over her childlessness. Then, a miracle, she does conceive, finally, when
she's in her late thirties, and has Camilla, and then just three years after
the miracle, the loss. Camilla would have been born when? In the early
fifties sometime. But gone before those years when Gregory came to
stay in Cummaquid. And these are the years, the very years, when the
notebooks break off. A silence of nearly seven years. It seems strange.
Wouldn't she have written, at least about the wonder of finding herself
pregnant, the months of waiting for her child? I look at the dates on the
notebook covers. November 1950–March 1951. Then January–October
1958. In between, silence. I open the journal for 1958 and find Gregory
on the first page:

January 14: Dennis's sister Dorothea died yesterday afternoon about
four o'clock; Louis called last night to tell us. Not unexpected; it's
been nearly three years since we heard she was ill. I have such a
jumble of feelings: sadness, of course, and pity for young Gregory, and
anger at both men who still will not name the demon she wrestled
with so long and gallantly—cancer of the breast. As if the very words
were tainted or shameful. Strange we cannot speak of what is central,
what has taken over our lives.

January 16: Back from Dorothea's funeral, a lovely service in the
chaste community church in Dover, a cold burial and a quiet sad
gathering back at the house. The neighbors had brought food of all
sorts; the women will bring meals for weeks, I'm sure. Louis unable,
I think, to comprehend he has a son who needs him. And young
Gregory, already so tall and manly in his new dark blue suit bought,
I'm sure, for the occasion, seems numb, frozen, like the girl in the
Danish tale with a sliver of ice in her heart. I am undone by the day,
go straight up to bed when we get home though it is only seven. It is
not just my sister-in-law I grieve for, but the sadness we cannot speak
of. Dennis is morose and heads for the parlor—this was, I remember,
his baby sister.

April 14: Two warm days have brought all the daffodils out. They nod
and say hello all up and down the lane. Spring will come regardless of
our unhappiness. I walked down to the harbor at dead low tide—note
the near bar is lower than last summer and has migrated decidedly to
the east. How clean the flats look this early in the season, too early for
the shore birds' migration, and the wise crustaceans are hidden away
until warmer weather.

April 17: Dennis spent two nights at West Marsh—frost has
threatened and he has flooded the bog, unhappy to be doing it so
late in the season and not totally sure water in place in time, but
hopeful. Important we get a good crop this year after investing in
that Darlington picker. The money continues to drain out. In dark
moments I consider the whole venture an expensive hobby, but would
never say that aloud to him. We could survive on my money if need
be, I keep reminding myself. Good news is the pump and gates are
working well and D cheerful about that after all the hours he put in
on them this winter.

April 27: D and I have invited young Gregory to spend the summer
here with us—he'll be home from St. Paul's in mid-June, and Louis
still burying himself in work, far as we can tell. Greg can work with D
on the bog, save us from having to hire someone part time. It would
ease my mind knowing D not alone all day and probably be good for
Greg to be away from that sad house.
    Louis distresses me so, cannot rage or cry so has become frozen
by grief. My D continues his evening disappearances to the parlor but
has begun talking of his sister, their childhood adventures. I realize

they were in some ways so alike, clever and whimsical in their take on the world, both feeling like misfits in that dour family Dorothea liked to call the "Tombstones." She must have brought light and air into Louis's life, at least until she got sick. Greg favors his father in looks and temperament, too controlled for someone so young.

I turn the journal pages looking for more mentions of Greg and find some starting in late June, mostly describing the work on the bog, a few that are more personal:

July 18: D and Greg late for supper after a hot day of ditch-clearing. D uncharacteristically silent in the presence of this silent boy, and Greg not so much rude or shy as folded inward—his way of coping? We did go down for a quick swim since it was still hot and the tide was high—D would not be persuaded—is it my imagination or is he uncomfortable around Greg? A reminder of Dorothea? Or some transplanted resentment of Louis, who took her away, who couldn't keep her alive? None of this makes sense but then when did the human heart ever make sense? (I edge away from thinking about my human heart and where it has led me.)

August 26: Greg upstairs packing his things. I brought up some laundry and wondered at how methodical he is. I think he's glad to be leaving, though not excited about going home or even back to school. I'm sad for my failure this summer to draw him out of his shell, remind myself he lost his mother only seven months ago and we were, after all, practically strangers—and still are, sadly. Some things can't be healed by others. Time will help, and he's young and on the brink of many changes.

And now Dorothea—my Dorothea, named for her grandmother—is awake and calling for my attention. I close the journals and head wearily for the stairs. My headache has not gone away.

The heat does not break for the weekend, and Gregory has actually arrived early, attempting—vainly, it turns out—to get ahead of the traffic. I send him down for a swim with Lesley and put together a cold supper of chicken salad served in cantaloupe halves, potato chips and sliced tomatoes seasoned with basil from Phoebe's garden. After supper I delight Lesley by suggesting we drive over to the Four Seas in Centerville for cones— with this old refrigerator she has missed the ice cream we always have at home. The excursion does not turn out well. The Four Seas is jammed with cars as it always is in midsummer, so we can't get the van in the parking lot and have to park across the street. Greg leaves the engine running so that he and Dorrie will have air conditioning, but it is fifteen minutes before we make it back with our cones. The dish of vanilla I have chosen for Dorrie has turned to soup which drips down the front of her shirt. We drive back to Cummaquid in silence and are met with a wall of humidity when we open the doors of the van.

"Are you getting tired of your pioneer phase yet?" Gregory says sarcastically when I finally emerge from getting Dorrie bedded down for the night.

"You can't judge things by today," I say, more irritated than I want to let on. "It's really hot, and that doesn't happen all that often. You've just driven seventy-five miles in traffic. Anyway, a front is supposed to come through tomorrow."

"I tell you, Anna, this is no way to live. Getting down here is an ordeal, and being home alone is no picnic, either."

We are sitting on the porch in the vain hope that a south breeze will come up. I am sweaty from making supper and doing the dishes and settling Dorothea for the night. Greg in the meanwhile has had a swim and has been reading the paper. He looks crisp and neat in his clean golf shirt and shorts.

"You miss your wifey?" Now I'm being sarcastic. I notice that I've borrowed Daphne's word. I try softening my tone. "I would think you'd like the peace and quiet at night. It must be easier to get your work done."

"Well, yes, but it takes a long time to get to it" (without me to fix dinner and clean up, I'm thinking), "and I worry about you down here. And I miss you."

There. He said it. I look at him with interest. It's been two weeks. "There's a fan in the bedroom," I say. "Do you think it's too darn hot?"

SATURDAY MORNING BRINGS no relief from the heat, and Greg has brought a briefcase full of work with him. He's grateful when I suggest that he retreat to the Sturgis Library in Barnstable, where there is air conditioning and a lovely antique table to work at in the quiet upstairs stacks. By the time he gets home for a late lunch, a hot gusty breeze has started turning up the undersides of the leaves, and clouds are piling on the western horizon. I feel edgy—I know there's a storm coming with what Lesley calls my "dog sense." I have to force myself to sit on the porch with Greg while he eats the sandwich I've fixed from last night's salad.

"Do you want to grill some steaks tonight, or shall I get some fish up at the marina?" I ask. Greg is wearing a seersucker shirt I haven't seen before. Again I marvel at how cool he looks. He never seems to sweat.

"What I'd really like is an air-conditioned restaurant," Greg says, "food optional."

"I don't feel right about leaving Lesley in charge at night yet, but hold that thought; Jeannine will be here in a few weeks." She has agreed to spend her vacation with us after her summer course is over, and already I'm savoring the idea of some free time.

"So you're determined to stay through the summer?"

"Of course. Jeannine's looking forward to some time at the beach, and I was hoping you'd take a few days off."

"Not possible, Anna. You know that. Besides, we'd all be packed in like sardines here."

"Not really. Jeannine can sleep in Phoebe's—the little corner room. It's just sharing the bathroom that will be different. And Jeannine's not a bathroom hog—she's got that big family at home, remember." Regardless of what I say it's obvious that Greg is not going to spend the week here. Lesley will be disappointed, and I don't want to be the one to tell her.

Gregory shifts his weight uncomfortably on the wicker sofa. "Anna, we've got to come to some conclusion about this house."

Here it is. I realize I've been waiting for two weeks for him to bring the subject up. "You know how I feel," I say cautiously.

"And you know how I feel. It's ridiculous, with all the stress you're under, to camp down here, away from your friends, from any help. . . ."

I sigh, wishing I had the words to say what I feel. "But that's just it, I'm not under so much stress here. Life is simpler. I'm away from . . ." How can I explain the freedom I feel here to Gregory? Away from the past, away from Needham and our lost life there, from pity, from Gregory's own icy grief I cannot melt, cannot heal. "And I do have friends here. Daphne would help me, any time I needed it." And Demetrius, I want to add but do not. And Phoebe. I think of Phoebe's journal, her pleasure in her own physical strength, that first summer when she helped Dennis clear the bog. "It's been good to be on my own—it makes me feel stronger to know I can cope—stronger than I thought I was."

"Look," Gregory is saying. He has put down his plate and is leaning forward toward me, in that habitual posture he assumes when he wants my full attention. "I was happy to indulge this whim of yours to spend some time down here. But enough is enough. I don't want to be saddled with this house, and I don't want you and the girls down here all summer. We ought to list the place before the season is over. Otherwise we'll be stuck with it for another year."

"I want to be stuck with it. Why do you hate it so much here? You haven't even given it a chance. You're so overworked this summer you've hardly had time to unpack, much less relax."

"Anna—" A sudden gust of wind distracts us as it sweeps the morning newspaper and all the mail onto the floor. A crash and the sound of broken glass sends me through the house to the parlor, where a vase full of black-eyed Susans I had placed on the window sill has fallen over. The pines and locusts on the hill above the house are tossing their branches. At last, the cold front. After all these days of heat, cool dry Canadian air. Now everyone will feel better, even Greg. There's a distant rumble of thunder, and I remember that Lesley is out on the bay with Daphne in her Beetle Cat.

I have an irresistible urge to go outside and meet the weather. "I'm going up on the hill to see if I can see the *Little Gull*," I call back to Gregory, who I can hear is stacking dishes in the kitchen.

"Who?"

"Daphne's sailboat. Lesley's out on the harbor with her. Check the windows if it starts to rain, will you?" I'm not sure Greg has heard me, but the wind gusts are stronger, and I want to get a view of the bay before the front comes through. I hurry up the hill to Phoebe's drift boulder, shed my sandals at its base, and clamber up.

The bay looks strangely divided. Sandy Neck is bathed in brilliant sunshine, the waters in front and to the east of me deep blue and tossed with whitecaps. To the northwest and rapidly sweeping down the harbor is a great dark shield of cloud, trailing veils of rain lit here and there by flashes of lightning. Underneath, a wide band of dark water moving faster than I would have thought possible marks the squall line.

With relief I catch sight of the *Little Gull* tossing on its mooring. I should have known Daphne would not take chances with the weather. She and Lesley are still aboard, struggling to furl the sail. The tide is near high; they'll have to swim to shore. I try not to think about the lightning moving inexorably in our direction.

I climb back down and start for the beach, but before I can get there the rain overtakes me. In seconds the few large drops splashing on the road dust turn into a downpour. I turn and dash for the house, with Lesley hard on my heels, bursting into the kitchen just behind me, dripping wet from her swim in from the boat. "I had my shower on the way home," she says happily, with more animation than I've seen in many a day. "Did you see? Daphne let me sail into the mooring. It only took me two tries. She says that's a lot better than she did the first time."

"You're dripping all over the floor, Lesley," Greg interjects, scowling.

"Yeah, Dad, it's pouring."

"Watch your tone, miss."

Why does he need to play the heavy now, I wonder. It's so rare for Lesley to feel this good about herself. "You checked the windows, didn't you?" I ask Gregory, hoping to take some of the heat off Lesley.

"What windows?"

"For heaven's sake, Gregory, all the windows. The windows where it's raining in. Do I have to write down instructions?" He has, at least, brought Dorrie in from the porch. She's anxious, I can tell. She shares my dog sense about when storms are coming. "I'll check the upstairs if you'll do down here. It's the parlor where it's apt to rain in." I run up the stairs more noisily than I need to—what is this obliviousness about their surroundings that all men seem to share? All the windows upstairs are wide open, and the north- and west-facing sills are puddled with water. I'll have to get towels out and soak it up, and then there will be more laundry to do. The same man who barked at Lesley for dripping on the kitchen floor. It's infuriating.

A tremendous flash and crack of thunder propels me back from the window in Phoebe's room, and before I can recover I hear Dorrie's wail of terror. I rush back downstairs, but Lesley is there ahead of me, squatting down in front of Dorrie and talking to her, telling her not to be afraid. It brings sudden tears to my eyes, watching the two of them, thinking back to the times when they were little, when it would be Dorrie comforting her little sister. Greg comes back into the kitchen from the direction of the parlor, carrying a wad of sopping paper towels. "You could try helping a little," he says sarcastically to Lesley.

"But Dorrie was scared," Lesley says, reddening. She looks briefly at me, flees up the stairs and slams the door to her room.

Gregory is heading back toward the parlor with a fresh roll of paper towels. I reach out and grab his arm roughly as he goes by, forcing him to turn and face me. I want to slug him. "Do you have any idea the effect you have on her?" I say. I'm so angry I am afraid I'm going to start to cry. "She was helping her sister. Isn't that more important than some wet windowsills? And if you'd closed the windows like I asked, they wouldn't be wet."

"Calm down, Anna. This is ridiculous."

"It's not ridiculous when you hurt our daughter. Do you ever think about how she feels? Today is the first time I've seen her that happy, that sure of herself, and you just—I think you ought to go up and apologize to her."

"This is ridiculous, Anna. Of course I think about what she feels. But she's gotten so sullen and rude—"

"She wasn't being rude; she was thinking of Dorrie."

"I don't know what's gotten into you down here. Why don't you go upstairs and clean up a little? Look at you; you're going native. Where are your shoes? And this discussion isn't going anywhere." Gregory speaks levelly, turning away from me and heading back to the parlor with the paper towels. I am left speechless with anger. He's done what he always does, deflecting the focus from himself to me. Me and my shortcomings. I stare after Gregory, wondering whether it's worth it to pursue him further, at least to get him to speak to Lesley. But no. And then it dawns on me that Daphne was right. This scenario—an incident, my angry accusations, Gregory's calm, even voice, that patronizing tone he might use to avert a child's tantrum, then the dismissal and retreat, and my—always!—my capitulation. Which of us is more to blame?

The downpour stops as suddenly as it started. I look for my sandals under the kitchen table, and then remember that I left them up by the drift boulder in all this soaking rain. I go out through the porch door, around the house, and up the hill, remembering, all at once, the way Phoebe looked that first day she brought me up here. A disheveled middle-aged woman with bare feet. Like me.

High Summer

Just above the tide line . . . dusty miller, beach peas, and
sandburs quickly take root, along with seaside goldenrod,
sand wormwood, bayberries, wild roses, and beach plums.

JULY 23: High summer. Another still, pale watercolor morning, only the slightest breeze ruffling the water into slightly darker pale blue stripes. How these days come one after another, like too many bouquets from a fond suitor! What shall we do with them all? We are running out of vases. Literally, too; my volunteer garden gone rampant. To stay indoors on such a day feels like spurning a gift. And so the dust collects and the mail piles up unattended to. I have been out and down to the second creek already, D sound asleep after one of his bouts last night and none the wiser. How peaceful it is! Only one thing moving in all that wide expanse of harbor, Barney Chilmark's lobster boat heading out to the bar opposite the point. I could hear the men's voices even though they were half a mile away.

July 24: Early morning low tide, dry air, fresh breeze, a bright blue day. So many clusters of baby mussels have gathered on the floor of the bay where the first creek runs out of the marshes. We are due for a shift in the shellfish population, metallic-tasting mussels replacing the blue-eyed scallops, so scrumptious, getting so rare. Even their shells, my favorites, are getting hard to find. Mussel shells remind me of baby feet, the same proportion between narrow heel and wide curved ball of the foot. Pry one apart and set the halves side by side, left and right. Baby feet, though a bit smaller. Preemie-size. Everything reminding me of babies these days, and my dread over seeing Dr. Miller. Will we ever have a birth certificate with an inked black footprint to remind me of mussel shells? Five years now. I begin to despair.

July 25: Out to tackle the back garden despite the dry weather. Things going wild. Tiger lilies faded and shabby-looking but Queen Anne's lace bobbing everywhere, black-eyed Susans, globe thistles topped with prickly blue balls, loosestrife shooting up to five feet back by the fence. Might root out all the Japanese lanterns; they look too artificial for my taste. Picked a Queen Anne's lace flower, really many flowers clustered together to form a broad plate. Puzzled as always by the one deep crimson one in the middle of all the white, maverick in the midst of the crowd, the way I feel these days when I go to Boston.

July 26: At last, at last, rain finally, at the end of a day so muggy and damp nothing would dry. Finally around nine o'clock it all came down as if we'd had a bucket dumped on us. All over in twenty minutes, but this morning the grass looks grateful. After it stopped, D and I stood out on the hill above the house and watched the lightning—quite a show, great jagged streaks across the sky and distant bright flashes, only the faintest faraway thunder. I love it when he comes out with me, which seldom happens anymore. It saddens me to think of earlier days and our long evenings of talk. A strange night, damper than ever and hard to sleep.

July 28: D back from West Marsh, berries have set, and looks like a good crop. Bees evidently did their work in June, despite the iffy weather. Five years since we embarked on this project and now, at last, a chance for a saleable crop. He's hired a young man from West Barnstable, in his teens but a good worker, cranberries in the family for a couple of generations, Portuguese and can find us pickers for the fall. Glad I didn't know how long before our investment would pay off; try not to think about the things that can go wrong—frost, weeds, bugs. D ready to leave the shop now but promises to wait until berries are ripe and it's picking season. A few more weeks and we're on our own.

August 4: Changeable day; a good soaking rain woke me around five, then by eight there were breaks in the sky, low fast-moving clouds— fog, with shrouds of it obscuring the neck at times—the air damp even with all the breeze. So much heat stored in the ground that it's seeping up and adding to the humidity. Finally around seven tonight that front that's been sitting just out of reach made it through and the air changed. A beautiful sunset with cloud banks violet-gray in places and rosy in others, D and I went down to the beach to see. Watched the sun slip under; decided to time it; it took about three minutes from touchdown to gone. Afterwards the western sky was yellow-green, except for a bright peachy semicircle of light where the sun had been. Afterglow. Now I know what that means.

I've been reading Phoebe's journal again, a few pages a day, up to 1944; she'd be—what? Twenty-seven, just about the age I was when Dorothea was born. Somehow I no longer think of "Aunt" but just Phoebe. High summer for me as well as her—in ten days it will be the first of August. Our time in Cummaquid is nearly half gone, the days sifting like sand through my fingers.

I'm startled by the thump of a ladder against the window ledge in Phoebe's room. Demetrius is here painting the house trim, a never-ending battle against the dampness and salt. I decide to tackle Aunt Phoebe's garden, an impossible tangle of wild flowers, quack grass, and vines. It will take days. I bring Dorrie out and park her in the shade of the locust tree at the corner of the house, set a picnic thermos of lemon-flavored iced tea for us to share.

It's companionable, having Demetrius nearby. He's working on the second floor windows with a hand scraper. I wonder if that's the same ladder Aunt Phoebe was on the day she fell, and if that thought crosses Demetrius's mind. Surely there were days when they were out here together like this, their work punctuated with bits of conversation.

"I've got iced tea down here when you want some," I say.

"Sounds like a grand idea," Demetrius says, making his way down to the ground. His hair is covered with little flakes of gray paint.

"Hold still a minute," I say, reaching up and ruffling the top of his head. "You're covered in paint." His hair is springy and soft under my hand, not at all wiry.

Again, that direct look, that smile. "That's a losing battle. I've a lot more scraping ahead."

I've embarrassed myself. What must he think, my touching him that way? But he pours himself a glass of tea and sits down in one of Aunt Phoebe's old Adirondack chairs. I settle myself in the other.

"Been thinking about that step out the parlor door," he says. "Be easy to fix up a little ramp there. I've got some spare plywood at home. Wouldn't cost anything."

"Except your time and labor. You have to let me pay you for that."

"How about you pay me with a couple of lunches?" He's doing it again, looking at me, smiling. I lower my eyes, thinking about his hair, and how I've been wanting to touch it since the Fourth of July.

"You're so tuned in to what Dorrie needs," I say. Daphne tells me your wife was in a wheelchair. I guess you've had some practice."

"Oh, yes, though she could do everything except run races in that chair. Hated being waited on, so I rigged up the kitchen so she could manage on her own. Lowered the counters and built a set of drawers down by the floor to hold her pots and pans."

"What was her name?"

"Marte."

"A Cape Codder?"

"New Bedford."

"You too? Demetrius sounds more Greek than Portuguese."

"It is Greek. My mother was Greek, but my father's family came from the Azores. I was born in Carver, but we moved to the Cape when I was about five. My father went to work for Makepiece, on the bogs."

"How did your parents meet?"

Demetrius gives me a mysterious smile. "My mother went to college at Bridgewater. It was unheard of in her family, that, for a girl to go to college. But she wanted to teach. She had an English teacher in high school who helped her get a scholarship. She taught at the high school in Carver and met Papa—his little brother was in her class. My grandfather wouldn't speak to him when Mama brought him home—bad enough he wasn't Greek and was Catholic, he was part Cape Verdean—that means African to most people. But by then they were in trouble, as we said in those days. So they eloped and had me. Mama had to quit teaching, but she started again when I went to school."

"And did you go to college?"

"No. Korea got in the way, and then I was married, and Marte was pregnant and we needed money. And then she miscarried a couple times and the arthritis got bad—one thing and another. Anyway, Mama educated me, from the time I was little. She read me Bullfinch as bedtime stories. When I was older we would read poetry together, and Shakespeare. She would make me memorize. She loved those old English poets."

"Do you have brothers and sisters?"

"No, I was the only one. That was also a disgrace to her family. They never spoke to her."

"She must have been lonely."

"She had me. I was her best friend, she used to say. And there were Papa's people, uncles and aunts and cousins, great feasts on the holidays. She converted and they made her part of the family."

"And who in the family had the green eyes?"

"Ah, too light for a Cape Verdean, you're thinking? We're a mixture, Portuguese, African, all the sailors from everywhere who made the islands a port of call. My father's mother had green eyes, though her skin was darker than mine. She would say there was a Viking in the family tree somewhere."

A sudden gust of wind makes us both look up. Storm clouds have gathered, and we can hear the first rumbles of distant thunder. A cold front is due. Demetrius pulls the ladder down and carries it into the garage. I wheel Dorothea around the house and bump her up the step into the parlor. A ramp would be a great convenience, no question about that. When I come back outside to gather up the tea and glasses, Demetrius is closing up his tool box and heading for his truck. "Tomorrow I'll talk less and work more," he says, smiling. "And tomorrow you must tell me your story."

Tomorrow. I am looking forward to it more than I have in a long time. Another gust of wind and the rain starts, a few big drops at first, then a downpour that soaks me before I can run for the house. After all the heat it feels wonderfully cooling. I tilt my head up and stand there letting the rain pour down on my face. Demetrius, backing the truck around, looks at me quizzically and then beams me a smile. "You look like Phoebe," he says.

When the rain shows no signs of letting up after lunch I fetch a few of the journal notebooks from upstairs and settle Dorothea and myself on the porch. Five years ago, just before Dorrie's operation. But the first name that catches my eye is Daphne's.

> December 29: Daphne over here drinking tea in the middle of
> her writing time, spitting mad, sparks flying all over my kitchen.
> Something about money, a trust her father set up for her daughter
> with Daniel trustee. Seems Daniel sends checks to the daughter and
> neglects to tell her what account they are from. Daphne kept getting
> up and pacing around the kitchen. "He couldn't stand that we lived
> on my money, those years he was in law school. And now, when he's
> making six figures and I'm trying to juggle accounts to pay my taxes,
> he can't stand for Susan to get anything from me. For me to have the
> pleasure." Says she could understand if he did it out of heat or anger,
> but it's something colder—bitterness, pride. Hurling herself around
> the kitchen, her anger making her awkward and she collides with
> the table, sloshing tea in both our saucers. "How awful to discover
> how little of my value was my own. Mortifying." Says she was denied
> credit by all the department stores when she got divorced, places her

family had shopped for generations. Even with things the way they are I see I've been protected by being married. Belonging to a family, even if the wrong one!

December 30: Lay awake thinking about Daphne and how glad I am not to be middle-aged anymore. How like adolescence those years from forty-five to fifty-five, so full of confusion and rage and blame. I was the same, exactly. Going back over all the old hurts and guilts and failures, the way marriage has failed us, and then we get to the real trouble, the childhood pain, the parental blindness. Wanting whatever it was we didn't get. Lashing out at everything, everybody, wanting to chuck it all. Longing for somebody, anybody who'll understand. Finding somebody if we're lucky, or unlucky. And eventually if we're luckier still, realizing there's only one ear, one heart. Our own, our own. Such a long journey. And when we finally get through it and feel at peace and happy with ourselves, it's our bodies we have to worry about. Dennis, those years of getting him through the day. And now that he's gone, myself. Waking in the morning and wondering if I'll be able to unlock these stiff old knees enough to totter across the room and look out the window at the birds.

It feels strange to read about Daphne through Phoebe's eyes, almost like eavesdropping on a conversation. A different Daphne, surely, from the one I'm getting to know, although I did see a flash of that anger the day we went walking on the trail in Yarmouth Port. And Phoebe herself, confessing her own frustrations with Dennis, something she almost never does. Our lives, so different from the outside, but in our hearts, perhaps, more alike than we might surmise. If I feel I have been eavesdropping on Daphne, did she feel the same when she read about me? I turn the notebook pages ahead to February, the month our lives changed forever.

February 23: Gregory called to cancel our meeting about the taxes. They have had a tragedy in the family, young Dorothea in a coma in the hospital for ten days, outcome still uncertain. Seems she reacted badly to anesthesia during a routine appendectomy. A sweet, self-possessed, musically gifted child is how I remember her, so resembling Gregory, same black hair and graceful way of moving. They may lose her. Gregory's voice was flat, tired, factual. I try to imagine Anna, and can't, except to be thrust back into my own nightmare. All back again. I bundled up and went down to the marshes and walked and walked, despite the windy raw weather.

February 25: Still no news from Needham. I have been living or reliving those terrible days with C—it has all come back, from the headache and fever (which I ignored and can't forgive myself for) to the spasms and our terror, the confusion at the hospital, how quickly she slipped away. The new vaccine we didn't trust, that would have protected her! My other guilt, of which I cannot speak. It overwhelms me now, when I should be praying (to Whom? to What?) for Dorothea, and Anna, and Gregory, who may have another unbearable death to endure, and little Lesley, who must be frightened and confused.

March 14: Gregory called again; I tell him I have finished the taxes and sent them off. He is the kind who soldiers on through any kind of pain, is not quite sure I am capable of simple addition, subtraction and division.

March 16: A miracle! Dorothea has awakened, is breathing on her own. Whether she will be the same Dorothea remains to be seen; she recognizes her mother but cannot speak and has major right side paralysis. Too early for a prognosis, the doctors say, but my heart goes out to Anna, who must endure whatever happens. But she has a strong core, I recognized that in her the first day we met.

There are more entries in the pages that follow, but I can't bring myself to read them; it's too painful to relive those months of false hope. And Phoebe, hearing about us, being thrust back into her own tragedy, the loss of her own daughter. I had forgotten about Camilla, born late, dead at three from polio. How I wish I had been able to find a way to speak to Phoebe about that! Or to speak to her at all, about all the happier things she knew and could teach me, about the garden, the ever-changing weather, the birds on the marsh. And now, before I had a chance, she's gone. No, not gone. Still here in these musty rooms, the mysterious noises in the night, a garden gone rampant, four stacks of mottled black notebooks filled with her small, spidery hand.

This evening the low storm clouds turn to fire, coloring the whole sky gold and peach and vermillion. I climb up on Phoebe's rock to see the sunset, the most dramatic by far of the summer. It's like watching a great glowing ball drop into the western end of the harbor. Behind it, a strip of pale blue marks the leading edge of the front dropping through from the north. As the brilliance fades and the clouds turn lavender and deep blue and then black, the strip of clear sky takes on an unearthly color, yellow-green.

That night my house dream comes again, a recurring dream I always recognize even though it's different in its details every time. We (or is it I?) move into a big old house, charming but badly in need of repair. A guest comes, someone I know well and want to please, this time a dark-haired woman I could not name, though in my dream she is an old friend. I show her through the house, the large rooms, the deep-silled windows (a stone house, though I've never lived in one), then open a door and find more rooms, dusty from disuse but sunny, full of light, rooms I didn't know I had, plenty of space for all the guests I want. I feel relieved and happy. All my friends—and suddenly there are more guests—all of them can stay.

Something wakes me, a soft sound, footsteps in the hall barely brushing the floor. In my half-dreaming state I think it is Dorothea—then I wake to the truth, as I did so many terrible nights that first year. "Lesley?" I call out. "Is that you?" There is no sound. I get up and make my way barefoot down the hall and open the door to her room. She is breathing softly, regularly, her hair a tangle on her pillow, her face turned to the window and the faint pre-dawn light.

In the morning Lesley is eating her cereal when I come into the kitchen after finishing Dorrie's exercises. Lesley has been better humored lately, up earlier and out and down to the beach with her drawing pad, or off sailing with Daphne. Despite my feelings of jealousy I have to be grateful. Just having a conversation with her before ten o'clock is something of a miracle. "Did you get up in the night, sometime in the early morning?" I ask.

"Nope, not unless I was sleepwalking. Why?"

"I thought I heard someone in the hall. Maybe it was part of a dream I was having."

"Maybe it was Aunt Phoebe. I think I hear her sometimes, when I'm downstairs with Dorrie and you're not here."

I stare at Lesley, usually so matter-of-fact. She hates what she calls "New Age crap," makes fun of her friends who believe in angels. But before I can think of what to say the phone rings.

It's Gregory, calling from the office, something he seldom does unless there's an emergency. "Anna. I'm glad I caught you home. Do you think you can have things tidied up by eleven o'clock Wednesday morning? Good news—I think we might have a buyer for the house."

On the Flats

*We cannot walk far in bare feet ... without feeling the
ripple marks which ridge the surface of the sand.*

L ESLEY KNOWS THAT the coolest place on a day like this, when the tide
is out and there isn't a breath of a breeze, is out on the flats. It's been
hot for three days now, too hot to do anything but read or sit around
in a wet bathing suit. She's learned to check the tides first thing, using
the chart Demetrius brought from the marina and Mom tacked onto the
pantry door next to her list of phone numbers. In summer people's days
revolve around the tide. If it's out they can't swim, at least not without
wading out about half a mile to the old channel. And sometimes Daphne's
sailboat is all the way out of water. Even when it's afloat there are sand
bars to skim over, going and coming. If they want to sail to Sandy Neck
they have to be sure to allow time to get back.

Daphne has been teaching Lesley about the shape of the harbor,
where the bars are and how the currents flow. It's weird how in some
places the wind is always stronger—in the channel opposite the marina,
for instance—and in other places they are sure to get becalmed on a quiet
day. Blind spots, where the shape of the shore blocks what little breeze
there is. Down by the first creek is the worst.

It was Daphne who suggested she should walk out onto the flats at
low tide and study the sand bars. They've had big tides all week, just a few
days after a full moon. Lesley checks the chart while she gets the Cheerios
down for breakfast. Low tide at 10:44 a.m. In an hour. Time enough to eat
a bowl of cereal and get out to the bar. She's already in her bathing suit.
She was up early this morning, early for her, anyway. It's too hot to stay
in bed. Mom is in the parlor, the coolest room in the house, with Dorrie,
doing her exercises. Happy to see Lesley up before the middle of the
day, glad to let her get down to the beach and into the water where she'd
love to go herself. "Take a dip for me, will you?" she calls as Lesley is
going out the door. It must be hard, Lesley thinks, every morning to know
she has to go through Dorrie's routine, the forty-five minutes of exercises, moving her arms and legs so they won't seize up, and no Jeannine

around to help her. Sometimes Dorrie's wet and smelly, too, like an oversized baby.

The tide is way out, farther than Lesley has ever seen it. The *Little Gull's* round bottom is resting on sand, and most of the quarter mile between the beach and the sand bar is out of water. The beach is already shimmering in the heat, but it's cooler out beyond the strip of beach grass where the sand is wet. A breeze is blowing out here, a south wind she hadn't felt on the beach at all. Daphne has been teaching her about the compass points and the winds. Each one means something different. The west wind is the normal summer breeze, a nice dry steady sailing wind. Northwest is cooler and stronger, a cold front coming through. An east wind usually means rain, and the south wind is damper, sometimes really hot, since they're on the north shore of the Cape and it blows over land. On the beach it means bugs, nasty greenhead flies that breed in the grass and sting when they bite.

No bugs out here, though, just acres and acres of damp sand, hummocks of seaweed, all sorts of creatures that spend most of their time under feet and feet of water. How adjustable they would have to be to go in and out of water all the time, their whole atmosphere totally changing twice a day! Lesley squats down to watch a hermit crab hurry out of her way, carrying its borrowed house on its back, a brown checkered periwinkle shell. She picks it up and watches it pull back inside as it rolls over in her hand. Its big seizing claw won't quite fit inside. Pretty soon it will have to move to a bigger shell. After a few moments its curiosity gets the better of it—two beady little eyes on long stems appear, legs emerge, and it traverses Lesley's outstretched hand. Moving crabwise, Lesley thinks, smiling to herself. But not crabby. Hermit crabs are enchanting little creatures, seldom shy, always wanting to be on the go even when they are in obvious danger, like being picked up by a giant. Not like lady crabs that pinch anything that comes close. They can really hurt.

Lesley starts as she feels something slithery jerk away from under her foot. She gets a quick glimpse before it buries itself, wriggling in and flipping little clouds of sand over itself until it disappears entirely. A baby flounder, flat and slippery, speckled all over and an exact match to the sand. Perfect camouflage. It can move like lightning. Not used to the tidal changes, this part of the harbor only exposed during moon tides, and not as good as a hermit crab at surviving out of water. It would drown in the air. There was a poem about that she read in school, about a fish breathing "terrible oxygen." Strange to think that what one creature can't live without is poison to another.

The last hundred yards before the bar are under water, a lumpy, uneven stretch with patches of seaweed she'd heard were the best places for quahogging. Demetrius told her that. He said he'd take her out some time and show her how to do it, using Aunt Phoebe's old long-handled clam rake and wire bucket. But he hasn't mentioned it lately. Quahogging sounds like fun but then her Mom would make chowder. She's seen what a quahog looks like inside, all gray and slimy and with that disgusting stomach full of sand and clam shit. The thought of eating one, even all cut up and cooked into soup, makes her stomach queasy.

Finally, at last, the sand bar. Pure sand, patterned all over with wavy ridges all going in the same direction, solid-feeling under her bare feet. No seaweed or shells of any kind, except for a few crab carcasses the gulls have dropped. The designs on the sand amaze her. They're like solidified versions of the little waves on top of the water on all but the calmest days. The lighthouse looms directly in front of her, close enough to swim to. She's three quarters of the way across the harbor. But she knows better than to try. She could probably get across the old channel right in front of her and walk over the big bar they call Horseshoe Shoal, but then comes the real channel, not very wide, but with a swift current that could take her and sweep her all the way around the point and halfway to Provincetown before she would be missed. But someday she will swim it, with Daphne following along in the *Little Gull* to make sure she is safe. Daphne promised.

She still feels uneasy when she thinks about breaking into Daphne's house. But it's been two weeks and Daphne has kept her promise not to tell Mom. Yesterday she took Lesley into the kitchen and showed her that the screen was back on the window, all repaired. It cost eight dollars, so Lesley owes her two days of feeding the cats. Next time Daphne will give her an extra key.

It doesn't take long to cross the bar to the channel. This was the old channel, Daphne said, not dredged anymore and pretty much filled in on the harbor mouth side by the big shoal. The water here is so clear, so many colors—depending on its depth, gold and green and greenish blue. Lesley feels drenched in color and light, the turquoise bands of water ruffled by the wind, casting rippling shadows on the tawny sand below. No one around anywhere near, just a few motorboats moving out in the big channel, marked by that dark navy blue that means deep water. The light stabs through her, a physical sensation that feels almost like pain except it's thrilling, wonderful. She strips off her T-shirt and takes a running plunge into the water, coming up gasping. It's much colder than what she's been wading through. It sweeps her sideways to the left. That means the tide has turned. It's starting to come in.

Lesley launches herself into her racing crawl, pitting herself against the current, hauling herself through the water until she runs out of breath. She hasn't made a lot of headway. She turns and swims in the other direction, with the tide this time, amazed at how swiftly she moves now through the water. She's not cold anymore, the water feels delicious against her skin, embracing her, holding her up. Salt water so much easier to swim in than fresh, more buoyant. At the lake at camp her feet would sink down until she was floating in a vertical position. A sinker, the swimming instructor called her. She said she'd float better when she got older and had a little fat on her bones.

The big bar on the other side of the old channel doesn't seem all that far away. She could swim to it, easy. She strikes out at a leisurely crawl, the pace she learned for her long distance swim. The current feels gentle but insistent, a little stronger as she gets out near the middle. She flips over and starts a backstroke, immediately feeling less winded. She has a clear view of her shirt, a bright spot of yellow sitting on the bar. She has floated a long way down from where she started. The bar looks much smaller and suddenly seems very far away. She's almost even with the edge of the bar and can see the entire space between it and the beach is being rapidly covered over with water. How far will she have to swim before she can touch bottom?

Lesley is afraid. She's getting tired, and there's nobody around. Swimming out this far by herself—it was a stupid thing to do. She remembers the water safety lessons she learned at camp. Take it easy. Don't panic. Don't fight the current—work your way in at an angle. She could swim a mile if she had to (she had, at camp, and had a felt badge with a fish on it to prove it). She turns on her back and kicks herself along, stopping every now and then to check her position. The yellow shirt is still there, a long way off to her left. Every time she looks the bar is smaller and farther away. She kicks harder and begins to backstroke. No need to panic. It's her best stroke and she can keep going a long time. She remembers the relay race at the final meet, the big lead she gave the team. They won. She swims what she imagines is a pool length and then flips over and feels for the bottom.

Finally, gratefully, she feels sand under her feet and is standing in water up to her shoulders. By the time she manages to wade back to the bar, her shirt is sitting on a small island. She puts it on quickly, shivering despite the heat. She hears the siren from up town start its plaintive wail. The noon whistle. Mom will be looking for her. Just hope to God she didn't come down the beach while Lesley was out in the channel. If she's lucky no one will have seen her. No way she could tell anyone. No way. Not even Daphne.

When she gets back to the house Dorrie and Mom are dozing on the porch, Dorrie in her chair in the corner and Mom stretched out on the wicker sofa with a notebook on her chest. A breeze has come up, but even so it is hot. Mom opens her eyes partway when she hears the screen door open. "Egg salad and peaches in the fridge" is all she says before dropping off again.

After lunch Lesley decides she wants to draw some of the plants in the herb garden. There's a little bit of shade and a nice breeze. She looks around for her sketch pad and then remembers she left it over at Daphne's on Tuesday when she went inside to get a drink. She puts on sandals and a shirt over her suit and slips out the parlor door and up the lane to Daphne's. There's a strange car in the driveway, an old-fashioned little green sports car without a top. Company? Lesley considers, then goes up to the screen door and peers in. Nobody in sight, no voices. She knocks tentatively and waits. No answer. Maybe they're down on the beach, though Daphne's always writing this time of day except on her day off, and that's tomorrow; she's made a date with Lesley to go sailing.

She knocks again, a little louder this time. Still no answer. Not even any cats—they must all be outside. She peers in again, can see her sketchbook right there on Daphne's work table where she left it. Tentatively she tries the handle of the screen door. Unlocked. It's just a few feet across the room to the table—she could be in and out in a flash.

Lesley has just picked up her sketchbook and turned to go when she hears footsteps from the direction of Daphne's bedroom. A strange man comes down the hall and turns, headed for the kitchen. He's tall and skinny and gray-haired and wearing nothing but white jockey shorts. He stops in his tracks when he sees her.

"What the fuck? Who the hell are you?"

"I'm sorry—I'm just getting my drawing pad. I thought you were down on the beach." Lesley feels her face go scarlet—it's dawned on her why no one answered the door. Two old people—too disgusting to think about.

Daphne materializes from the corridor, wearing a long shirt and looking not mad exactly but strange. "I'm really sorry," Lesley begins again. "I thought you were down the beach and I just wanted . . ."

"It's okay." Daphne says, looking not at Lesley but at her guest. "This is my neighbor Lesley Dylan from across the street. Lesley, this is Paul."

Lesley doesn't mention the man to her Mom, even though the little green car is still in the driveway the following morning, and still there when Lesley comes up from the beach for lunch. No, her mother says, Daphne hasn't called about going sailing. At two o'clock when the tide is plenty high enough for the boat to get over the bar, Lesley heads down to the beach again. The *Little Gull* is not on its mooring. It takes a few minutes for her to spot the sail. It's all the way across the harbor by Sandy Neck, moving past the row of cottages, headed for the point.

The Spotlight

. . . the mill of the surf is relentless and constant.

D ENIAL IS A useful survival strategy. I'm an expert at it, and I use it now. "I can't talk about the house now—I'm busy with Dorrie," I say to Gregory in a voice that feels strangled. "I'll call you at home tonight." I have no emotions yet about what he has said. A buyer for the house? The last time we talked about selling it nothing was decided. Or so I thought. I'm relieved that Lesley has disappeared up the stairs while I'm on the phone. If I don't say the words, they won't be real. Not yet.

The day is muggy and hot with thundershowers expected, so Demetrius will probably not be here to scrape paint and listen to my story. Dorrie's morning routine wears me out. I abandon the breakfast dishes in the kitchen sink and retreat to the porch, one ear cocked for the sound of Demetrius's truck. Too restless to start on any household projects, I fetch one of Phoebe's journals from upstairs, but even that doesn't engage my mind. By eleven thirty I'm making sandwiches for lunch and eating with Dorrie, even though Lesley is not back from the beach. Afterwards I give in to my weariness and stretch out on the wicker sofa.

How many more days do I have left to lie here looking out on the back garden, tumbling over with bloom right now, with late daylilies and airy white cosmos and Phoebe's volunteer black-eyed Susans that have cropped up everywhere? People are coming to look at the house. I should be cleaning, hiding the accumulated mail and magazines and carrying Lesley's beach shirt and sandals upstairs, tackling the heaps of clothes on her bedroom floor, wiping down the bathroom sink and sweeping the sand up from the kitchen floor. I can't just throw the clothes in the closet, either—they'll want to look in the closets. Damn them, and damn Gregory. I lie there motionless, trying to outwit the anger roiling around inside me, and fall asleep in spite of myself.

When Lesley finally comes in and announces she isn't going sailing with Daphne after all, I take advantage of the chance to go the market, leaving the girls at the house. As I drive down Kettle Lane past Daphne's, I notice a dark green MG in the yard, an older model, beautifully restored. Lesley is in the kitchen when I come in carrying the grocery bags, slumped at the table in a way that makes me realize her good mood of the past two weeks has vanished. "I wonder who's at Daphne's," I say casually.

"That's Paul," Lesley says. "Paul the small."

"Who's Paul?"

"Some friend of Daphne's. He's a schmuck."

"And is he small?"

"Not really. Paul the tall. Paul the tall schmuck."

"I take it you've met him? And you don't like him?" I'm full of curiosity, surprised that my daughter would know something about my friend that I don't know.

"He doesn't like me. He told me to get lost."

"He said that to you? What did Daphne say about that?"

"She didn't hear. She was back in the bedroom or somewhere. He just said what was I doing there. And then Daphne came out and introduced us. He's got a neat car, though."

An hour later Daphne is at my porch door, as if my curiosity had conjured her up. "Can you come to dinner tonight?" she says without preamble.

The invitation surprises me; it's so unexpected. "You mean all of us?" I say.

"Well, actually, I mean just you. Can Lesley stay with Dorothea?"

"I'm sure she will. I'll talk to her about it. When would you like me?"

"About seven-thirty. Give you time to feed the girls. Paul will be there. I want you to meet him."

"Ah. The green MG. Are you going to tell me anything about him before I get there?"

"What's to say? He's perfectly wonderful. But I'd rather you found out for yourself."

"At least tell me how you met him. What does he do?"

"He's guest directing at the Cape Light Players in Harwich. Carolyn Richards introduced us—my editor at *CapeNews*, remember? I went with her one night; she knew some of the cast and they invited us to go to Clancy's with the company."

"And you got to talking."

"Yes, we did. When we got there, there was a great blue heron standing right outside the window. They have a floodlight, you know, to light up the marsh, and this huge bird was just standing there in the light.

We both went over to look at it, and he said, 'I can imagine you like that, all by yourself in the spotlight.'"

"It's the legs. You must have been wearing shorts."

"Thanks, but no, I was in my once-a-year dress, as a matter of fact. Well, you'll meet him tonight. See you at seven-thirty." And she is off across the yard leaving me feeling—how? Amused, surprised, and yes, envious.

The rain never materializes, but by evening the air has freshened, the humidity carried off on a gentle western breeze. Daphne greets me at the door, a bit nervous and flustered, looking for all the world like a bride giving her first dinner party. All she lacks is the frilly apron. I follow her out to the deck, where Paul rises to greet me, smiling at me and taking my hand tenderly as if it were something fragile. "Ah, Anna," he says. "How well the name suits you."

"Hello," I say, feeling awkward. What does one say at such a moment? I've heard so much about you? So you're my friend's lover? Are you worthy of her? Hello seems as appropriate as anything. I'm struck by how much alike they look, the two of them, standing there in the early evening light with the pond lavender and silver behind them. Both tall and spare and long boned, both with that shock of graying hair, though Daphne's is salt and pepper all over and Paul's is, I would guess, skillfully colored, nearly black on top with attractively graying temples, swept back from his face like hers, though more carefully arranged. Two compelling, restless, elegant, androgynous figures. They could be brother and sister.

"*Anna* means grace; did you know that?" Paul says, still smiling at me. His eyes are piercing, knowing, intensely blue, nothing like Daphne's. But then Daphne seldom looks directly at me, I realize. She's usually gazing at some point just beyond me, out on the horizon. This is an attractive man, I think to myself. No wonder Daphne is smitten. His attention makes me nervous, as if he were coming on to me, as the kids would say. But probably he acts this way with everybody. He is, after all, in the theater.

Daphne refuses my offer to help in the kitchen; she wants me to stay and talk to Paul. We sit down and watch the lavender sky turn to rose behind the darkening trees. I am nervous, though I couldn't say why, and ask the appropriate questions about where Paul is from and the play he is directing. He has a new play in rehearsal, he says, by a woman whose first work was a hit at the New Play Festival in Louisville last year. Controversial stuff, some rough language, not your run-of-the mill summer stock material.

"And you, Anna, tell me about your life."

The question I dread among people like Daphne and Paul. "There's nothing to tell. I have a disabled daughter; she takes most of my time and attention."

"Ah yes, Daphne told me. But you, Anna, are a people person, I would guess."

"I don't have much time for people these days."

"Don't disparage yourself. Love drives your life—do you know how rare that is? Your face says welcome, don't be afraid. You're like the pond down there, a beautiful calm place. Does your husband know how lucky he is?" He's looking at me intently. What does he want from me? What has Daphne told him? I look away, nonplused. He seems to sense my discomfort and shifts his attention to Daphne, who is approaching from the kitchen with the bottle of wine. She refills my glass and sits down, gazing at Paul. She adores him, that's plain. How happy she looks, I think enviously. How young.

"And my Daphne here is freedom. Athena. Isn't she something? So strong, so sure, so big inside."

"And you?" I say, wanting to cut the tension. The electricity between them is so strong it is beginning to embarrass me.

"Power. Fame. I'll do anything for it. Obviously that's why I love directing. It's making a world, my world. That's what the theater is, you know, as Shakespeare tells us, a little world. It contains everything."

There's something a little too pat about what he's saying, I think. It sounds like a speech he's given many times before. To post-performance audiences, probably.

"When you work in the theater it gives you everything," he goes on. "Where else can you practice your art and if you're lucky enjoy a certain fame, and at the same time have the most intimate, the most personal one-on-one relationship with all those people in the audience? What is theater but baring the soul, showing yourself naked to those strangers out there in the dark?"

But that's not intimacy, I think—it's a one-way transaction. I shift in my chair. The no-see-ums that invariably appear at sunset are beginning to attack my ears.

"But that's just it; the light's on you and they are in the dark," Daphne says, putting into words what I am feeling. "They aren't baring their souls to you."

"How wrong you are, my darling" Paul answers, reaching out and putting his hand on her arm. "To be up there on that stage, to feel what comes back to you from those people—you know when you've touched someone, maybe even changed a life. Sometimes it's so strong it's like a wave breaking."

"Does the wave ever knock you down?" I ask, not sure of what I mean, but wanting to be part of the exchange.

"Of course. When you lose control of the emotion, when you fall out of the part—"

"There's that word, control," Daphne says impatiently. Obviously they have had this discussion before. "How can you be feeling an emotion and control it at the same time? Is it really you they're seeing? Your soul, your pain? Or is it the character you're playing? Someone you're hiding behind?" She picks up the bottle and refills our glasses.

Paul is obviously enjoying their exchange. "You can't hide. You have to find the places where you and the character overlap. Then he comes alive. You can't fool an audience. If you're not honest, if you don't feel what you're playing, they know it."

"And the tide goes out."

How happy I am, sitting here sipping good cold Chardonnay, watching the day's color fade from the pond, and listening to these two, their minds circling round each other, declaiming, arguing, defining, competing in a sort of intellectual equivalent to the playful wrestling of infatuated teenagers. The air around us is highly charged, sexual. How wonderful to be able to talk this way with someone you love. But I could never do it; I don't have Daphne's lightning quick mind, her wit, her love of a challenge. And am I the only one being bitten by gnats?

DAPHNE APPEARS AT my door again about ten the following morning, as I hoped she might. Lesley fades out of the kitchen without saying hello, which seems odd to me. Daphne follows her out into the yard, which seems even odder. I fix us both a cup of tea and settle us on the porch when she comes back inside.

"Sorry," she says. "I wanted to apologize to Lesley. Did she tell you I stood her up yesterday? We were supposed to go sailing."

So that explains Lesley's mood. I'm relieved; for once it wasn't something I did.

"Well, what do you think?" Daphne asks.

"About?"

"About Paul, Silly."

"I think you're both head over heels."

"Isn't it crazy? I never expected this to happen again, not here. It's played havoc with my writing schedule."

"Is he still here?"

"No, he's at rehearsal. The play opens next week and runs two weeks, and then he's back to New York."

"Then what?"

"Too early to tell. I won't let myself think about it. He's the first man I've known who doesn't mind that I'm competitive. He doesn't love me in spite of it; he loves me for it."

"I could see that last night. That discussion about acting—it felt a little like a tennis match."

Daphne throws back her head and laughs, exposing her throat, which looks surprisingly unlined considering she must be ten years older than I am. Then she leans forward and gives me a thoughtful look. "You know, my father taught me to compete, that winning was a way to get attention and to please him. He used to play cards with me. I was a shark at casino by the time I was four years old. He never eased up so I could win—he always played to the hilt—so finally when I did win it felt wonderful, a real victory. And he loved it when that happened. Of course what he did was make me unfit for 99 percent of the men in the world, who might want all sorts of things from a woman, but not competition."

"Well, you don't seem to threaten Paul."

Daphne laughs. "Not at all. But maybe it's because he knows how to win in the end. All he has to do is brush the back of my neck with his lips and it's all over."

"I love seeing you so happy," I say. She does look happy, relaxed and young. Again I feel a stab of envy.

"I love it too. I can't believe it. Who would believe this could happen to me here, now? It's a miracle, a gift."

"Well don't ask too many questions, just enjoy it."

"I am, I am. I'm basking in it. Am I acting like a fool?" She's looking at me coyly.

"Yes. But that's okay. The world needs fools. I'm jealous."

"Don't be. Just be happy for me."

"I am, I am. And grateful too, for reminding me that life is full of surprises."

What I don't tell Daphne is that I lay awake for a long time last night trying to sort out my roiling emotions. Part of it was being so physically charged by the two of them, the intense verbal exchanges of two minds that moved so swiftly, that were so utterly engaged. And feeling the sexual tension that underlay everything they said. But there were other things I was feeling, less obvious, harder to acknowledge. Something about Daphne's behavior with Paul bothered me. She spent the evening bustling around, refilling glasses, making innumerable trips back and forth to and from the kitchen, too anxious to please. And all the while honed in on Paul, looking for approval. That was it. It was as if her solid core, that sure center that makes her seem so maddeningly remote at times, had dissolved away, and not only her happiness but her very sense of self suddenly was in the hands of this handsome, fascinating, and utterly narcissistic stranger.

And there was more—my reaction to Paul, the pleasure and alarm I felt every time he turned those intense blue eyes in my direction. This is a dangerous man, I thought, shifting over, trying to get comfortable, turning the pillow to the cool side. What if he came after me, appeared in my kitchen, brushed his lips across the back of my neck? How vulnerable I am, I thought ruefully, and no wonder. I have become a machine, a function, something to keep Dorothea going, with a little energy left over for Gregory and Lesley. How long has it been since Gregory and I have made love? What is it now—once every three or four weeks, maybe, and nearly always at my instigation. And did he ever look at me with that kind of naked hunger?

I don't want Paul to take over Daphne's life. I know that, but do I know why? Jealousy? That's part of it. I don't want him turning her head. There was something unseemly about his flirting with me while she was in the kitchen getting the wine, even though he probably treats every new person he meets the same way, testing to see if he's making an effect. Looking for himself, for the way I saw him. Not looking at me at all. Is he like that with Daphne, too?

And what is she getting out of it, besides the obvious sexual wave that's bowled her over? I fear for her. And so I lay alone in Phoebe and Dennis's sagging double bed, picturing the two of them standing on Daphne's deck silhouetted against the pond, tall, dramatic, and elegant. They could be brother and sister, I thought again. They could be twins. But there's a difference. His elegance is superficial, carefully orchestrated, hers effortless and unconscious and bred in the bone. Don't get involved with him, I want to say. He'll use you; he'll hurt you. But of course I won't say it; it's too late and she wouldn't listen to me anyway. And how much of my fear is for myself, that he'll take up so much of her life that there will be no room for me?

Of course, all the anxiety was probably a way of avoiding what was really bothering me. Gregory's words from the morning call came back to me like a blow. I forgot to call home, I realized, raising my head to look at the clock. Too late, almost quarter of two. What has Gregory done? Has he listed the house, and how could he do that without telling me? What sort of person would talk about buying a place he's never seen? A contractor, someone who builds on spec, who'll divide the land, maybe even raze this house to the ground? The thought propelled me out of bed and down the hall to Phoebe's room. I pulled back the old-fashioned chenille spread and lay down on her narrow cot. It was a long time before I fell asleep.

The Stillstand

Eleven thousand years ago . . . instead of Cape Cod Bay there was a huge, stagnating mass of ice.

I FORGET TO CALL Gregory Monday night, a Freudian slip, perhaps. I don't call him on Tuesday, either, mainly because I haven't figured out what to say. I dial home finally at six-thirty Wednesday morning. He doesn't like it, I know—it disrupts his morning routine. I can imagine him at our bedroom closet, selecting one of his immaculately pressed shirts hanging there in a precisely spaced row. "Anna?" he says. "Are you all right down there?"

"We're all fine. Well, the girls are fine. I'm not. Who is this buyer for the house? We haven't decided to sell—we've hardly talked about it. Don't you think we should have discussed it?"

"Take it easy, Anna. I was going to discuss it with you—it's just that these people popped up out of the blue. They're clients of Ben Talbot's. He knew we had this house on our hands, and he mentioned it to them. They're going to the Cape today to meet with a real estate agent, and they liked the sound of the place."

I make a mental note of the phrase *on our hands*. Like a burden, a white elephant, something awkward to get rid of. "You told Ben we were putting the house on the market?"

"Well, yes. We talked about it this spring, didn't we? I thought the only question was when."

"That wasn't the only question. Who are these people?"

"Their name is Woodbine. A young couple, three little children and from what I gather lots of money. They're looking for a place with some acreage on the north side, beach access, quiet street, all that."

"How can they know they're interested without seeing the house?"

"I think they liked the sound of seven acres backing up to a marsh. They'll probably remodel the house."

"Sure, or tear it down and build one of those starter castles." I'm beginning to imagine the Woodbines, the quintessential Yuppie couple with a BMW and an SUV, three kids and a nanny, bringing in a

Boston architect to design some monstrosity with seven bathrooms and Palladian windows and decks everywhere. The thought makes me angry. "Doesn't that bother you?" I ask Gregory. "Don't you think it would upset Aunt Phoebe?"

"Aunt Phoebe's dead, Anna. Nothing is going to upset her."

"Who's the realtor?"

"Northside. That place right there in the middle of the village. They'll be there today, at eleven. Does the house look presentable?"

"I don't see what difference that makes, if they're going to tear it down."

"Simmer down, Anna; you're not making sense. Look, I've got a killer day ahead of me and I'm running behind. I'll call you tonight to see how it went. Good luck."

Good luck. I'll show him good luck. As soon as Gregory hangs up I call Northside Realty and leave a message on their machine: "This is Anna Dylan on Kettle Lane, in the Turnstone house, the one you were supposed to show today at eleven. There's been some misunderstanding, I'm afraid. The property's not for sale."

At eight o'clock Demetrius is knocking on my porch door, smiling in at me. "Come out and see, Anna." I'm about to take Dorrie back to her room to bathe and dress her but I follow him out to his truck, where he is unloading something heavy, big and square. "Here we are. It's the ramp for Pegasus. I'll just take it around and see how it fits."

By the time Dorrie and I arrive in the parlor after her exercise routine, the ramp is in place, wide and solid. No more bumping up and down steps. I wheel Dorrie in and out twice, just to test it. "It's wonderful, so easy," I call up to Demetrius, already up on his ladder, painting. "Now we'll spend more time outside. Thank you."

"No trouble," he says. Dorrie waves her good arm and makes her humming noise; she recognizes his voice but can't locate him; she doesn't have the muscles to raise her head and look up in the air. She likes Demetrius. It's funny what strong opinions she has about people and how clear her preferences are from her limited repertoire of motions and sounds.

I can't spend this day working in the garden and drinking tea with Demetrius; I have a list of errands to run in the village and over in Hyannis. And I have to take the girls: Lesley needs a new bathing suit; the Speedo we bought in April is already too small. Shopping with Lesley is never a pleasure these days. Nothing pleases her, and with Dorrie along it's worse. If I find the averted eyes discomforting, Lesley feels mortified and angry. The happier, more open Lesley I had a brief glimpse of for the past two weeks has disappeared again, and I don't know why. Perhaps even she doesn't know why. Daphne's fascination with Paul hasn't helped. In any case I will not subject us to the crowds in the mall. Instead we head for the small sporting goods store in the West End across from the high school, where they carry the nylon racing suits I know Lesley likes. I leave her to make her own selections and wheel Dorrie over to the front corner of the store, where I idly look through the sale rack of warmup suits. There was a time, not so many years ago, when I played on our club tennis team, when I might be in the market for a new warmup suit or a new pair of shoes. How quickly life changes. For the hundredth time I chastise myself for being out of shape. But that's not strictly true. I have plenty of upper body strength from lifting Dorothea and guiding her through her daily routine.

By the time Lesley emerges with a suit that is the "least gross," as she puts it, it is well past lunchtime, muggy and still, and when we get back to Kettle Lane, Demetrius is gone. Lesley grabs the bag with her new bathing suit and disappears into the house, leaving me to contend with Dorrie. By the time the car is unloaded and I'm wheeling her up the new ramp, Lesley is back outside, the porch door slamming behind her, on her way to the beach.

GREGORY CALLS BACK at seven, just as I'm clearing away the supper dishes. He's seething; I can hear it in his voice. Some men yell when they're angry, but Greg gets more and more controlled. He speaks slowly and carefully, as if to someone who's a little deaf or isn't fluent in English. It interests me that he's freer to show anger over the phone than when we're talking in person. Come to think of it, so am I.

"Ben called me into his office tonight, Anna. The Woodbines telephoned and said you'd canceled the house showing. Please tell me there's been some mixup. What's going on?"

"No mixup. I called Northside and told them the house was not for sale."

"What are you doing, Anna? It was all arranged. By the way, after they left the realtor they did drive down the street. They're not sure which house it was but they loved the street and the beach."

"Well, they'll have to wait for something else to come on the market. This house is not for sale." Even as I say the words I'm surprised at myself. If Gregory were here in the room, would I have the courage to defy him?

"For pity's sake Anna, use your brains. We can't keep that place as a sentimental gesture."

"I'm not being sentimental. I'm living here, and I want to keep coming here. I'm not ready to let it go. I might never be ready. And it's not like we can't afford it."

"I thought you would have come to your senses by now, living down there without any friends around, with those antediluvian appliances and no help."

"I have help. Lesley's here, and Demetrius, and Daphne's right down the street if I need her. Do you know what Demetrius did today? He put in a ramp by the parlor door. Now we can just roll Pegasus out into the yard."

"Pegasus?"

"Dorrie's wheelchair. That's the flying horse, in Greek mythology." I can tell I'm making no sense to Gregory.

"I know who Pegasus is, Anna. I think you're getting a little peculiar down there. We'll talk about this some more the next time I come down. By the way, it probably won't be this weekend. I have to go back to Washington tomorrow."

"Peculiar how? Like Phoebe? Don't count on changing my mind about the house. Both our names are on the deed, remember."

"Damn it, Anna, this isn't like you. I don't like it." Gregory's calm, level voice is actually beginning to rise. "I will not have you defying me."

How dare he? I hang up without saying another word, and the minute I do, I feel not angry or guilty but amused. Never in our married life have I hung up on Gregory. What does he mean, this isn't like me? This is me. It's just a voice I haven't used in a long, long while. I immediately pick up the phone and dial Daphne's number so that if he calls back he'll get a busy signal. Besides, I want to tell her that Gregory and I have actually had a fight, or an argument, or at least a heated discussion. She'll probably congratulate me for that.

But Daphne's machine recites its recorded message. Either she's out, or writing, or Paul is over there. I hang up, check Phoebe's phone list, and dial Demetrius's number quickly before I have a chance to change my mind. I'm not sure what I will say to him, and it makes me nervous. He picks up the phone on the second ring. I remember Daphne saying he lived in a tiny house, an old hunting shack on the marsh.

"Demetrius? It's Anna. I just wanted to thank you again for the ramp. We've been using it all afternoon—it works great. Will you be back to paint tomorrow? I owe you a couple of lunches, remember."

"Weather sounds iffy. There's talk of more rain. I'll be over mowing weeds at West Marsh in the morning—then we'll see."

"How about I bring lunch to you there? We can have another picnic."

"You want to go to that trouble?"

"Less trouble than building a ramp. I'll see you tomorrow around noon?"

"Noon's fine."

When I hang up the phone, I'm feeling happy, excited even. The conversation with Gregory has faded from my mind. This time I'll make something more memorable than ham and cheese sandwiches and Oreo cookies. A blueberry pie—I was going to make one tomorrow anyway, using the recipe I found in Phoebe's file that calls for half raw and half cooked berries. I'll pick up a fresh baguette in the morning and use it to make subs with the turkey breast and Swiss cheese I bought in the deli on Monday, shredded onion and lettuce, fresh tomato slices, some Durkee's dressing. A little pickled three bean salad on the side; there's plenty left over from tonight's supper. I start in on the pie pastry and hunt up a basket from Phoebe's collection and two gingham napkins from the sideboard in the dining room. Maybe in the morning I'll pick up a bottle of chilled wine. Why not? This is a thank-you present. By nine o'clock the pie is done and I've used it to lure Lesley down to the kitchen and get her to agree to babysit Dorrie for an hour in the middle of the day. As I climb the stairs to bed, I realize that all evening I've forgotten to stay angry at Greg.

Demetrius is right about the rain. I am awakened by the rumble of thunder, and by seven it is pouring. I think ruefully about the blueberry pie. But then the storm passes, the sky brightens, and by ten the rain has stopped and a few ragged holes in the clouds promise a better afternoon. I make lunch for Dorrie and Lesley and arrive at West Marsh a few minutes before twelve. Demetrius is out at the far end of the bog with Uncle Dennis's weed cutter. I set the basket and cooler inside the door of the bog house and walk out to greet him.

"Where are your girls?" he asks, looking beyond me back toward the van parked next to his pickup.

"Lesley wanted to stay home," I lied, "so I left Dorrie with her. She gets tired of being hauled around. So it's just me."

He gives me a look I can't read. "I'd like to finish this section," he says. "Just a few minutes more."

"No hurry. I'll just watch unless you've got a job for me."

"Ever been on a bog?" Demetrius asks. "Come on over, if you want. There's a plank across the ditch, up there by the corner."

I make my way gingerly across the temporary bridge and step onto the bog. The ground is not what I expected, not boggy at all, but firm and solid under the thick mat of green vines, so dense they feel springy under my feet. Springy—the word makes me think of Demetrius's hair. Up close I can see the berries, still small and white this early in the season. Out of curiosity I reach down and pick two or three sprigs from the vines. The leaves are tiny ovals thickly arranged along the stems. The bottom halves of the stems are bare, wiry and brown. A stiff, energetic sort of plant that pleases me somehow, that seems like a miniature of the sturdy cascading shrubs that line our porch in Needham. Cotoneaster. Cranberries are evergreens, I remember, except in winter they are not green, but a lovely deep red, the color of wine.

Demetruis kills the engine of his weed cutter and leaves it in place while he walks over towards me. It's that ingenious machine Uncle Dennis designed, balanced there on a bicycle wheel and two tubular legs, hardly anything touching the ground to crush the vines. I think about stories I've heard of Uncle Dennis's inventions. A tinkerer, Gregory used to call him, not meaning it as a compliment. *My Rube Goldberg* is what Phoebe wrote in her journal. "Think you'll have a good crop this year?" I ask Demetrius.

"Looks pretty promising. This section's sparser than the main bog. This I call Cove bog—built it just about fifteen years ago. I've had some trouble keeping it level, but we resanded this winter and reset the vines, and it'll come along in a year or two."

"What's that yellow stuff growing over there by the big ditch?"

"Dodder weed. A headache. That I'll have to root out by hand. We don't use herbicides anymore the way we used to. Have to think about the aquifer."

"Aquifer?"

"Yup. It's our water supply for the whole Cape. It's like a series of underground freshwater lakes. They get toxic, we're all in trouble. Here, let me finish this and we'll go have that lunch." Demetrius heads back to the cutter, starts the engine, and continues his steady progress, walking first away and then toward me as the circles grow smaller and smaller until he reaches the center. He moves easily, gracefully, with no sense of hurry. How differently people work, I think. I tend to tackle long, tedious jobs slapdash, with bursts of energy punctuated by numerous breaks, rushing until I make myself tired and then stopping partway through out of fatigue or boredom. I admire people who work as Demetrius does, with steadiness and grace.

Unpacking the picnic lunch I feel foolish about the cloth napkins, the wine. Demetrius chooses iced tea but I open the bottle anyway and pour myself a paper cup, to steady myself I say silently. It's been an emotional couple of days.

"All right, now. It's your turn to talk about yourself," Demetrius says when we are settled with our plates of salad and sandwiches. We are in the doorway of the bog house sitting on some old crates.

"There's not a lot to tell; I've had a very ordinary life. Privileged but uneventful. I grew up in Cincinnati and went to Wellesley. Greg and I met my junior year, his first year of law school. We got married right after my graduation, and then we just did what people do, worked and then had babies and moved to the suburbs."

"And what did you do, those years you were in the city? And what city was it?"

"Boston. Well, Cambridge, actually. I taught English for a while, to adults, just part time, English as a second language."

"You liked teaching? My Mama was an English teacher."

"I remember. Yes, I did like it. But then we moved, we got a house that needed a lot of work, and then I had Dorothea and Lesley. I was a stay-at-home mom, and I liked it that way. I just missed the women's movement, I guess. And Greg is very old-fashioned about what women ought to do." I'm saying things I've never put into words until now, I realize. I pour myself another cup of wine.

"And not do?"

"And not do. Not that I wasn't busy, what with the girls' activities and community work and all that. And then Dorrie got hurt and since then she's been my primary job. Of course we've had help. We sued for malpractice and got a big settlement so we could afford to hire somebody. This is the first time I haven't had anyone to help." I've been talking about myself too much. Greg would be annoyed. But Demetrius doesn't seem to be—he's the one asking the questions. It's so pleasant here, sitting in the doorway looking out at the bright expanse of the bog, with a cooling breeze and good food and this attractive man beside me, looking at me with attentive green eyes. I feel totally relaxed. Maybe it's the wine.

"And how are you with being here all on your own?" Demetrius is asking.

"Better than I thought. Maybe it's that there are so few other demands on my time down here. But Jeannine—she's our live-in helper—is coming for two weeks in August and I have to admit I'm looking forward to being spelled a little. I get tired, I mean physically tired." I dip back into the picnic basket and set one of the pieces of blueberry pie in front of Demetrius.

"You made pie? This is a special occasion. And my favorite kind, with the raw berries—Phoebe used to make this."

"It's her recipe."

"For this I'll have to build another ramp." He's silent for a few moments, savoring the pie. Then he looks at me again. "Anna, how do your husband and Lesley feel about you being here?"

I don't know how to answer the question. "Greg's been too busy this summer to notice I'm gone," I say. And Lesley? Have I ever stopped to wonder what Lesley thinks?

"Foolish man," Demetrius says quietly.

I have been so caught up in my own thoughts that I have to think for a minute what he might mean. "I should tell you, Gregory is determined to put the house on the market. He arranged for some couple to come look at it yesterday."

"And what did they think?"

"They didn't. I canceled on them. I told them the house was not for sale. I don't want to sell. I want to be here. Gregory is furious at me, but he has no right—" And before I know what is happening my eyes are flooded with tears.

Demetrius stands up and comes over to me. "Come," he says, taking hold of my hands. "Can he sell if you don't want to?"

"No, he can't. Both our names are on the deed. And the house is really Dorothea's. It's a good place for her to be, and for me, away—away from—" And I am crying hard now and Demetrius is pulling me to my feet and taking me in his arms and holding me. For a long minute we stand there unmoving. We are almost the same height; my face is against his ear. His hand is on the back of my head, pressing me close. Then he lets go and I turn to look at him. And then one or the other of us moves just slightly and we are kissing, a long, sweet kiss, more tender than passionate. I feel a great loosening in my body, as if an ice jam had broken up and let go.

And now I see this is what I wanted all along, this the reason for the carefully prepared lunch, for leaving the girls at home, the blueberry pie, the bottle of wine. We are poised on the brink of a great rapid, about to drop down into that wild ride there is no way to stop.

But Demetrius stops. "No," he says. "This isn't right. You're angry at your husband. Think about what you are doing, Anna. There will be consequences."

"I don't care about the consequences."

"But you will. Go home, Anna, and think—think hard. Then if this is what you want, come to me."

"Is this what you want?"

"Oh, yes, Anna. For a long time now. But I have less to lose. Go home and think, and if you decide *yes*, come to me. Not here. To my house. I'll be there. But you must think. Promise me, Anna."

"I promise." And he is out the door of the bog house, stopping by his truck bed to pick up a shovel and heading back over to Cove bog.

A Spring Tide

What is taken away may appear in another place and
form.

THERE ARE TWO moments in every love affair that no one ever forgets:
the moment of recognition, of being pierced through the eye by Cupid's dart as the Elizabethan poets used to say, and the moment of inevi-
tability, of yielding and knowing that no force on earth can stop what the
two of you have begun. Recognition can come in a blinding flash at first
sight, or it can gradually impose itself on our attention like an unknown
object glinting on the horizon, catching our eye when we're looking at
something else and disappearing when we try to locate it, flashing again
as soon as we look away.

That's how it was with Demetrius. I wasn't looking to love a Cape
Cod cranberryman, sixty-one years old, Aunt Phoebe's handyman, who
rode around in an ancient blue pickup and spent his days outdoors clearing
irrigation ditches and wrestling with sluice gates.

Much of my private pleasure these days comes from reconstructing
those glints and flashes. Demetrius on the porch that first day, squatting
down eye-level with Dorothea and naming her wheelchair Pegasus. Or on
the Fourth of July, holding the lollipop for her, and I, noticing the thick
curly steel-gray hair on the back of his head and thinking how alive it
looked, wanting to touch it. Waking later that afternoon on Phoebe's quilt
in the yard to find him watching me. (When did you first know? I asked
the first time we made love, one of those troubling questions women seem
to need to ask. Was it the day of the picnic? I wanted you that day, yes, he
said, and looked away, uncomfortable.)

How to describe falling in love like this, in middle life? When the
iron gates are about to close, the rest of the way set, all wonder, all surprise behind us? There are only the clichés, though thinking that makes
me remember something Daphne said once: "Clichés get to be clichés
because they are true." To be reborn. To be loved, at forty-three, by a man
inappropriate in every way according to the social rules I'd unconsciously absorbed: From a world I know nothing about, too old, so different

from the type I normally think of as handsome, slight and dark, and no taller than I am, and, as my mother and some of my friends would put it, not of my class. Uneducated, except of course that isn't true. He's read everything, English poetry going back to *The Wayfarer*, the classics, Shakespeare, Melville, Thoreau. And books on the history of science that would mystify someone like Daphne, let alone me. And every word he's read, it seems, has engraved itself on his mind, the lines of poetry waiting there in his head to weave themselves into his conversation. That I didn't expect.

Nor did I expect the tenderness with Dorothea, which is really what won me, that and the ease with which he lives in his body, the energy that radiates from him. Do other people feel that? Or is it just me, caught up in that mysterious attraction none of us can explain, that sets every nerve on alert? Our bodies, from the first touch, Lord knows, recognized each other as if they had come home at last after a long and harrowing journey. Our conscious minds had nothing to do with it. And then, surprise of all wondrous surprises, our minds, tagging breathlessly along behind, discovered each other and we became friends.

"With my body I thee worship," the Anglican service says. Somehow Gregory has always found sex hard to confront, impossible to discuss. It is unimaginably lovely, having my body looked at frankly in the broad light of day and found beautiful, not being allowed to be ashamed of the marks of age it is beginning to wear. "Oh, God," Demetrius says, uncovering my heavy breasts, softened from nursing two children and marked like my belly with the silver lines of long-past pregnancies. "You are so beautiful. It stuns me," he says.

It angers him when I disparage myself, when I complain about how I look. "I always have fifteen pounds I want to lose," I said one night. "I'm too generous everywhere. My friend Margaret, from up home—she's five ten—calls me *softig*. I always thought that was a tactful way to say overweight."

"No, stop talking about yourself that way," Demetrius says. He is genuinely angry. "You are beautiful. Perfect. Ask any man who looks at you. A man looks at you and imagines—you were meant to be seen naked."

"*And therefore is wing'd Cupid painted blind,*" I say gratefully, kissing one eye closed, then the other, but all the while I believe him. We are on Phoebe's quilt spread under the little stand of pines at the top of the field closest to the harbor, just out of sight of the house. It is reckless to meet in the middle of the night, but when have lovers not been reckless?

It is buggy out here under the pines, but we don't care. The moon, not quite full, is shining on my face, but Demetrius is in shadow. I shift him sideways so I can see him better.

"*My face in thine eye, thine in mine appears,*" he says.

Did Gregory ever make me feel this way? I try to remember how it was, those first months we were together, before the children. Passion we had, yes, but passion in the dark, separate, not framed on either side as it is with Demetrius with these searching looks, these words, this laughter. As if sex were something meant to be sealed off from our rational waking life, inexplicable, uncontrollable and irrelevant as the strange wild dreams we sometimes wake from and are afraid to talk about. Gregory, whose physical modesty first amused and then saddened me, though it was his reticence, his mysteriousness that first attracted me. I thought it was just shyness. I thought that lovemaking would somehow open a door for us. But his inner core remains, after nineteen years of marriage, as much a mystery as ever. How tragic that it has taken me forty-three years to understand what it means to know and be known, body and soul. Carnal knowledge, a phrase that no longer sounds ugly to me, but beautiful.

I go home after the picnic at West Marsh and think, as Demetrius made me promise. But I'm not really weighing choices, I'm rationalizing, as we all do at the beginning. If reason had anything to do with it, I think, smiling, the human race would have died out long ago. On good days Demetrius shows up in his truck and works on the house. His demeanor is just as it was back in February at Phoebe's funeral: polite, taciturn, deferential. I might well have dreamed the encounter at the bog house. Finally, after nearly a week, I appear out by the garden one afternoon with a pitcher of tea. "I've thought," I say. "And the answer is yes."

Demetrius finishes drinking a long draft of tea and turns to look at me. "Well then," he says.

"I'll have to come during the day. I can't leave the girls at night."

"For lunch, then, tomorrow? No. Come Wednesday. It's the new moon. There'll be a spring tide."

I don't ask why the spring tide is important. Perhaps it has some romantic symbolism in his mind. "I'll be there," I say, "and I'll bring lunch."

"You know Thacher Shore? You go past the Land Trust sign and it's a dirt lane off to the left. The second one after an old salt box—you'll see it. No road sign, but a mailbox with my name. Just go all the way down to the end." Demetrius puts his glass down on the tray and heads back to the window frame he is painting. Nothing about his manner has changed at all. But adrenalin is pulsing through me; my hands have gone cold, though it is a hot day.

"Twelve, then?"

"Twelve. On Wednesday."

How QUICKLY LOVE teaches us how to lie. It helps to be the sort of person who does not have secrets in ordinary life. I have already lied to Demetrius about why the girls were not with me at West Marsh, and now I lie to Lesley, telling her I have been invited out to lunch on Wednesday by an old friend. When Gregory calls Tuesday night I tell him the same thing. "Who?" he asks.

"No one you know. Selena. Selena Thacher. She's someone I knew at Wellesley, before I met you. She transferred after sophomore year." The lies proliferate, the elaborate lie more convincing than the simple one. And we have not even begun. But now I must write the name down so I will remember it, which I do, in my date book. *Selena* for Phoebe's friend who gave her the lap desk and the notebooks. *Thacher* for Thacher Shore.

I spend a large part of Wednesday morning deciding what to wear to my—what shall I call it? Assignation? Rendezvous? Tryst. I like the sound of *tryst*. My yellow shift, a simple column of linen that stands away from my body, cool on a hot day, with my amber necklace for good fortune. My new tan sandals. Underwear is a problem; everything I have here is practical, mostly cotton, at least a year old. I pick out the least worn bra. The one pair of nylon panties I brought from Needham, beige and unadorned with lace. Pray they don't show through the yellow linen. And how does one prepare one's body to be seen by a near stranger? What soap, what cream, what perfume can transform forty-three years of living into beauty? And so I shower and wash my hair, shave my underarms and legs with more care than I've used all summer, use the blow drier even though it is a warm day. Dab Bellodgia behind my ears, at the back of my neck, between my breasts. By the time I finish dressing I'm perspiring and in need of another shower. My hands are ice cold.

The dirt road to Demetrius's house is longer than I expect. There are no houses along it that I can see. The lane winds through scrub oak and cedar, and yellowed grasses grow up between the two sandy tracks. The van is heavy but doesn't have four-wheel drive. What if I get stuck out here in soft sand? But Demetrius has a truck. He would know what to do.

One last turn and I see I have arrived. A small, weatherbeaten cabin tucked in among beach plums and bayberries, with two tall cedars shading it. Unpainted cedar shakes, curled with age, cover the walls and the roof. Beyond it, through the trunks of the trees, I see the bay stretching out to the horizon between a sandy bluff on one side and a faint row of houses leading to a lighthouse on the other, foreshortened from this angle but recognizable as Sandy Neck. To the right, perhaps a half mile away, I spot the long boardwalk where Daphne and I walked and talked about our daughters. But the vast marshes have disappeared under water. The spring tide. At the very edge of the water is a smaller building, some sort of shed or boathouse, perhaps. And Demetrius is there, coming through the door, walking up the little slope toward me in his deliberate way and smiling.

"This is where I live," he says simply, taking the picnic basket from my hand and leading me across the narrow porch that faces the water and through the door of his cabin. It is two rooms, simple and un-adorned except for a large basket of dried flowers on the scarred pine table, hundreds of tiny blooms packed tightly together, their colors faded with age.

"Did your wife do that?" I ask. She has been on my mind, on my conscience. Perhaps by mentioning her I might exorcize her ghost.

"Yes. It's old now but I like it. It's the one thing I brought of hers from the other house."

"Then she never lived here?" I ask, feeling relieved.

"No. I sold the big house when she died, used the money to pay down the loan for West Marsh. Though we came sometimes in the summer to boat or swim. Marte loved the water. Swimming was good for her." I think of Dorothea, her pleasure in the bath, in the few times I have taken her into the water on the beach on Kettle Lane. "All the family used this place in the summer," Demetrius is saying, "and the men would come in duck season for a few days. It was a ritual, no women, just us men and boys."

"And do they still come in duck season?"

"Some do. The old men are gone now, so it's not the same. Not all the stories. But two of my cousins, and some of the nephews sometimes."

I look around the small room where Demetrius obviously spends most of his time. An L-shaped kitchen in the rear and along one side, a small pine table where he eats and which probably doubles as a desk, a sagging sofa with a faded brown slipcover, a tiny bedroom off to the side with barely enough room for an old iron bed and a small chest of drawers. Bookshelves built into the walls under, over, and beside the windows. A bathroom, no doubt, out of sight beyond the bedroom.

Demetrius puzzles me by continuing to stand in the middle of the room holding the picnic basket. "Come with me," he says finally, heading back out the door and down a small slope to the other little building. He leads me inside, and I see why he wanted me here at high tide. It is set on low pilings on the very edge of the marsh, and now with the tide all the way up it is almost in the water. Two wide doors open out onto a ramp that is half submerged. A boathouse, this must have been. Demetrius has fitted the wide opening with screens, and more screening forms a solid line of windows around the other three sides. A futon on a wooden frame is set up as a sofa facing the water. A ladder nailed on the wall to the side of it leads to a narrow loft above. A narrow table is built into the wall under the windows, with an ancient thumb-back chair in front of it and a few books propped along its back. Two battered wicker chairs. Nothing else. Except Demetrius has brought flowers in, the Queen Anne's lace and black-eyed Susans that are in bloom everywhere along the roadsides right now, set on the table in a Mason jar along with clouds of sky-blue sea lavender, just coming into bloom on the marshes. The little house is airy and full of light, surrounded by silvery blue water reflecting the gentle motions of the waves on the walls and rafters. We could be on a boat, at sea. I understand about the spring tide.

"Is this where you sleep?" I ask, feeling awkward, having no idea what to say.

"In the summer, yes, unless the no-see-ums are too bad. They can come right through the screens. But it's cooler here than in the house."

"It's magical, like being out at sea." I can almost feel a rocking motion, watching the play of reflected sunlight. I imagine Phoebe here, or myself as Phoebe. She would have loved this place, everything about it. She would have brought the wild flowers from her own garden, gone out on the marsh with a knife to cut the sea lavender, pausing to marvel at how it grows like miniature flowering trees rising above the tough fibrous fields of sea grass, covered by the tides twice a day and yet surviving, bearing hundreds of tiny star-shaped blossoms the exact color of the sky.

And so we became lovers, crossing that divide all lovers cross, sharing our picnic lunch with the grave, shy politeness that precedes the plunge into intimacy, the oddness of having to negotiate everything, from deciding when to put down the peaches and the wine glasses and embark on the kiss that will start it all, wondering when and how we will undress—ourselves or each other?—even, upon reaching that moment when we must lie down, having to get up and unfold the futon frame, one on a side, and having to figure out who will lie where. So scary, and comical, and lovely. And then the fear and excitement of touching, being touched by a virtual stranger after nineteen years of knowing only one man. The strangeness dissolving into discovery and ease, into oneness and joy, into a tenderness so deep it feels bottomless. The sweetness of holding his head on my breast as he sleeps, the deliciousness of sliding, finally, into sleep in the safety of his arms.

When we wake the tide has receded a long way; we are surrounded by the brilliant green of the marsh grass. I move my arm just slightly so I can see the dial of my watch. Three o'clock. I must get home, and now. Demetrius is not asleep. He has been watching me, I know, the way he did back on the Fourth of July. "How do you feel?" he asks.

I consider. How do I feel? Not guilty. Not ashamed or fearful, and though I know I will pay the piper somehow, probably sooner than later, not worried. "Happy," I say. "Wonderful. Like I've come home." And there's something else, a shedding of an image I've been carrying of myself as a good woman, virtuous wife, self-sacrificing mother, someone people point to with admiration, even if it's mixed with pity. I turn and take Demetrius's face—beloved face!—in my hands. "And like I've joined the human race rather late in the game," I say. "Like an ordinary sinner."

It is nearly four o'clock by the time I get home. I apologize to Lesley, explaining that my friend and I got talking about college and lost track of time. She's justifiably annoyed but doesn't stay around to complain; she is already in her suit and quickly disappears down to the beach for a swim. I am irritated to find she has parked Dorothea in the parlor in front of the TV, watching snow and listening to static, but I'm hardly in a position to reprimand her about it. I turn off the set and wheel Dorrie out the parlor door, down Demetrius's ramp and into the shade of the locust trees on the north side of the house. She doesn't like leaving the TV, but soon begins studying the gently swaying patterns of sunlight and shade on the grass. I wheel her up to Phoebe's Adirondack chair and sit down facing her, taking her good left hand in mine. She smiles her lopsided smile. How I wish I could make her—myself!—understand all the emotions I am feeling, that I could bring her a taste of the huge physical joy still warming my body, something she will never have a chance to know, wishing I could tell her everything. But of course she can't understand, and if she could, if she were normal, I could not tell her. It would devastate her, Lesley too, if she ever found out. I should feel guilty, or at least apprehensive, but I don't. I get up out of the chair and stand behind Dorrie so I can rub her shoulders and back. She hums with pleasure, and I lean down to kiss her on the ear, feel the sweet silkiness of her hair against my cheek. "I'm happy, Dorrie," I say simply. "I'm happy."

Kayaks

*Once they are spread upon the beaches, the loose sands are
never stationary. . . . They move with the wind-driven
water.*

WHEN YOU'RE A kid no one believes your time is worth anything,
Lesley thinks. Mom's two hours late and what does it matter? Let
her try that on Dad and see what he says, especially if she made him miss
an appointment. Trouble is, she didn't tell Mom she was supposed to be
down by the second creek over an hour ago, or why. Mom would spaz if
she knew.

She met Phil out on the sand bar two days ago, when she walked out
there to take a dip and get away from the heat. He paddled up in a red
kayak and said *hello*, came up on the bar, talked to her for a while and then
let her try his boat out for a few minutes. A lot harder to get into than a
canoe—she tipped the whole thing over and swamped it the first time she
tried—but easier to paddle once she got the hang of it. She loved the feel
of it. It was more like being in the water than on top of it, so quiet and
smooth, the only noise the soft dip and splash of the paddle. The best part
was he said he had another one, his brother's, and they could go paddling
together if she wanted. He lives in a house that backs onto the second
creek and they keep them in a boathouse next to their dock. She was
supposed to meet him at three and now it's after four—he'll think she's
blown him off for sure.

But when she gets to the beach, there he is, paddling his red kayak
halfway between the beach and where the sandbar will be coming up in
the next hour or so. It takes awhile for him to notice her, but finally he
sees her and waves and starts moving in towards shore. Lesley walks down
the beach towards the creek. She'll be happier if no one on the lane sees
them together.

"I'd given up on you," Phil says, as he beaches his boat on the edge
of the creek.

"I'm sorry," Lesley says. "I had to babysit my sister and my mom was
two hours late."

"You got a kid sister? I'm the baby in my family, thank God. My brother takes all the flak."

Lesley could kick herself for mentioning her sister. She doesn't want to get into all that. But it doesn't matter—Phil isn't waiting around for an answer to his question—he's too eager to get going. "Come on," he says. "Walk up the creek and I'll meet you—you'll see our dock. It's the third one up on your side."

Fifteen minutes later they are all set, paddling back down to the harbor in two identical red kayaks. Lesley is beginning to get the hang of it, though her arms are already tired. Phil showed her how to paddle using her shoulders, not her elbows, but it's hard to remember to do it. "Want to go to Sandy Neck?" he asks.

Lesley is leery of being seen from the beach by her mom or one of the neighbors. "How about up this way?" she answers, looking beyond the creek to the east, away from Kettle Lane. "What's around that point?"

"A big inlet—you know the bridge on Keveny Lane?"

"No."

"It's cool. Lots of birds this time of year. Don't think we can make it under the bridge right now—the tide's out too far—but I can show you where it is."

Phil's right about the birds. They see a whole flock of cormorants, a pair of great blue herons, and best of all, a mother swan with three babies, almost full grown but still wearing their gray juvenile plumage. "That's Blair Swan," Phil says. "She was here last year too. We call her Blair after my aunt. She's got triplets. How'd you like to have three little sisters to babysit?"

Sisters again. Lesley changes the subject quickly. "I better get back. I got to get home." Then she adds boldly, "Think we can do this again sometime?"

"Sure. How about tomorrow? High tide's about one, I think, so how about after lunch? We can paddle down to the marina and go under the bridge into the marsh."

Lesley knows she should tell her mom about the kayaking, but the thought of mentioning Phil puts her off. It's the following Monday before Mom confronts her as she's flying out the door to the beach. "Daphne tells me she saw you out on the bay in a kayak yesterday," she says. "With a boy. Want to tell me who he is?"

"Just a boy. His name's Phil Petersen. He lives over on the second creek."

"How old is he?"

"I don't know. Thirteen, I think."

"I'd like to meet him. Would you like to ask him over here sometime?"

"Mom," she answers, drawing the word out with an exasperated whine. "He just asked me to go kayaking. He's got two of them—one belongs to his brother."

"You know I like to meet your friends. And what's more important, I need to know when you're out on the harbor in a boat. That's a safety precaution pure and simple. You know Daphne always lets me know when the two of you are going sailing." What did Mom have to bring that up for? She probably wouldn't be sailing with Daphne any more, with that guy Paul practically living over there.

"Yeah, I know. I got to go."

"Going kayaking?"

"Yeah, I guess, if it's not too windy."

"You're wearing a life vest, aren't you?"

"Sure. Phil's got two," she lies.

But when she gets to the beach there's no sign of Phil. She walks over to the creek and finds him sitting on his family's dock. The kayaks are nowhere in sight. "Sorry," he says. "It's my brother's day off. He's over on Sandy Neck somewhere with his girlfriend. She's down for the week."

"Is he in college?"

"Nah. He's only seventeen. He's supposed to be a senior next year but he bagged a couple of courses. He's kind of a party animal. Hey, speaking of that, he's having a party on the beach tonight, late, around ten. Any chance you could come?"

"Not till ten?"

"Yeah—most of his friends wait tables and that's as early as they get off."

A party. She's been invited to a party on the beach that doesn't begin until ten. Does Phil think of her as a girlfriend? She looks appraisingly at him. He's shorter than she is by an inch or two, skinny and babyish-looking with a funny haircut, shaved up the sides and pointy on top. Kind of cute, though, in a boy sort of way. A party on the beach, with blankets and a fire like in the movies. Would he try to kiss her? And if he did, would she mind? "I don't know. But I'll try," she says. There's a funny little pause, as if Phil doesn't know what to say. "How old are you, anyway?" Lesley asks.

"Fourteen. How about you?"

"Same here." No way she's going to say twelve.

She'll have to sneak out, and that will involve going to bed early enough so Mom will think she's asleep. And she'll have to figure a way to get dressed so if she gets caught going outside she'd be in her p j's. It's going to be a hot night—she could say she needed to cool down. She packs her gym bag with jeans, her beach sandals, and a sweatshirt, and when Mom is busy in the kitchen feeding Dorrie supper she carries the bag up the hill and hides it behind the big rock. She always sleeps in a T-shirt and boxer shorts anyway—they'll do as underwear. She takes a long shower and washes her hair. Should she wear it up or down? She settles for a pony tail and the gold hoop earrings Dad gave her for Christmas last year. She's so nervous her hands are sweating. She wishes Katy were around to talk to. Besides, it would be so fun to tell Katy she was meeting a boy. On the beach, at ten o'clock at night. Even Katy has never done that.

It's nearly ten-thirty by the time she gets to the beach. Leave it to Mom to spend the evening up in Aunt Phoebe's little office, right next to Lesley's room. She makes her getaway when Mom goes down to check on Dorrie, sneaking down the stairs and through the dark parlor and out the door before Mom comes back into the hall after turning out the lights. Once she's on the beach she can see the glow down by the creek. The boys have built a campfire of driftwood on the sandy spit that has formed on the far side of the creek, so Lesley has to wade across. It takes a few minutes to locate Phil. There are more people here than she expected, most of them arranged in pairs and foursomes on beach towels and blankets, just like she imagined. Phil calls her name and motions for her to sit down between him and a much older-looking boy with longish dark hair.

"Hey Jake, I told ya she'd come. This is Lesley. She's my kayaking buddy."

"Hey Lesley. You got good taste, brother. Where you from, Sweets?"

Sweets. No one has ever called her anything like Sweets. She can see the family resemblance now, though Jake is much bigger, with muscled arms like someone who lifts weights, and longer, darker hair. His chin is stubbled with the beginnings of a beard, and he's drinking a can of beer. It hadn't occurred to her there might be beer. "I'm from Needham," she says uncertainly.

"Make yourself at home, pretty lady. Where'd you get that hair?"

At this point the girl sitting on the far side of Jake leans over and introduces herself. "Hi Lesley, I'm Joanie. How old are you, anyway?"

"Fourteen."

"Jail bait. Too bad," says Jake. "Help yourself to a libation, anyway."

What is a libation? And what is jail bait? Lesley looks confusedly at Phil, who smiles and says, "Coke or beer?"

"Coke, thanks." She's grateful to see that's what Phil is drinking. She's feeling out of her element. Some of the couples on the blankets are smoking, and there's a funny smell in the air that she suspects is pot. She learned about it in their drug unit at school. Pot smells like burning rope. That's got to be what it is.

One of the older-looking boys is noodling on a guitar, fiddling with chords, not playing anything recognizable. Lesley wishes he would play a song so everybody could sing. Mostly people are talking about things that happened at work, making fun of customers they had, mentioning names she doesn't know. A few of the couples go swimming. Why didn't she think to bring a bathing suit? When Jake and Joanie head down to the water, Phil moves closer to her and rests his arm loosely across her shoulders. Now what?

"Hey, want a hot dog or a marshmallow?"

"Sure—a marshmallow, I guess."

Phil fetches her a long peeled stick and a couple of marshmallows from the plastic bag near the fire. "I'll toast it for you," he says, putting one marshmallow on the stick and carefully holding it over the fire.

"Here, let me," she says, taking the stick from him, grateful for something to do. She's feeling very strange, here with all these older kids. What if her mother checks her room before she goes to bed? She spears a second marshmallow onto the stick and holds them in the flames until they catch fire. Black as pitch and crispy on the outside, all gooey on the inside, that's how she likes them. The trick is getting them done just right and then out of the flames before they melt and fall into the fire. And then not burning her fingers when she takes them off the stick.

Jake and Joanie come back from their swim and wrap themselves up together in a couple of beach towels, Joanie sitting between Jake's legs, he with his arms around her from behind and nuzzling her wet hair, kissing the back of her neck. Lesley tries looking everywhere except at them, getting more and more uncomfortable. "I've got to get back," she announces finally. "I'm going to get killed." When she gets up to go, Jake stands up and gives her a crushing hug and then a little pat on the behind that makes her feel weird. Phil says he'll walk her home, but she tells him he doesn't need to. She's wondering what she would do if he tried to kiss her. She runs all the way to the big rock, strips out of her jeans and sweatshirt and replaces them in the bag, which she'll have to remember to get in the morning, makes her way carefully into the house and up the stairs, and slips into her bed gratefully. She's committed enough crimes for one night.

THE NEXT TWO days bring rain, so she doesn't have a chance to see Phil. She thinks about him a lot and spends even more time going over her brief conversations with Jake. He called her Sweets and noticed her hair. Hard to imagine that Phil would look that grown up in a couple—three—years, so muscular, so confident, so dangerous. She spends a lot of time in her room looking into the dim mirror over her pine bureau, trying her hair different ways. The second evening she appears downstairs with her hair up. She's put it in a ponytail and pinned it up. Her mother looks at her quizzically. "Looks nice," she says. "Makes you look grown up." It's the first time her mother's noticed her in a while—she's been in a funny mood for the past week, not cranky but kind of distracted.

On Thursday the sun comes out again, and Lesley goes down to the beach in the late morning. The tide is low, so she doesn't expect to see Phil. She heads out to the sand bar for a swim and has just started back to the beach when she spots him coming toward the bar on foot. Somehow seeing him makes her feel embarrassed. "Get home all right?" he asks.

"Sure. I didn't get busted."

"Think you could get out Sunday night?"

"I don't know. My Dad's coming down—he may still be around on Sunday. What time?"

"Oh, around ten again. Jake's got a friend with a beach buggy—he's going to take us out to Sandy Neck. The back beach. It's Joanie's last night here so it's kind of a celebration."

"Isn't that a long way, to the back beach?"

"It's about twenty minutes to the parking lot—then you drive on sand—depends on how far up the beach you go."

"That would be so fun."

"Tell you what. If you can get out, we'll pick you up down at the end of your street, on 6A. Kettle Lane, right?"

"That's right. What time?"

"Say ten? Think you can make it?"

"I'll sure try. I've never been in a beach buggy."

GETTING OUT ON Sunday night is easier than she expected. Dad left early in the day, right after lunch. He and Mom were getting into it over something—she could hear them arguing in the bedroom Saturday night. And Mom is watching—or listening to—some movie on television. She hardly looks up at nine-thirty when Lesley says she's going to bed. This time she has to be extra careful going down the stairs with Mom right there in the parlor. She finishes dressing in the garage, hoping the fleece pullover she brought will keep her warm enough. The weather has changed since the rain, damp and foggy at night, and the back beach faces Cape Cod bay. It could be pretty windy out there.

Walking down to the end of Kettle Lane is scary. It's pitch dark except for a couple of lights at Daphne's house. Lesley walks swiftly on the other side of the street, her hiking hat pulled low over her face in case Daphne happens to look out and spot her. She's about ten minutes early. She doesn't know what to do with herself when cars come by, and there are a lot of cars since it's Sunday night and the weekenders are heading home. If she stands out in plain sight, one of the neighbors might see her, but if she hides back next to the privet hedge on the roadside, the boys might miss her and drive right by. She wishes she had brought her watch. It seems like a lot longer than ten minutes.

Finally she spots the beach buggy, a funny sort of jeep with a roll bar and big wide tires. The open back is loaded up with kids—five or six of them. Phil calls to her, offers her a hand, and she climbs aboard and sits down beside him. Jake and his girlfriend are up front with the driver, so Phil is the only one she knows. Everyone is all jammed together so she can't even straighten out her legs—they're all tangled up with Phil's, along with a couple of other people's. Phil looks different to her tonight, more like a little boy. A kid brother. He looks younger than me, Lesley thinks. She never thought about how they looked together when they were out kayaking, but it's different here with all these older kids. Is he going to try to make out with her? She doesn't know if she wants him to or not. She feels all jangly inside, part excited, part scared to death.

The ride out to Sandy Neck beach is unbelievably bumpy. She clings to the side of the jeep for dear life. She hasn't met the driver— the owner, she guesses—but he's going awfully fast down 6A, with all its blind corners and narrow turns. It's a relief to get out of the traffic and onto the beach road, which looks pitch dark but is good and straight, at least. They stop to move a wooden barrier by some sort of deserted ticket booth, then head across the empty parking lot. What an odd sensation to drive off the end of the pavement and right onto the beach. The bumping stops, to be replaced by unexpected swerving motions as the wheels try to get a purchase in the soft sand. Things smooth out as they move down closer to the water where the sand is damp and more solid. Lesley stops feeling nervous and begins to enjoy the sensation of being out on the beach at night. It's lighter than back on the lane, the sky patterned with faint stars peeking through broken clouds, the white ruffles marking the small breakers looking iridescent against the dark water.

They drive a long way down the beach, more than a mile, Lesley guesses. It's warmer than she imagined it would be, so she's glad she wore her bathing suit under her clothes. Finally they stop near a notch in the bluff above the beach, where a path leads back into the dunes. Jake and Joanie, another strange girl and the driver, a short sturdy guy with acne and a dirty blond ponytail, get out of the front of the jeep—they must have been mushed with four people across, Lesley thinks. They come around to the back and begin unloading bags of food and two big coolers as everybody else jumps down and begins spreading blankets and towels in a row under the bluff. No fire tonight, Phil explains. They're not supposed to be out on the beach after dark.

"Hey, you guys, have a drink," says Jake, lifting two small bottles out of the biggest ice chest and twisting off the lids. Wine coolers. She takes a taste. Sweet, like soda pop, with something bitter underneath. How much will it take to get her high, or drunk? She hasn't got a clue.

"Let's go swimming first," she says to Phil a little desperately. "I remembered to bring my suit this time." She strips off her fleece top and T-shirt, her jeans and boxer shorts. The way Jake is looking at her makes her feel weird, so she turns and runs for the water, surprised at how rocky the beach is, glad she thought to wear her Tevas. Phil catches up to her just as she is about to plunge under a wave. There are real waves here, though it's surf in miniature compared to what she's seen over at Nauset, little breakers that roll in, pretty but not quite strong enough for belly surfing.

"Watch this," Phil says, leaning down and running his open hand rapidly through the water. His hand glows, outlined with streaks of greenish light, like the brief shimmer of the sparklers she and Mom lit for Dorrie on the Fourth of July.

"Wow. That's amazing!"

"It's phosphorescence. It's really bright tonight. Sometimes you can hardly see it. It has something to do with plankton."

Lesley dips her hand into the water, tries writing her name in cursive. *L.* By the time she gets to *e* and *s*, the *L* has faded. Beautiful light, but only there for a moment, gone before she can be sure it's there. She turns onto her back, kicking up a great turmoil of splashes, all outlined with light. Phil joins her as they kick themselves away from the beach, laughing at the noise, the brief lovely flashes of light. When they stand up, the water is deeper than Lesley expects, almost up to her shoulders, swaying her gently up and down with the motion of the waves. Then Phil is ducking her under, coming after her, tangling with her as she pushes up gasping for air. And then his arms are around her, his face in her face, kissing her on the mouth, then back under water and pushing away from her before she can register what happened. Kissed. He kissed her, quick and soft and wet. She doesn't know how to feel about it, certainly not what to say. But then they are both distracted by two new lights, from down the beach in the direction of the parking lot, a car coming towards them, its headlights forming two beams in the misty air. They crouch down in the water so only their heads show, not moving or speaking, like two deer caught by the side of the road.

But it doesn't pass. It stops in front of the jeep and a man gets out with a flashlight and a uniform, not a policeman's but something else. "Shit," Phil says. "It's a Smoky."

"Smoky?"

"Yeah, the conservation police. We're not supposed to be out here after dark. Ken might lose his permit."

Lesley follows Phil out of the water and back toward the jeep, trying not to imagine what might happen next. Underage kids with liquor. Will they get arrested? Will she have to call her Mom from the police station? But when they get back to the others, they see the coolers have been closed and replaced in the back of the jeep, covered with a heap of towels and beach blankets. The Smoky, who doesn't look a lot older than Jake and Ken, is writing down Ken's name and registration number but doesn't seem interested in interrogating the rest of the kids. He gives them what Lesley guesses is his standard lecture on beach regulations, warns Ken he'll lose his permit if he's caught again, and follows them back to Sandy Neck road.

Lesley shivers all the way back to Cummaquid in spite of her fleece pullover. They're going to continue the party down on their own beach, Jake says before climbing into the front seat, but she begs off, asks to be let out at the end of Kettle Lane. She doesn't look at Phil, and he doesn't try anything else on the way back. He's probably as much at a loss for words as she is, she thinks. Funny, she feels pretty much the same, except for the huge relief over not being arrested. And yet she passed a milestone tonight. It doesn't seem real—does under water count? First kiss, and no girlfriend around to call up tomorrow and tell.

All the lights are out as she makes her way back up Kettle Lane, even Daphne's. No sign of life at her house, just the faint glow of the night light from Dorrie's window. She strips out of her clothes and wet bathing suit in the garage, puts her damp T shirt and boxers back on, and cautiously opens the screen door to the porch, tiptoes up the stairs. By now she has memorized the creaky places and knows how to avoid them. She's finally calmed down and is just drifting off to sleep when she hears something— voices, steps across the parlor, up the stairs. Should she be scared? Before she can decide whether it is real or she has dreamed it, she is asleep.

August

*What will the sea do with all the debris it is taking from
the present land?*

It's LIKE LIVING in another body, the way I've been feeling since—how
long? A week ago Wednesday. I'm drunk on happiness, giddy as a child
on the first real spring day, light on my feet as if released from years of
dragging the heavy weight I've been carrying so long I no longer think of
it as separate from my body, all the sadness and anger I have not let myself
feel for the past five years.

I wake at dawn, mornings, full of energy, plunging into the day,
tackling Phoebe's disheveled gardens with a gusto I only fantasized about
last spring, taking long rambles along the lanes and down the beach on
afternoons when I can corral Lesley into sitting with Dorrie. I've lost five
pounds in ten—nine—days without even thinking about going on a diet.
Can falling in love crank up the metabolism? People are starting to tell
me I look wonderful. Daphne has noticed—even Lesley said this morning
I looked thinner.

Demetrius and I have been together twice since that first afternoon,
one quick meeting at his house on the marsh on Friday and—crazy as
it was—once up on the hill this past Sunday night. I have told no one.
I carry my secret with me like some precious talisman that might disappear if I dare convert it into language. The last time I remember feeling
this way was the week I discovered I was pregnant with Dorothea. Too
magical to be believed, let alone shared. I left the doctor's office feeling as
though I might spill over any minute. It was two days before I broke the
news to Gregory.

Gregory. I haven't thought of him in days. Part of me wants to share
what has happened with Daphne, but another part is reluctant. I want
to hug this secret happiness to myself. Besides, there's something about
Daphne's manner when Demetrius's name comes up in our conversations.
It's not that she dislikes him, or mistrusts him exactly, but there's
something, some history there, something she has not been willing to
talk about. Perhaps like Gregory she blames him for Phoebe's accident.

Or maybe I'm imagining it, using it as an excuse to postpone sharing my treasure. Besides, Daphne has been so caught up lately with Paul, we've hardly had time to say hello, much less have heart-to-heart talks.

Today I've been working in the back garden all morning, deadheading and pulling weeds and grass from around the perennials. Dorrie has been keeping me company, happy to be out after the rains we've had, enjoying the crisp air that makes me realize that it's August. I've taken her for a walk down to the beach and back—too windy to sit down there or think about taking her into the water. I've parked Pegasus where she can watch the monarchs landing on Phoebe's butterfly bush. I've counted seven. They must be in the middle of their migration. I am taking a break with one of Phoebe's journal notebooks—the last one, as it happens, before the long silence that has me so puzzled. The day sounds much like today. Looking up from the page to the garden in front of me, it's hard to place myself in time. It could be now or then.

> September 18: Clear, cool, and windy as it always is after a
> northeaster, with a two-day stiff breeze that doesn't want to die.
> Found a sunny spot in the lee of the house, so I'm snuggled up against
> the little dooryard garden enjoying the tumble of white cosmos all
> bent over from the storm but blooming even more furiously than
> usual, and the morning glories that have finally decided to show up,
> making their entrance like belles come late to the ball. Flaring skirts
> of the most astounding blue, as if anyone could miss them!

> September 22: Work crew all lined up for the harvest. Crop a little
> late this year after all the cool weather; good quality but not as
> abundant as last year, D says. He seems more cheerful lately and
> stomach bothering him less than last week. I pray no more benders
> at least until after the harvest. Had a visit from Thelma Turnstone
> yesterday. Not sure what she was doing here except nosing around.
> Heard D was ailing but arrived well after the fact so she didn't have to
> do anything as troublesome as bring a casserole. After she left, I went
> over to West Marsh to look at the crop. Only one D out on the bog; I
> found mine sound asleep in the bog house. Let him lie and helped for
> a while with weeding the ditch borders.

> September 24: Grapes are ripe and I spent all morning picking and
> boiling and straining and this afternoon putting up jam. D ailing
> again and in bed and complaining about the smell—seems ominous

to me when one is sickened by the smell of wild grapes. Carried four jars over to the bog house.

September 26: Doctor has been by to see D who can't seem to hold anything down and is visibly jaundiced. Wants to put him in the hospital for tests—is worried about his liver function—but he will not hear of it. Finally able to keep down some chicken broth and toast but that is all, and must be persuaded to try even that. Appetite has left him. I have been back over to West Marsh to apprize D of the situation. He assures me he can manage things; crew will start as soon as they're done in West Barnstable. Thank God for him, and I do, every day.

September 28: D still too sick to go to work but has ventured down into the parlor for the day. A crisp blue day, sky almost as deep as the morning glories. I've been out to the bar to clear my head. Fish are still running in the harbor—I could see where they were ruffling up the water, and the gulls and especially the graceful little terns were swooping and diving with great excitement, crying their urgent little cries. A great year for blues, I was told by a fisherman out on the bar. And as if to prove it, D arrived unexpectedly about five o'clock with two lovely filets, all cleaned and ready for grilling. My D had no appetite for anything as strong as bluefish, so I invited D to share, but Marte waiting for him at home. I cooked and ate outside despite the cool air and early sunset. Equinox is past; winter will soon be arriving with its gales.

So Dennis was already feeling the effects of his drinking as early as the 1950s. It shouldn't surprise me, remembering the comments Gregory has made about those summers just a few years later when he stayed on Kettle Lane. So many years you had, Phoebe, of trying to hold everything together by yourself. Of course you had Demetrius to look after West Marsh, but he couldn't help you with Dennis, with the illness, the isolation you must have felt. And yet the tone of the entries, at least when you are writing about the beach, the weather, the panorama of seasons, doesn't change. *D* and *D*. Dennis and Demetrius. It's not always clear which one you mean.

Equinox is past; winter will soon be arriving with its gales. The last words for more than six years. That winter arrived with Phoebe's pregnancy. Was she already expecting when she wrote that last entry? There's no mention of it. Perhaps she was and didn't know it yet, too preoccupied with Dennis's illness to think about the calendar, though I remember being suspicious within days of conceiving my girls, the odd tingling sensations in my breasts, the overwhelming sleepiness, the sudden aversion to coffee. I try to remember when Camilla's birthday was, and can't. Sometime in late spring or early summer. That Phoebe might be pregnant and never record it seems out of character.

I close the journal and wheel Dorrie back around the house, smiling as we make our way up Demetrius's ramp. It's time to bathe her, and myself, start doing something about dinner. And time to come to grips with what I have been cleverly avoiding thinking about for days: Gregory arrives tonight, for the first time since everything changed. I've been afraid to think about it. Will he look at me and know? Will my skin, my slimmer body betray me? Will he thrust me away in disgust in the middle of lovemaking, knowing that I've been with another man?

Supper, I must think about supper. Phoebe's mention of bluefish makes me think about getting something at the upscale little fish market at the marina, not bluefish, which neither Gregory nor Lesley can stand, but striped bass, possibly, if any of the sports fishermen have brought one in, or one of the delicious prepared dishes the proprietor is known for, flounder roll-ups or perhaps seafood lasagna, stuffed with chunks of lobster and scallops. The tender local corn which is still available. Tomatoes out of the garden, and some of the herb rolls from the fish store. Dessert—I'll have to buy something ready-made up town. This means three stops, and it's after four and Lesley is still not back. Probably out kayaking with that boy again—Phil, was it? She told me his last name but I can't remember it. I'll have to go down to the beach and see if I can spot her.

Just as I've worked myself into a state about Lesley, she appears at the kitchen door. I remind myself not to take my nerves out on her; it's Gregory I'm worried about, and Lesley hasn't even bent any rules; it's only a little after four-thirty. I explain to her where I'm going and escape before she can complain about the fish. She can have corn and tomatoes for supper.

I buy the last four slices of seafood lasagna at the fish market along with a bag of herb rolls and head over to Yarmouth Port for the corn, piled on a wooden stand in front of an old colonial house with a handwritten sign and a metal money box. I've never seen anyone in the house or yard; whoever lives here trusts in the honor system. As I'm counting out my change from the cash box, I decide to drive into the center of Yarmouth

Port and stop at the new coffee bar for some of their oversize chocolate chip cookies. Lesley will like those, and it will make up for having fish for dinner. On the way back I find myself making a left turn, then a right, and driving up the dirt track to the bog house at West Marsh. Demetrius is just loading some bee boxes onto his truck. He's surprised to see me.

"What are you doing here?"

"I don't know. The car just found its way over here. I can't stay. I've got supper in the car—Gregory's due tonight." I look longingly at Demetrius. If he asked, I would manage to concoct some sort of story so I could follow him home, but of course he doesn't. He just turns and walks toward the bog house with me following right behind. The door is open; he hasn't finished loading his truck. I can see his lunch cooler and rubber boots by the door. I follow him in, shut the door behind me, and slip wordlessly into his arms.

"Are you frightened to be seeing your husband tonight?" Demetrius asks when we finally pull apart. He's looking intently into my eyes. I'm having trouble meeting his.

"Yes, I guess I am."

"It will be all right. You're not wearing a scarlet letter, you know."

"How did you know that's exactly what I've been worried about? You don't think he'll sense somehow? Notice I look different, or act different, or something?"

"No. I might. But then I've been making a study of you. I love you, you see."

I'm in the car and all the way back on Route 6A before the tears come, though whether they're tears of fear or guilt or joy I couldn't say. "I love you, you see," he said. He's never said that before.

I'm startled to see Gregory's gray Buick in the driveway when I get home. He's two hours earlier than I expected. No time for mental rehearsals. But I'll have the bustle of dinner preparations to hide behind.

"You're early," I say, setting the bags of food down on the kitchen table.

"Where have you been?" Is that a simple question, or an accusation? Guilt is making me imagine things.

"Just running around getting things for supper. Seafood lasagne, how does that sound? It's all prepared; I just need to heat it up. Want to take a swim first?" Silly question; it's too cool and breezy, and the tide is out anyway.

"No. I just couldn't face the traffic. I went in to the office early this morning and left a little after three. That's the secret, I guess, to get ahead of the mob."

I have run out of things to say, at least for now. I busy myself with lighting the oven, arranging the lasagne in a baking dish. Gregory settles himself on the porch with this morning's *Boston Globe*. He must have left for the office very early if he didn't even take time to read the paper. I glance at him as I walk across the porch on my way to the garden for tomatoes and basil. He looks tired, his face pale, an indoor face. And there's more gray in his hair than the last time I noticed. Men and their newspapers— their wall of defense. As a newlywed I never understood Greg's need to hide behind that wall when he first came home from work. Later when I was a housebound young mother starved for adult conversation, it felt cruel. I learned to let him be, though, to have the time to decompress, as he used to call it. But sometimes he'd never emerge. Even at the dinner table he'd stay distracted, his eyes darting away. We never sat and chatted over wine the way I imagined we would do. And now I'm the one who's hiding.

By the time supper is ready things seem more nearly normal and my nerves have dissipated. I decide to serve the food buffet style so we can eat on the porch, where the late afternoon sky is fading beautifully from deep blue to pale gold. We all are more relaxed out here, especially Lesley, who tends to feel she's being scrutinized whenever we sit at the table.

"So what have you been up to, Punkin?" Gregory asks Lesley. It's his pet name for her, her baby name. He hasn't used it in a long time.

"Not much," she mumbles, working on her second ear of corn. She eats the kernels around the ear instead of typewriter style like Greg. I wonder whether anyone has done some sort of study on the psychological significance of that. It's a relief to have Greg's attention turned on her instead of me.

"Tell your Dad about the kayaking," I prompt.

"Oh, yeah, I've got a friend who's been lending me a kayak. It's so fun. Do you think we could get one, maybe, next summer?" I notice she's neglected to mention the gender of her friend. I look at her appraisingly, her strawberry hair combed for once and pulled back off her face in a pony tail, her long legs looking smooth and brown in her white shorts. Graceful legs, long like Gregory's, legs I wish I had. She's a beautiful young woman as Daphne reminded me, even chomping gracelessly on corn. She's grown up this summer while I wasn't looking. I must have a talk with her, about boys, about what lies ahead for her. This boy Phil, whom I haven't even met. Does he see her as a buddy, another child, or is he smitten with her? Or worse, does he see her innocence as a challenge?

Greg, I notice, has ignored Lesley's question about next summer. "Where do you go in the kayak?" he's asking.

"Oh, everywhere. Over to Sandy Neck. There's lots of little creeks over there that wind all over the place. And lots of birds. We saw a swan the other day, with three babies, except they were almost grown up. They're gray, did you know that, when they're immature?" Immature, not a word Lesley would choose herself, a bird watcher's term, something she must have heard Phil say. I start to feel more kindly towards this unknown young man. If he's interested in birds he can't be all bad. Thirteen, did Lesley say he was? Probably still a little boy, but on the brink. Too bad young girls can't be camouflaged like baby birds, hidden away until they're old enough to think about mating. Lesley with those legs and her flaming hair, her budding breasts, hard for anyone to miss, let alone teenage boys flooded with hormones.

"So what do you make of Lesley's new friend?" Gregory says as we are getting ready for bed. "Is she reliable? Do you think Lesley's safe out there on the harbor?"

I don't want to be the one to tell Gregory that this friend is a boy, so I duck the issue. "Of course she's safe. She's had all that canoeing at camp, remember, and she can swim a long way—across the harbor if she has to."

"Even so, this friend, what's she like?"

"He. His name is Phil."

"A boy? How old? Are you sure she's safe with him?"

Safe. He's used the word twice in the last minute. Is every father this obsessed with safety, or only the ones who've lost a child to something there's no protection from? "To tell you the truth, Greg, I haven't met him. I only found out about him a couple of days ago because Daphne saw them together out on the harbor."

"What's she doing sneaking around seeing some boy?"

"Greg, please, it's not like that. They're buddies, that's all. Don't upset her by getting on her case about him. She was so relaxed at supper, didn't you think? I'm glad she's found someone her own age, especially since Daphne's—"I stop. I have no right to discuss Daphne's love life with Gregory.

"Daphne's what?"

"Daphne's too busy to take her sailing. She's been having a lot of company lately."

I am careful when we get into bed not to send Greg any signals. He drifts quickly off to sleep but surprises me by waking me in the first gray light of dawn, and I surprise myself by responding with more passion than I would have imagined. A wordless coming together it is, framed on both sides by sleep.

It isn't until Saturday night that things go awry. It's my fault, really—Greg has been so maddeningly agreeable. The day is lovely, warm and still, and the four of us head to the beach together for the first time this summer. Greg is not a beach person, but he spends time with Lesley, playing frisbee with her in the water, even offering to keep an eye on Dorothea so I can go for a swim. Both of us are on the lookout for the mysterious Phil, but he doesn't show himself. I'm grateful to Greg for not grilling Lesley about him or worse, teasing her about having a boyfriend.

But by evening I'm cross and out of sorts. Guilty, probably—how could I be unfaithful to such a model husband? And the matter of the house has still not been settled. It hangs like a presence between us.

We're up in the bedroom after supper. The air has taken on a chill and I'm changing into long pants and a sweater, and Greg is reorganizing his suitcase in his maddeningly methodical way. I can tell he's annoyed at the way I've left my clothes piled in a heap on the chair. I'm unforgivably sloppy sometimes, but why is he so compulsive? So closed in about his feelings. The way we made love this morning almost furtively. So different from Demetrius.

"I noticed you never answered Lesley's question about the kayak last night," I start in.

"What question?"

"Whether she could have one next summer."

"Anna, you know how I feel. We're not going to be here next summer."

"And you know how I feel."

"I can't believe you're still carrying on about this nonsense."

"And I can't believe you think you have the right to make unilateral decisions about things that affect all of us." I shove the bureau drawer shut and head for the door.

"Keep it down, Anna." Greg is right; my voice has been rising. The last thing we need right now is to make Lesley feel she's in the middle. She's just now settling in here; she's happy for the first time in ages. She doesn't need to worry about it all being snatched away. Or am I projecting my feelings onto her? It's my life that might be snatched away.

"—early tomorrow morning." Gregory has gone on, saying something I didn't catch.

"What did you say?"

"I said let's not argue the last few hours I'm here. I've got to leave early in the morning; I've got court Monday. Oh, and did I tell you I probably won't be down next weekend? We'll be right in the middle of the case, and you know how that is. Anyway, Jeannine is coming next week, isn't she? She'll be here to help out."

"Fine. Yes, Jeannine. Fine. We'll be just fine without you." I open the bedroom door roughly and start down the stairs, angry and relieved in equal measure, already calculating how, and how often, I can manage to steal off to see Demetrius while Jeannine is here.

Gregory is off right after breakfast the following morning. We have had little to say to each other since last night. The issue of the house is still unresolved. I am wild to see Demetrius; I need some antidote to my frustration. But how, and where? Lesley doesn't appear downstairs until I'm in the middle of Dorrie's exercises. I follow her into the kitchen to let her know her father has left. "You had a fight last night, didn't you?" she says accusingly. She thinks I've driven him away. Maybe she's right. I look at her, hunched over her cereal in a torn T-shirt and her father's boxer shorts, her hair hiding her face. If she seemed like a young woman last night, she's regressed again to the sulky girl of last spring. This isn't the time to bring up the issue of the house. Before I can think of what to say she is clattering up the stairs. Ten minutes later she is back down, striding through the parlor in a bathing suit and sweatshirt. "I'm out of here," she says, slamming the screen door behind her and heading for the beach.

I leave Dorrie again in the middle of her routine and dash to the phone, dial Demetrius's number in Yarmouth Port. I don't expect that he'll be there, but he answers on the fifth ring.

"Can you come tonight?" I ask. I know I sound more than a little desperate. The last thing I want is for him to think I'm going to get dependent and clingy.

"Are you all right? Did something happen with Gregory?"

"Just the usual go-round about the house. But I'm feeling—I don't know what I'm feeling. I just want to see you. Can we meet like last week?"

There's a perceptible pause. "You know that's dangerous, Anna."

I know. It's not just the chance of Lesley or the neighbors spotting us. Demetrius has to leave his truck at the public landing down by the creek and walk along the beach. It's unusual for anyone to park there at night, and the neighbors over there could spot the truck, even call the police. "Please" is all I say.

"Okay. But this is the last time. Eleven-thirty again?"

"Yes. Anyway, Jeannine comes on Tuesday so we won't have another chance. You'll have to entertain me during the day."

"I'll entertain you any time, morning, noon, or night."

"Night then, tonight."

This time he's not up on the hill when I arrive. I have to wait fifteen minutes, wondering what has happened, whether someone arrived at his house, or if perhaps he changed his mind. But then there he is, coming up towards Phoebe's rock from the direction of the beach, a little out of breath.

"I'm sorry I'm late. There was a couple parked down at the landing. I left the truck over by the marina instead."

"But that's over a mile away."

"Not so far along the beach. Anyway, I'd walk a million miles—"

"Don't be silly. But you're right. This probably isn't a good idea."

"Next time I'll come by boat, like the rum runners during Prohibition."

"Were you a rum runner?"

"I'm not that old, Anna, but my Papa could tell stories. You know the boathouse where we—" We are smiling and touching each other's faces by this time, and then he's peeling off my sweatshirt and bending to kiss my breasts. I want to hear about the rum runners, but not now.

It's nearly one o'clock by the time I get back into the house. I look in on Dorrie, tiptoe up the stairs, and listen for a moment by Lesley's door. All is peaceful. I decide to sleep on Phoebe's narrow cot instead of the double bed where I lay last night next to Gregory. Before I turn out the light, I pick up the book of John Donne's poems, still on the top of Phoebe's desk where I found it back in February, the week she died. I leaf through the pages, thinking of Demetrius. He quoted Donne to me the other night, out there under the moon. *My face in thine eye, thine in mine appears,* he said. My eye lights on an odd title, "Love's Diet." Donne dares compare love to anything, I think, smiling as I read the opening lines, thinking of the pounds that have melted off me lately, wondering if Phoebe is somewhere in the room with me, directing my eyes to this particular page:

> *To what a cumbersome unwieldiness*
> *And burdenous corpulence my love had grown,*
> *But that I did, to make it less,*

And keep it in proportion,
Give it a diet, made it feed upon
That which love worst endures, discretion.

Discretion. What I've been lacking today, certainly. What I've been trying to acquire all my life, to please the people I love, or thought I loved: my mother, Gregory. How much alike they are, it dawns on me for the first time, at least in the way I've always felt around the both of them, as if I might commit some unforgivable gaffe any minute. The way they both are so visibly uncomfortable around Dorothea. Our daughter, our beautiful firstborn, repository of our hopes and dreams, what is she to Gregory now? He went off this morning without so much as looking in on her. Dorrie, my love, the embodiment of a terrible medical faux pas, indiscreet with her sagging face, her spastic flailings, her humming and drooling, her desperate cries. And we must live, every day, with her to remind us, so indiscreetly, that our lives are not under our control. No wonder even our close friends turn away. How strange that both our families, Gregory's and mine, different as they are, taught us the same lesson: Control what you can; avoid the messy, the damaged; avert your eyes and will them away; keep danger at bay with responsibilities well and carefully met, with punctuality, beautiful manners, immaculate grooming, perfectly folded shirts. As I drift off to sleep, I think of Phoebe again. She grew up on Beacon Hill, came from that world as well, and threw it over for this out-of-the-way place and an alcoholic dreamer of a husband, the privilege of balancing barefoot on a rock, eyes sweeping across the harbor, up there by herself in the wind.

The Bog House

It is easy to destroy a salt marsh.

WE ARE LYING together on the cot in the bog house after making love. Demetrius is dozing in my arms but I am wide awake, happy, perfectly relaxed, the electricity diminishing but still there, still flowing as I study his face, the shape of his skull growing familiar under my hands, the faint bulge of his forehead, the neat arched edge of the socket under his brow. His head is narrower than Gregory's, more neatly made, the skin smoother, darker, narrow brows lying close as I smooth them with my fingers. How greedy my hands are, hungry to know this face, each bump and line and mole.

Some corner of my mind, the rational part not quite edged out by my huge bodily happiness, is amused at the scene. How like teenage lovers we are, sneaking away to this shack, holing up with the spiders. The dark rafters above us are covered with their webs. One could lower herself down on us at any moment. What if someone came, the local police or real teenage lovers, or Lesley even, looking everywhere for me because something has happened to her sister, finding us, a sweaty middle-aged man and woman, naked and spent, having thrown off the thin quilt in the heat of our lovemaking? It doesn't bear thinking about—it's too terrible and funny.

Demetrius stirs; I shift his heaviness off me; we are pressed together by the sagging springs of the cot. "Turn," he says thickly, and fits himself behind me, wrapping his arm around me, pressing me back against himself. "We fit together very well," he says to the back of my head. "I love your hair. It flies everywhere. Not under control like the rest of you."

"You think the rest of me is under control?"

He chuckles into my hair. "Not now I don't." And he shifts again, turning my body back toward his, raising himself above me and smiling the smug eternal smile of the conquering male, which somehow doesn't annoy me but pleases.

"You like that, don't you? Having me under your control."

"Yes," he says, freeing an arm and brushing the hair away from my eyes. "Now turn and I'll rub your back."

"Tell me about your wife. How long ago did she die?" It no longer bothers me to think about Marte, or ask about her.

"Three years ago. She'd been sick for years. She was diabetic—went to her kidneys. And she'd had arthritis a long time, since her twenties."

"Do you have children?"

Demetrius stops rubbing my shoulder and is still for a moment. "No children. The arthritis came on right after we got married, and they had her on a lot of medicine. They warned her not to get pregnant, with the side effects, and the diabetes—she just couldn't risk it."

"I'm sorry. You have a way with children, with my girls anyway. And you're so good with Dorothea. I guess you've had a lot of practice taking care of your wife."

"I helped her get around, yes. But she wasn't helpless. She suffered a lot, but she made room for it. She used to say the pain was like a selfish houseguest, someone you didn't like but had to make room for. She loved to read and would read aloud to me in the evenings."

"Like your mother."

"Yes. I loved that. And she worked with flowers, dried flowers. She had a shop in Dennis, making bouquets and wreaths and things. They had a catalogue and sent her things all over the country. She had a gift for it."

"She could do that with arthritis?" I ask, remembering a long-ago attempt at arranging dried flowers, the way the brittle stems would break off, the petals shatter when I touched them. That basket of faded flowers Demetrius keeps on his table in memory of her. He must have loved her, in spite of everything.

"She started it as therapy, to keep her joints from stiffening. And loved it, and just kept going."

"It sounds as though you loved her."

"I did. I hated her sometimes, but also I loved her."

"Hated her?"

"Of course. She was an invalid most of our married life. We couldn't really be married a lot of those years, if you know what I mean, much less have children. I would get into rages sometimes. Sometimes I'd go out on the bog at night and just rage at the sky. If it was winter and the stars were out, I'd rage at Orion. I wanted to fight, for him to come down out of the sky and pull his dagger. I had so much anger in me I could have beaten him, I was convinced." Demetrius shifts a little and begins rubbing my other shoulder. "Do I sound like a crazy person?"

"Life makes us all crazy sometimes."

"What do you do when you get angry about Dorothea?"

"Oh, I don't get angry. I did at first, I guess. But I spent a year in therapy. I've made peace with it."

"You can't have."

"No, it's true. It's a long time since I've felt really angry about anything."

"Then it's worse than I thought."

"Are you saying you want me to get angry? Why? Why now, when I've worked so hard to make peace?"

"Because the anger is there; I can feel it in your house. It's real. Maybe you don't give yourself permission to get angry. But you've given it away, to Lesley. Lesley has your anger, and I'm not sure she knows what to do with it."

I sit up, moving away from Demetrius's hands, which he has been running smoothly down my back in long, soothing strokes. I'm anxious and confused. How did we get from my innocent question about Marte to Lesley? Lesley, whom I keep trying not to think about these days, this stranger in my house who looks so different, feels so—so angry. Who's regressed, after a few short weeks of cheerfulness, to the sullen child she was back in May. The tension between Greg and me—she feels it. And feels hurt by Daphne's preoccupation with Paul. I've hardly given Lesley a thought, barely know or care where she is half the time, especially these past two weeks. But Jeannine is here now. I'm freed up to spend time with her. I'll plan an outing with just her, go clothes shopping for school, maybe, with dinner and a movie after.

"I've got to get home. It's late," I say to Demetrius. It's been a lovely afternoon, but now my mind is elsewhere. The mood is broken. My family needs me.

It is five o'clock by the time I get back to the house. I brace myself, rehearse the story I've made up for Jeannine. But there's no need; it would never occur to her to ask why I'm late. She, Lesley, and Dorothea are in the parlor, watching a snowy rerun of *M*A*S*H* on television.

JEANNINE ARRIVED ON Tuesday afternoon. She will stay until the beginning of Labor Day weekend, have a few days at home, and then move back into the Needham house with us the following week after classes start. I'm confused by my feelings at having her here. I'm free to come and go much more than I've been able to all summer, and it's a relief to have someone else to talk to besides Lesley, who's retreated to monosyllables. But her arrival marks the beginning of the end of our time here. Up to now I have not let myself imagine leaving this place, going back to my old life, perhaps not ever living here again. What if I threw everything over to stay here, told Gregory I was not coming home? Could we make a life here, the girls and I? Would Demetrius be a part of it? Could we live together, here in Phoebe's house, would he want that? Would Lesley adjust? And what sorts of obstacles would Gregory, clever lawyer that he is, throw in my way if I told him that's what I wanted? Is that what I want? Could I really change my life?

Those questions were swirling in my head on Tuesday afternoon as Jeannine's blue Honda turned into the driveway. I tamped down a little sense of invasion as I watched her step out of the car, hesitate a moment, and run for the steps when she saw me waving from the porch. She looked different, a little older, more sure of herself. She had a new haircut, shorter, flattering, her thin hair fluffed in soft bangs that hid her high forehead. "Hi Mrs.—Anna!" she cried excitedly, then turned to Dorrie, who regarded her curiously. She didn't remember her, but if Jeannine was disappointed she hid it well. "Hey Dor, how you doing?" she asked. "You been swimming? Will you show me the beach?" Dorrie smiled her halfsmile doubtfully, then reached out and patted Jeannine on the arm and began to hum. Perhaps she did remember her after all.

I led Jeannine upstairs to her room, Phoebe's room, thinking with some regret that I was losing my retreat. I've taken to sleeping in there, even though the bed is narrow and the mattress sags. I've cleared off the top of Phoebe's desk for Jeannine and packed the books and papers into two cardboard cartons, which I've set temporarily on the attic stairs. The journal notebooks I've piled in the master bedroom on the far side of the bed. I'll have to move them again before Gregory comes back for Labor Day.

We spent the rest of the afternoon touring the yard and neighborhood, Jeannine jauntily pushing Dorrie up the lane, pausing to gasp when we got to the top of the rise and she saw the view of the harbor. We descended to the beach, where Jeannine doffed her sneakers, rolled up her jeans, and ran to the water like a child. "It's freezing!" she called back to me happily. I could tell she was going to like it here. I explained about the tides, the currents, the way the sand bars appear and disappear, the reason why the old lighthouse is so far away from the point, conscious all the while that I was repeating what Phoebe told me that long-ago day I came here for the first time. I told her about Demetrius naming the wheelchair Pegasus, my lover's name awkward and delicious in my mouth. On the way back to the house I pointed out the glacial erratic, but I did not show her how to climb it. It's Phoebe's rock, Phoebe's and now mine.

That evening I grilled salmon for dinner and served it with corn from the farm stand and tomatoes from the garden. Jeannine took over the chore of feeding Dorrie and drew Lesley out with questions about what she's been doing all summer, questions I never dare ask. Lesley ran upstairs while Jeannine and I cleared the plates, reappearing in a moment with her sketchbook. It was the first time in a long time I'd seen her drawings. She's working in pen and ink now, mostly botanical sketches, a few of Daphne's cats and the row of houses on Sandy Neck. One of the big rock I'd love to frame and hang in Phoebe's room. "Hey, girl, you're a pro," Jeannine said, putting my thoughts into words. Saying what I never take the time to say.

MY LIFE LIGHTENS miraculously as Jeannine, helpful and easygoing as always, immediately fits into the daily routine. I'm grateful to let her take over Dorrie's morning workout, using the extra time to get caught up with the garden and tackle some long-neglected chores like cleaning the refrigerator. Every second or third day I manufacture an errand in town, a visit with a friend, and spin jubilantly down Kettle Lane to West Marsh or the house in Yarmouth Port for an hour, maybe two, of lovemaking (always first, will we ever outgrow our eager need to touch each other?), a quick meal, another installment of intimate talk, the sweet quiet moments in each other's arms before we have to go our separate ways.

My imagined special time with Lesley doesn't materialize. I can't interest her in shopping for school clothes. It's obvious she's trying to fend off every thought about summer ending. On Friday she does agree to go off to the mall with Jeannine and Dorrie, much to my surprise. As I help load Pegasus into the van I notice the green MG is not in Daphne's driveway. It's been ages since we've talked. It's time to tell her about Demetrius. The moment the van drives off I head across the lane. Three o'clock, almost the end of her writing time. Perhaps she won't turn me away.

"Ah, it's you," she says, arriving at her screen door flanked by cats, as usual. "Long time no see. I'm sorry I've been so taken up."

"I've been taken up too. That's what I want to talk to you about."

"I see you have company—Jeannie, did you say her name was?"

"Jeannine. An angel on wheels." I collapse into Daphne's wing chair, vacated for the moment by Hephaestus. "I'd forgotten how much work she saves me. I want you to come for supper and meet her, when you can—maybe this weekend? Greg's not coming down."

"Monday might be better. Paul's here this weekend, and the opening's coming up a week from Wednesday. He's pretty high maintenance right now, what with the last-minute glitches and jitters."

"Monday then." I pause, look at Daphne appraisingly. I want and don't want to say what I came to say. I decide to buy a little more time. "You know, I've been reading Phoebe's journals again, and I've come to that place where they just break off. Six and a half years, it is. Do you think she just stopped writing?"

Daphne turns her desk chair away from me for a moment, looks out through her slider toward the pond. "I wondered about that; she was so faithful otherwise, never missed more than a couple of weeks. She puts me to shame, and I'm supposed to be the professional writer."

"Do you think she lost some of the notebooks?"

"Burned them, maybe."

"Why would she do that? There's nothing very incriminating in any of them, that I can see."

"Aren't we all criminals one way or the other?" Daphne is smiling cryptically at me. I feel my face go hot. Does she know, suspect what I've been up to? Or is it just my guilt, the way I got defensive when Greg asked me the other afternoon where I'd been.

"Do you know something about Phoebe—some reason she might burn her journals? Did she tell you why?"

"No, we never talked about them other than her telling me she wanted me to read them. She never showed them to me while she was alive. Maybe the missing ones are hidden somewhere, under the mattress or behind some books or somewhere. Where did you hide your diary when you were a teenager?"

"I never dared keep one. My mother would have found it, wherever it was." I take a breath and then commit myself. "Speaking of hiding things, there's something I want to talk to you about. Could I trouble you for a glass of wine?"

Daphne gives me another one of her unreadable looks and gets up and heads for the kitchen. "Should I have a glass as well? Is this going to get unpleasant? I think I know what you're going to say, and if it's any comfort to you I've been feeling awful about it."

"What?" Now I'm genuinely confused. Daphne is back in a flash with a half-full bottle of Merlot and two glasses.

"I know I hurt Lesley's feelings, that day I went off sailing and forgot about her. And I suppose she told you about walking in on Paul and me that day. And then I went and ratted on her by mentioning that boy she's always with." She's pouring me a generous glass of wine, nearly up to the rim, but I don't tell her to stop.

"No, it's not about Lesley. She was upset about the sailing, you're right, but she blames Paul more than you. He's not her favorite person right now. As for that boy—Phil—I'm awfully glad you told me. I need to know when she's out in a boat. I think she was embarrassed to tell me because he's a boy. But they're just buddies. It's good for her to have a friend her own age. She's only twelve." I take a big gulp of wine, waiting for an opening to change the subject.

"Only twelve? When I was only twelve, I was French kissing under the bushes after school in Central Park."

"But you were one of those depraved city kids. Lesley's from a leafy suburb, remember. Things move slower there."

"Yeah, right," Daphne says with a snicker. "The garden of Eden."

There's my opening. I take another slug of the wine. "Speaking of sin—"

"Were we?"

"Well, I was. I mean I want to." I'm stammering around, trying to figure how to get the words out, and then I just do. "I'm having an affair."

"*Et tu, Brute?* Who the hell with?"

"You can't guess? It's Demetrius."

Daphne's look changes from amused interest to something darker and more confused, but her voice remains as light and bantering as before. "An older man, huh? Or is it the Lady Chatterly syndrome?"

"Don't make fun. This is serious. I really love him; he's wonderful. You can't imagine how wonderful he's been with Dorrie, all along, and he's not just some nature boy, some hunk with muscles."

"Hardly a boy of any sort."

"I know. I've never been attracted to someone that much older before. It's as if we've known each other forever, as if time were irrelevant."

"Soulmates. You're talking in clichés, you know."

"All right, soulmates. And you were the one who said clichés get to be clichés because they are true. He's real. He's complicated, not at all what you might think. He knows poetry."

"He quotes John Donne."

"How did you know that?" I try to read Daphne's face, but she's looking back out at the pond. A terrible realization is slowly dawning in my mind. My half-sensed feeling that something about Demetrius bothered Daphne—could it be? By now I've had enough wine to ask her outright. "Did you and Demetrius—?"

Daphne takes a swallow of wine, sighs, turns back again to me. "No, Anna. Not me. Can't you guess?"

"No, Daphne, I can't guess. Tell me, for God's sake. Is he involved with someone else?"

"Not anymore. She's gone. Go home, Anna. Look again. Read the journals."

D and *D*. *My two D's,* she wrote that day she went to West Marsh. "Phoebe?"

"Phoebe."

I'm not sure what I say to Daphne after that, or how I get back to the house or what silent words of gratitude I offer up because the girls are still out at the mall or what excuse I write on the note I leave on the kitchen table. Thank God Jeannine has left the keys to her car in case I need to go out while she's off with the van. I back out of the driveway, struggling with the Honda's manual transmission and grinding the gears, driving too fast down the lane and along the twisty stretches of 6A toward West Marsh. Demetrius is still there, out on the far bog. When he sees the strange car drive up, he heads in. I don't stop to call or wave, but march toward the bog house. The door is closed and padlocked, and I didn't think to bring the key Demetrius gave me. I stand there by the door angry and shivering as he heads my way, my back turned to him, locked out. Then I'm crying. This is the last place I should have come. I've got to get away. I turn and run back to the car. Demetrius is still halfway across the bog, walking in his deliberate way; I'm not sure he has recognized me and I pray he has not. It takes me three tries to get the engine to turn over, what feels like forever to jam the gear shift into reverse. I'm halfway back to the road when I hear his voice, puzzled and unsure, calling my name.

Storm Warnings

... inhabitants know well the power of gale winds and surf, and the long-term, inexorable march forward of the ocean.

THE GIRLS ARE still not back when I return from West Marsh, thank God. I've got to figure out a way to get control of myself. I drop Jeannine's keys on the kitchen table and walk straight through the house and out the parlor door, trying not to think about the ramp, head up the hill and stop, looking out across the harbor. Phoebe's rock looms above me, but I have no impulse to climb up. Phoebe's rock, not mine. Phoebe's house, Phoebe's life. Phoebe's man, it turns out. This sister, mentor, wise-seeming woman I have so wanted to be. The warm accepting mother I never had. And all the while I never knew, never suspected. My anger at her makes me catch my breath. The strangeness of it—the age difference. He so much younger—when did it start? Who gave the first signal? How long did it go on? How could he? Is he an opportunist, taking advantage of a lonely old woman so he could get—what? West Marsh? The house? And now going after me, has it all been calculated? I sit huddled miserably in the late afternoon sun, my back against the rock, grateful for its warmth as a chill settles in the air. Has everything Demetrius has done been part of some plan—did he persuade Phoebe to lend him the money for West Marsh and then forgive the debt? Has he been planning his conquest all along, from that first morning when he propped the newspaper so cleverly against the back door where I couldn't miss it? His attentions to Dorothea. Pegasus. The ramp. And Daphne, why couldn't she have said something before it was too late? But that isn't fair. She didn't know. I kept it from her until today.

I hear the crunch of tires on gravel. The girls are home. I need to go down and greet them, do something about dinner, but the thought exhausts me. By the time I am back through the parlor door, Lesley has arrived in the kitchen and Jeannine is headed around the house with Dorrie's wheelchair. I can't face them, not tonight. I avoid the kitchen and Lesley, linger in the hall until Jeannine comes in, framing my story, more lies. A terrible headache, sick to my stomach. Can she manage dinner? Nothing for me, thanks anyway. I just want to go to bed.

Amazingly I fall deep asleep, but by two in the morning I'm wide awake, prowling downstairs for aspirin and something to eat. The big glass of wine on an empty stomach has left me with a real headache. I'm at the kitchen table surreptitiously spooning Cheerios into my mouth when Jeannine appears. "You okay?" she asks sympathetically.

"Much better, thanks. I shouldn't have gone to bed so early, though—I feel slept out. How was the mall?"

"It was okay. I got Lesley some butterfly clips for her hair—hope that was all right."

"Sure. It's the first time she's been over there all summer. Did Dorrie like it?" I feel guilty I haven't taken her anywhere except the supermarket.

"Yeah, she did. Lesley got upset, though. There were some kids that ragged on us."

"Oh, no. She can't handle that."

"She swore at them, but then she calmed down."

"We haven't run into that for a while."

"It always throws me. If they're little kids it's easy—they're mainly just curious. If you answer their questions, they're usually all right. But the older ones—eleven, twelve, thirteen—it's tough then. But then they're tough on each other at that age, aren't they? Oh, did you hear the weather report? There's a hurricane down near the Bahamas that might come up this way."

"It's that time of year. The weather people always dramatize them. They mostly all go out to sea."

"You sure? I talked to my Mom tonight, and she's freaked out about it."

"Not to worry. If it really comes this way we'll send you home if you want."

"Want me to make you some tea? Might settle your stomach."

That's right: I'm supposed to have an upset stomach. Jeannine must wonder what I'm doing eating cereal. I feel exhausted again, beg off, and head back upstairs to spend the rest of the night tossing in my bed, rearranging pillows, staring at the ceiling. Tomorrow, the next day, I'll have to have an encounter with Demetrius. What to say, what to ask. I don't know. I don't want to see him and feel the familiar pull, or worse, discover it's dissolved away.

Two days go by and there is no word from Demetrius. Maybe he really didn't know it was me at the bog house, but by now he must be wondering why I haven't appeared or at least called. It's the weekend—maybe he thinks Greg is down. By Saturday night I can't stand it anymore. I decide I ought to return the key to the bog house. That would put a sense of closure on things. I could just say I've realized it was a mistake, that I hoped he could understand. I'll go Monday and just tell him and hand back the key and that will be it.

Late Sunday afternoon Daphne shows up at the porch door. By the time I get downstairs she and Jeannine are chatting away in the kitchen like old friends, and I remember ruefully I had invited her to dinner Monday. It's the last thing I want to do. But she seems to read my mind because she's begging off tomorrow night, something about a press reception at the theater with Paul. Then she asks me if I want to walk out on the flats with her. It's an offering of sorts that I can't refuse. Besides, I've hardly been downstairs for two days; the air will clear my head.

"You okay?" she asks as we head down the lane toward the beach. She's walking so fast I'm having trouble keeping up with her.

"Not really. I was really mad at you. I felt betrayed, and then I realized you didn't know anything about us."

"I had a couple of inklings. But I think of you as such a straight arrow—I admit I was surprised." We've reached the beach and are crossing the soft sand and heading down to the damp strip below the high tide line. Daphne turns right, along the beach toward the creek where Demetrius parked that first night he met me up on the hill by the rock. Am I ever and always going to relate everything to Demetrius?

"I'm sorry. I'm just kind of overthrown—overwhelmed. I don't know how I feel about anything."

"You know, Anna, it all happened a very long time ago."

"How long ago?"

"Oh, way back in the fifties. And it didn't last very long—a few years at most."

"The fifties? He was just a kid then."

"Old enough, evidently."

"But they spent so much time together, all those years, right to the end. They just stopped it and kept on working together and being friends?"

"They did. They stayed friends. That's kind of a miracle, I think. I've never been able to pull it off with any of my lovers."

"You sound as if you've had quite a collection."

"Not that many, but an eclectic collection for sure. Picking men is not my strong suit."

"What about Paul?"

"Well, he's temporary. We both know things won't last once he's back in New York. And sometimes I think that might not be all bad."

"You getting tired of him?"

"Not by a long shot. But guilty about all the work I'm not doing. Am I walking too fast?" She slows a bit to let me catch up. By now I'm audibly puffing. "Far enough. Let's turn around and go back." We walk back more slowly, for which I'm grateful. Grateful too, for Daphne, for what she has come to tell me. My thoughts, my feelings these past two days. I've been feeling betrayed by everybody. Maybe Demetrius isn't a con artist. Maybe he was going to tell me, sometime soon, about Phoebe. I don't feel he's been deceiving me, not now. Strange, it's Phoebe I feel deceived by, as if she's the one who should have let me know.

After supper Jeannine and Lesley turn on the evening news for the latest report about the hurricane. It's skirted the Bahamas and is headed north northwest. People in low-lying areas of Georgia and the Carolinas are being encouraged to evacuate. Category Four, a big one. Bob, its name is, an innocuous name, hardly conjuring up destruction and danger. Women's names were better. Hurricane Daphne has a better ring. I laugh out loud, thinking about the emotional storm she's stirred up in me these past few days. The old black and white TV is incredibly snowy. It might be a blizzard we are looking at instead of an intriguing white swirl of cloud with its single ominous eye.

I spend another nearly sleepless night, but by morning my mind feels clearer. I must make an effort to think rationally. I need to get myself back on track, reassume my share of the daily burden of care I've foisted off on Jeannine, give Lesley some time and attention. I need to take a breather, extricate myself from this headlong affair with Demetrius, think about what I'm going to do. Who am I kidding? What was it Daphne said, so coolly, about Paul? "He's temporary." Could I ever say that? Still, in just two weeks it will be time to move back to Needham, and life will resume the way it's always been. Won't it? Could I build a different life? Impossible to do without an act of demolition. How much destruction am I willing to set in motion? I need time to think. Time away from Demetrius, until I can decide what to do. I will return the key, the way I planned. Explain that I'm confused. It's true; I am. He'll understand. Won't he?

I'm up early on Monday morning, before Jeannine stirs, drinking coffee and mixing pancake batter for breakfast. I dig my key chain out of my purse and am just unclipping the stubby padlock key to the bog house when Jeannine appears. We share a quiet half hour of pancakes and coffee before Dorrie wakes, demanding her share of the morning. Jeannine tells me about her summer program. She's excited about it, that's clear; her voice is animated. She's been working with very young infants, diagnosing muscle weakness and developing rehab programs for them. A new emphasis on early intervention. Her voice becomes progressively louder and more confident as she talks about it; she thinks she has found her speciality. My heart sinks, unaccountably. Did I think she was going to devote the rest of her life to Dorothea? A few more months and we'll be looking for her replacement. Back where we started.

But for now she is here. This morning we tackle Dorrie together, which delights her, working two sides at once to the beat of a local rock station on the radio. It's fun, I have to admit, working as a team. I remember those first months when so many of my friends and neighbors came to the house in shifts, following a schedule I wasn't allowed to worry about, the physical drudgery lightened by banter and neighborhood gossip. I'd forgotten in the intervening years, forgotten all that generosity, that gallantry, so many friends, neighbors, even friends of friends I barely knew, giving their time, distracting me from the horror I was trying not to face. But one by one the helpers fell away. Pitching in during a crisis is one thing. But what to do when the crisis goes on and on, becomes a permanent condition?

Lesley is up, finally, heating up the leftover pancakes in the toaster oven when I pass through the kitchen on the way out to the van. She's reverted to sleeping late, but I'm too intent on where I'm going to comment on it. I drive over to West Marsh without really dwelling on what I might say. It's a letdown to see Demetrius's truck is not there. He could be home, working somewhere else, running errands in Hyannis—he could be anywhere. But just as I'm about to drive by without turning in I see his blue truck heading towards me from the opposite direction. I wait by the entrance to the track up to the bog house, then follow him in.

"That was you, the other afternoon, wasn't it?" he says, coming around to my side of the car and waiting for me to step out. I'm rooting around in my purse, looking for the key to the bog house, which doesn't seem to be anywhere in the cluttered detritus that has accumulated on its bottom. Finally I give up, realizing I've lost the reason for coming over here.

"It was. You're right. But I remembered something and had to leave. No, that's not true. I didn't know what I was going to say, so I left. I was very upset." I'm standing by the car by now, making no move toward the bog house. If I go inside, I'll lose my resolve.

"Upset at me?"

"Upset at something I learned about you, yes. I was talking with Daphne."

"I see."

"You can guess what she said?" We are standing as if rooted, five feet apart, looking searchingly at each other. We're always circumspect when we are out in plain view, but there's something different in our postures now, both of us, a wariness.

"Are you going to tell me?" Demetrius asks. He's being cagy. He doesn't want to tell me what I don't already know.

I'm not in the mood for tactics, and I've never been any good at them anyway—being married to a lawyer has taught me that. "Yes, I'll tell you. She said you and Phoebe had an affair. She didn't just blurt it out. I thought—I thought for a minute maybe it was you and she, and . . ."

At this Demetrius bursts out laughing. "Come, Anna—can you really imagine Daphne would go for me?"

"And why not?" Now I'm laughing too, at my quick leap to his defense.

"You're angry about Phoebe? Anna, it's all ancient history, many years ago."

"I know; Daphne told me. It was just not knowing about it. I thought I knew so much about you, and about Phoebe. She's been like my friend, there at the house, as if she's there with me. And then to find this huge fact, this whole other dimension—it threw me. I've been beside myself."

"You're jealous."

"I guess you're right. It doesn't make any sense, but I am." What I'm thinking, but don't say, is that I don't know which one I'm jealous of. "Why couldn't you tell me?" I ask, searching his face, which seems closed to me, shuttered, like Gregory's face.

"I thought about it. But it wasn't just my secret, and Phoebe's gone. What would you have thought of her if you knew?"

He's right. My anger up there on the hill, what I'm feeling now, it's not just jealousy. Phoebe and Demetrius—it seems—unseemly. The age difference, the gulf between their backgrounds. How I hate myself right now, the snobbery behind what I feel, what my mother, Gregory, what everyone I know would feel, if they could see me now.

I have not answered Demetrius's question. "Will you come inside?" he asks.

"I don't think that's a good idea, not today. In fact, I came over here to give you the key back. I need some time to get my feet under me and figure out what I'm feeling. But now I can't find the key. I think I left it at home, on the kitchen table."

"Well that's something. Come inside for a moment, anyway." And so I do, and he holds me silently and gently for a long minute and then lets go. Part of me is sorry, but I turn and walk back out to the car like a good girl. I'm not angry anymore, not relieved, not anything but numb. He doesn't follow me outside but waits in the doorway, watching me as I climb back into the van. "I'll wait to hear from you," he calls after me.

"I'll call you," I say.

"Soon?"

I don't answer.

That night I lie awake for a long time going over it all again in my mind. Demetrius and Phoebe. It hurts to say the two names together. It's not sexual jealousy as I first thought, but the pain of realizing that someone I thought I knew and understood is a stranger, or at least has a dimension I knew nothing about. That's a betrayal we don't talk much about, though it destroys friendships more often than we'd like to admit. No anger like that of a friend kept in the dark. How could they—two people I love—keep this enormous secret from me? As if Phoebe could have sent me messages from the grave. As if Demetrius should be faulted for never mentioning a long-ago affair. Maybe what I really mean is how could I have known them and never guessed?

By Wednesday the hurricane is taking up most of the local news. The storm has skirted the outer banks, headed briefly out to sea, hesitated, and then set itself on a course that puts us in harm's way. I decide to suggest to Jeannine that she go home for a few days. Her mother has called twice, obviously anxious. She can come back Sunday night or Monday, all being well, and still have her last week of vacation. We take a last trek to the supermarket for supplies and I'm amused by the families waiting in line with carts loaded with food, gallons of fresh milk, cartons of ice cream even, when the biggest problem most of us will have is surviving several days without a refrigerator if the power goes out. We buy bread, onions, carrots, cans of tuna and soup, batteries for Lesley's Walkman, the last box of candles on the shelf, charcoal for cooking out on the grill. I send Jeannine off by two o'clock so she'll miss the rush hour traffic around Boston.

I have not heard from Gregory. If he's in the middle of a case, he might not even know a storm is coming. I have no impulse to leave. The worst that can happen is that we'll have to live without power for a few days. We might have to cook outdoors, heat kettles of water on the gas stove for washing, get along with candlelight in the evenings. Lesley's reaction, when I ask her if she wants to stay, is "Cool." She wouldn't miss it. I feel the same way.

I cook an early supper, inventing a casserole from the leftover chicken and rice, fresh green peppers and tomatoes, making some tapioca pudding to use up the milk and eggs which are likely to spoil if we lose power. At sunset I walk up the hill and climb up on the erratic to look at the harbor. Most of the boats usually strung along the beach have disappeared, though the *Little Gull* is still riding boldly on its mooring. The air feels heavy, fraught with something palpable, the water like silvered glass, eerily still.

The Northeast Quadrant

Hurricane winds whirl in a counterclockwise vortex.
When the storm itself strikes the land, . . . these winds . . .
play havoc with everything exposed upon it.

THE BIRDS KNOW the storm is coming. I wake at five thirty to a perfect
stillness, a suggestion of dawn showing where the clouds are thinnest
in an otherwise gray sky. No wind at all. But flocks of sparrows are wheeling in and settling in the three big cedars between the porch and the road.
I throw on shorts and a shirt and let myself out through the parlor door,
cut across the yard to the big rock, and step out of my sandals because the
climb is easier in bare feet. By now I know where all the handholds are.
The bay is dead still, the clouds hanging low over it. The air is heavy and
damp. It seems hard to breathe, even up here where there is nearly always
a breeze.

Then I see a figure in the water, wading out in a bathing suit. It's
Daphne, going out to the *Little Gull*. She wades out to shoulder height,
her arms held high over her head, something in one hand, then begins to
swim, a one-armed crawl. She's going to bring in the boat. She's gauged
her angle to take account of the current, at its strongest now at half-tide.
She half-swims, half-floats, swiftly meeting the bow of the boat, where
she hauls herself partway up to release the mooring and fasten her tow
line. In a moment she's swimming sidestroke, pulling the boat, heading
doggedly for the beach with the boat bobbing lightly behind her, ignoring
the current that is sweeping her sideways.

How can she dare swim out like that, alone at daybreak? She might
need help with the boat. I scramble down from the rock and hunt for
my sandals in the long damp grass. By the time I get to the beach she
has walked the boat back to the path through the marsh grass and has
brought it as far up on shore as it will go.

The no-see-ums are fierce, honing in on my ears and scalp. They must
be worse for Daphne, with so much exposed wet flesh. "Need help?" I call
out, not wanting to startle her.

"Oh, Anna, it's you. No thanks. I'm going to pull the boat up on the beach at high tide—you might come down and help me then. I wanted to get it in and off the mooring before the wind starts. You can help me with these sail ties, if you want. I'm going to take the sail off and haul up all the loose equipment."

We struggle with the knots in the sail ties; undo the stubborn little cords holding the sail to the wooden rings encircling the mast; unsnap the worn canvas boat cover; and fish the rudder and tiller, the paddle, and a bucket full of extra ropes and sponges out from under the deck.

"How did you learn so much about boats?" I ask, remembering that Daphne grew up in Manhattan.

"I spent a lot of time over at the boatyard asking questions. Jim Pauley—he hauls the boat in and stores it in the winter for me—he loves to talk about boats and sailing. No one sails right except for him, he's convinced. I saw him at the post office one time, and he said, 'Glad I ran into you. You need to tighten up that outhaul before you hoist the sail next time.'"

We're standing on either side of the *Little Gull*, stretching the boat cover between us and trying to force the brass rings around the edge over their fasteners, one by one. It's a tight fit.

"How'd you learn to sail?" I ask.

"By the seat of my pants. I'd been once or twice, years ago, and I bought a book and read it cover to cover. I was nervous—I bought the boat and didn't go out in it for nearly a month. Finally one day I just decided to do it. It took me forever to get the sail up. I was halfway across the harbor, sideslipping like mad, before I remembered to put the centerboard down."

"You didn't even take someone else with you?"

"No, I was too embarrassed to let anyone see how incompetent I was. I'd been out a couple of times with a friend who sails. But you don't learn to sail from a book, or from watching somebody else. It's physical learning, like learning how to drive. Each boat has its own way of going, its own feel."

Daphne has finished stuffing the sail into a blue nylon bag; she straightens up and pulls the drawstrings snug. I help her carry the equipment up the path to a wheelbarrow she has left at the edge of the sand. How matter-of-fact she is, I think. Does anything frighten her, this hurricane, for instance? How comforting it would be to have her in the house with me during the storm, but I hesitate to ask her. I felt confident, excited even, when I sent Jeannine home, but now I'm losing my nerve. Gregory hasn't called. He's probably back in Washington, where the storm won't be dominating the airwaves the way it is here. Most likely he hasn't even heard about it. It's just as well—he'd only have insisted we drive back to Needham. Too late now. Despite my anxiety I'm not sorry.

Demetrius is here, of course, but given the way we left things he might not come by. No, that's not right. He'll show up if he thinks we need help. Will he ride out the storm at home, all exposed over there on the marshes with nothing to break the wind? Will our boathouse—I smile ruefully, thinking about the word *our*—will a storm surge float it away or break it up into a pile of sticks? Or the cottage, even? I can't call him, much as I'd like him here with us. Besides, he's probably at West Marsh, safe from the waves and blown-down trees. I pray that's where he is.

I agree to come back to the beach to help Daphne pull the boat up at high tide, around ten-fifteen. By ten o'clock a breeze has risen, not much, but enough to make me want to look at the harbor again. A few drops of warm rain have begun to fall, and the leaves of the locusts make a rustling sound, showing their silvery undersides. When I reach the crest of the hill I see the water is beginning to break into whitecaps. It could be an ordinary breezy day, except for the long gray ropes of cloud that are moving swiftly across the harbor from the east.

Daphne is already there, sitting on the deck of the boat looking out at the water. "Are you ready for the storm?" she asks me.

"I think so. We've got candles and our little radio. I haven't taped anything up. On the news they always show people taping windows."

"That's to keep the glass from flying around if the window shatters. It might help to do it on the windward side. They think it will come in around Providence or New Bedford, so that means a southeast wind for us, at least through the worst of it."

"Oh, I just assumed it would come off the water. Southeast—that's the porch side. And there are a couple of big trees on that side of the house. But I don't think I have any tape."

"Don't worry about it. Just stay on the leeward side and away from the windows."

"You sound like such an old salt. Ever been in one of these before?"

"I was here for Gloria, staying in a motel in Hyannis. It was when I was house hunting. It wasn't bad except for not having electricity for two days."

"You want to ride this one out at my house?"

"Thank you, but I've got a lot to keep track of at home. The cats, for one thing. I don't know how they'll react. Are you frightened?"

"No, actually. I'm rather excited, really. Tornadoes always terrify me—I've been through plenty of tornado warnings, living in Ohio. But this doesn't feel life-threatening, just immense and inevitable."

Daphne smiles. "Yes. I feel sort of the way I did the day I woke up and found myself in labor. Anyway, I'm right down the street if you need me."

When I get back to the house, there is a red truck in the driveway with a flashing yellow light on its top. A tall, dark-haired young man in a fire hat and a yellow slicker that is too short for him is knocking on the screen door, looking quizzically in at Dorothea, whom I left at the table in the kitchen. He starts when I come up behind him, as if he were expecting something dangerous to happen. How young he looks! Is he here to protect us from the storm? Suddenly my father's words come into my head: "All the cops look like children." Firemen, too. This boy looks too young to ever have lived through a hurricane.

"We're here to carry out an evacuation order, Ma'am," he says. Being called Ma'am makes me feel middle-aged. "We're evacuating this area. You're being asked to proceed to one of two shelters we've got set up, at Barnstable High School or Marston's Mills Elementary. You're in danger of being stranded in here if the road floods back down by the marsh." The speech is so obviously memorized, the young man so ill at ease, that I have to suppress an urge to laugh.

"Surely we're not in danger of being flooded out. We're a long way above the harbor, and the marsh, too."

"No, Ma'am, it's just that we won't be able to get to you. This is a class three hurricane, real dangerous." He is trying very hard to look grave, but his anxiety—a combination of anticipation and fear?—forces him to smile.

I interrupt him by indicating Dorothea, pushed up against the table in her wheelchair. "If you don't mind, I think we'll ride it out here. My two girls are here—I've got a daughter in a wheelchair, you see, and being in a shelter with a lot of other people would be upsetting to her. We have candles, and a portable radio, and I have a neighbor just down the street. It will be less frightening for my daughter if she's on familiar ground, take my word for it."

"Well, Ma'am, it's your decision. But you don't know how these storms can be."

"I'm not afraid we'll be injured. The worst that could happen is that a tree could fall on the house, but we'll stay on the lee side."

"I hope you have a house to stay in," he says, turning uncertainly and making his way down the steps.

I have a moment of uncertainty myself and call after him. "Thank you, we'll be fine. Don't worry. And good luck." It's a ridiculous thing to say, but I'm trying to make up for his sense of failure; he wasn't able to persuade us. His anxiety touches me. He looks for all the world like a young man facing his first battle.

Almost eleven o'clock. I'm listening to the radio, tuned now to the local news. The storm is just south of Providence. Landfall is expected around New Bedford or Fall River sometime after two o'clock. I'm just thinking about going upstairs to wake Lesley when she appears in the kitchen, walking heavily on her heels, her hair a tangle. She sits down at the table and rests her head on her arms as if she's unable to keep herself awake. "What's it like out?" she asks.

"It's just starting to sound like a windstorm. The fire department came around; they want us to evacuate to the high school because the road might go underwater. How do you feel about that?"

"Mom. No way."

"That's what I said. I told them we'd ride it out." Lesley smiles at me from under her hair, a conspiratorial smile I remember from when she was a little girl. It's the first time in a long time I've had the feeling that we agree on something. "Want to walk down to the harbor with me?" I say.

"Okay," she answers, surprising me. She gets up from the table and goes out to the porch, where her windbreaker hangs next to the door. She puts it on over her T-shirt and boxer shorts and sweeps her long hair out of her face with a graceful gesture.

"Want something to eat first?"

"Yuck. No. I'm not awake. What about Dothie? Is she going to be all right?" Dothie. Her childhood name for her sister, a name she hasn't used for a long time. Lesley showing concern for Dorothea? What has happened during the night to turn my daughter back into herself?

"She's fine. I'll put her in the parlor with her tapes."

The locust trees are beginning to toss and moan. No doubt about it now; a storm is coming. We make our way down to the beach, leaning sideways into the wind. The harbor is dotted with whitecaps now, with gusts flinging swift-moving dark patches across the water. The scud is moving faster, still from the east, low and menacing. The *Little Gull* is sitting high up on the marsh grass where we dragged it, its round blue bottom outlined in yellow. How like Daphne to choose that bright glimpse of color, visible only when the boat heels over or when it's sitting aground, like now. I think about her kitchen cabinets, plain pine on the outside and finished a rich antique red inside. What was it she said about them? "It cheers me whenever I open them. Sort of like knowing I have on red underwear."

On the way back to the house Lesley leaves the road and hops over the stone wall into the field at the property line. I know where she's going. "Be careful," I call after her. "Don't stay out too long. I'll worry."

"Mom," she answers, flinging the word to me over her shoulder. By the time I reach the parlor door and turn around, there she is on top of Phoebe's rock, standing straight up with her arms in the air, beseeching, perhaps, or expressing joy, or maybe both.

Dorothea's good eye meets mine when I step inside and her face brightens. She's anxious, humming her nervous hum. Can she feel the storm coming? Or has my mood infected her? Can she feel the barometric pressure lowering, the way I sometimes think I can? I squat down in front of her, smile at her, ruffle her hair. "It's okay," I say. "Just a big storm. Lots of noisy wind, but we'll be fine." She does not return my smile. How much does she understand? Are there words, still, in her mind, locked in so she knows they are there but can't reach them? The thought brings tears to my eyes. She understands more than people think, that I'm sure of. She won't believe my words about the storm because she can read my body. She can feel that I'm anxious. I decide to turn the television on. It will distract her, and I want to hear the news.

All three of the network stations have given themselves over to weather bulletins. The hurricane is eighty miles south southeast of Providence. Authorities have closed the storm gates in Fall River. It's estimated that approximately thirty fishing vessels didn't make it back in time and are stranded on the outside. A printed scroll of safety measures for the storm rolls across the screen: stock up on matches, batteries, a portable radio, ice, candles, drinking water, non-perishable foods. Ice. Why didn't I think about buying a bag of ice? And extra batteries. We have one new set. Lord only knows how much is left in the ones in Lesley's radio—she plays it all the time. It's too late now to go out in the car.

All at once the television picture fades to an intense point of light in the center of the screen. The power has gone out. This is it. The radio we must ration. Dorothea begins her humming again. The sound grates on my nerves. Why does she have to feel frightened? Why can't I explain to her what is happening? How can I calm her, when I'm not calm myself? Tears sting my eyes. I can't get through to her, locked in as she is, can't even guess what goes on in her mind. Once again I feel overwhelmed, asking myself the question I've asked so many times before: Will I ever get used to losing what she once was? Knowing I never will.

Gregory. I think of him off in Washington, unaware of us. It makes me envious, angry too, the way he can get away, leaving all the decisions and drudgery and coping to me. Couldn't he have arranged his life some other way, shared the burden? But he didn't. And here I am, alone. I imagine him arguing back, reminding me in his maddeningly logical way that it was my choice to be here. Ridiculous to send Jeannine home and stay alone with the girls to ride out the storm. And to tell Demetrius to leave me alone. And then my mother's voice chimes in: You've made your bed, now lie in it.

Where is Lesley? I open the parlor door to call up the hill and find her right there on the ramp, flushed and smiling, her hair whipped into tangled strings, her windbreaker blown open and the flimsy nightclothes under it plastered to an unfamiliar woman's body.

"I love this," she is saying. "I went up on Aunt Phoebe's rock. It's really something up there."

"I bet." I don't scold her for being careless. Something keeps me from telling her I saw her, some instinct that she needs to keep that private moment of communion to herself, along with a wish that I could have done that, scrambled up and stood there fronting the storm without holding on. My brave daughter. Like Phoebe.

Noon—and the wind has shifted around to the southeast, though its intensity doesn't seem too different from an hour ago. Lesley has brought her little radio into the parlor and is keeping Dorothea company. I'm worried about the batteries, but the sound of voices is comforting to all of us, even Dorothea. I find myself pacing around the house, entering rooms with some purpose which I forget once I get there. I can't sit still, restless as our old dog back in Ohio, who used to anticipate thunderstorms by panting and pacing. I'm still irrationally irritated at Greg for not calling, for leaving us in the lurch. How like him never to be at hand when I need him.

I'm being ridiculous. It was my decision to stay, and just an hour ago I was feeling grateful Greg hadn't called. We can do this. Phoebe did it, more than once. More than anything I want to be outside, to watch.

By one o'clock the rain is a fine mist blurring the windows. Lesley and I make our way back down to the beach, half blown there by the wind. The storm has begun in earnest. The wind eases somewhat once we start down towards the water with the hill behind us, and the tall banks of rugosa roses on either side of the path afford some shelter. The tide is halfway out. Sandy Neck has disappeared behind a cloud of gray mist and the wind is whipping up trails of spray across the harbor. The Higgins's big sailboat, left on its mooring, is lying over on its side in the shallow water. The *Little Gull* is safe, though, resting smugly on the marsh grass, its tell-tale fluttering wildly in the wind.

By two, the gusts are getting frightening. The incessant whine of the wind grates on my nerves. According to Lesley's little battery radio the eye has come ashore above Buzzard's Bay. That puts us in the most dangerous place, the northeast quadrant. Every few minutes the house shudders, as if someone were pushing against it. Could it shift off its foundation? The storm door on the parlor side keeps blowing open—evidently the metal catch has given way. I try to bend it back with a knife; the door holds, but in a few minutes it's banging again. Do I dare go outside and prop something heavy against it? A cement block—I saw one in an odd place—where was it? The barn? The porch? Out by the garden? Not on the porch, and I don't dare go out to the barn. Demetrius would know—why isn't he here? Because I told him not to be, I remind myself. But this is a hurricane. Why won't he come the way he always does, to check up on us, make sure we're all right? We're on our own. No one is coming to rescue us. We'll have to fend for ourselves.

I find two gallon cans of paint on the floor of the pantry closet, obviously several years old and looking as if they have never been opened. I go outside and set the paint cans firmly against the storm door, then fight my way fearfully around the house to come back in through the porch. The wind feels like something solid as I round the corner of the house, the two big maples on the porch side rocking and tossing, one of them sweeping the power lines. What if the wires come down, fall on me? Are they live, dangerous with the power off?

In a few minutes the parlor storm door is banging again. The wind is still getting behind it and has nudged the paint cans across the step. Do I have to stand here and hold it shut through the whole storm? Then Lesley has an idea. She disappears into the kitchen and comes back with a ball of heavy twine. She ties it to the handle of the storm door, threading it through the back of the front door, and ties it around the leg of Aunt Phoebe's heavy walnut sideboard. The door still bangs but it will only open an inch or so. The glass might break but at least it won't tear off its hinges.

By now gusts of wind are shaking the house. The windows rattle; the rain sounds like handfuls of sand being thrown against them. I send Lesley upstairs to lock the windows while I take the ones on the first floor. It stops some of the rattling. The wind whistles down the chimney, causing the tin stovepipe cover in the kitchen to pop and rattle. Then it blows across the opening like a child with a glass bottle, making a low moan. Something wooden is thumping against the house but I don't dare go outside again.

I make us tuna sandwiches for lunch, washed down by big glasses of milk, since it won't keep if the electricity stays off. We eat in the parlor where it's quieter, and then I wheel Dorrie back to her room, hoping to settle her down for a nap so she'll sleep through the worst of the storm. She's anxious again—her humming is louder and more insistent. She clings to me with her good arm as I hoist her up and onto the bed. I lie down beside her and rub her back, wishing there were someone to rub mine, to soothe me. Every now and then we both start as the wind gusts, feeling like it might shove the house off its foundations. I lie there beside my daughter, my anxiety replaced by an overwhelming fatigue.

What feels like moments later I wake to the sound of rifle shots. It's too early for hunting season, I think stupidly. But it isn't shooting; it's the sound of trees cracking. Dorothea, bless her, has fallen asleep. I slip carefully off the bed and head for the parlor, but before I get there the sound of breaking glass propels me toward the kitchen. Wind is howling through the house—one of the maple branches has come down and crashed through the porch windows. I don't dare go in there.

I pull the kitchen door shut to stop the wind, turn the lock and head for the parlor. Lesley isn't there. Where is she? Upstairs? Not in her room, nor in Phoebe's little room, nor anywhere in the sound of my call. And now Dorothea is awake, wailing; I have to go back and comfort her. But where is Lesley?

Then I hear her on the porch, knocking frantically on the kitchen door. As soon as I turn the lock she bursts into the kitchen, into my arms. She's frightened in spite of herself, and so am I. She went over to Daphne's, she says, and then down to the beach, was just passing under the locusts when two big branches came down.

"How could you go out there without telling me?" I shout at her angrily. "Don't you have any sense?"

"But you were asleep."

"Well, you're all right, anyway. How's Daphne?"

"I didn't go in. The MG's in the driveway. You should see down the beach. It's crazy. You can't see Sandy Neck at all, and the Higgins's boat is blowing over, and then up, and then over. It's going to be a mess."

She's still holding me, there in the kitchen, and I can hear that Dorrie is approaching hysteria. I should go in to her, but Lesley doesn't let me go. We huddle together, listening to things hitting the window, more than just rain now—leaves and small branches. Then a big crack and a crashing sound startles us apart. One of the maples has fallen over on the corner of the porch, right through the roof. The wicker rocker where I read my morning paper, in the corner where I like to station Dorothea and Pegasus in the sun, is hidden in a welter of leaves and branches. Lesley is clinging to me and crying. "Where are the birds?" she says. "Where do they go? What if they come back and their tree is gone?"

Now Dorothea is wailing in earnest. Lesley follows me when I go in to her. I lie down on the bed, holding my terrified daughter from behind, while Lesley climbs in behind me. We lie there shivering, listening to the howling wind, the cracking branches, the noise of leaves, branches, sheets of rain slamming into the house. Dorothea is shaking, but gradually her cries subside to moans and then humming as I sing to her, the old lullabies the girls loved years ago. "Sweet and low, sweet and low, Wind of the western sea," I sing. "Over the rolling waters go." Lesley joins in. I don't know how long we lie there, the three of us like nested spoons, frightened and alone in this old house that feels more and more like a ship lost at sea.

Then, imperceptibly, the crisis passes. Rain still pelts the windows, but the wind has a different sound, and most of the cracking has stopped. Dorothea has fallen asleep again. I doze myself for a while, until I feel Lesley get up. I carefully lift my arm from around Dorothea and slip out of bed. Every muscle in my body feels stiff, as if I'd spent the day doing heavy lifting. I'm surprised by the tears that spring to my eyes as Lesley draws the quilt gently up to cover her sister's shoulder.

We tiptoe through the house to survey the damage. Everything is all right upstairs except for a stain on the bathroom ceiling. It's hard to see out. All the windows are smeared with water and salt and bits of leaves. We decide to venture out to survey the damage. The maple on the southeast corner of the house will have to be taken down. It is leaning heavily on the porch roof where it fell, crashing through the corner and breaking three of the windows. Everything on that half of the porch is sodden from the rain: chair cushions, the woven straw rug, a week's worth of newspapers, a stack of Phoebe's old magazines. I'll have to call a tree man to cut down the maple. It will need ropes and pulleys, not a job Demetrius could tackle by himself.

Demetrius. Where is he? Is he safe? And is he thinking about us, whether we've come through all right? Did he and Phoebe sit out the last hurricane together, here in this house? Why isn't he here now?

The lane is almost obliterated by fallen trees and branches—no one will be driving in or out any time soon. Our locust grove looks terrible; at least half of the trees have been split or are broken ten feet off the ground. The cedars near the top of the hill have lost a few branches but look relatively untouched. Even with the dark storm clouds scudding by, the yard is much lighter than it was with so many trees gone. I look over towards Daphne's house. Her front yard is a tangle of locust trunks and branches. One tree has fallen on Paul's car.

It takes over an hour to clear the porch and haul the wet papers and magazines to the garage. I stand the cushions on end on the floor, drape the wet rug over the back of the sofa. My favorite spot in this house—how long before we'll be able to use it again?

Evening comes, bringing breaks in the clouds and a mild breeze replacing the wind. We grill a steak outdoors. By eight o'clock darkness has begun to fall. We take one last walk to the beach even though it involves clambering over fallen trees. The *Little Gull* has weathered the storm, though the cover has torn away and she is full of rain water. The Higgins's boat is not so lucky. It is lying on its side, its metal mast bent by the force of the wind trying to roll the hull over. By the time we get back and I settle Dorothea, it is pitch dark and there is nothing to do. I try to read by candlelight, but it is too dim. By nine we are all in bed. It's too early to sleep, and I'm too wired in any case. That fallen maple, the hole in the porch roof, the windows—they are going to be expensive to repair. Greg will have a fit, especially since we can't show the house in its present disarray. It's an ill wind, I think. We'll have the house for another year, at least.

I smile. We came through on our own, not unscathed, but safe. I feel closer to Lesley than I have in a long time. She was braver than I was, and I'm grateful she was here. Phoebe would have been proud of her. Phoebe would have loved being here.

Sometime in the middle of the night I am startled awake—by what? Not Dorothea, or Lesley stirring down the hall, or branches against the window. There is no wind at all. I listen and hear nothing but perfect stillness. Perhaps it was the silence that woke me. The only sound is the quiet tick of my battery operated alarm clock. Somewhere far away a bird is singing, a mockingbird probably, other than the owls, our only night singer. Yesterday morning was like this, perfectly calm without a breath of wind, Daphne making a broad wake in the silvery water as she swam out to get her boat.

Bright sunlight wakes me about seven, a green smell of crushed leaves, fresh like the new-mown hay I remember from June at my uncle's farm in Ohio. The power is still out. The milk in the refrigerator is barely cool and won't keep through the day. I should try to get some bags of ice somewhere.

By eight o'clock I spot Demetrius in the yard, gazing at the fallen maple, and feel a huge wave of relief. He came. I'm not in this alone after all. The truck is nowhere in sight. I run down the porch steps, wanting to throw my arms around him, but something stops me. He's assumed his role as hired man, polite and distant.

"Surely you didn't walk over here?" I ask.

"No, no. The truck's down the lane. Trees down all over. The fire department's got volunteers out clearing the roads but it'll be awhile before they get in here. Need anything from the store?"

"Just ice, but I bet there isn't any. You all right? I worried about you getting flooded out." I follow him around the house to the locust grove. It looks like a disaster, not a tree untouched. Even the leaves hang desolate and wilted.

"I'll have to cut about half of them down," Demetrius is saying. "The rest I'll trim back and they'll put out new branches. And new ones will spring up—look, there are already some seedlings here. All I have to do is mow around them and they'll grow faster than you'd believe."

The pines are less damaged, just a few branches down. And the cedars, surprisingly, hardly at all, considering how dense they are.

"Is the power out all over?" I ask, thinking about the food in the refrigerator, how foolish I was to forget to buy ice.

"I'd say so. All over the Cape, they're saying. There's a driving ban too, for nonessential drivers. I'm essential because I've got a chain saw. I'll work on clearing the lane for you and try to get back later to cut back those branches and board up your porch windows."

"How are things at your place? The boathouse still there?"

Demetrius gives me an intent look, the faintest of smiles. "Should be. We were lucky with the tide. Haven't been home. I rode the storm out over at West Marsh." He heads back down the lane and in a few minutes I hear the whine of his chain saw.

I'm anxious to know how Daphne is but don't quite dare to knock on her door with Paul there. And there's plenty to occupy my mind. I'll have to resurrect my camping skills, heat some water on the portable grill, survey what in the refrigerator can be salvaged. The milk will have to go, but the eggs should last all right. Last night's steak was the last of the raw meat, but there's always canned tuna. Mayonnaise will have to be thrown out, too. No driving, no hope of ice. With the trees down we're trapped in here anyway. The phone line dead, Greg frantic, maybe, the TV news always exaggerates disasters. Funny, I don't feel trapped or frightened or even annoyed. There's something satisfying about having survived one of Nature's major convulsions. Living without electricity, all the conveniences that serve to insulate us from the natural rhythms of the world out there. Having to go to bed because it's too dark to see. Hearing none of the familiar mechanical sounds a house makes at night, the clicks and hums of all our convenient machines. The perfect peace of waking to a morning as it must have been years ago. And of knowing, with no confusion, what the important things are. Food. Water. Shelter. And the people we love, come safely through in the circle of our arms.

Aftermath

*After a storm . . . the swelling, churning breakers sweep
toward us . . . opaque and brown . . . with the torn and
powdered substance of the land.*

MY ENTHUSIASM FOR the simple life doesn't last long. The weather for
the next few days is cool and crystal clear, but by the third day the
air smells faintly sour. All the leaves that weren't blown off the trees wilt
and turn a dull greenish brown and begin to fall. I am as sick as the girls
are of canned tuna and soup, and the drudgery of heating pots of water on
the charcoal grill has become tiresome. I spend most of my days trying to
tackle the yard, cutting up branches with the lopper and raking leaves out
of my ruined gardens. The physical work consumes me, which is just as
well. I have too much to do to dwell on the future. Once I've washed the
supper dishes in cold water and settled Dorothea, I fall into bed exhausted
and sleep until first light. It's only that early hour before sunrise when I
let myself ponder what I've done and what lies ahead. That's when my
Knoxville grandmother's voice echoes in my head: "Them what wants to
dance have to pay the piper."

When the phone lines are reconnected on Thursday, I spend most
of the afternoon indoors on the phone, leaving a message for Greg to
say we're fine, calling Jeannine to suggest that she wait until the weekend
to come back, contacting the insurance company about the porch and
trying vainly to reach a tree man. The electricity is still out after three
days, and the only sign of Demetrius I've seen is late that first afternoon
when he cleared Daphne's driveway and cut down the tree that left a siz-
able dent on the hood of Paul's green MG. Dorothea seems unfazed by
the changes in her routine, but Lesley resists my pleas for help in the
yard and makes herself scarce, retreating down to the beach for hours at
a time.

On Friday I wake before dawn to hear the welcome sound of the
refrigerator running. The power is on! Dorrie is awake, too, unusually
early. It's only nine o'clock by the time she's dressed and fed bread and
jelly. I'm boiling water for my last bit of coffee when Demetrius turns

into the yard. I run outside and give him a kiss through the window of his truck. This time I don't care who's looking, I'm so glad to see him.

"Well," he says, embarrassed but smiling. "How about a grocery run? They'll be mobbed. We better go early." It feels like that day back in May, the two of us and Dorrie, filling the cart with milk and orange juice, vegetables and hamburger and the makings for barbecued chicken. I'm happy, relaxed even; all my anger at Demetrius is gone. This feels natural and right, loading bags of groceries into the van while the man I love lifts my daughter into her seat, straps her in carefully, folds her chair, and sets it in back. My doubts about him have vanished, like the great whirling wind that tried to overwhelm us but didn't.

Demetrius and I are still unloading the car when the phone rings. The sound fills me with guilt and annoyance. It must be Gregory again with more questions about the damage. But when I run inside to get it, it's not Gregory.

"Anna? Can you come over?" Daphne's voice is almost too soft to hear. She doesn't sound like herself at all—has she been crying?

"You mean this afternoon?" I say, thinking how odd she sounds, how odd for her to call at all, let alone at eleven in the morning.

"I mean now. Can you come? Please?" There's no mistaking the break in her voice. Something has happened. I go back outside to find that Demetrius has lifted Dorothea into her chair and wheeled her up the hill under the little stand of pines. He starts to say something about lunch outside, but I don't wait for him to finish.

"Daphne wants me over there right now. Something must be wrong. Can you watch Dorothea?"

"Of course. Unless you think I should go."

"I don't think so. She must have heard us when we drove in. And she asked for me."

Daphne's front door is open, but she's nowhere in sight. I find her sitting on the edge of her bed. She's been crying, a lot. She smiles at me sheepishly, but her face looks distorted, the mouth turned up but the eyes like holes in a tragic mask.

"What has happened to you? Are you all right?"

Her smile grows a little wider. "I'm trapped inside a cliché," she says, laughing ruefully. Her voice is slurred; she has trouble pronouncing the word *cliché*.

"Are you drunk?" I ask, incredulous.

"Not officially. Daddy always said, no candy before ten o'clock. I just had a little valium. And a little glass of scotch. Don't worry; I'm not trying to do myself in. Just get a little numb."

"What in God's name has happened?"

"Oh, not much, just the plot of a drugstore novel. Successful writer falls for narcissistic bastard. Bastard seduces and abandons, after getting a lot of freebies from writer. Think we'll get movie rights?"

"Paul?"

"The very one. Oh, God, when am I going to learn?" Now the tears are starting in earnest. Daphne lies back crosswise on the bed, then begins to laugh. "You know, it's true, that song? I've got tears in my ears."

Now I'm laughing too, but mainly from relief. A lovers' quarrel. Nothing dangerous. Daphne is crying again and muttering under her breath: "Oh shit, shit," she is saying. "Men are such shits. Life is so shitty. How could I let this happen again? So stupid. Such a cliché! Shit!" And she rolls over on her stomach and grabs her pillow and begins to sob, the way my girls used to do, the way I did that day, months after the fact, when the full realization of Dorothea's condition hit me. I do the instinctive thing, the thing I did when the girls were little and got crying like this, and start to rub her back. It feels amazingly solid under my hands, all bone and muscle. I've never seen her exercise, other than those morning walks down to the marsh. How does she stay so strong?

"You know," Daphne says, her voice muffled by the pillow, "the worst thing is I keep thinking no one will ever touch me again. I'm fifty-four years old. Who's going to want to touch me? It was three years; I thought it didn't matter so much, that I'd got over the longing. You know what I think now?"

"What?" I say stupidly. She's talking; it will be good for her, calm her down; I want to keep her talking. I start to rub her back some more, but she rolls over and sits up, holding the pillow in her lap, punching it every now and then for emphasis.

"We never get over it. Wanting someone to touch us. Sex, being held, sleeping next to another body, hearing that breathing in the night. We get old and ugly and people leave and betray us and die, and we still wake at four in the morning with all that longing." She lets out a huge sigh. "Oh, God, I can't bear thinking about it. It isn't fair. It's like when I was little and went to the dentist once with my father. I told him I couldn't wait to grow up so it wouldn't hurt anymore. Haven't we all believed we'd get old and not feel so much? Not care? You know what I think? I think we feel more. Oh, God."

I knead Daphne's shoulder muscles with my hands, trying to work out the knots of tension. What she's saying scares me. I don't know what to say.

"Where's Dorothea?" Daphne asks suddenly. "Is Lesley watching her? You didn't leave her by herself?" She's beginning to come around; she's out of her own pain enough to think about somebody else. It's a good sign.

"Don't worry about her. Demetrius is over at the house. He was helping me unload groceries and was going to stay for lunch anyway. I'll give him a call. I'm not going anywhere. You're going to eat something, and then you're going to sleep off this little bender you're on. Can you get up? Why don't you take a shower."

"Okay. That's a good idea," Daphne says docilely. She's calm now; the tears and the talk and the back rub have done their work. How like my own children she seems right now! How like little children we all are, when these storms come over us.

Fifteen minutes later, when I come back into the bedroom with a cup of canned beef broth and a toasted cheese sandwich, the only lunch I could assemble from Daphne's sparsely stocked kitchen, she has showered and put on a nightgown and gotten into bed. "This is ridiculous," she is saying. "It's the middle of the day. But I'm so weak; I feel as though I'm convalescing from some long illness."

"It's the valium. Greg took some once when his back went out and fell sound asleep on the living room floor. How much scotch did you have?"

"Just one. One glass. Kind of a big glass. Do I have to eat the sandwich?"

"Take a bite, anyway," I say. This mother-daughter scene we seem to be enacting is beginning to amuse me.

I close the bedroom door softly behind me and retreat to the kitchen, where I finish off Daphne's sandwich and clean up after our meager lunch. Then I run back over to ask Demetrius if he can stay part of the afternoon. He says he'd be glad to—he'll work on cutting up the downed locusts. Lesley should be back from the beach soon, looking for lunch. I don't tell him much about Daphne, only that she's very upset and needs to talk. I head back to her house, grateful to Demetrius for not asking any pointed questions.

It is four o'clock by the time Daphne emerges. She shuffles out onto the deck, where I'm sitting reading her copy of *To the Lighthouse* and watching the birds take turns at the feeder. Her face looks a little ravaged, but she has gotten dressed and seems almost herself again. The desperate little girl has disappeared. She flops into the chair beside me and looks out over the pond. She seems to be avoiding my eyes.

"Feel better?"

"Yup. A little hung. A new experience for the middle of the day."

"Hardly the middle. It's after four."

"Ye Gods. A whole day shot. The last of many, I might add." The edge is back in her voice.

"Want to talk about it?"

"It's like I said. A cliché. So like James, that one in New York, the one with the ear. Paul just swooped down on me, so intense, you know? He wanted me; he thought I was wonderful, so strong and free—you know what he called me? His pioneer woman. Me, who grew up in the East Seventies. Boy, I fell for it."

"He's an attractive man."

"It wasn't that. It was the attention. The phone calls. You know, he called me five times in one day. It was the day they started rehearsals on *Burn This*. He was so excited—he had to tell me about it, and he kept saying how lovely it was, the intimacy, being able to share. Oh, shit."

"So what happened?"

"He took me to the party the night after the opening. There were a couple of people there from New York, publishing people one of the actors knew, up here on vacation. Anyway, they knew my work and made a big fuss over me. Paul was furious, wouldn't speak to me all the way home in the car. That was his party, you see. He was supposed to be the star. He acted as if I'd planned it. I didn't have a clue what was wrong till he started calling me names, hot-shot has-been flash-in-the-pan one-book bitch, he called me."

"You have to admit it has a nice sort of rhythmic *je ne sais quoi*."

She misses my attempt at humor. "And after that he wanted to make love. Wanted to fuck, I should say. Nothing tender about it. It was like saying 'Take that, and that.' He wouldn't talk. I couldn't wait for him to be gone the next morning."

"But he was here, wasn't he, for the hurricane?"

"That's just it; I'm so stupid. He called the morning of the storm, all freaked out because he's been staying on the water, over in West Dennis. He thought he'd get washed away. So dumb me, I said come on over. And then that damn tree fell—"

"Poetic justice."

"—and you'd think I'd arranged it, the way he ranted. He ranted and swore, and then wouldn't speak to me. He drank all of my gin and went to bed. I ended up sleeping on the couch. And then with the damn storm and the fucking trees down everywhere he couldn't get out. He was here for another whole day. It was like a scene from *No Exit*."

"So that's why you got Demetrius."

"He was down the lane, sawing trees. I went down and pleaded with him—told him it was an emergency. I don't know what he thought. But bless him."

"Yes, bless him. But Paul—do you think he'll call, or show up and apologize?"

"Oh, he probably will. I don't care. I had this before; I was married to it. I know all about it. Little digs, little insults, little punishments every time I got to shine, got to be the center of attention. I had a whole marriage of it. Get a story published, and Daniel wouldn't sleep with me for three weeks. Win the Chambers award and he has an affair. I don't need this, Anna."

She stands up and crosses over to the deck railing, looking intently at the pond as if there were some new species of bird out there. The trees look forlorn, stripped of most of their leaves, despite the bright sunshine. Then she turns and looks at me, finally. I'm wondering if I should say something about the misgivings I felt that night we had dinner together and decide against it—I'm afraid she'll change her mind and leap to his defense. I've seen it happen before with other friends. Besides, I can feel her gathering steam. She comes back to where I'm sitting and stands there looking down at me. I can practically feel the heat of her anger. "There's one sun in Paul's universe, and he's it," she goes on. "It's his show. And my God, the time he stole! What happened to my discipline, my work schedule? Me on the phone two hours a day? I was demented."

"Can you really just quit him cold turkey?"

"I don't know, but I'm going to try. It was sick; some sort of fusion. But I've got to get unfused. Defused. Why did I fall for it?"

"Maybe you're not as tough as you think."

"Well, don't tell anybody. Oh, damn. Oh, God. Oh, shit."

"Are you going to be all right if I go home? I really ought to rescue Demetrius."

"I'm not suicidal, if that's what you mean. Just pissed. At Paul, at me. I'm going to turn on the computer and start writing. Might as well make use of all this energy." And with that Daphne goes back into the house, sits down at her desk, feels around with her foot for the switch on her surge protector.

"I take it that's my cue to exit," I say, giving her a quick hug from behind. "But you take care. And call me, hear?"

"I will, honey chile," she says, mimicking my Southern phrasing. By the time I slip out the front door she is clicking away furiously at the computer.

The Key

*The surrender of these old ice-built lands was due only
partly to the attack of winds and waves . . . the rising sea
flooded them . . . capturing them without a battle.*

THE STORM RUINED everything, Lesley thinks, making the lane look like a war zone. Half the trees down and the rest of them looking all dead. The wind and the salt dried out all the leaves and now the trees and bushes look like late fall except with no color, just brownish gray and withered. Maybe they'll all die from the shock of it. She's been sleeping late since the hurricane and spending a lot of time on the beach. It's been too cool to swim, and Phil's not around to go kayaking. She walked down the beach and up along the creek to Phil's the day after the hurricane but no one was there, the house all locked up with all the deck furniture taken in, like they'd closed up the place and gone home. He hadn't even told her he was leaving, like he didn't care if he saw her again or anything.

She sat on the beach for a long time after that, trying to imagine what it would be like to ride the hurricane out over on Sandy Neck. From this far away all the houses look okay. And there aren't any trees near them to blow down. What she really wants is to sail over there and take a closer look, but Daphne hasn't even rigged her boat again since the storm. It's back out on the mooring, but the rudder and the sail aren't in it. At least that Paul hasn't been around ever since the truck came and towed his car away. Paul spent the hurricane at Daphne's house. Lesley was glad when she saw the MG all bashed in by that tree. Serves him right.

Her mom has been acting weird. For the last two weeks she's been gone half the time and making her babysit Dorrie, not really saying where she's been, whispering on the phone to who knows who, probably not Daphne with that Paul over there all the time. Dad will be back tomorrow, and Jeannine is coming back to the Cape on Sunday. Something is going on between Mom and Dad, something they keep arguing about. The weekend is going to be tense. She'd like to be anywhere else, back in Needham, maybe. Maybe she could go home with Dad Sunday night.

She wishes she were old enough to stay by herself, without anyone around to tell her what to do.

She's been taking long walks in the afternoons to look at the storm damage. Today she's headed toward West Marsh. It's kind of a long way, more than two miles up 6A. She's got a key in her pocket as an excuse, one she found on the kitchen table a couple of weeks ago. The tag on it is all creased and dirty with the words *Bog House* just barely readable. She thought about showing it to Phil and his brother, taking them there some night when they sneaked out again. It would be a great place for a party. But now Phil's gone, so what's the point of keeping it?

The main road isn't as messed up looking as Kettle Lane. The leaves are all wilted and dead, but only a few big trees are down. The sound of chain saws whining is everywhere, like an invasion of giant bees. A huge maple must have fallen across the road and just missed the cute little Cummaquid post office. A cutoff stump is leaning across the sidewalk, its roots high in the air with hunks of asphalt hanging off of them. Endless lines of cars are winding up and down 6A in both directions. People going to the store now that the power is back on, or just out looking around. Lesley is glad for the bumpy narrow sidewalk so she doesn't have to dodge the cars, but they make her feel weird, like everyone is gawking at her. One old car full of boys slows down and whistles and hoots at her. It's a relief to turn into Blackberry Lane and away from the traffic. Just one more turn, another right. She's almost there. It's farther down the road than she remembers, but then she's only been over here a couple of times, and that was in the car.

Then, finally, there's the bog opening up on the right side of the road, flat as a pancake and a funny shade of green, not looking at all harmed by the hurricane, the ramshackle shed still standing with the old Model A truck inside, the bog house all closed up with the wooden shutters down over the windows. No sign anywhere of Demetrius. Just as well— she doesn't know what she'd say to him and she doesn't really want to give back the key. Probably out with his chain saw like everybody else cutting up trees. She should turn around and hike back, but she wants to rest a little. And wants to see if the key really fits the padlock on the door. Maybe it doesn't; maybe it's just an old one of Aunt Phoebe's that Mom found in a drawer.

Lesley looks around before heading up the dirt track to the bog house. There's no place to hide, but nobody seems to be around. When she gets to the door, she fishes for the key in the pocket of her jean shorts, then looks around again before she tries it in the lock. At first it doesn't seem to fit, but after a couple of tries the padlock clicks open. She lifts it out to free the hasp, cautiously opens the door and slips in, pulling the door shut behind her. It takes a few minutes for her eyes to adjust to the darkness. All the shutters are closed tight, for the storm, probably. But then the room forms itself around her, familiar from the day they had the picnic with Dorrie, the day she saw the marsh hawk. She feels shivery and cold. Demetrius could show up any time and find her trespassing. She idly makes her way around the room, touching an old flannel shirt, the rubber fisherman's overalls hanging on the wall. She's conscious of the same guilty excitement she felt that day she and Sally snooped around in Jeannine's room back in Needham and she found the report about Dorrie. Not much to see here, though, other than stacks of wooden boxes and rakes and spades and cans of oil and gasoline. She peers through the door into the smaller room in back. A mattress with a couple of quilts. Demetrius must sleep here sometimes. No bathroom. She wishes there were one because she needs to pee. What does Demetrius do? But he's a man. He can just go behind a bush anywhere.

Then she hears the truck outside, and she almost does pee, right in her pants. Demetrius. He'll see the open padlock. The door of the truck slams and she slips into the little back room and waits, trying to think up a story for why she's here. She can't let him think she's snooping. He'll tell her mom, and then her mother will light into her, ground her forever. She hears footsteps on the gravel. She found the key in the kitchen, she'll say (true) and wanted to return it. It's always better to mix up some truth with a lie. She needed a bathroom (also true) and that's why she came inside. She just got there five minutes ago. She's really sorry about trespassing (truest of all!) and hopes he doesn't mind too much. But the footsteps seem to be fading. She waits, conscious of the sound of her breath, the beating of her heart, sure she'll end up wetting herself. After a few minutes of silence, she peers out through the crack where the wooden blind doesn't quite cover the back window. There he is, walking away from her around the perimeter toward Cove Bog. Looking for damage, downed trees and branches, probably. Pretty soon he'll be at the far end and will turn back. She'd better make her getaway now.

She slips back out the door and carefully replaces the padlock, slipping the key into her pocket, remembering the time she locked Daphne's key in her house. She's almost back to the road when she hears Demetrius calling her name from the far path. More panic. She can't just run away; he'll get suspicious. She keeps walking, pretending she doesn't hear him, but he calls out again and she has to turn around. She'd sell her soul for a bathroom. She has to go so badly she squeezes her legs together like when she was a little kid. It brings on a weird sensation in the front of her crotch, focused and powerful, that seems to have nothing to do with having to pee.

"Hey Lesley," Demetrius is saying as he comes up to where she is standing. "What brings you all the way over here? Were you looking for me? Something wrong over at the house?"

"No, I was just out walking. I didn't think you were here 'cause the bog house is all closed up. You don't have a bathroom in there, do you?"

"No such luck. Plenty of woods around, though."

"That's all right. I can make it home, I think." The desperate urge really does seem to be going away.

"How about a ride home?"

That would mean he'd come in and talk to Mom, probably, and she'd get chewed out for walking so far, but on the other hand she really does have to pee. "That would be nice," she says in her polite lady voice that always makes her feel like her own grandmother back in Ohio, her mom's mom, always harping about manners. "But don't you have things to do?"

"Not really. I was just checking on things. I stopped by to get some more fuel for the chain saw. I'll be right out. Wait in the truck if you want."

So he has been out sawing trees, Lesley thinks as Demetrius emerges from the bog house, a red metal gas container in one hand and a can of oil in the other. They say very little on the way back to Kettle Lane. One of the things she likes about Demetrius is he doesn't feel the maddening need most adults have to make small talk with kids. She likes how quiet he is. Sometimes he startles her when she spots him up on the ladder painting, so quiet she didn't even know he was there. She likes the feeling of having him around, close by, but not asking her things, not pressuring her. It makes her feel safe, taken care of even. She wishes her own dad were more like him, the kind of man who puttered around the house fixing things. Building things like the ramp for Dorrie. Like the tree house she longed for when she was little, that she and Dad were actually planning, making little drawings, when Dorrie got sick. After that she knew better than to ask about it. But it was hard to imagine her dad out in the yard hammering and sawing, even if Dorrie hadn't gone into a coma.

Demetrius doesn't come in the house, just waits in the truck while Lesley hops out and then drives off. "Was that Demetrius just now?" her mother asks, coming down the hall from Dorrie's room just as Lesley is emerging from the bathroom. She looks tired, old all of a sudden, like she hasn't been out in the sun for a long time.

"Yeah, he gave me a lift home. I went for a walk up 6A." No point in saying how far if she isn't asked.

"That was nice. I hope you thanked him," her mother says, sounding like her own mother, Lesley's grandmother. The polite lady voice. She looks intently at Lesley for a moment before turning towards the kitchen. "Can you do me a favor?" she asks wearily. "Could you finish getting Dorrie ready for supper? She's all dressed but she needs her hair combed. And if you could bring her out to the kitchen I'll work on supper. I've got my Italian chicken in the oven. And I'll make biscuits, or maybe corn bread?" Her mom is going overboard now that the power's back on. She's smiling, but her eyes look funny, strangely shiny, like they're going to spill over with tears.

Dorrie is lying on her bed, all dressed except for her shoes. Mom must have given her a bath and washed her hair; she smells of shampoo. It's a funny time of day for her to have a bath. Maybe she got her period. It's weird to think Dorrie's had it for years when Lesley's been waiting nervously to get hers, knowing it could happen any day, probably when she's out somewhere wearing white shorts. Dorrie had just got hers when she went into the hospital. She told Lesley all about it even though Lesley was only seven and really too young. Lesley wouldn't believe her at first. She thought her sister was teasing her again. But then Dorrie showed her the book Mom had given her and read part of it out loud and explained what some of big words meant.

Now Dorrie smiles when she sees Lesley, that funny lopsided smile she has. Lesley smooths down her sister's hair, which is still damp and really does need combing. First the shoes, though. Dorrie's legs are so skinny, like sticks. And so limp. It's hard to get her feet inside her shoes, like dressing a doll. Playing with dolls never appealed to Lesley. She much preferred her stuffed animals. Dorrie was the one who liked dolls. The attic playroom had a whole row of them that she never let Lesley touch, even when she'd outgrown them. But Lesley didn't care. Dolls just seemed like a lot of work to her, like Dorrie herself these days. She wheels the chair over next to the bed, then sits Dorrie up, scoots her over to the edge with her legs hanging down, hoists her up by the armpits, balances her on her strong left leg and plops her more roughly than she means to into the chair. "Pegasus," Lesley says to Dorrie, who grins lopsidedly and makes loud noises. "That's right, Pegasus!" Is that what she's trying to say, Lesley wonders. Does she even know what the word means? Will she ever be able to dress herself, say words?

But of course Lesley knows the answer. Mom and Dad sat her down ages ago, when she was nine or ten, and told her that Dorrie would probably always need to be taken care of, washed and dressed and pushed around in a wheelchair. What they didn't say, but she knows it anyway, is that someday she'll be the one doing it all, years from now when her parents are dead. No wonder Mom looks tired. She's got her all day, every day, especially this summer with Jeannine not around. Even so she hardly ever asks Lesley to help, just now and then as if it was a special favor. I should chip in more, Lesley thinks. She's my sister, still my sister. She turns Pegasus toward the door. "Supper, Dorrie," she says. "Here we go." Together they roll down the hall towards the kitchen and the comforting smell of corn bread baking in the oven.

A Changed Landscape

*If the earth's lingering ice sheets completely finish their
melting, . . . they will drown whatever remains of the
Cape and Islands.*

SOMETIMES WE'RE REMINDED that everything is temporary. So much
has happened in so short a time I'm reeling from it. All the neighbors
can talk about is the hurricane, in the obsessive way people have after a
near-disaster, starting with themselves and then moving on to the tragic
and funny things that happened to people they know or have heard about,
recounting over and over the tree that just missed them, the friend of a
friend whose newly purchased boat ended up on the rocks in front of the
former owner's house. Now that the power is back on we'll all romanticize
the drudgery of heating water and cooking outside, the boredom of evenings without television or a lamp to read by. The storm has introduced
me to more of the neighbors. We're outside all day stacking branches,
sawing up tree trunks, raking leaves, comparing notes on the damage as
if we were competing. Slowly we're getting used to the strangeness of
the landscape. The endless whine of chainsaws is becoming intermittent,
the biggest of the downed trees finally cut into manageable lengths and
hauled away or stacked for splitting into firewood for winter. The withered
leaves rustle and let go in the night breezes, cluttering the lawns with
faded gray ghosts of themselves. Only the grass has stayed green, growing
thick and shaggy. No one has time to cut it; there's too much else to do.

I see the changes, am startled every morning by the unaccustomed
sunlight where the locust grove used to be, commiserate with other folks
on the lane about the mess. They accept me as one of them. But all the
while I'm barely conscious of the physical world around me. It's my inner
landscape I can't get used to. More than anything else I am overwhelmed
with longing for Demetrius, now that I've told him I want time to think.
Who am I kidding? My naked joy when he showed up the morning after
the storm, there for anyone to see. Our trip to the Stop and Shop with
Dorothea, so like that first time back in May. I ache to be with him, have
to restrain myself from driving over to West Marsh and pulling him bodily

into the bog house. Gregory is due for his vacation week, and Jeannine will be back on Sunday. Now that Demetrius has cleared away the top of the fallen maple, boarded up the three broken porch windows, and stapled tar paper over the hole in the corner of the roof, he's been making himself scarce. We've talked about the repairs, about cutting back the locusts, but not about ourselves.

Soon Gregory will be here. And soon, too soon after that it will be time to go back to Needham. Needham and my life there, the way it was. Will that mean the end of everything between Demetrius and me? If Gregory prevails, and we sell the house, my life will go back to its old pattern. What if I refuse? What if I tell Gregory I want to leave him and live here? Could I, with Demetrius and the girls? I can't think about it now; it's beyond imagining.

On Friday afternoon the phone rings. Jeannine is sick with a cold and is begging off. She won't be here to act as buffer between Gregory and me. Perhaps it's just as well. We must settle the question of the house. And I need to think about the bigger question of the two of us, our future. But not this afternoon; I'm exhausted. When Lesley gets home I ask her to help with Dorrie while I cook a good supper, her favorite chicken casserole. I'm glad Greg is waiting to drive down after the traffic and won't be here until nine or ten. It gives us one last dinner together, just us girls, without tension hovering over the table.

Gregory doesn't arrive until nearly eleven, and by then it's raining. He goes upstairs to bed as soon as he finishes his plate of warmed-over chicken. I follow after I'm sure he's safely asleep and spend a fitful night, awakened over and over by the driving rain showers that come and go. In the morning the stain on the bedroom ceiling has grown, but when we inspect the porch downstairs it is dry. Demetrius's temporary patching job has held.

After breakfast we make a tour of the yard to assess the damage. Greg is appalled by all the broken trees. "At least Phoebe's man's been on the job," he says, gazing ruefully up at the black tar paper covering the hole in the porch roof, the plywood nailed over the broken window. Phoebe's man. If only he knew. What an odd thing to call someone he's known since childhood. A distancing name, condescending. The lopped-off crown of the ruined maple is heaped in pieces by the garage, waiting to be cut up into firewood or fed to the chipper. What is left of the trunk is stubbed off, leaning awkwardly toward the house. From this angle we can see its rotten core.

As we pick our way through the devastated locust grove, it's obvious Greg's imagination hadn't grasped the power of the wind from my telephoned descriptions. "Good God, Anna," he says, surprising me by taking hold of my arm and looking intently into my eyes. "Why did you stay here for this? What must it have sounded like, all these trees breaking! The girls—you weren't safe! Why did you do it?"

That word again, safe. "We were safe. Nothing happened. We didn't do anything foolish."

"Weren't the girls terrified?"

I think about us all curled up together on Dorothea's bed. "We were scared for a while, yes, but exhilarated too. It was exciting. I wouldn't have missed it, and I don't think Lesley would either."

"I should have insisted—I should have come to get you."

"I'm a big girl. You don't have to take care of me, and you were out of town anyway," I answer crossly. In spite of myself, I'm touched. I put an arm around Greg's waist and give him a hug.

Then he breaks the mood. "You realize this is going to lower the value of the house," he says, "not just the damage, but the yard. It looks like hell. Now we'll have to wait until spring. And the whole market will probably be depressed for a while. Hurricanes scare the bejesus out of people."

"Good. Then maybe this argument won't have to happen so often."

"Anna—"

I won't listen. I turn away from Greg and make my way through the rain back to the house, Phoebe's house. My house.

My dodge doesn't work. Things go downhill from there, and I'm sorry I've carried our quarrel back where the girls can hear us. Greg catches up to me in the parlor and grabs my arm again, this time more roughly. This time he isn't looking at me, but I can see the struggle in his face between control and anger. His courtroom face. Control wins out; it always does. "Anna, what is this behavior? What has happened to you down here this summer? You're not yourself."

"This is myself. You're just not used to me not caving in to everything you want."

"Is that how you see me, always having to have my own way?"

"Think about it. How many times in the past few years have I argued with you about anything?" I turn and face Gregory. More than anything I want him to look straight at me, the way he did out there among the wrecked locusts.

"You came down here and spent the summer, didn't you?" Gregory lets go of my arm; I can see him processing his actions, realizing he's acting the heavy with his body if not with his words. He's facing me now, but still not looking directly at me. His eyes shift to the side, where the blank television screen offers no challenge.

"Look at me, Gregory!" I'm losing control; I can feel it. "This is me. Why can't you hear what I say, what I want? I needed to be here this summer, to get away. I've been happy here, away from the pressure, away from—"

"Away from me?"

"Not you; away from the pity, and all those friends we had who avoid us now, those people who knew us before." But even as I say the words I know I am lying.

Is all marital fighting so predictable? We've said all this before; I feel a sense of *deja vu*. The quarrel ends the way it always does, with Greg's voice sounding more and more level and logical, though he is white around the mouth from the effort, and my voice rising into that register I hate, the voice of an emotional, hysterical woman. Nothing is resolved. The rain is falling in sheets now, trapping us in the house together. We spend the rest of the morning avoiding each other, Greg working in the parlor, I surreptitiously reading Phoebe's journals, which I have stored under the bed. As I go upstairs, Lesley is just coming down for breakfast. She stiffens and looks away as we pass each other. She has heard us fighting, and there's no doubt who she blames.

> September 14: Grief is like a long, serious illness—there comes a day, long before you are truly well, when you know you will survive. Not that the pain is gone. God knows, it's worse than ever, but now I can feel it. It's welcome, after the numbness.
>
> Yesterday, halfway around the marsh on Commerce Road, a flood of tears. I tried to outdistance them and startled the great blue. He took off with a slow, deliberate flap of wings, lifting his heavy body into the air against the odds.
>
> It's a luxury to feel anything after such a long time. There's a sensual pleasure, a release in tears. A letting go. It happens, now, two or three times a day and leaves me exhausted and relieved. And then for a few hours at least I don't feel the pain. The gift along with all this weeping is that now the memories come flooding back, and I can let them. Camilla—I can say her name. I can see her in her little red and white ruffled dress. She loved that dress, and the necklaces

I would make for her out of pop-it beads. Her little white sandals I
have hidden in the attic and can't bear to throw away.

D cannot speak of her yet.

September 1958. A little over a year after Phoebe lost her child. I
recognize what she describes, the numbness, the images of freezing and
thawing. For me it's been five years. Is that what this summer has been
about, the return of feeling after years of ice, of not daring to feel because
it meant unbearable pain? Depression is the freezing of emotions, my
therapist taught me, a defense mechanism to fend off pain that can't be
borne. But it must be borne, sooner or later. Demetrius has given me
passion, and laughter, and self-acceptance. And this place, this beautiful
landscape, has welcomed me and healed me, with Phoebe as my guide.
But the pain is still there, and I can't avoid it much longer. I can sense it
waiting, up there just ahead of me.

It is painful, being here in bed with Greg. We both lie stiffly,
pretending we are asleep. I can feel the frustration radiating off his body.
In all our years of marriage, we've never developed the skills for mending
a quarrel, perhaps because we both come from families where quarreling
wasn't allowed. Our arguments peter out, unresolved. Greg stonewalls; I
capitulate. I lie beside him unmoving, feeling nothing but cold resentment.
Nothing as warm as anger. Not even guilt, though heaven knows I should
be consumed by it. How could I betray this man? Most of my friends are
halfway in love with him, and why shouldn't they be? Tall and lean, with
his shock of silky dark hair just beginning to recede and turn gray. An
elegant man, immaculate-looking even in a golf shirt and khakis. A good
provider who works himself to death for us. Or works himself to death to
avoid us. Who startled me today when he looked straight at me because
that's something he never does.

It frightens me to feel so cold toward him. There was a moment,
out in the yard this morning, when I felt something—a rush of gratitude
because he was worried about us. Because he took my arm and looked me
in the face. But now I feel nothing but resignation.

What would happen if I turned to him now and told him I have a
lover? That I can't endure the coldness between us any longer? That I want
a divorce? Would he look at me then? And what if he agreed? Is that what
I want?

The Antidote

*. . . of all the processes of geological creation, none washes
and renews the earth's supplies as thoroughly as the sea.*

APHNE CAN TELL by the left-leaning slant of the red channel marker
that the tide has turned. She keeps her eye on the sail for signs of
luffing, pointing as high as she can into the wind. It feels wonderful to get
the *Little Gull* rigged again and back out on the harbor. She hasn't been
sailing since before the hurricane, that time with Paul, though why she
thought he'd take to a Beetle Cat she can't now imagine. Paul's idea of a
sailboat was one with a galley and a head and mahogany trim, or at the
very least seats so he wouldn't have to endure what he called "sprawling on
the floor and ducking every goddamn two minutes" when she came about.
Her mental editor, always on the alert, notes she's thinking of Paul in the
past tense and she smiles. A good sign.

It's lovely being out on the water without the whine of motorboats
everywhere. Most of them were hauled out before the storm and won't
reappear since it's nearly Labor Day. She wedges the mainsheet into the
jam cleat so her hands are free and leans back beside the tiller, which
responds easily to the pressure of her arm. The *Little Gull* skims along
effortlessly, going with the tide. The gentle slap of water against the hull,
the creaks of the mast are hypnotic. The trauma of the past week seems as
far away as the shrinking shore behind her. Her desperate afternoon with
Anna might have happened to someone else.

Phoebe sailed with her to Sandy Neck once, she remembers now,
on a day very much like this one. She took to it right away even though
she hadn't been in a sailboat since she was a girl, since those summers she
spent on the North Shore (funny how a trace of Beacon Hill surfaced
in the vowels when she said "North Shore," meaning Manchester-by-
the-Sea). Scrambling around when they came about bothered her not a
whit. She had good natural balance and an instinct for timing. Nimble for
someone who called herself a creaky old lady.

That day—it must have been four years ago and sometime late in
August—Daphne had only had the *Little Gull* for a couple of months

and was just starting to feel at home in her. They'd packed a picnic, loaded some towels and beach chairs and an umbrella under the deck, and set off for the point in a good steady breeze. They'd sailed smartly up on the beach, unloaded their gear, and anchored the boat on the edge of the channel, elated to be the only people there. They'd swum and eaten their picnic and gone for a long walk around the point, climbing up into the dunes, spotting the faint needle on the horizon that was Provincetown Monument, and marveling at the wreck of tangled steel that had once been a signal tower, twisted grotesquely and blown down by some long-ago winter storm.

That was the day Phoebe told Daphne about her daughter Camilla, and about Demetrius. And Daphne told Phoebe about Susan. Two women with lost daughters. They had hugged each other, even cried, there on the edge of the dunes, looking out across Cape Cod bay. "This is the cure," Phoebe had said. "The perfect antidote—to plunge into the world. To look out across some great expanse—funny how grief curls us up inside ourselves. A view like this," she said, her eye moving out from the sugary sand they were sitting on, over the rounded, many-colored stones at the water's edge, the green-gold of submerged sand bars blending into every shade of blue stretching out to the horizon, its line of demarcation from the sky just beginning to blur in the afternoon haze. "I need the ocean to look at."

It must have been the following summer when Phoebe brought up the subject of Camilla again. Lost daughter. Only three when she died. The irony, the year of the last really bad polio epidemic, before the vaccine became widely available. That's when Dennis really started going downhill, when he'd disappear sometimes for days, leaving her in that empty house. She said some nights she couldn't stand being inside and would take a pile of quilts up on the hill and just lie there looking up at the stars. Demetrius lost to her as well. It ended, then.

Daphne thinks of her own story, not that it could come close for tragedy. Susan—how had it happened? Every teenage girl hates her mother, and most probably see her as the villain if there's a divorce. But the rift never healing, even later, after college, after law school. Susan went as far away as she could. Stanford, Berkeley Law. And now, how many years without so much as a holiday call—six, seven?

Daphne hauls in the sail and shoves the tiller away from her, turning the *Little Gull* into the wind, then quickly reaches forward to pull up and fasten the centerboard. She ducks instinctively under the flapping sail as the boom swings back and forth. Momentum carries the boat neatly up on the beach fifty feet short of the point. A perfect landing, and on only one tack all the way from Kettle Lane. Daphne feels a little swell of pride, even though there's no one around to see.

She should take Anna sailing one of these days, she thinks as she sets the anchor firmly in the soft sand and pushes the boat out to catch the channel current. Maybe when her helper gets here. She can't imagine what it must be like to be tied down that way to an eternally helpless child, like having a toddler only much worse, all the physical drudgery and no end to it, ever. Yet Anna doesn't complain. Could she do that, Daphne wonders. All the nightmare worries she dwelt on that year she was pregnant: Down's, malformations, cerebral palsy, some rare unpronounceable genetic disease. Could she, if she had to? People do, don't they? She thinks about moments she's seen Anna with Dorothea, the way she rests her hand on the girl's shining cap of hair. She loves her, in spite of everything.

Like Phoebe with Dennis. His drinking, the cirrhosis, his overwhelming neediness those last years. Yet Phoebe loved him. Trying to explain it to Daphne once, she quoted C. S. Lewis— marriage as an endless conversation. The old stories, the bantering—did it make up for the drudgery? The irony that both of them would turn to Demetrius. Anna's affair a surprise; she seemed at first so conventional, but after that appalling dinner party Daphne can understand why. Anna deserves some human warmth after living with that automaton. Her anger at finding out about Phoebe and Demetrius not so hard to understand when Daphne thinks back to her own surprise that day Phoebe told her, right here on Sandy Neck where she is now. Anna mostly angry because she never guessed. Who would imagine, with the fifteen-year age difference, especially in that generation? Now that she knows, Daphne wonders if she's broken Phoebe's trust. She likes Anna, is beginning to treasure their friendship. Should she tell all of Phoebe's secrets? Whom do we owe more to, the living or the dead?

With supper over, Daphne lingers on the deck above the pond with a cup of coffee. She's promised herself to work tonight to make up for the day on the water and hopes the caffeine will be enough to keep her going. She can't concentrate at night the way she used to. A sign of age, probably. Aging: She's just beginning to think about what it might mean. What would it be like (should she use *would* or *will* as the verb in that thought?)

now that she's up here away from any family? Who is she kidding? What family? The cousins in the city? Susan, out there on the West Coast?

Isolation has never frightened her, even when she was a child. Still, it would be (*was*—she's thinking of Paul again, using the past tense) wonderful to wake in the mornings to the available warmth of familiar arms, the everyday miracle of sex, someone there when she needed another voice, another mind to define herself against. But always? All day long when she was trying to think, to write? She chose a solitary profession, or rather, it chose her. Being alone doesn't bother her; she finds it freeing. That's the first thing she and Phoebe discovered they had in common.

It's peculiar, how Phoebe has been on her mind all day. She needs to talk to Anna about the journals; she'd like to get them back before Anna leaves and it's nearly Labor Day. There's a story there, though what she'll do with it isn't clear to her yet. Not a memoir; some of what she knows she can't reveal while the relatives are still alive, not that they deserve protecting. Fiction, it will have to be. A short story, centered on Phoebe's calm exterior, her hidden secrets? Or is there enough drama in that quiet life to make a novel? How much more alluring it is to think about Phoebe, to plan a new project, than to buckle down to the task at hand, finishing the draft of *End of Days*. It tires her to think about it. Perhaps the whole idea was a mistake and she should scrap it.

Daphne laughs to herself. By now she's familiar with all her avoidance strategies—artful dodges, she calls them. Getting through these final chapters is such a slog; it's been weeks since she's felt that energy surge that comes when she's writing well. She knows why, of course. The story hits too close to home. The estranged daughter, back home in Vermont to sort through her dead father's things. The revelation that makes her realize she'd misjudged him all those years. The sense of reconciliation, comforting even if too late. Like it might have been with her own father. Except when he died there was no revelation. Her mother did the sensible thing and went through his things herself, packing up his clothes, even his cashmere coat, and giving them all to charity. Daphne loved that cashmere coat. If she shortened the sleeves it would have fit her perfectly. His personal papers, mementoes—surely he had some—must have gone down the trash chute.

Her mind takes the logical jump to her own future death, her own daughter going through her things. What would she think; what would she find? Maybe all this dwelling on Phoebe isn't a distraction from the novel after all. Funny how the center of attention in her writing seems to be shifting, from youth and passion and being caught up in the sweep of history, to something more inward. Aging and regret, that's what this one is about. Parents dying. The impossibility of knowing who they were, the struggle to escape seeing them only in relation to ourselves. What do we do with all the regret?

Foolishness. Daphne crosses to her work table, switches on the computer, listens impatiently to its whirrs and hums as it boots up and greets her with its annoying little tune. She starts by proofing yesterday's work to prime the pump, and by nine-thirty she's banged out three and a half pages of adequate if not brilliant text. Mostly description, mostly based on her own father's den in their Seventy-third Street apartment. Men had dens then; women had sewing rooms, though not, of course, her mother, who sent everything out to the dressmaker, even hems. They'd both have home offices now. And a family room for the children, or in her case, child. Kneehole desk, always stacked with papers though he never sat there. The red leather chair and ottoman where he did sit, that her mother hated.

A sense of claustrophobia is what she's after. Claudia, the daughter in her story, associates the den with serious conversations having to do with lapses in her behavior or upsetting decisions, like whether she should be sent up to Massachusetts to boarding school. The atmosphere isn't really working, Daphne can tell. But she's got words down on the page; that's a start. She'll firm up the sentences, flesh out the imagery tomorrow. Add a childhood reminiscence or two. That bit about boarding school, what her cousin Ellie on Staten Island told her when she asked what it was. Ellie's mother, Daphne's Aunt Liz, used it as a threat whenever Ellie misbehaved. "Any more sass like that, Miss, and you'll find yourself in boarding school," she would yell in exasperation. Ellie was ten, maybe, Daphne only about five, following her cousin everywhere, idolizing her. Boarding school, Liz told Daphne, is where they strap you to a board and throw you off a dock and let you float away. Terrifying prospect when she hadn't even learned to swim. No wonder, ten years later when her parents seriously considered boarding school (it was possible for them; unlike Aunt Liz, her father had married up), she'd reacted with a flat refusal and a great slamming of doors.

When the phone rings, it startles her. It's nearly ten—no one she knows would be calling at this hour. Paul? Tonight is the night the play closes; probably he's heading back to New York tomorrow. The thought freezes her in place as she is about to pick up the phone. What in the world would she say to him? Better leave well enough alone. She listens to the four rings, waits through the pause while her recorded message plays, and then hears a voice. Not Paul. A woman's voice, faint, hesitant, sounding only vaguely familiar. But what it's saying, or asking, is "Mom?"

In Harm's Way

*For a distance of a hundred miles south of the moving ice
front the air was chilled.*

A T LEAST LESLEY knows what the fight's about now. It's about the
house, whether they should sell it or not. Dad wants to, and Mom
doesn't. She keeps bringing up Aunt Phoebe, like she's still alive or something. Lesley's been thinking all week that she'd like to go home, but if the
house got sold, she'd be really upset about not coming back next summer.
She's had her heart set on a kayak. And Phil—if he doesn't come back she
might not ever see him again. She doesn't even have his winter address.
She can't say anything because the only reason she knows about the house
is she's been eavesdropping. What her parents don't know is if she lies
down next to the grate on the floor of her room she can hear everything
that goes on in the parlor below.

Dad left kind of early on Sunday. He was supposed to stay down this
week but he's got a big case that he can't get out of. Mom didn't seem too
upset when he told her. He didn't think about if Lesley was upset. And
Jeannine isn't coming back today after all. She called Friday night to say
she had a horrible cold. It was probably the truth; Lesley answered the
phone and Jeannine's voice was all harsh and crackly. She isn't the kind of
person to make up lies to get out of things anyway, not like some people.

At least the rain has stopped. It's gotten warm and muggy but it's
still all cloudy and foggy and looking like it might rain again any minute.
Lesley stays in bed until she's sure Mom is through exercising Dorrie. She
promised herself on Friday that she'd help out more, but she really doesn't
feel like it this morning. After her bowl of cereal she's restless; she hasn't
done much of anything since her long walk on Friday. A swim would feel
good. She puts on her new Speedo bathing suit, standing on the bed to get
a glimpse of herself in the small mirror over the dresser. The reflection surprises her. She looks like a grown woman, with boobs and a real waistline.
She could be sixteen, maybe. Those boys in the car that whistled at her on
6A—what if they knew she was only twelve? Well, going on thirteen. She
hops down off the bed, fastens the velcro straps of her Tevas around her

feet, throws her father's baggy Harvard sweatshirt on over the suit, and clatters down the narrow stairs and out the parlor door.

The tide is up pretty far, about a half hour past high. Lesley gasps as she plunges in. The water is icy, much colder than it's felt all summer. The hurricane must've brought in water from way out in the North Atlantic. It's too cold to stay in long. She shivers as she sits down on her towel. The air temperature is warm but it's still cloudy. No sun today, it doesn't look like. Maybe tomorrow. Her eye is caught by a spot of red far across the harbor close to the point. A red kayak. Phil! His family must have come back over the weekend. She wishes he had come around to tell her he was back, but then he never did come to her house, just always took the chance of seeing her on the beach. Too far away now to spot her sitting here on the sand. She'll have to catch him later.

By the time lunch is over, the sun is out after all, but the temperature has dropped too far to think about another swim. Some kind of front has come through, with a little band of dark gray clouds and rain, followed by a fresh northwest wind that is kicking up whitecaps on the harbor. Lesley keeps thinking about Phil, about that night over on Sandy Neck beach when he grabbed her underwater and kissed her. She's got to see him, make sure he's really back. She could take a walk past his house, maybe, go by the road, maybe pretend she's out for a jog. But he'd never buy that—he knows she never jogs. She'll take Dorrie with her, push her in the wheel-chair, give Mom a break. It's time she told Phil about Dorrie anyway. The thought scares her. Maybe he'll be grossed out. But he seems too nice for that. Maybe he'll just take her for granted as part of Lesley's family, like his own brother, Jake the dropout.

Mom is amazed, that's the only word for it, when Lesley offers to take Dorrie for a walk. She has about a million questions about where they're going. "Just down 6A a ways," Lesley says. "To the post office. I've got postcards to mail." It's nearly two before they set off. Lesley has showered and washed her hair and put it up on her head, the way Mom said made her look grown up. She's wearing a new T-shirt, balanced off with her frayed jean shorts, so she won't look too dressed up, like she hasn't put all kinds of thought into what she looks like. She clambers back up on her bed to take another long look in the mirror. The jean shorts are old and worn but her legs look nice.

By the time she gets downstairs, Mom has Dorrie out in the yard in Pegasus. Dorrie's wearing her gross flowered cotton pants and an old tennis hat of Mom's to keep the sun off her face. She smiles at Lesley

and moves her hand up and down in the funny way she has, glad to be
going somewhere. Lesley wheels her down the middle of Kettle Lane
without meeting a single car and turns onto the narrow sidewalk along
the north side of 6A. It's hard going. The surface is lumpy and there are
places where roots have worked their way up through the asphalt. It's
much farther down 6A to Phil's road than it seems when she goes the
beach way. Lighthouse Lane, it's called. It's almost as far as Blackberry
Lane, the turn to West Marsh. And Phil's house is a long way down the
lane, practically to the beach. Lesley's not sure which house it is at first
since she's always approached it from the water side, but then she sees
the boathouse down on the creek, and the red kayak pulled up onto the
grass beside it. Phil must be back from Sandy Neck. She feels the inside
of her stomach clench in a funny way, her hands turn cold and wet with
sweat. Before she has a chance to back out, she wheels Pegasus across
the flagstones to what looks like the kitchen door and knocks hesitantly,
peering through the screen.

The face that materializes on the other side of the door doesn't look
familiar. Lesley has a moment of confusion before she recognizes who it
is: the boy with the beach buggy, Ken. He doesn't seem to know who she
is, either. "Hey, gal," he says, opening the door and smiling, then taking an
instinctive step backward when he gets a look at Dorrie's face under the
wide-brimmed hat.

Lesley's used to it by now, that unconscious way people turn aside
when they see Dorrie's twisted-looking face. They're trying to figure out
what's wrong with her, Lesley knows. A cripple? Retard? She's heard
the words, sometimes said out loud, sometimes muttered to friends.
Sometimes she just imagines them silently crossing people's minds. They
hurt just as much, spoken or not. She's learned to take the offensive,
explain before she's asked. "She's my sister Dorrie," she says. "She got
paralyzed during an operation. I'm Lesley, remember? I went with you to
Sandy Neck beach back a couple of weeks ago."

"Hey gal, yeah," Ken says, looking doubtful.

"Phil's friend," Lesley prompts.

"Yeah, now I remember," he says. "Kettle Lane."

"You got it," Lesley answers. It feels funny, this kind of banter. She
can hear herself sounding like those older girls on the beach the night of
the party.

"Does she talk?" Ken asks, gesturing towards Dorrie, who is looking
up at him with an uncertain expression.

Lesley hates it when people talk about Dorrie as if she wasn't there. "She makes noises but she doesn't really talk," Lesley says. "But she understands a lot of what's being said. You can talk to her if you want."

"I'd rather talk to you, Sweet cakes."

Sweet cakes. Phil's brother Jake called her Sweets, that night on the beach. Then, just as she is thinking about him, Jake walks into the kitchen, followed by another boy she's never seen before, a tall, rangy, athletic-looking boy with short spiky blond hair. They're both carrying empty beer bottles.

"Phil here?" Lesley asks hesitantly.

Jake edges his way around Ken and puts his arm around her shoulder. "Won't we do, Sweets?" Sweets again. "Who's this? You babysitting her?"

"This is Dorrie. She's my sister. She got hurt in the hospital, during an operation. Her heart stopped and now she's paralyzed." For years her mother's been saying the easiest thing is to just tell it like it is. Maybe she's been right.

"Wow. That's major."

"It happened a long time ago. We've gotten used to it. Is Phil here?"

Jake's arm is still around Lesley's shoulders. Now he turns and propels her through the kitchen towards the porch beyond. "Phil's not here . . . not right now. Why don't you have a drink and wait for him? How about your sister? She like beer? How old is she, anyway? Hey Worm, this is Phil's squeeze, Lesley. Cute, huh?"

Worm, if that's his real name, looks her up and down, his eyes lingering on her chest in a way that makes her feel squeamish inside. He smells like beer. So does Jake. She's not sure about the other one, Ken. She wonders where Phil is. Out with his parents, probably. There aren't any cars in the yard except for Jake's old truck and Ken's beach buggy. She should have recognized it from that night on Sandy Neck.

Lesley is beginning to feel more and more uneasy. Jake asks her again if she wants a drink. "Got any juice?"

"Sure, Sweets. Let me get it."

"Hey Jake, let me help," Worm says. They disappear into the kitchen and come back a few minutes later with two glasses of orange juice. "Your sister like one?"

"No thanks. She has a special cup she uses." No way Lesley is going to try to get Dorrie to drink from a regular glass in front of these guys. She takes a big slug of her own orange juice. It tastes good; she's thirsty; she drinks the rest of it down quickly. "Where did you say Phil went?"

"Didn't say. Isn't baby brother a little young for you, Sweets? How about me?" Jake sits down on the sofa beside her. Now his arm is around her neck and he's pulling her towards him.

He's going to kiss her, she realizes. What's he doing? He must be drunk. He doesn't know what he's doing. She pulls away from him with some difficulty and stands up. "I've got to get home," she says, trying to sound less scared than she feels. "Tell Phil I came by, okay? When he gets home?"

The tall boy, Worm, seems to find her very amusing. He keeps laughing—Lesley isn't sure why. She steers Dorrie back to the kitchen and towards the door, grateful that no one blocks her way. The three boys are all out on the porch now, talking in low voices. Then out of nowhere they're all around her. "Come on, Babycakes, stay awhile. You just got here," the one called Worm is saying. "Party with us. Your friend Phil won't be back. He's gone back to Holliston with his folks. It's just us working stiffs here." She feels funny, lightheaded, wired up from being scared, probably. She's got to get back outside. She pushes an arm out of her way (it's Ken's, she thinks) and backs out through the screen door, keeping Dorrie's wheelchair between her and the boys. Jake hangs onto the arms of the wheelchair for a moment. Is he teasing her or is he going to hold her here? Why is she feeling so weird, like something is wrong with her eyes? She pushes the chair against him, throwing him momentarily off balance, and makes her escape out into the yard and back towards the street. The boys are about to follow her when a car comes down the street from the direction of 6A. All three of them duck back into the house. A moment later the same car passes her again in the opposite direction. An older couple, probably just sightseeing or scouting For Sale signs, what Daphne calls peepers. They drive down Kettle Lane all the time, annoying the people who live there. But this time Lesley is grateful.

She rolls Dorrie down the lane, going too fast and making the wheelchair bounce. Dorrie sets up a loud sound, something between a moan and a hum. By the time they reach 6A Lesley's head is spinning. She stands there on the corner, trying to think what to do. She hears a motor behind her and turns to look. It's Ken's beach buggy with all three boys aboard. Lesley feels a jolt of fear, and then another wave of dizziness. She might really pass out. What should she do? The boys pull out onto 6A and turn right, calling to her but not stopping, thank God. She's got to lose them. But first she has to find a place where she can sit down, or lie down. The sunlight is beginning to hurt her eyes, the patches of shadow on the road are running together. She hesitates for a minute, looking carefully up and down to check for traffic, then crosses 6A and turns left. Fifty yards down on the right side is Blackberry Lane, the way to West Marsh. If she can get off the road before the boys come back they'll never find her. She needs to get to the bog house where Dorrie will be safe and she can lie down. If Demetrius is there he'll drive them home. And if he's not, she has the key, still in the pocket of her jean shorts where she put it on Friday.

Her head is feeling worse and worse. She's beginning to lose track of time, of where she is. It seems forever before she gets to Cove Road, the last turn. A few feet from the corner she wheels Dorrie up into the tall grass on the side of the road and sits down. Her head sinks between her knees, falling forward with a jerk that startles her awake. Her eyes focus for a moment on her sister. Dorrie is humming, looking at the flowers on the side of the road, the many little blue and yellow butterflies that flit from one to another. Dorrie is stretching out her good left hand—she wants to touch the butterflies. Lesley does too, but her arms feel heavy, as if they were paralyzed. The butterflies quiver there, tempting, just beyond her reach.

Someone drives up and stops. Lesley lifts her head. How long have they been there? Could she really fall asleep sitting up? Demetrius, she thinks. But it isn't Demetrius. It's the white beach buggy, with Ken and Jake and the other, the tall one with the awful name, all standing there smiling at her though she doesn't remember them getting out of the truck, something in their faces she doesn't dare to read.

"Please," Lesley says, wondering why the boys don't know what she wants. "Down there." Her tongue feels thick in her mouth, like it's been paralyzed. She reaches into her pocket and pulls out the key and hands it to Jake. "Please . . . I'm sick."

"Don't worry, Baby, we'll take care of you," somebody is saying, Lesley isn't sure which one.

"What's this say? *Bog House*. Hey, I know where she's going. The cranberry bog—it's just down here on the right."

"Come on, Baby, we'll drive you there," someone is saying. The van, Lesley wants to say but her tongue won't work any more. Then they are lifting her up, propping her in the back of the truck, and lifting Dorrie wheelchair and all and setting her on the truck bed. Two of the boys crouch beside the wheelchair to keep it from rolling while Ken drives slowly down the road and turns onto the track at West Marsh. Let

Demetrius be here, Lesley is praying with what is left of her mind. But there's no blue truck, no sign of him anywhere.

Someone is reaching under her arms, lifting her up and out of the truck, setting her down, lifting her up again in his arms like a little kid, carrying her somewhere dark, somewhere she's been before, laying her down on some sort of bed. It smells of mildew. She's grateful to be lying down, that she can stop fighting the overpowering urge to sleep.

She wakes out of a dream of drowning, fighting her way up to the surface to feel herself held down, arms over her head, hands everywhere, lifting her shirt, running down her front, pinching her nipple, hurting her. She gets to cry out once before the hands are over her nose and mouth, smothering her. Someone is laughing. Pulling at her shorts, slipping them down, yanking at her underpants, someone raising her knees, pushing them far apart, now down on her, probing at her, shoving against her, hurting her. Behind it, the laughing. And further away, an awful animal noise, somewhere between a moan and a scream, going on and on and on. She's fully awake now, flailing like a drowning person fighting for air, still not knowing where she is but knowing what. Someone is raping her. She struggles harder, breaks free from the hand over her mouth, screams once again before the hand clamps down. Then the laughter breaks off, footsteps, shouts, scuffling sounds and a voice she knows, a man's voice, shouting "No! Not again!" Then a sound she doesn't understand, sharp and dull at the same time, jolting her from a distance like a blow through a pillow, and the force she's been struggling against lets go and collapses onto her, heavy and inert, pinning her down.

Damage

*The land lay locked in frost . . . swept by winds and
storms and often cloaked in fog.*

L ESLEY DOESN'T REMEMBER, thank God. At least her conscious mind
doesn't. She dreams, though, and wakes struggling. I hear her through
the walls, two rooms away, and get up and go to her two, sometimes three
times a night. The night light in the hall is on all the time now, as it was
when the girls were little.

She may never remember. It's not just posttraumatic amnesia. It's
from the drug those boys gave her, rohypnol, roofies, the date rape drug,
it's called. What does the word *date* have to do with my twelve-year-old
daughter? Or the word *rape*? Technically, we are told, she wasn't raped
in the usual sense. They called it *incomplete penetration*. Stopped just in
time. Technically, Lesley is still intact, though surely not a virgin in the
usual sense, now that she's been deceived, drugged, held down and gagged,
spreadeagled and attacked (the map of her struggle there for all to read on
her body, even if she couldn't tell us in her own words). Violated. Thank
God she doesn't remember.

But Dorothea does remember. Technically, she *was* raped, not just in
the usual sense, was penetrated, first with a thrusting penis and then the
wooden handle of a hoe. She is not intact, her internal organs bruised,
her vagina nearly ruptured. The words keep swimming around in my
mind. *Attacked; not intact.* More horrifying even than the usual horror.
Something the cruelest sadist would hesitate to do to an animal.

I am thrust back into that other time, five years ago, when we weren't
sure she would even survive. The numb shock, the denial, the need to
blame. But so much worse now because I know who's to blame. Those
boys, yes, but also myself. I wasn't paying attention. Does Gregory blame
me? Of course he doesn't know the depth of my guilt.

Dorothea is not the same. She's gone away to someplace far inside
herself. Catatonic, almost, or like the most severely autistic child, gone
from the world of human contact. But I will fetch her back. I have to. I
spend all day with her, these days, working with Jeannine on her exercises.

Mornings are hardest. She flinches and cries out the first time we touch her. Sometimes when I take her arm to put it through a sleeve, or to balance her in the bathroom, she jerks away. She doesn't look at any of us, doesn't smile her crooked smile. But she will come back to us. She has to.

Jeannine has been a godsend. She's been here, staying at the house since the day we brought Dorothea home from the hospital even though she had another week of vacation. She's devoted herself, not just to Dorrie but to me, taking over most of the cooking, staying downstairs to keep me company in the evenings when Gregory isn't home, teaching me how to crochet, a skill she learned from her grandmother, who used it to calm herself all through World War II. Now that her semester has started, I worry she'll fall behind in her classes, but she says it's no problem. I thank God for her, the only other person besides Lesley and me that Dorrie doesn't find terrifying. Even Gregory, being a man, sets her screaming. He's taken to avoiding her, which fills me with sadness.

Gregory has changed, too. He looks older, more stooped, weary. He's not sleeping well, and when he does, sometimes I wake to the sound of him grinding his teeth. He feels to blame. He's the girls' father; his job is to keep them safe. I know much of his anger is focused on Phoebe's house and my insistence on staying there. He hasn't come out and blamed me directly, but I know that's how he feels. "God, I hate that place," he said when the police were questioning Lesley about the bog house.

And I? Have I changed? I can't even think about myself. I feel shut down, numb. The girls consume me. When I think of Demetrius, my gratitude for what he did is overwhelmed by my guilt. If I hadn't been so caught up with him, if I had paid attention, none of this would have happened. Would it?

Lesley has started school again. It has helped some, but she comes straight home every day and spends the afternoons alone in her room. There was no way to keep the story out of the papers. The girls' names were suppressed, but the boys were fair game, all over eighteen. Not boys, but surely not men. What in God's name do I call them?

Lesley told the police what she did remember, in the hospital the day after the attack. She was confused, groggy from sedatives, strangely uncurious about how she got there or had gotten hurt. She didn't know about Dorrie, or that Demetrius had spent all night at the police station being questioned, and none of us knew, then, that the boy was there in the same hospital, upstairs in the ICU. They sent two women officers from the rape team. One sat with me through the exam Lesley mercifully dozed through. *Rape kit*, they call it, what they use for what they do.

Lesley had gone over to see her friend Phil, she told them. She'd seen his kayak out on the bay and thought his family was back. I didn't comment on the oddness of her taking Dorrie with her. But Phil wasn't there, or his parents, just his brother—Jake, his name was—and the other two. She'd met Jake before, and one of the others, on the beach. They lied to her, told her Phil would be home right away. That's how they got her to come inside. They gave her some orange juice and brought some for Dorrie, too, but Lesley hadn't wanted her to drink in front of them because Dorrie always made such a mess. Oh Lesley, I thought, if only you'd given it to her! If only she could have amnesia! What are her memories like, locked there inside her silent mind? Is there a way to erase them? All I can do is try to replace them with something safe, loving looks and touches that don't terrify, a sure, familiar everyday routine. But this is something I don't talk about with Lesley, who feels guilty enough, even though she is not to blame.

There's enough guilt to go around. My glimpse of Demetrius as I drove up just as the EMTs arrived, sitting in the back of a police car, his face wet with tears. Jeannine, who somehow thinks she's at fault for staying home with a cold. And Greg, whose grim silence frightens me, who has plunged himself into the only thing he knows how to do. He has withdrawn from his big Washington case, spent the past two weeks mostly on the phone. The corporate lawyer learning his way around the grimy world of criminal law. He does not talk to me about what he's doing, and I don't ask. And I? Have I felt the full impact of my guilt? Will it ever end?

Today I am not with Dorothea, though. Today Gregory and I are in Barnstable, sitting in the big gray courthouse I've always admired, looming over the village with its imposing columns I am surprised now to see are made of wood. I am grateful for the beauty of the old-fashioned courtroom, its warm paneling, the incongruous gilded cod that hangs over our heads.

I concentrate on the elaborately carved moldings behind the judge's bench, avoiding looking over to the right where the boys are sitting with their parents and lawyers. Only two of them. The other one, William Hendricks, is still in the hospital, out of danger now, no longer in a coma, but with possible residual brain damage. It's too soon to tell. Despite myself I find some justice in that. Lesley didn't know his real name. She'd only heard his nickname and couldn't even remember that, except it sounded like something awful. His parents are here, though, along with Jake Petersen's. Jake, brother of Phil, the boy Lesley went kayaking with all summer. I never bothered to seek out and size up his family, just blindly trusted him with my daughter, caught up as I was in my own madness. Phil is not here. What must he think of all this? Brothers. Was he, would he be equally dangerous?

Demetrius isn't here, either. Not in the courtroom, anyway. Most likely he will be called as a witness later, assuming there is a trial. He spent all night at the police station, that first night and part of the next morning, being questioned. They were waiting, I realize now, to see if the Hendricks boy would die. Gregory went to see Demetrius the next afternoon, once we were sure Dorothea was out of danger, to thank him. I persuaded him to go. He was sitting in the hospital looking so lost. I was aching to see Demetrius myself, but I wouldn't leave the girls. I had to be there when Dorothea woke up.

The hour Greg was gone was terrible. Images of the bog house kept flashing through my mind, Dorothea discarded on the floor like a heap of old rags, moaning or screaming, those three monsters clustered around Lesley, holding her down. Unspeakable. What if Demetrius hadn't arrived when he did? And what if those boys—men, really, full-grown, and three of them—what if they had turned on him? And behind all those images, the thought of Gregory and Demetrius talking. What would they say? My two men, betrayer and betrayed. Would it come out somehow? The question fills me with self-loathing. My life doesn't matter, not now. Nothing matters except finding a way to make my girls whole again.

When Gregory came back, he offered only the briefest outline of their conversation. Demetrius was shocked and regretful. "He kept apologizing," Gregory said.

"For what? Think if he hadn't shown up when he did."

"I know. But he kept saying he's not a violent man. He can't believe he nearly killed that kid."

"With good reason."

"Yes. I told him we'd take care of the legal side for him. He argued with me about it, but I think he'll agree. The only lawyer he knows is Flannery, and he's not equipped to handle something like this."

I couldn't ask all the questions I wanted to ask. What did it do to Demetrius to have Gregory there, offering to help? And does Gregory wonder why Lesley was at the bog house in the first place, or why she had the key? I want to know about the key, too, why she took it, though I know

where she got it. Off the kitchen table, that day I was going to return it
and left it there instead, unconsciously on purpose.

They don't make courtrooms beautiful like this any more. It has the
atmosphere and layout of a church, the heavy oak pews where we are
sitting, the jury's chairs arranged sideways almost like a choir stall, except
the judge's desk is where the altar would be, and behind, instead of a cross,
a range of bookshelves hold thick leather-bound volumes. A temple to the
law, this is, that holy abstraction to whom we appeal for redress. A place
where we behave as we do in church, silent and attentive, standing and
sitting on cue, because we feel small and powerless.

I do not want to be here. I tense my muscles to keep myself from
gathering my jacket and handbag, edging past the other people beside us,
and running out of the room. Gregory says it's important for us to be here,
as the girls are not. To put human faces on the victims' family, if not on the
victims themselves. I look sideways at Gregory. He looks grim, impassive.
A lawyer's, not a father's face.

Today is just a severance hearing, so the proceedings are brief.
The Petersens are petitioning for a separate trial for Jake. I know the
impression they want to make. Jake, one of the summer people, from a
good family, mixed up with two no-good locals who surprised him with
the drugs. Maybe they don't realize that being one of the summer people
is not an advantage in this courtroom. I don't buy Jake's innocence anyway.
The boys were on something when Lesley got there, cocaine and beer and
amphetamines, jazzed up and high. The police questioned Lesley carefully
about the orange juice: Who suggested it? Who actually brought her the
glass? It was Jake, she said, but the other boy, Kendricks, went into the
kitchen with him to get it, and they were laughing when they came back.

It's over in what seems like seconds. The bailiff commands "All rise."
The judge comes in, looking the way I imagined he would, a broad man
with a thick shock of gray hair over a florid Irish face. The lawyers present
their arguments, and the judge promises a ruling before the end of the
day. That's all; it's over for now. It's ridiculously simple and quick. No
witnesses; that will come later. As we file out into the narrow hall, I catch
a glimpse of the Petersens, the father looking defiantly at Gregory, aware,
probably, that he is a lawyer and used to courtrooms, the mother's head
down, looking at the floor.

When we emerge onto the courthouse lawn, we can see the harbor
spread out before us half a mile away. The sun is out. It's October and
the leaves are starting to turn. The fog that cloaked everything with dew

this morning has burned off, and a strong breeze has come up from the northwest, scattering whitecaps over the deep warm blue of the bay.

We won't stay for the judge's ruling. Gregory and I are in separate cars because I need to go by the house and pack up the clothes and food we left there six weeks ago in our hasty departure, and he has an early afternoon appointment in Boston. I feel nervous about seeing the house again, but as soon as I turn into the driveway I relax. Despite everything I'm glad to be back. The garden is a tangle of weeds and flowers, the last of the black-eyed Susans bending to the ground under their own weight, and behind them, airy pale blue asters that must have volunteered. I think sadly about sitting out back with Demetrius those summer days, drinking iced tea. Will that ever happen again? I can't think about it, or him.

The house is less welcoming, though I'm relieved to see the workmen have finished repairing the porch roof and replaced the broken windows. Someone—Demetrius, most likely—has repositioned the wicker furniture we had left stacked in the corner. All my feelings for him I've packed away, avoided all these weeks—there's no avoiding them here, where his handiwork confronts me everywhere I look. He wasn't in the courtroom today. Now I can admit my disappointment. Will he show up here, and if he doesn't, do I dare seek him out? And if I did, what would I say?

I have to struggle to open the kitchen door. It's cold and damp inside, with a musty smell. I open the refrigerator. It will need cleaning out. There's a half-full carton of very sour milk on the top shelf, and a malodorous head of slimy lettuce and furry carrots in the vegetable drawer. A cucumber from the garden has collapsed into a puddle of repulsive brown liquid under the lettuce. I close the drawer and the refrigerator. Time to deal with that later. I fetch a plastic garbage bag from under the sink to use for dirty laundry and head upstairs.

Everything takes longer than it should. I look around Lesley's room at the scattered clothing, the no longer wet bathing suit that has left a faint white ghost on the floor, and dissolve into tears. Her sketchbook is open on the unmade bed, along with three or four tee shirts she must have tried on and discarded. Going to see that boy, Phil, and thinking about how she looked. She was wearing those raggedy cutoffs, the ones that Gregory thinks are indecent. I leaf through the pages of the sketchbook. A few portraits of Daphne's cats. Lots of line drawings of plants, the cattails on Daphne's pond, the wild pea vines and poison ivy that line the path to the beach, very professionally done. About three pages back, a quick sketch of a boy's face. Phil. I close the book and add it to the take-home pile.

I gather up very few of my own summer things, hoping I'll be back before I'll need them. I don't have to pack for Gregory; he never leaves anything here. Back downstairs, I tackle Dorothea's room. It doesn't take long; she doesn't have very many clothes. How I wish I could yell at her for strewing around her T-shirts! It's much colder in here than it is upstairs. Cold and lifeless. I sit down on the neatly made bed for a minute while my eyes blur with tears.

I've been dawdling, and now it's after one o'clock. I'm cold and hungry, and anxious about Dorothea, whom I haven't left this long since the whole ordeal started. I heat a can of soup from the cupboard for lunch, which warms me a little, and call Jeannine in Needham to let her know I've been delayed. Everything's fine, she reassures me. Dorrie's okay, not agitated. She looked right at Jeannine while she was getting her dressed, a job I usually do. Maybe we've turned a corner. Maybe.

There's still the refrigerator to tackle. The kitchen is freezing. In another week or so there could be a hard frost. It's time to drain the pipes. Demetrius still has his key to the house. Will he want to keep coming over here, taking care of things? I'll have to talk to him about it. I haven't spoken to him since those first few frantic days, blocked him out of my mind, but now, here, the longing comes back. We can never, not now, not after what has happened. Does he feel the same way, as racked with guilt? Now, here, in Phoebe's house, my house, I long to comfort him. Comfort myself.

I can no longer postpone the refrigerator. I decide to warm the kitchen by heating up the stove. What a strange appliance, burning both gas and wood, with one foot in the nineteenth, one in the twentieth century! Janus, it ought to be called. That's something Phoebe would say. Phoebe—if only she were here, maybe she could tell me what to do.

There's no wood in the box on the porch or in the parlor next to the fireplace. I head out to the garage, where Demetrius always keeps a stack along the inside wall, out of the weather. The garage doors are unlocked, I notice, as I struggle to raise the latch and pull them open. Careless, though there's nothing inside but a very old lawn mower and a few garden tools. But when I swing the door open, there is something else there. A bright red kayak, with a beautiful wooden paddle resting inside. Scotch taped to the back of the seat, an envelope with a name scrawled in pencil in an uneven, childish hand: *Lesley*. It's not sealed, so I open and read it: *Lesley—This is for you. Dad is selling the house and we won't be back next summer. I'm so sorry what happened. Phil.*

Confrontations

As the ice wasted northward, it bared a widening scene of desolation.

A T FIRST I am so angry I want to smash the thing. Do they think they can buy Lesley off by giving her an expensive present? Or that we'd let her own something that would remind us all what they have cost us? I slam the garage door and stalk into the house. I will call them and let them know what I think of their kayak. Damn them! Damn Phil, who sounded so safe, damn him for having that brother, for not being there that day, and the parents, where were the parents? I pull the phone book out of the kitchen drawer and look up Peterson. I don't even know the father's first name. There are two whole columns of Petersons. But wait, it's Petersen with an *e*, and there are only six of those. Jacob Petersen, father of Jake, with a Yarmouth Port address, Lighthouse Lane. I dial the number before I think what I might say, so I won't lose courage. But by the time the phone has rung three times and I hear someone pick up the receiver, I think better of it and quickly hang up.

Maybe it would be wiser just to return the kayak sometime when the family isn't there. But that would take help, a truck or a van, and someone to help load it aboard. Demetrius. Do I dare call him, or go find him and ask? I've been longing to see him all day. I hoped he would be at the courthouse. Up in Needham, with the girls to worry about, I could go for days without thinking about him, but sitting in that courtroom this morning I had to face that he is tangled up in everything that has happened, that it might destroy his spirit, not to mention ruin him financially. What is he feeling about it all? Anger, or guilt that it is somehow his fault? And the questions I'm not ready to even think about: How do I feel about him? And what does he feel about us? How can there be an *us* now?

I force myself to finish cleaning the refrigerator first. It isn't too bad once I have dumped out and washed the vegetable bin, though the slime makes me want to gag. There is little else that has gone bad, just the milk and a leftover cube of moldy cheese. Thank God there wasn't any meat. I do a half-hearted job of wiping out the inside. My hands are freezing and

I have decided not to heat up the stove after all. I notice the clock—a little after two. I need to leave the Cape before three if I want to miss rush hour. I load up the car and drive down the lane, noting with regret that Daphne's car is in her driveway. She will wonder why I haven't stopped to see her. A real friend she's been, all summer, to me and the girls. I haven't even thought to call her, and now there's no time. But at the end of Kettle Lane I don't turn right, toward Boston, but left, down 6A to Yarmouth Port.

There is no sign of life at West Marsh, so I drive with some trepidation over to the cottage on the harbor, not at all sure how I'm going to react. Demetrius's truck is there. He appears at his door with a guarded look on his face, as apprehensive as I am, evidently, about meeting. He looks smaller than I remember, smaller and older. I step out of the car before he has a chance to open the door for me, and start to talk quickly so I don't have to cope with the images of earlier visits that are flooding over me. "I have a couple of things I need your help with," I say hastily. I can't look at him. I gaze out over the marsh instead. The little boathouse is already shut up for the winter, looking lifeless, the wooden blinds lowered and fastened tight. I remember the light that first day, how it bounced off the water and came in through the screens and danced over the walls and flashed in our eyes. Now the water is far away across the marsh. The tide is out, and the grasses have flattened, turning yellow and dying.

Demetrius does not approach me. He does not come and take me in his arms. "Down for the hearing?" he asks.

"Yes, and I've been back to the house. There were some things I needed to get."

"I wondered. Went by to check a couple times. How are the girls?"

"They're okay, physically. Lesley's back in school. But Dorothea— she's still recovering, and—oh, Demetruis, she's still so scared all the time. She remembers. Lesley doesn't because of the drug they gave her, but Dorothea does, even with her—with the way she is."

"I'm sorry; I'm so sorry." Hearing his words I begin to cry. More than anything I want him to put his arms around me, but he doesn't. I force myself to look at his face, but he just stands there where he is, looking frozen, looking miserable. Like all of us he feels responsible, even though he's the one who saved them—thank God he was there, I think for the hundredth time. If he hadn't shown up, what might have happened?

"It's not your fault. Good God, Demetrius, what if you hadn't come when you did? We're so grateful, so sorry that you've gotten dragged into it." I'm using that marital word, *we*.

"I keep doing it, bringing terrible things to your family, over and over again. You—I'll see about getting someone to keep an eye on the house."

"Don't you want to do it anymore?" I'm so dismayed by his second sentence I forget how confused I am by the first.

Demetruis turns away from me and looks out over the marsh, just as I have been doing. "It's not that, it's too many things. I should never have loved you. It's all happening again. It would be better—easier—if we didn't see each other any more."

"What do you mean, happening again? Do you mean loving Phoebe?"

"That, too."

I wait for him to elaborate but he doesn't. "Do you mean the way Phoebe died? That wasn't your fault. You know how independent she was."

I see the tears shining on his face in the afternoon sun. I badly want to take him in my arms, but I don't dare move. Demetrius runs both of his hands through his hair and turns toward me. I can't read his expression. "I feel bad I hadn't taken care of the ice. But I hurt her long before that." I remember Marte, his wife. He wasn't free to love Phoebe, and perhaps his guilt finally led him to break it off, just at the most painful time, when she had lost her child. But now he's saying something else, something about Gregory, only he calls him Greg.

"What about Greg?"

"All this—it must make him remember."

"Remember what?"

Again Demetrius pauses for what seems like a long time. He looks past me at the car. "What brought you over here?" he asks. "You said you need help with something?"

And so I ask him to drain the pipes, saying we won't be down again until the trial, which won't be scheduled for several weeks at the earliest, and then I tell him about the kayak. He isn't at all surprised about that. It seems he was there mowing the lawn when Phil appeared, dragging the kayak up from the beach. Phil asked Demetrius not to tell anyone about it; he wanted Lesley to find it after his family had gone. They've put the house on the market and already have a potential buyer, the same family, as a matter of fact, that wanted to look at Phoebe's house back in the summer, that Gregory and I had such a row about.

"I can't—we can't let Lesley accept anything from that family," I say bitterly.

"Why not? Think about that boy. He wasn't even there. Besides, I don't think his parents know. There's a notice up at the post office about a missing kayak. I think he told them it got stolen, or he left it on the beach and it drifted away on the tide."

This gives me pause. I've been wrong, probably, condemning the whole family for what one of them did, the parents for not supervising when Jake is, legally at least, an adult. Perhaps my anger is misplaced, and I'm the one guilty of lack of supervision. I feel a strong need to meet the parents, the mother at least, and size her up. And a need to let them know about the kayak. We can't accept it. Gregory would be livid about it, I know. He'd consider it some sort of a bribe. I look at my watch. Quarter of three. The Petersens were in the courtroom today, so maybe they're still here. And I must leave here before I give in to my feelings. I remind Demetrius once again about the water pipes and tell him I need to get back to Needham. "We'll never be able to repay you," I say, forcing myself not to look back as I turn the car around and drive away. We have not touched each other.

Negotiating the long uneven track back to the main road takes all my attention. It's a few minutes before I can evaluate my feelings. I feel numb, but tears are running down my face. I suspect they will flow off and on for a long time. It will be hard, but not impossible. Already we seem to be setting some ground rules. It's a question of not touching, of averting the eyes. It isn't until I am back on 6A that I realize he never answered my question about Gregory.

Lighthouse Lane runs into 6A just down the road from the village green in Yarmouth Port. It comes up suddenly, and my wheels squeal as I make the turn going a little too fast. I drive more slowly down the narrow lane, trying to read the house numbers as I go. The Petersens are close to the end, on a rise above a winding tidal creek. It's an attractive, well-kept house, long and low and built of redwood, looking as if it belongs in the Pacific Northwest. There's a small car in the driveway, expensive looking, teal blue, a BMW convertible. I pull in behind it and follow the flagstone walk up to a porch door, mindful that Lesley probably took this same path that terrible day six weeks ago.

Mrs. Petersen comes to the door. She's changed into jeans and is obviously busy getting ready to move. Stacks of taped and sealed boxes line one side of the porch. She has an open round face framed by wisps of short brown hair. She greets me quizzically if politely, but when I identify myself she backs away a step, keeping the screen door between us. She doesn't tell me her first name. "I'm not sure we should be talking," she says, sounding more afraid than angry.

"It's not about the case—it's about your kayak," I say, thinking how ordinary this woman seems, and how nice, even under these difficult circumstances.

"Phil's kayak? You know where it is?"

"Well, yes. I found it in our garage this afternoon. With a note. Seems he wants to give it to Lesley. I don't think, under the circumstances, it would be wise for us to accept it."

Mrs. Petersen pauses. It's a long pause. I can feel her weighing things in her mind, trying to decide what to say. She looks past me out to the street, trying to ascertain, perhaps, whether my husband is in the car. Her husband doesn't seem to be around. Maybe she's hoping he'll arrive in time to bail her out of this difficulty. She's a diffident woman, probably used to checking with her husband before she does anything. I saw him at the courthouse today. I remember his face when he looked at Gregory, rage simmering just under the surface. An angry man who can't stand losing control. Well, he's lost control now. I feel a little rush of sympathy for this woman. This isn't the sort of family I'd been imagining: loud, disorganized, careless. This family is obviously well-to-do and doesn't make messes. Everything in sight on the porch and in the yard is perfectly tidy, right down to the neatly taped boxes. But perhaps they're hiding a secret, abuse or violence. Or maybe this family is not all that different from ours, nice people who've been blind-sided and now are staggering, trying to regain their bearings. Maybe it isn't their fault that Jake did what he did. And they have another son, a son who watches birds, who cares enough about Lesley to give her his most valued possession.

"I wondered about his story," Mrs. Petersen is saying. "He's always so careful with his things, and he said he left the boat on the beach, down below the tide line. I knew he would never do that."

"So this was all his idea?"

"It must have been. Jacob would never let him do it if he knew, not while this case is going on. In fact we probably shouldn't even be talking to each other."

"You're probably right. It certainly is very generous of Phil. It's just I don't think—"

Mrs. Petersen's eyes are tearing up. "He really cares about Lesley. He's been devastated. He wasn't even here, you know, that day. We were all home in Holliston except for Jake."

At the sound of that name I feel myself getting angry again and cut her off. "You know, you're right—we shouldn't talk about it. The kayak's in our garage on Kettle Lane. Maybe you can get your husband to pick it up sometime."

"Oh no, I can't tell Jacob about it. He'll be furious with Phil."

I consider the implications of what she has said. Perhaps my image of an abusive father is not so far off the mark. I think about Gregory, who wouldn't be abusive but who surely would be angry. "I don't want to cause any trouble, for you or us," I say. "I'll tell you what I'll do. I'll not say anything about it to anybody. After all, it was a fluke that I opened the garage door—I only went in there to get some firewood, and we won't be back down until—quite a few weeks, at least." I don't want to mention the word *trial*. "You talk it over with Phil, and if he wants to take the kayak back he can come get it, and Lesley will never know. Otherwise we'll settle the question later, after—"

"After the trial," Mrs. Petersen says, finishing my sentence. She gives me a beseeching look. I think she wants to say she's sorry. I know I do, but I turn and walk back to my car instead.

As I'm opening the car door, I remember something. "What did the judge decide?" I ask. "We got the severance," she answers. "We're hoping Jake—"

I shut the door and back out of the driveway before she can finish her sentence. It's already after three according to my dashboard clock. I'm going to hit traffic on 128. When I reach the end of the lane, I pause for a moment and then turn left before I can change my mind. Demetrius. I need to tell him about the kayak, to leave the garage unlocked. I could call him from Needham—that would be the easiest, the safest thing. But the call would appear on the phone bill. And that sad little exchange we had, both of us afraid to touch, to look, even. For weeks I've kept him out of my thoughts, too numb to remember love or anticipate loss. Now that I've seen him, I still don't know what I feel. It's impossible, now, that there will be anything between us, anything like what we had. Those meetings, all that passion, the crazy happiness—it seems like years ago. Right now my emotions are frozen. Will I wake up to longing again, and if I do, will I have to learn how to survive without him? And what about him? He's retreated so far inside himself, so burdened with guilt, but guilt for what? Terrible things, he said, over and over. And something about Gregory. "It must make him remember," he said. Remember what? I have to ask him what he means.

Maybe he'll be gone, I tell myself as I turn again onto the narrow track to the cottage. But the truck is still there, and Demetrius is behind it loading some boards. "You came back," he says over his shoulder.

I pull up beside him and lower the window. He turns to face me but doesn't come over to the car. He's not going to put me at my ease. I tell him about my encounter with Mrs. Petersen, explain about the kayak, and ask him to leave the garage unlocked through the weekend. "If that's what you want," he says. "I'll do the pipes tomorrow. Anything else you can think of?"

"That's all, unless you see something that needs doing. But I have a question. I pause a moment, then open the car door and get out, crossing the space between us. "What did you mean about Gregory remembering?"

"I meant the same thing happening again. There. In the bog house."

"I don't know what you mean."

"He never told you? About that last year he worked there?"

"No."

Demetrius is silent. I can't tell if he's unwilling to go on, or if he's having trouble forming the words. He won't say more, and I'm not sure I want to confront what he isn't telling me. "I need to get home to the girls," I say lamely.

I have just turned back toward my car when he speaks again. "I should have seen it coming," he says. I should have stopped it but I was new on the job. Worried I'd make things worse for him. Then that day Dennis and I were gone all day, over to Wareham." He stops.

"And what—?" I can't bring myself to ask the question.

"Ask Gregory," he says finally. Then I feel his hand on my arm. "They buggered him. Right there in the bog house."

My mind caroms wildly off the word, which almost makes me want to laugh, it sounds so strange coming from Demetrius. A British insult, isn't it? A word I never hear, quaint almost. But nothing quaint about what it means. They buggered Gregory, not the man I've been living with but a gangling, grieving fifteen-year-old. Held him down and forced him. Like Dorrie and Lesley. "He never told me," I say quietly.

He pauses again. "Wouldn't have told us if we hadn't walked in on it. Made us swear not to tell his father. Nobody knew, except us, Dennis and me and—"

"—and Phoebe."

"Yes, Phoebe. She had to know. She took care of him. Then she and Dennis came up with some story he could tell his father and he went home."

"He never saw a doctor, or pressed charges?"

"People didn't press charges in those days for that sort of thing. Even girls, and for sure not a teenage boy. You figure what everyone would make of it. Greg won't like that I told you." He still has hold of my arm. I turn and lean against him, hiding my face. For a brief moment his arms hold me, then he releases me and steps away. My body has not forgotten him.

"Oh, Demetrius, I don't know if I can keep it a secret from him," I say. I'm too stunned to think right now. I need to get home. "I need to see about the girls. I'll call and let you know before we come back down so you can turn the water back on."

"Take care of your girls."

"I will. And you take care of yourself."

Then I'm on the road back to Needham with the late afternoon sun in my eyes. The last part of the drive is brutal. Route 128 is clogged with rush-hour traffic. My mind is full of flashbacks as the car crawls along—Jake in the courtroom, looking slicked up and boyish, the bright red kayak jumping out at me when I open the garage door, the feel of Demetrius's body that moment he held me in his arms. And images of the bog house—my daughters being stripped of their innocence right there where Demetrius and I made love, and where Gregory—where Gregory became the kind of man he is.

I arrive home with sun-dazzled eyes and a bad headache, anxious over Dorothea. She's been all right, Jeannine says, but she clings to me and whimpers when I hug her. At least she is comfortable with Jeannine. At least she missed me when I wasn't here. At least she's come back enough for that.

Jeannine has started supper. Spaghetti sauce is simmering on the stove. Gregory called to say he will be late, she tells me, so we eat early. Jeannine offers to do the dishes with Lesley's help, and Lesley pitches in without complaining while I settle Dorothea down. She is looking at me more. Maybe we're making progress, at least at home with people she knows. Maybe one of these days taking her outside in her wheelchair won't throw her into a panic. One step at a time, one day at a time. I retreat gratefully upstairs to my bedroom and lie down in the semi-darkness. Two Advils have dulled my headache but it has not gone away. I stare up at our wedding picture, the handsome young couple smiling down at me from the top of Gregory's chest of drawers. What has that secret cost him all these years? Precise, careful Gregory, always in control. Tidy, like the Petersens.

Hostage to Fortune

Many of the world's great cities would be as sand castles
built on the shore to enjoy a fleeting existence between
advances of the tide.

DAPHNE IS SURPRISED to see Anna's car go by the house. Ironic, she thinks, that we've been such confidantes and now we haven't even spoken since the day Anna called in a panic. She needed to get to West Marsh—the girls were in trouble and she might need Daphne later. Then waiting for the sound of a car, or a phone call, but there was nothing until late the next afternoon. She heard Anna's car, finally, and ran over to find her ready to leave again. Still only the sketchiest details about what happened. No, she didn't want company at the hospital. They were moving Dorothea by ambulance to Mass. General. Lesley was okay, physically okay at least. They were all going home to Needham. Then not a word, not even a call, for all these weeks. It has hurt. What she knows she has pieced together from the articles in the newspaper. She called Needham once and left a message with the girl, Jeannine, but Anna never called back.

Daphne knows she shouldn't be angry, but she is. She decides not to go over there. All her life independent, rationing her time, even as a teenager never subject to the common female addiction to rehashing everything on the phone. But she has missed Anna. Especially now. She forces herself to stay at her computer, but her mind isn't on her work. Anna doesn't call, and sometime after two Daphne hears the car going back down the lane. Maybe a trip to the grocery. When it hasn't returned by five, she feels snubbed and disappointed.

Walking back up the lane from the beach the next morning, she spots Demetrius in Anna's driveway, lifting a bag of tools from the back of his truck. Despite herself she stops and asks about the girls. Demetrius doesn't have much to report. Yes, the Dylans were down for a court hearing, no, not the trial, which won't happen until sometime after Christmas. Lesley's all right but Dorothea is still having aftereffects, physically all right but scared. What Daphne wants to ask, but doesn't dare, is whether they'll be back next summer. She'll need Anna next summer. What if she doesn't come back?

October already. She's got to finish a draft of her novel in the next couple of weeks. If she's lucky, she'll be able to start on a rewrite before Christmas. Christmas, and Susan will be here. Then it will be January, and everything will change. Susan here, and then the baby. She a grandmother, living in this little house with a daughter who never could stand her—and a baby. She tries to remember Susan as a newborn, the endless feedings and sleepless nights. But that was a world and an age away, in the middle of Manhattan with a baby nurse for the first month and friends down the hall and her mother two blocks away and dropping in daily. Five days in the hospital, with nurses to teach her everything, and comforting back rubs at night, then the bustling professional at home who took over. New mothers in those days were expected to have help. They needed their rest. This baby will come home on the third day, and Susan, highly competent Susan with opinions on everything—here Daphne smiles to herself— Susan will find out she's not quite in control. Not that Daphne is of a mind to horn in and take over.

One phone call out of the blue, and everything in her life changes. Her first reaction was no way. Thank God she didn't say it out loud. Of course she couldn't refuse, though how she will cope is beyond her. She never was a natural mother, resented the time and attention Susan took, and those days it was so easy to find help, to escape the clinging relentlessness of a small child. And yet, and yet . . . a little girl, Susan said. She had the test and opted to find out. A girl.

The call came, ironically, the night before everything happened at the bog house. Daphne almost didn't pick up the phone, and it had been so long since she'd talked to Susan that she didn't recognize the voice right away. She sounded so different, young and unsure. It took Susan several minutes to come round to the news. Pregnant. No, not married. Not planned. Not artificial insemination or anything like that. She wouldn't answer any questions about the man. Married, no doubt. Married, most assuredly, older, most probably, with other children as well as a wife to protect. No, he didn't know, and Susan wasn't going to tell him. She was leaving San Francisco and would eventually apply to a firm in Boston, but not right away. No, she hadn't considered an abortion, not for a minute. She wants this child and wants to change her life. Could she stay in Cummaquid, have the baby here, get her bearings for a few months? Yes, the right thing to do, and the right time. She's been thinking for a couple of years that she needed to change her life, and now life is forcing her hand.

Oh, Susan, Daphne thinks, that's a lot to put on a baby. And not to tell the father. He has a right to know. Will she put his name on the birth certificate, or will she write "father unknown"? Whatever she decides could come back later to haunt her, not to mention her daughter. She's a lawyer, for God's sake; she ought to know that. Daphne leans back in her desk chair and shifts her view to the pond outside. I'll have holes in my tongue from biting it, she thinks. Susan already knows what I'd say—I don't have to tell her. Except that internalized mother in Susan's mind is probably fiercer, more unbending, than the older, wiser woman Daphne feels she is now. A grandmother! A little girl. If only Anna were here. Or better still, Phoebe.

She's certainly not getting any writing done. She's physically restless; maybe a few minutes outside will settle her down enough to concentrate. She stands up and crosses the room to pick up Hephaestus, who's sound asleep in the wing chair, as usual. He's lazy. He'd sleep all the time if she let him, never go out at all if she didn't carry him to the door. As always she's surprised at how heavy he is. If Mistress Quickly is the size of a newborn, he's more like a six-month-old. A fat cat, her biggest by far. But not really fat. Big-boned, double-pawed, the only cat she's ever owned so heavy on his feet she can hear him padding across the room behind her on his way to the feed dish. Long and sleek and muscular, he pours out of her arms and lands on the front step, looking up at her with something resembling exasperation before ambling off under the rhododendrons.

Daphne walks down the little slope to the edge of the pond. It's at its most beautiful this time of year, especially on a day like today when there is no wind and all the colors are reflected in the water. Scarlet leaves of sumac and poison ivy form a brilliant rim below the more muted russets of the scrub oaks, the few remaining yellow leaves on the locusts. The cattails have burst open, spilling out their cushiony white interiors. Susan. A baby. How will she be, now that she needs me, Daphne muses. There was always a power struggle between them, from the time Susan was a baby. Never wanting to be held, arching herself backward with such force that Daphne nearly dropped her once. Never wanting her hand held, even in the street. Tantrums when Daphne insisted, throwing herself to the sidewalk. Daphne could swear Susan enjoyed the disapproving frowns of passersby, her humiliation. Bad mother. Now they'd be in this little house together, on Daphne's turf, wedged into her jealously defended space, her carefully regimented day. They'll never survive. Susan always at her worst when she was feeling dependent. Was all that my fault, Daphne wonders, or is that just how she was? How will the two of them negotiate living together, and with a baby, night feedings, colic maybe, no sleep? She hates going without sleep. Writing is going to be out of the question.

At least she has the guts, Daphne says to herself. And then it all comes back, that long-buried time in New York, she riding on a wave of brand-new celebrity, Daniel's resentment and how it took her by such surprise, the chill when she would get home from a weekend book tour—Susan was how old then? Four, maybe. Then the award, chatting with James at the dinner, the big man with the big reputation, stories in *The New Yorker*, so flattering. She was ripe, of course. Her first affair. Then finding herself caught. She hadn't thought through what she'd expected him to do about it. He'd done the responsible thing, at least in the context of those times, organized it all, the trip to somewhere in Pennsylvania, the money. He hadn't gone with her and was surprised that she expected him to—it went without saying that the affair was over. He'd arranged for some woman he knew to drive her, an editorial assistant or something. Daphne always suspected that it wasn't the first time he'd had to do it. She remembers how long the ride was, the silence, her shame and terror, the woman at least knowing enough not to chatter. The thing itself not too bad—the man had given her something so everything was blurry after the shock of seeing the instruments laid out on the tray. She told her husband it was a reading at a college—Bucknell, just an overnight trip. He never suspected. It was years before their marriage finished falling apart, and by then Susan was twelve, old enough to blame Daphne for driving her Daddy away.

Susan at twelve. Daphne can barely remember her those years puberty hit and all the rebellion. Daphne had thrown herself into her writing, under the terrible pressure to produce after a promising first novel. The second took more than three years, and even with her reputation it didn't make a real splash. At least there was money enough, what with Daniel's child support and her advance, for a full-time housekeeper. By then Daphne was something of a name around town—funny how socialites like to have creative people around. Lots of parties, editorial luncheons, readings at colleges, a couple of distracting love affairs. Then the long dry spell, her decision to get out of New York. The right decision, a kind of cleansing, it has been, her immersion in the clear ocean air, her stripped-down life. She'd gotten rid of everything, everybody extraneous. Until

Paul, and she was just getting back on her feet after that disaster. Now Susan, and a baby.

Daphne turns away from the pond and climbs the slope back to the house. Hephaestus is waiting for her on the doorstep and pushes his way inside in front of her, making straight for his chair. Her computer hums, calling her back to work. Nearly ten. She backtracks to the beginning of the chapter and begins to delete words and phrases, her first attempts to say anything always so full of redundancies. If she's lucky, the process will give her a running start and she'll be able to finish the chapter before evening.

JUST AS SHE's lifting the pan of stir fry off the stove the phone rings. Probably Susan, who has taken, uncharacteristically, to calling once a week or so with some logistical question about the move or obstetricians or her own symptoms. Their conversations for the first time ever are almost chatty, with Susan reporting her progress in deciding what to put in storage and trying to hide her blooming pregnancy under long jackets. But this time it isn't Susan. It's Anna. The delight Daphne feels at the sound of her voice is followed hard on by anger. Her "Oh, hello" comes out curtly, even though she regrets the chill in her voice. Where has this woman been now that she needs her? But of course Anna doesn't know that Daphne needs her.

The conversation is puzzling. Will Daphne be home tomorrow? Anna's coming down to the house and wants to see her. The water is off for the winter—that, Daphne realizes, is what Demetrius was doing over there this morning. Anna coming back again so soon, something strange there. She has the grace to apologize for her long silence. The girls are better, at least Lesley seems all right, but Dorothea is still frightened all the time and won't relate to people, even Jeannine or Anna herself sometimes. *Disconnected* is the word Anna uses.

"It's so unfair," Daphne finds herself saying. Hasn't Dorothea—and Anna, for that matter—endured enough damage? How can there be more?

But Anna has changed the subject to Gregory. Those summers when Gregory lived with Dennis and Phoebe—did Phoebe ever talk about them? She said something in one of the journals about making it up to Gregory—does Daphne know what she meant?

"I don't remember, really. That was pretty soon after she lost Camilla, you know. So much happened. It was a hard time." The years of the missing journals, Daphne is thinking, but Anna is asking about Gregory, not Camilla.

"Did she ever tell you why she stopped writing in her journal?" Anna asks.

"She burned them. Too painful, or maybe too private." Daphne wishes Anna would change the subject, but she persists with the questions.

"Did she ever tell you what was in them?"

"Not really," Daphne says softly. Conscious of the lie, she elaborates. "They were about Camilla. I think later she was sorry they were gone."

"And she never said anything about Gregory, those summers he was there?"

"Not much. Just when she was making her will. She talked about the house, and about you. She really liked you. She said the two of you had an affinity. She was glad Gregory married you. She said she thought you might bring Gregory back."

"Back to the Cape?"

"I'm not sure. Back here, or back to himself, maybe. Sometimes she said she was sorry he was so disconnected." *Disconnected*: The same word Anna used just now for Dorothea.

"I want to see you, Daphne," Anna says. "I'm so sorry I haven't called you. I've been so wrapped up in the girls I haven't talked to anyone. I'll be down tomorrow, just for the day. There are some things I need to take care of in the house, and the water's off. Could I use your bathroom, maybe trouble you for a cup of tea?"

"Only if you'll stay for lunch."

"In the middle of your writing time? I'm honored."

"We have a lot to catch up on. I have some things to tell you, too."

Before falling asleep Daphne thinks about Anna's questions. Gregory. He must have said something to Anna. Maybe something did happen between him and Dennis—something to do with the drinking—but Phoebe never talked about it. She felt guilty about Gregory for some reason. Those years . . . she probably was in no frame of mind to mother a motherless teenage boy. So hard to imagine Gregory as a boy. A cold man. Handsome, capable, but closed in. Disconnected, as Phoebe said. Oblivious to Anna's warmth, or her need for love and comfort. And now this tragedy with her children, damaging them again, not just Dorothea but Lesley too. Would we dare have them, children, if we knew ahead of time how they will break our hearts? Little Camilla lost, Dorothea damaged, and now Lesley as well. Her own Susan, lost to her for years, now coming back—maybe to be lost again, and more painfully. And a baby, a little girl, new life, a chance to start over. Daphne, don't count on it, she admonishes herself. She remembers that day years ago when she and Phoebe sailed to Sandy Neck and sat on the dunes talking about their daughters. Hostages to fortune, Phoebe called them. Have them, love them, pray for their safety, but we can't save them. They are out of our hands.

Daphne is startled out of her train of thought by a small body landing on the bed. Mistress Quickly, light-footed little cat, jumping up in the middle of the night the way she always does, climbing over her to curl up next to her hip. Daphne reaches out her hand and caresses her, a soft white ball, getting old and arthritic now, the hop up onto the bed more and more of an effort. Hostage to fortune. She thought cats would be no trouble, so undemanding, so easy to leave alone in the house, but she knows and loves them, every one, with their odd quirks, their comforting little bodies, their brief little lives. She cups the silky head in her hand and rubs behind the ears the way Mistress Quickly loves.

The Lap Desk

Although . . . the glacier would appear to be standing still,
the body of moving ice actually would bring a continual
supply of new debris to the front, where the front edge,
melting, would drop it.

I CAN'T NOT ASK Gregory about it. I wait until we're alone in the bedroom and the house is quiet. There's no way to keep Demetrius's name out of it. I start by saying I had spoken to him about turning off the water and he'd said something that puzzled me. "He said it's happened again," I say. "What did he mean?" Gregory disappears into the bathroom, but I follow him there and persist. "What did he mean?" I say again.

"I haven't any idea," Gregory says, his words muffled. His back is to me; he's brushing his teeth.

"He mentioned you," I go on. "It must have had something to do with you."

"God knows what goes through the man's mind. He feels to blame. How the hell did those kids get into the bog house?"

"You know the answer to that. Lesley had the key. It was Phoebe's key from the kitchen drawer. I'd left it out on the table, and Lesley took it, and . . ." My voice peters out, defeated by the lie in the middle of what I'm saying. "You're changing the subject."

Gregory turns on the water and spits into the sink. "He must mean those boys I worked with—two brothers and a cousin, or something. They didn't like me, thought I was a snot. They beat me up one day when the men were gone."

"And that's it?" It shocks me that Gregory might be as adept at lying as I am.

"What else could it be, Anna? God damn it, can't we talk about something else?" Gregory rinses his toothbrush and replaces it in the holder, then escapes around me into the bedroom. He's wearing his new Brooks Brothers pajamas. They still have the crease marks on them. A handsome man, with his hair thinning just a little, graying attractively at the temples, every bit as handsome as the bridegroom in the picture on his dresser. Still going to bed in the same kind of pajamas he probably took to St. Paul's.

"Demetrius said again, that it's happened again." I take a breath, and then ask. "Did those boys rape you?"

"Jesus, Anna. What did Demetrius tell you?"

"Nothing."

"Then can we drop this now?"

I can't tell him I know; it seems so important to him that I don't. It's a long time before I can fall asleep. My head is still aching, and I can tell by his breathing that Gregory is awake, too. How sad that he could never tell me about that summer; what a commentary on our marriage. So long ago, and he still can't talk about it, to me, or maybe even to himself. What kind of a marriage is this? How much of what we say to each other is lies? More to the point, how much do we avoid saying at all? Gregory so impenetrable, this distance not something that crept up on us—it's been there since the beginning. My reason—my excuse—for Demetrius. And I, have I been any more truthful? What have I done with my loneliness, my despair? Soldiered on, good wife, good mother, keeping the family together while all the time I was suffering inside. I think of that puzzling thing Demetrius said to me back in the summer—Lesley has my anger, and she doesn't know what to do with it. I shift in the bed, turning away from Gregory to face the window. As so often happens when we are both pretending to be asleep, he turns at the same moment in the opposite direction. We need help, the two of us, and Lesley as well. She seems all right, but God knows what she has buried. Back in August I thought about going to see someone, to decide about Demetrius. Now that's over, has to be over, but I still need to. We need to. Together, a family counselor. I'll make some calls in the morning and figure out some way to get Gregory to agree.

The one time we did try therapy, about a year after Dorothea's operation, Gregory hated it. He only agreed as a concession to me. I was worse off than he was in those days, deep in denial about the permanence of Dorothea's condition, so heavily invested in her I had been, my beautiful firstborn, child prodigy, though we were both still in shock. Dr. Collier, her name was. She tried getting us to talk to each other, but Gregory ended up addressing her, talking about me in the third person. He canceled the one private session she scheduled with him—because of a crisis at work, of course. How many sessions did he come to—three, four maybe? I kept going a few months more after he dropped out. How uncomfortable he was in that little office off Harvard Square. Not knowing the ground rules, maybe, no established precedents to look up, as in the law.

What did it do to him, that summer Gregory was fifteen? Still grieving over his mother, the awkwardness of living with Dennis and Phoebe, the bullying by those older boys—what did Gregory say their name was? Being attacked like that, the degradation and shame. And then, never telling, living with it, burying it deep. Maybe he has blocked it out of his mind. No wonder he's thrown up a wall between us. But could confronting it now change anything, change the way he is? Would therapy help, or is it too late? It's worth a try. If we could talk about what he felt, what he went through, maybe it would help both of us get the girls through, heal them.

If only Phoebe were here to talk to! She was there, she knew. There might be something in the house, those missing years of the journals hidden somewhere maybe, though why then would she tell Daphne she burned them? Maybe she told Daphne something in confidence. I could talk to her. Dorothea seemed better tonight, almost back to normal with Jeannine, good enough to do without me for a few hours. A quick trip, just for part of a day, Thursday, maybe, when Jeannine doesn't have any classes, a chance to look in the attic, maybe find some answers. But what are the questions?

On Wednesday evening I reach Daphne. We'll have lunch together and have time to talk. I've missed her friendship, and no matter how hard she tries to hide it I know she feels hurt by the way I've shut her out. Thursday morning I stay around long enough to help with Dorothea's exercises. It's such a relief to have Jeannine back in the house, and not just because she shoulders so much of the physical load. She's been spending time with Lesley, too, trying to draw her out, asking her to help persuade Dorothea that it's all right to go outside, chatting with her after supper about clothes and music, French braiding her hair. The way Dorothea might have done, Lesley's lost big sister.

My trip to the Cape is a pleasantly swift ride down highways devoid of traffic. The fall colors in Needham are beginning to fade but are at their height further south. I decide to take the old road along the north side instead of the mid-Cape, the old King's Highway, still rural and beautiful, mostly devoid of tourist traps and shopping centers. The maples, planted to replace the magnificent elms that died in the sixties, are changing in the piecemeal way they do, splashed with patches of bright yellow, orange, and green.

As I pass the courthouse in Barnstable, I think about the trial looming ahead of us. What will happen, and what will it cost us—the girls, especially? Will it be the end of our life here? And why have I come back so soon? I've given myself noble reasons, but isn't it really the memory of that moment Demetrius touched me? In my heart, my body, nothing has changed. There's a small chance he might be at the house. I can't seek him out this morning—it's too dangerous. I'll sort through the house, the attic, then maybe stop to see him just before I go home, late enough so it will be impossible to stay.

It's after eleven by the time I get to Kettle Lane. There's no sign of Demetrius. I swallow my disappointment. Inside it's slightly warmer than two days ago, thanks to the sunny weather, but still cold and damp. I leave on my jacket and climb upstairs, then turn the key that's always in the lock and open the door to the attic.

It's been weeks since I've been up here. In early August I made a few desultory attempts to look for Phoebe's missing journals, but I was always defeated by the trapped heat, the sheer volume of boxes and pieces of furniture. So many heaps of papers and books. At the very least it's a fire hazard. It's time to start going through it. I clear a space on the nearest cot and carry over a cardboard box of papers. Accounts from West Marsh going back who knows how far. Ancient Christmas cards, household bills, old magazine articles Phoebe had clipped to read or file, yellowing and curling at the edges. I start separating the papers into two categories, one to look through later and one to throw away. The second pile grows slowly. Even the West Marsh accounts might be of value to a local historian, someone. Hard to think about throwing away a life, two lives.

It's nearly one o'clock when I get to the wooden chest all the way back by the far window. It's made of pine, covered with dusty rough paint in a light shade of grayish blue. Milk paint, probably original. No one has tried to pretty it up over the years. The first thing I see when I open the lid is a worn pair of child's sandals, white with buckles and straps and a pattern of pierced holes in the leather. Lesley had sandals like those when she was a toddler, that summer we went to Knoxville. Underneath is a cardboard dress box with the name *Slattery's* printed on it. Inside the box, a worn yellow blanket with the satin edge loose and raveling. A blankie, like the ones my girls held and loved and could not sleep without. Seeing it makes me cry. They should have buried it with Camilla, I think, to comfort her. Below that, a hand-knit sweater with tiny heart-shaped buttons and a couple of little smocked dresses.

The rest of the chest is full of toys, blocks, mostly, a couple of wooden pull toys, a baby doll worn from play, and a primly dressed little girl doll looking like it's never been touched. At the bottom, under the blocks, another wooden box, beautiful polished walnut with a top cut on the diagonal and attached with delicate brass hinges and an elaborate lock decorated in filigree. I recognize the box from the description in Phoebe's journal, the very first one. It's her lap desk, sent as a wedding present by her Southern friend—Selena, wasn't that her name? I stand up, hug the lap desk to my chest, and pick my way back to the stairs, down to Phoebe's little room at the end of the hall. There, in the top lefthand drawer mingled in with the paper clips and old stamps, is the peculiar brass key I noticed back in May. It slips into the lock without sticking and the desk clicks open.

Opened up, the two halves form a square writing surface covered with worn green leather. At one end are two little drawers and an empty round hole that could hold a bottle of ink. In one of the drawers is an ancient fountain pen, a few well-worn pencils. There's nothing in the other one. Then I remember what Phoebe's journal said about the secret compartment. It takes me a few minutes to find it; it involves lifting out a piece of wooden trim below the drawers and releasing a hidden catch. I reach into the space and pull out a little packet of letters and another envelope.

I read the letters first. Three of them, all from Selena, and all referring to Camilla. The first, a cheery letter of congratulations. Phoebe obviously had written to say she was pregnant. The second is a short note of sympathy:

> *Dearest Phoebe,*
>
> *I cannot yet comprehend your news. I'm so sorry I won't be able to get there in time for the service, but I want nothing more than to see you, if you and Dennis will have me. Do not refuse me; it's as much for me as it is for you. I could arrive by train in Barnstable on August 26. I will happily stay at an inn if that will be easier than having me at the house. Please let me know. In the meantime, every thought and prayer is with you. I hope the daisies have arrived; they are the cheerfulest of flowers and will always remind me of you and your beautiful Camilla.*
>
> *Forever your loving friend,*
> *Selena*

The other letter is longer. It was obviously written after Selena's visit.

Dearest Phoebe,

I am writing this on the train so I hope you can read my shaky script. I did not want to leave you today and you have been on my mind every minute since my last glimpse of you sadly waving as the train pulled out of the station. Thank God I came! It is still hard for me to believe Dennis could be so cruel and destructive. He was not himself. As you said, he was wild with grief. He will regret it later (I think he already does) and the terrible hurt to you. He dearly loves you still, and that love shines through his pain and even the cruel words. And you love him, that is clear in spite of everything that has happened. I pray that the two of you can learn to comfort one another and find a way to go on.

When I get home, I will send you the picture of Camilla you enclosed in your Christmas card. Then you'll have at least one to treasure. It's the reason I sent the daisies. I'll also start planning for your visit to me. You still haven't seen darkest Alabama.

Your loving friend,
Selena

So that's why there are no pictures of Camilla in Phoebe's house. Dennis. It seems impossible that he could do anything so hurtful, but then maybe he had no other way to express his grief. I try to remember the time I saw him drunk, that weekend he took me over to West Marsh all those years ago. Not a violent person even when he was drinking, though he could say some nasty things to Phoebe. Then I remember Gregory's silent fury, his vow not to bring the children back to the Cape.

Gregory. His anger at Dennis, and at Demetrius. Now it makes sense. What Gregory does with anger or grief is to fold it up, quash it down, hide it under his perfectly pressed pinstripe suits, his immaculate shirts. Will it, could it ever erupt the way Dennis's did?

I turn to the other envelope, lift the brittle flap. Inside, a folded document with an embossed state seal. Camilla's birth certificate, with the print of her little foot. I remember the day Phoebe wrote in her journal about mussel shells being the same shape. Another, smaller envelope containing a curl of soft dark brown hair. And a black and white picture. Camilla, taken when she was perhaps two years old, sitting on the ground in a white sunsuit with a crown of daisies on her head, smiling up at the camera, her hair under the flowers a mass of dark curls. Strange, I think, that she should have such dark hair, when Phoebe was fair-skinned and sandy-haired and all the Turnstones were blonds or redheads with freckled pale faces. Gregory's dark hair comes from his father's side, as does Dorothea's. I look again at Camilla's picture. Impossible to tell the color of her eyes, but even on her round baby face the brows are already distinct, perfectly formed, two gracefully arched wings drawn neatly across her forehead. And then I know.

The Back Beach

The beach is littered with fallen giants.

I HAVE TO SIT there on Phoebe's cot for a few minutes before I can bring myself to turn the birth certificate over. There are the names: Camilla Gardener Turnstone, and Phoebe's and Dennis's names. Of course that's what it would say. I fold the document and replace it in its envelope along with the picture and the lock of hair. Oh, Phoebe, now I understand everything—why you broke things off and why you stayed friends. "It's happening again," Demetrius said, full of guilt for the damage he thinks he's caused. But what about his losses, then and now? Since that brief touch on Tuesday, all my longing has come back. The worst thing I could do now is give him encouragement and take it away again. I will not go to see him, even to ask about Gregory. It will be better, for both of us.

I'm very late for lunch at Daphne's, and there is much I need to ask her, much more than I thought when I left Needham this morning. What I don't count on is that Daphne has momentous news of her own. After asking for a detailed report on the girls, she tells me. Susan, the daughter in San Francisco, is arriving in six weeks. Pregnant. Planning to stay at Daphne's until after the baby is born. Astonishing, given what Daphne has said about Susan in our talks over the summer, her ambition, her lack of interest in getting married, her coldness to Daphne herself. Even more astonishing is the way Daphne seems to accept the idea of Susan showing up out of the blue, actually living with her, and especially the baby. She's thrilled about the baby; it shows all over her face, excited as any other prospective grandmother. We spend the whole of lunch talking about it. Daphne wants me back. She'll need me there across the lane, she says, to give advice, and to escape to when the going gets rough.

I hug Daphne, trying to imagine her as a doting grandmother, changing diapers, walking the floor with spit-up on her shoulder. Impossible. But stranger things have happened. Look at me, I tell myself. Who could have predicted the life I've led for the past five years? And this summer?

I wait until we've finished our lunch, a Caesar salad topped with lobster meat and a loaf of crusty whole wheat bread, glasses of Sauvignon blanc. Daphne has made a real effort with this meal. I remember that day just after the hurricane when I made lunch for her, when there was nothing but bread and cheese and canned soup in the house. "Now I've got some things to ask you," I say, "things about Phoebe." My palms are sweating, I'm so anxious. "Could we maybe take a little walk? I'm stiff from the drive down and sitting up in the attic sorting papers, and I've still got the drive home."

"Sure," says Daphne, carrying our plates and glasses to the sink to rinse and stack. "Are you up for a hike? I've been wanting to go out to the back beach. It's a bit of a drive."

"You don't mean Nauset?" I ask.

"No, no, Sandy Neck, the back side. It can seem like Nauset with the kind of breeze we've got today. I'll lend you a hat. It's just about fifteen minutes, if you've got enough time."

The back beach. I've never been there. It requires a town beach sticker in the summer and I never bothered to get one. We have our own beach and it seemed like too much of a trek to take Dorothea all that way. Then I remember that Lesley's been there. She admitted it when the whole story came out about her and Phil. That was where she went one of the nights she sneaked out to meet him—Phil and his brother Jake, and one of the other boys, the one with the jeep. She talked about how beautiful it was, trying to distract me from my anger at her recklessness, not knowing that I was thinking of my own recklessness. That was the night—the very night—I met Demetrius up on the hill.

I shouldn't take the time, but I badly want to find out what Daphne knows. We decide to take both cars so that I can leave for home without coming back to the house. That will save half an hour of driving and put me on the road by four, too late to miss the traffic but with time enough to get home for dinner. And I'll be less tempted to backtrack to Yarmouth Port and Demetrius. I run back to Phoebe's to close up the house. I decide against taking the letters or the picture or the birth certificate with me, so I carefully replace the envelope in the secret compartment and carry the lap desk back up into the attic and put it where I found it, in the wooden chest at the far end. I do not want Gregory coming across these things and asking questions.

I follow Daphne down 6A. The road to Sandy Neck beach is a sharp right turn just after the Sandwich town line. It extends northeastward back into Barnstable for more than a mile before ending with a small gatehouse, two large parking lots, and a weathered bathhouse. It's nearly deserted now that the swimming season is over. There are just three other cars in the lot, and the only people in sight are a woman and a man far down the beach and at some distance from each other, walking dogs. The view out over Cape Cod bay is magnificent, the water in the clear October air impossibly blue. Whitecaps are rolling towards shore from the northwest with a steady roar that blends with the wind. If the surf lacks the ground-shaking thump I remember from Nauset, it gives the same exhilarating sense of power. The beach is strewn with seaweed and rounded stones of every color. In spite of the bright sunshine the wind has a bite, a hint of coming winter. I'm grateful for the knitted hat Daphne insisted upon lending me.

"Let's turn right and walk with the wind," Daphne is saying. "There's a path through the dunes about a mile up where we can cut through and walk back on the marsh side. That way we won't feel the wind so much." And without waiting for a response from me, she sets off at a good clip with me breathlessly struggling to keep up. We make our way across the soft sand to the damp, stony strip below the high tide line. The footing here is firmer, and walking is less of an effort. We are a good quarter mile from the parking lot before I get up my courage to ask any questions. I start with Greg. Though I wouldn't believe it last night, it's the easier subject.

"Did Phoebe ever talk about those summers Gregory stayed at the house, when he worked for Dennis?" I ask.

"She mentioned him being here—he was just a teenager, wasn't he?"

"Did she ever mention anything happening to Greg?"

"What do you mean?"

"About him getting hurt? About him going home?"

"I don't know what you're fishing for, Anna," Daphne says, pausing a moment to give me a chance to catch my breath. "She was sorry he didn't like it here, I know that. There was some bad blood between him and Dennis, I think."

"How about him and Demetrius?"

"I don't know about that. Demetrius was working at the bog even back then, wasn't he? But she never said anything about him and Gregory. What's this all about?"

I have no desire to tell Daphne anything she doesn't know; it seems disloyal, so I ignore the question and change the subject. "Tell me about Camilla."

"What is this? Gregory didn't know Camilla, did he? That was before, wasn't it? I mean, Camilla was gone before Greg . . ."

"Why didn't Phoebe have any pictures of Camilla around the house?"

"What are you asking, Anna? Obviously something's upset you. Did you find something today in the attic? Did Gregory say something?"

"No. I mean yes and no. Gregory didn't say anything and I did find something in the attic. Letters, from Selena, that friend of Phoebe's from college. You know, she's in the journals, in the early ones. She's the one who sent the lap desk."

"Ah, yes, Selena. Phoebe loved her. They kept up all those years. I thought she might be at the funeral."

With a stab of guilt I realize that Selena, if she's still alive, might not even know Phoebe died, has been dead for—what is it?—eight months now. No one in the family recognized the name, or identified her as someone who should be notified. I must write and tell her.

Before I can think of what to say to Daphne next, something on the beach up ahead catches my eye. It's large and shapeless, lying just below the wrack line left by the last high tide, something brownish and soft, like cloth, a tarp, maybe, or part of a sail discolored by the sand. Seagulls gathered in a ragged cluster complain raucously and fly a little way off as we approach. "What's that?" I ask Daphne, who has noticed it too. With the wind coming from behind us we get very close before the stench hits us. "God, what a stink," I say. It's something dead, but what? Too shapeless to be a fish or a seal, too solid to be an oversized jellyfish. Up close we can see the dark leathery skin. In places where the birds have eaten it away there's a gelatinous lighter layer underneath, bubbles of fat. My stomach flips over.

"Ocean sunfish," says Daphne. "I saw one once, a live one, when I was out sailing by myself. Nearly fell out of the boat."

"It's huge."

"It looks even bigger in the water. The one I saw was just under the surface, like a giant shadow. I thought it was a shark."

"It doesn't have any shape. Is it swollen up, do you think?"

"That is its shape. It's pretty dead. Your classic vile body. Come to think of it, it's about the size of a body, some really bloated drowning victim maybe. But give the birds a go, and the salt air, and there won't be much left in a few weeks, not even a smell."

It's a relief to leave the horror behind and start again down the beach. The wind carries the stench a long way after us. I've spent all day poking among the dead: Phoebe, Dennis, Camilla. There's no way not to think about what happens to bodies, the ones we bury in polished wooden caskets with their guaranteed waterproof liners. Rotting, reeking, desiccating, reduced to bones and hair. John Donne's "bright hair about the bone." Our irrational need to preserve what can't be preserved, when it would be so much cleaner, more meaningful, to let the people we love dissolve back into the earth, evaporate into the air.

Another several hundred yards, and Daphne points to a sign indicating a path leading away from the water. We turn and follow it up through the soft sand into the dunes. The going is much harder here, even on the faint double track worn by the four wheel drives. We sink into sand almost up to our ankles and have to stop every few minutes to catch our breath. Once we've cleared the row of dunes lining the beach there is much less wind, and no water in sight ahead or behind. We could be in the middle of a desert.

"Whoa," I finally say. "Let's take a break. I'm too out of shape for this." It's true. For weeks now the only exercise I've had is my morning physical therapy session with Dorothea. Daphne is puffing too, and only too glad to sit down. We collapse into the soft sand at the side of the trail.

"Well, back to the matter at hand," I say. "Have you ever seen a picture of Camilla?"

"Have you found one?"

"Didn't your mother ever tell you it's rude to answer a question with a question? What are you avoiding telling me?"

"What are you avoiding asking me?"

"Touché. But first answer my question. Did Phoebe ever show you a picture of Camilla?"

"Yes, she did." I wait for Daphne to elaborate, but she doesn't. She's tracing circles on the sand with her finger, in imitation of the many circles around us, drawn by the blades of compass grass blowing in the wind.

"Then you know what I know," I prompt.

"Which is?" It's out of character for Daphne to be so coy. She's protecting Phoebe, I realize, honoring a promise she must have made. I just have to plunge in.

"Demetrius. She was his. It's written on her face. Did Dennis know? Is that why he tore up all the pictures? Selena said something about that, in a letter I found, so she sent back a snapshot that Phoebe had mailed to her."

"Yes. That's the one Phoebe showed me. She made me swear never to talk about it, but I think she wanted me—wanted someone to know. Now you must swear. Does Gregory know?"

"I don't think so. He's never so much as mentioned Camilla. Do you think Dennis knew from the beginning?"

"He must have. They'd tried for so many years. Dennis had his faults, but he wasn't stupid. But they never talked about it. They just lived with it, the way people do."

"Yes, they do," I say, my mind's eye flashing back to the reeking hulk we encountered on the beach. The things we don't talk about. The things Gregory and I never talked about. The questions we don't ask because knowing the answer might destroy us.

Suddenly I'm very, very tired, too tired to go any further, at least today. And the sun has swung down and is shining in our eyes. "I've got to get back," I say. "I've got a long drive ahead of me." I stand up, a little unsteady in the soft sand. "Which is the quickest way back?"

"Same difference either way. We're almost to the other side, and there's a road there along the edge, much easier walking." Daphne gets up and starts off toward the marsh. After one more steep dune we can see the whole western end of Barnstable harbor laid out before us, a wide expanse of waving grasses, crisscrossed by creeks and drainage ditches and punctuated here and there by tall, feathery plumes. "You won't say anything to Gregory?" Daphne asks.

"Of course not."

"How about Demetrius?"

Demetrius. I have tried so hard all day not to think about him. What this must have meant—the whole of it, the miracle and the terror, his own wife childless, working every day with Dennis and wondering what he knew, what he might do or say, and then the loss, so sudden, so soon. So much more terrible even than the things we've endured, our losses, Dorothea, both girls losing their sense of trust, their innocence. I will have to tell him I know, if we are to have anything left, a friendship if nothing more. It would never survive with a secret like this between us. But how, and when?

Daphne stops and turns around to face me on the path. The slope of the dune erases our difference in height and places us eye to eye. It's the first time I've really given her my full attention in weeks. She looks older, weathered but magnificent, like an aging goddess, with her tall, spare body framed by the deep green marshes, the brilliant sand, the incredibly blue October sky. I cannot lie to her, either, not if I want to keep this friendship I treasure. "I have to talk to him," I say. "But I'll leave you out of it. I'll tell him about finding the picture. That's really how it happened. I knew as soon as I saw it. Does Demetrius know that Phoebe told you?"

"Probably. Phoebe didn't keep secrets from him. That's what they had, even after they lost everything."

We slip-slide the rest of the way down to the bottom of the dune. The loose sand gives way to a firm dirt road leading back along the marsh edge to the parking lot where we started. We have little else to say to each other. When we reach our two cars, Daphne surprises me by giving me a hug. "Are you all right?" she asks.

"Yes. This wasn't as hard as the other." The other secret, I mean. Daphne knows what I mean without asking.

"Be safe, my friend," she says, letting me go. "And come back. I'll need you here next summer to teach me how to cope. You're a world champion coper, you know."

I am too tired and overwhelmed to respond, even with a joke. It will be probably be months before I see her again, the only one who knows the whole story, who understands. I hug her wordlessly and start toward my car. Then I turn back. "There's something else," I tell her. "Gregory, that last summer he worked for Dennis, some boys at West Marsh raped him. Demetrius was foreman but he and Dennis were away for the day. That's why Gregory never came back."

"Oh, God," Daphne says, "so that's why."

"That's why a lot of things, maybe," I say, the thought forming in my mind as I say the words. "Now I really do have to get home. I'll call you when I know the court date."

The Outwash Plain

Across the desolate landscape, these huge, dirty derelicts
marked the wake of the vanishing ice like grounded
icebergs.

IT'S NEARLY SIX by the time I get home, and Gregory's car is in the
driveway, a surprise because he's hardly ever home this early. Jeannine
is in the kitchen about to put a casserole in the oven. Dorothea is with
her, pulled up to the kitchen table, swaying a little and wearing her half-
smile. It takes her a minute to notice I'm in the room, even though I've
called her by name. I walk over to the table and make sure she can see me
before I reach out and take her hand. I've learned not to touch her before
she's ready; it brings on the fear. But she's not fearful now. Then I notice
the earphones on her head, blended in with her black hair. She's wearing
Lesley's Walkman. Now that I'm next to her I can hear the music: Bach,
one of the orchestral suites.

"Lesley's the one who thought of it," Jeannine is saying. "She brought
it downstairs after school. Dorrie fought it at first, but now look at her."

I place my hands on the earpieces and gently lift them off Dorothea's
head. She's still smiling, but she's looking at the machine lying on the
table. I can tell she wants it back, but she hasn't stiffened, hasn't cried
out. Her whole body looks more relaxed than it's been in weeks. Have
we turned a corner? "I missed you today," I say, lowering myself to get
in her line of sight. "I'm home now. Almost supper time. Love you."
Dorothea smiles again, at me this time, and then shifts her gaze back to
the earpieces, which I gently replace on her head. Music! Of course. Why
hadn't I thought of it? And a Walkman. Leave it to Lesley to come up
with that idea.

Lesley, as if on cue, clatters down the stairs and comes into the
kitchen. "What do you think, Mom?" she says.

"It's wonderful. Thank you for thinking of it. I suspect you're going to
have trouble getting her to give it back, though."

"That's okay. She can have it. My birthday's coming up. Maybe
somebody will get me something newer. Hint, hint."

I get up from the table and give her a hug. Miraculously she does not pull away. "Message received," I say. In three weeks she'll be thirteen, a teenager. Hard to believe. The five—going on six, now—years since Dorothea's operation have flown by so fast, and Lesley's been growing up the whole time while no one was looking. Seven then, and now nearly thirteen. A woman. Any day now she'll get her period. I was how old? Twelve, nearly thirteen. Her body in my arms is more solid; she's filling out, growing into her height, the bone structure of her face beginning to solidify into its adult shape. Older now than Dorothea was when everything stopped for her. And she's changing in other ways, as well. Here in the kitchen with us, gathering silverware out of the drawer to set the table without being asked. Giving her Walkman to her sister, though (here I chuckle inwardly) it seems she has ulterior motives. Her bad dreams come less often—at least she has not awakened me for the past couple of nights. Will the memories always come back to frighten her in the night? We need to do what I decided to do on Tuesday, see someone, all of us, as a family, keep all of this from being buried like so much else. Like what I found today in the attic, hidden away in a secret compartment. And in Phoebe's heart. And Demetrius's.

"Where's your Dad?" I ask Lesley, remembering my surprise at seeing his car in the driveway.

"Upstairs on the phone," she answers. "He's been on for ages. I need to call Becky."

I make my way upstairs and into our bedroom, where Gregory is just hanging up. "Who was that?" I ask. Gregory is usually terse and efficient on the phone. He's sitting on the edge of the bed making notes on a yellow pad. He finishes what he's writing before he turns to me.

"Where the hell have you been?" he asks. "Jeannine said you went back down to the Cape. Why, when you were just there Tuesday?"

I haven't thought about what I was going to tell him. I say the first thing that comes to my head, a combination of truth and untruth, as usual. "Daphne invited me to lunch," I say. "She was upset I didn't go over there on Tuesday, and that I haven't called her. And Dorothea's been so much better. Jeannine had the day off from school so she could sit. And I thought I'd work on the attic, clear it out a little before it gets too cold. It felt good to take a day off." I'm doing too much explaining, more than necessary. It's what I always do when I lie. I cross into the bathroom and run some water to wash my face. "Daphne has big news. She wanted to tell me in person—that's why she called me," I continue. I explain to Gregory about Susan and the baby.

He's surprised. "She has a daughter?" he says.

"I told you about her last summer." It didn't register, of course. He would file it under women's gossip, not something he needed to remember.

"If you say so. She just never seemed the motherly type to me."

"Lots of people who aren't the motherly type have children."

"I'll give you one thing, Anna—you're a good mother." He's still sitting there on the bed, not looking at me, running his eyes over the notes on the yellow pad. He has said this before. It used to be his usual response back when I still asked him if he loved me. I guess he thought it was an answer. I dry my face and walk back through the bedroom and into the hall. Gregory calls after me as I reach the stairs. "Welck's coming tonight, around seven-thirty. He'll want to talk to Lesley, and to you. We've got a trial date. March 11."

Welck. From the D.A.'s office. Up from the Cape, interviewing me. And Lesley. I don't want him upsetting Lesley. Gregory doesn't like him. He doesn't even use his first name, the gulf between corporate and criminal law not something he wants to cross. I don't like him either, haven't liked him since the first time he came to the house. He wanted to meet Dorothea, except he didn't put it that way. "Assess the situation" is how he put it. But Dorothea isn't a situation. She's a person, I wanted to tell him. He had trouble looking at her. He never spoke to her, just talked about her as if she were deaf or not in the room. And Lesley's given her deposition. They sent a woman for that, thank God. There wasn't much she could say anyway, except for what went on at the Petersens. The bog house she doesn't remember. The fatigue that has been building up all day hits me. I pray I can keep my wits about me.

We eat supper hastily, and I enlist Lesley to help Jeannine clean up while I get Dorothea settled. I want to make up for being gone all day. The doorbell rings and I hear the men talking in the hall, but I don't hurry Dorothea into bed. It soothes me to spend time with her. She, at least, will have no questions about where I've been and what I've been doing. I brush her hair the way she loves, singing to her all the while. "I see the moon and the moon sees me," I sing. She loved that one when she was little. "And the moon sees the one that I want to see," I go on, thinking of Demetrius alone there on the edge of the salt marsh, his crippled wife, his doomed love, his lost little girl.

The men have settled themselves in the living room, a room I avoid whenever I can—the Steinway waiting forlornly in the corner makes me too sad. Crossing the hall I can hear Gregory's voice, the controlled anger. "No," he's saying. "Not possible." When I reach the doorway I see that Welck has settled himself in the wing chair where I usually sit. He's pulling some papers out of his briefcase. He's a solid-looking man in his fifties, not handsome but well put together. He obviously works out and has his hair styled. Tinted, too, probably—his hair is all one shade, like stainless steel. There's something steely in his face as well, especially now when he's clearly annoyed. He would be a formidable opponent in front of a jury. "I've been telling Mr. Welck he can ask you anything he wants to know about Lesley," Gregory says, standing and moving towards the hall. "I'll get us some coffee." So Gregory has refused to let Lesley be interviewed again. Thank God for that.

I seat myself on the sofa across from the lawyer. I don't like being left alone with him. My hands are sweating, and I feel like a witness on the stand. "I'm not sure what I can tell you that's not in the deposition," I say, forcing myself to look Welck in the eye. I wish I could remember his first name. "Lesley was drugged—well, you know all that. She can't remember anything after she left the house."

"What was she doing over there with her sister? Did she drop by often?"

"No, she didn't. She thought her friend Phil was there. The younger brother. She'd seen his kayak out on the harbor. His family had been gone—they went home after the hurricane—and she hadn't seen him for a while. They used to go kayaking together." Mr. Welck is watching me intently. My hands feel like ice. He can read my body language, I know it. Do I need to tell him Lesley had a crush on Phil? Did she? She's never admitted it. Should I tell him what I've always suspected, that taking Dorothea for a walk was just an excuse to go by his house? Should I mention the little pile of rejected T-shirts I found on her bed?

"Do you have reason to suspect something was going on between Lesley and that boy?"

"Going on?"

"You know what I'm saying. It's something the defense might very well suggest. We know she was meeting him at night at beach parties."

"Twice," I say angrily. And then I lose it. My voice cracks, and tears blur my eyes. "Is this why you wanted to speak to Lesley? To break her down, to get her to confess to some—she's twelve years old, for God's sake. It's statutory rape, isn't it? You've got the medical report. She was, she is a virgin—what else do you want? Is this going to turn into a trial of Lesley—of her innocence?" My voice has risen. I look up to see Gregory standing in the doorway with three cups of coffee on a tray. He is glaring at me. Then I realize it's not for Welck's benefit but for Lesley's. She's somewhere in the house, up on the stair landing if I know her, listening. She can probably hear everything I say.

"Anna," Gregory says. He sets the tray down on the coffee table in front of me and hands a cup to the lawyer. I make no move to offer the cream and sugar. After an awkward moment he gets up and comes over to spoon two full teaspoons of sugar into his cup. His hair is definitely dyed.

"I'm sorry to upset you," he says to me, settling himself again in the wing chair, "but the defense will try to distract the jury from the facts of the case with all sorts of innuendoes. It's my job not to let that happen. You need to be prepared, and so does Lesley."

"I know," I respond wearily, "but can't we wait until it's closer to the time? I don't want her to relive it any more than she has to." I'm beginning to see how this man has earned his reputation. I'll be pressured by the defense. Better an outburst here than in the courtroom. I'm feeling overwhelmed with exhaustion, and just now I hear the unmistakable click of Lesley's door closing upstairs. I need to go to her. "Is there anything else you need to ask me?" I say.

"I think that's enough for now," Welck answers, taking another sip of his coffee and offering me an apologetic smile. Maybe there is some human kindness after all, under the steel.

Lesley doesn't answer when I knock on her door. I open it gently and peek in. She's turned off the lights, though it's only a little after eight, and is lying on her stomach with her face turned away from me. I can tell by her rigid posture that she's been crying. I sit down on the bed beside her and begin to rub her back. "It's all right," I say, though of course it isn't. Maybe nothing will ever be all right again. "That's the lawyer who will be arguing at the trial. We have a date—March 11. He wanted to talk to us about what kind of questions will be asked."

"Are they going to ask me questions?"

"Yes, they will, Lesley. Remember, I told you. You're underage, so they'll clear the court. There won't be anyone there except the judge and the lawyers and the jury, and us." And the boys, I think, but I don't mention them now. "Except for that you won't even be in the courtroom."

"But what if I want to be? Can't I sit in the back where no one will see me? It's about me! It isn't fair!"

"Believe me, you don't want to be there. You know, Lesley, at a trial a lot of things get said, not because they're the truth, but just to hint at things that might be true, to make people look better—or worse."

"And they want to say I'm some kind of slut, don't they! That's why you got mad, isn't it!"

"They won't say that. They can't say what isn't true. You know it isn't true, and your father and I know it."

"Some of the kids at school are saying it."

The words make my heart stop. I thought things were getting better at school. After weeks of coming straight home and going to her room, Lesley has started spending afternoons with girlfriends, talking to them on the phone. That new friend she mentioned, Becky—they talk almost every evening after supper. "Saying things to you?" I ask.

"Well, they did when all that stuff was on TV. It's been okay lately." Lesley turns and sits up and throws her arms around my neck. "I'm sorry, Mom. I didn't mean for anything to happen! I'm so sorry Dorrie got hurt. It's my fault. I was telling lies, all summer, and sneaking out, but I didn't do anything really bad! I'm sorry!"

"Oh Lesley, it's not your fault! Never think it's your fault. I'm sorry too," I say, thinking how much more I have to be sorry for than I can ever tell her. I sit there awkwardly clutching her to me, my big, solid, nearly grown up girl, her childhood behind her now, gone forever.

By the time I get back downstairs, Welck has gone. Gregory is still on the living room sofa, looking over a pile of papers. "What else did he say?" I ask, reclaiming the wing chair.

"Just that he wants to use some expert testimony. He wants another physical and psychological evaluation of Dorothea, to see if there's been permanent damage. And he's adamant about wanting her in the courtroom. He wants the jury to see her. The boys may try to claim she consented."

"Oh, Gregory, do we have to?" I think about Dorothea's terror in the hospital, and in the doctor's office later. "It's like they're raping her all over again."

Gregory sighs and puts down whatever he's been reading. "I know, Anna," he says, "but we have to help him nail those boys. You'd be amazed at how hard it is to get a conviction. Think of that case in New Jersey. We've got to protect the next girl this happens to." Amazing, I think, how Gregory can look beyond the personal agony to the legal implications of what happens in the courtroom. His noble devotion to the law. It's one of the things that made me fall in love with him all those years ago, the way he could look beyond the need to win, and fix his attention on what a case would mean to the body of law of which it would become a part. The long view, divorced from any personal stake he might have in it. A rare quality, almost unheard of in a young man. Yet it's that same trait that makes him seem cold when I need empathy. I'm not being fair. He does feel. He's in agony too. "Did Lesley overhear you?" he asks.

"I think she did. I talked to her about it. Oh, Gregory, she seems to think what happened is her fault. And the kids are saying things at school. I think we need to get her a therapist. Or maybe we all need to go."

"You feel you need therapy?"

"Yes, I do. I think we all need it. This is just the last straw—there's been stuff going on since—since forever. We don't talk. We aren't honest."

"You think I'm dishonest? That I need therapy?" Gregory looks at me with genuine surprise.

"Not dishonest, but you hide things, your feelings. And I'm not saying you need therapy, not just you anyway. We all do. Me, you, Lesley, all of us."

"Lesley's certainly learned how to hide what she's doing. Honestly, Anna, how could she sneak out at night without you knowing?" He's doing it again, shifting the focus away from himself.

I bristle. "So all this is my fault? How much of an eye do you keep on her? That's when you're even home." As soon as I say it, I wish I could take it back. I'm too tired for a quarrel, and what I need to be doing is persuading Gregory about the therapy. I say I'm sorry and go on.

"Look, Gregory, we all have secrets, things we don't tell anybody," I say.

"And what are your secrets?"

That startles me. Does he know about Demetrius? Of course not, I reassure myself, but he's waiting for me to answer his question. "I'm not honest about what I feel either, how I feel about Dorothea, what all that has done. And Lesley—do you realize that Lesley's whole childhood has gone by, that she's going to be thirteen in a couple of weeks? I feel as though I've missed everything about her for the past five years. Almost six. I don't really know how she's felt, whether she felt left out. Or even how she feels now. Tonight's the first time I've seen her cry about the rape. She thinks it's her fault."

The effort of what I'm saying drains the last bit of energy out of me. I'm not sure I can get out of this chair or climb the stairs, but I feel relieved to have the subject out in the open. Now if only I can get Gregory to agree. "If I find somebody—a family therapist—will you agree to go?" I ask. Gregory is gathering up the pile of papers on the table in front of him. I can tell he wants to get out of the room.

"Not that woman we had before."

"Okay, not her. A family therapist. A man if you like. I'll talk to Dr. Aldrich and see who he suggests. Okay?"

"Okay, if you think it would help Lesley, I'll go."

"Thank you," I say. "I'm whipped; I'm going to bed." So Gregory is agreed, and I am committed. Maybe I'll be able to come up with some answers, about the children, our marriage, the future, which at this point feels as precarious as the edge of a cliff. There is nothing more to do or say, at least for now. I head down the hall, peek briefly in on Dorothea, and slowly climb the stairs to bed.

The Courthouse

New England's mainland paid well with its substance
for these ramparts of earth which now help to shield it
from the attack of the open sea.

THE GIRLS AND I follow Gregory down from Needham on the first day of the trial. Jeannine comes too, to help out with Dorothea and to drive the girls home when Lesley's testimony is over. We come to a compromise with Welck about Dorothea: She will appear in the courtroom, but only while it is cleared for Lesley's testimony. He wants her there the whole time, not just for the jury but for the press, but he lets us have our way. We don't want her gawked at, or television cameras thrust in her face, or her image repeated over and over on the evening news.

I wait with the girls and Jeannine during the first hour of the trial, in one of the small conference rooms off the hall. I hate to miss the opening statements, but I want to be with my daughters. It's my place. Finally around eleven o'clock we hear noise in the hall and Gregory appears, followed by Welck. There's a short recess, and then the closed hearing will begin. Gregory's face looks pale and grim. He motions me out into the hall for a moment to tell me how things are going. The defense is suggesting that both girls consented to physical contact, that Lesley was so flattered by these older boys' attentions that she would do anything they wanted. On the other hand, our expert witness made it crystal clear that Dorothea could not have granted consent. Having Dorothea appear so soon after his testimony will have a dramatic effect on the jury. Dramatic effect! How will this day affect her?

I feel the whole ponderous machine of the law grinding over us, fearing the damage it can do. Dorothea's limitations paraded, displayed. And now Lesley in the witness box, her innocence on trial, along with her crush on Phil, that first sweet crazy love that sweeps us away and makes us reckless. That party on the back beach, how different it looks from the perspective of this imposing courtroom. Boys with beer and pot, underage girls sneaking out and trespassing on the beach at night, breaking all the regulations. And Lesley going over to the Petersen's house, entering willingly, and then later telling the boys where to take her, a deserted bog house where they'd be out of sight. Obvious what she had in mind, the defense will say. Anna, stop second guessing, I tell myself. Reality will be tough enough.

Welck comes back to tell us the girls will be brought in through the door near the judge's chambers, avoiding the crush of people out front. We follow him down the corridor, Lesley and I walking together, Jeannine pushing Dorothea just behind us, and Gregory bringing up the rear to ward off the public or the press. This will be the first time Lesley will have to confront those boys since it happened. Not Jake, who's not on trial, but the other two, Ken and the one called Worm, William Hendricks. Jeannine wheels Dorothea in and stations her where the prosecutor directs her, up front near the clerk, in full view of the jury. And of the boys. What are they thinking now, I wonder, seeing her helplessness? Do they feel shame? Their faces are impassive. It's hard to tell what is going through their minds.

Sitting there watching Lesley make her way to the witness box, I can see her as a stranger might. She's a beautiful young girl. Young woman. She certainly looks older than thirteen, despite my attempts to hide her budding figure. Her incredible hair is pulled back from her face with two barrettes, and she's wearing her navy blue blazer and a plaid skirt she detests. It could be a parochial school uniform. The judge speaks kindly to her, making me suspect he's a man with daughters. She looks more self-possessed than I expected, and although she speaks softly as she takes the oath, her voice does not waver. Her testimony does not take long, thank God. There is much she can't remember. In cross-examination, the defense attorney tries as best he can to suggest she went looking for a party. She sits there unmoving, not looking away as he approaches and asks again, "Tell us, Lesley, why did you go into the house when you knew you would be alone with three older boys?"

"I was looking for my friend," she answers. "They told me he'd be home soon." She does not hesitate or raise her voice or look away. I'm proud of the way she handles herself. She outfaces the lawyer. Her father's daughter.

On redirect, Welck has just a few questions for Lesley. "How old were you, Lesley, last August 26?"

"Twelve."

"At any time did your sister Dorothea tell you that she wanted to be with these boys?"

"Dorrie can't talk. I was taking her for a walk. She likes to be outside and ride in her wheelchair."

"If Dorrie can't talk, how do you know when she likes something?"

"She smiles sometimes, and she hums."

"Hums?"

"Yes. But sometimes she hums when she's worried about something, or a little scared. It's a different hum."

"Did she hum the day you took her over to the Petersen's house?"

"I can't remember."

"And what if she's very scared—what does she do?"

"She moans and sometimes she thrashes around. And sometimes she cries."

"And did she do any of those things on that day, August 26?"

"Not at the house. I don't remember later."

I'm grateful that the judge lets the session run long so that Lesley's testimony is over before the break for lunch. By one-thirty Jeannine and the girls are in the van and on their way back to Needham. Gregory and I stay behind. Our day is far from over. When we file back into the courtroom, I'm happy to see Daphne has found a seat near the back.

The next witness is Jake, who has agreed to testify against his buddies in exchange for having his case continued without a finding, which means in effect that he gets off scot-free as long as he stays clear of the law. I was outraged when Welck told us about it, but it was the best guarantee the other two would be convicted of anything other than drug possession. Assault and battery, aggravated rape, indecent assault on a minor. They could get twenty-five years. Watching Jake in the witness box makes me realize that he's paying a price no matter what happens. For the moment he looks younger than Lesley. His hair has been clipped so short the scalp shows through in back. He sits there uncomfortably, unwilling to meet anybody's eye, certainly not his former friends. His parents are halfway back on the center aisle, his mother with her eyes cast down, the father sitting ramrod straight, expressionless. Phil is not there.

Jake tells his story convincingly enough, though I don't buy it. I remember Lesley's account, that Jake offered her a drink, that William Hendricks, the one called Worm, followed him out into the kitchen, that they were both laughing when they came back. Jake was the one who put his arm around Lesley, who tried to keep her from leaving the house. But he manages to sound innocent, somebody who was, yes, high on drugs but just going along for the ride. He's a year younger than the other two, and has no arrests as an adult. Juvenile records are sealed, so whatever he did before this past year doesn't count.

The defense's cross-examination of Jake is merciless compared to his treatment of Lesley. Ken's attorney asks right away about the plea bargain. Despite the prosecutor's objections, Jake ends up looking every bit as guilty as the others, just luckier. He was waiting his turn; another few minutes and he would have been committing rape.

By the time the judge declares the day's session over, I can barely keep my eyes open. Out in the corridor Welck is noncommittal about the chances for conviction. Gregory is angry. "That little weasel's testimony might backfire," he says in the car going home. "Everybody hates a snitch." Despite my worries about the girls, I give in to exhaustion and fall asleep. Next thing I know we are turning into our driveway in Needham. It's a relief to be able to hug my girls and know their part of the ordeal is over. Dorothea doesn't seem to have been affected by her appearance in the courtroom. Lesley is silent. What she's thinking is hard to fathom. I tell her how proud I am of her performance. It's a bad choice of words, I think as soon as I have said it.

"It felt so weird," Lesley tells me. "Like no matter what I said it would be a lie. Even my clothes were a lie." Oh Lesley, how right you are, I am thinking. How can I tell her I was trying to hide her considerable sex appeal, something she's still unaware of for a few more weeks or months, if we're lucky?

"But you didn't lie," I tell her. "You told the truth exactly as you remembered it. That's all you can do." She's right, though. Being questioned under oath, is it ever possible to do it without doubting everything that we saw and did? I think about something Gregory said about trials early in our marriage: They're not about facts; they're about appearances. *Performance* is the right word, exactly.

ON THURSDAY WE take two cars to the Cape again because Gregory has to go to in town to the office for an early meeting. He'll join me in mid-morning, and we'll stay in Cummaquid for the night. Before I leave, I have a loud confrontation with Lesley, who wants to come with me. None of my arguments hold water for her, and she ends by storming up the stairs and slamming her bedroom door. She hasn't had a tantrum like that in months. In a way it's reassuring. She's feeling her emotions, at least.

Just as I'm sliding along the smooth oak bench in the courtroom, I hear Demetrius's name called. He is the first witness of the day. I'm suddenly terrified—and grateful that Greg isn't here yet. What if it should somehow come out that Demetrius and I were lovers? What would that do to his credibility, not to mention to Gregory? Sitting there alone on the hard wooden bench, so like a church pew, I feel the full brunt of what we—what I—have done. Sneaking out and meeting in the bog house, the very place where those boys—it's sordid, horrible. Something I'll have to live with the rest of my life.

And yet looking at Demetrius, I feel nothing but longing and sadness. He approaches the witness stand dressed in the same old-fashioned suit he wore at Phoebe's funeral. As always he moves calmly and deliberately— if he's nervous, there's nothing to reveal it. He looks smaller than I remember, older and more tired. He tells his story calmly. He arrived at the bog house about four o'clock and noticed the jeep parked outside. He carefully describes what he saw when he went inside: Dorothea curled on the floor, moaning; the three boys clustered around Lesley, Ken holding her arms over her head, Jake standing near her feet, Kendricks on her. No doubt at all in Demetrius's mind about what was happening. Jake and Ken lit out as soon as they caught sight of him, but Kendricks was oblivious to the fact that he was there. Demetrius picked up the first thing that came to hand, a hoe lying on the floor, and struck him on the back of the head with the handle. The same hoe they used on Dorothea, I realize with horror. Thank God Gregory isn't here for this.

He arrives just as Demetrius's testimony is ending and slides in beside me. "What's going on?" he whispers in my ear, glancing up at Demetrius with mild dislike. "Did he make any points for us?"

The sports metaphor disgusts me. This is not a game, I want to say to him—it's our lives. Ours and our girls'. "A few, I think," is all I say.

The last witness for the Prosecution describes the physical evidence that Dorothea was raped and the injuries she sustained. Severe internal and external bruising. A tear high in the vagina. The presence of semen, with a DNA match to William Kendricks. I have to use all the strength I have to sit where I am and not burst into tears. Gregory sits motionless beside me, but I can see the effort it is costing him, the clench of his jaw.

Ken and William do not testify when the defense presents its case. The gist of their argument is that no one actually saw who injured Dorothea. They do not pursue the argument that Dorothea consented, for which I am grateful. Lesley is another story. She's pictured, once again, as a reckless girl looking for a party, willing to do anything. Statutory rape, yes, but the sex was consensual. Jake is depicted as someone who would say anything to save his own skin.

By the time the summations are over and the jury is charged it's nearly four o'clock. The crowd spills into the corridor and beyond, out onto the courthouse lawn. Gregory and I run the gauntlet of cameras and reporters and head outside for a breath of air. My body feels stiff and sore from sitting all day with every muscle tensed. It's bright outdoors, the sun at a higher angle in the sky than it was the last time I noticed. The air has an edge, but spring will be here before long. Maybe one of these days this long nightmare will be over.

Daphne approaches us hesitantly until I notice her and smile. Then she comes up and gives me a firm hug. I thank her for coming. After my long neglect of her, it wasn't something I expected her to do.

"Of course I came. If you like, I'll wait for the verdict as well. Do you need to have a conference or anything?"

Gregory excuses himself to go find Welck. Daphne and I stand on the grass looking out across the harbor opposite. From this angle we can see right over Sandy Neck to the bay beyond. The sun feels good on the side of my face. I feel almost hopeful. I look around for Demetrius, but he's nowhere in sight. I wonder what he's thinking, what all this has cost him. He seemed self-possessed up there on the witness stand, but weary. I've missed him all these months. All the longing I haven't let myself feel hit me today, sitting on that hard oak bench. Tears sting my eyes, but I force myself to smile at Gregory, who is coming toward us across the courthouse lawn.

The jury takes just under two hours to reach a verdict. We spend most of the time across the street at the Tavern, where Gregory orders himself a scotch and Daphne and I have a glass of wine. We are about pay our check and cross the street again when Gregory's pager goes off. It's Welck, saying the jury is coming back in. It all happens faster than we expected. Kenneth Smith, on the charges of assault and aggravated rape, indecent assault of a minor, not guilty. William Kendricks, guilty.

And so it's over. One of the three will be punished; the other two will go free. Hendricks will probably get three to five, Welck tells us later, and be out in two. I think of the ordeal my daughters, all of us have endured all these months. Two will go free. Tears blind my eyes. I stand up at the sound of the judge's gavel and walk swiftly toward the back door, not waiting for Gregory, who, I know, will want to speak to Welck in the front of the courtroom. Instead of heading outside I turn down the narrow corridor that runs the length of the building. I'm not sure where I'm going, but I want to get away from the television news crews waiting out front, hungry for a reaction from the victims' mother. Outrage is what the viewers will expect, outrage and fear. Strangely, I don't feel either. Ken should have been found guilty. It is an outrage, but not a surprise. Welck told us how hard a conviction would be. There is no help for it. Certainly I don't need Jake to be in prison. His eyes, there in the witness box, his inability to look at the friends he was betraying. The family—how will they come through this? That father, the anxious mother trying to hold everything together, and Phil, guilty only of caring for Lesley, trying to make it up to her with the sad little note, the kayak still hidden in Phoebe's garage. I don't need an eye for an eye. Jake's father will make him suffer enough, I suspect. A rigid man like that can't admit to feeling helpless—he'll turn it to rage. Anger turned outward, not hidden like Gregory's.

Halfway down the corridor I hear footsteps behind me and turn to see Demetrius. He's still here, after all. He must have followed me. No one else is in sight yet, but in a moment the hall will be filled with people. "Here, come in here," Demetrius says, opening a door. It's a small conference room, the same one where we waited for the girls to be called. He doesn't say anything else, but puts his arms around me and pulls me to his chest. I raise my face to look at him and then we are kissing, the first time since last August. We stand there motionless for a long moment, my emotions a confused mixture of rage and sadness and longing for comfort. Then I hear a noise by the door and look over to see Gregory, just a slice of his body as he backs out and closes the door behind him.

Up in Smoke

As the glaciers moved they incorporated into themselves
whatever materials were not tightly enough in the grip of
the earth.

I BREAK AWAY FROM Demetrius and follow Gregory out into the hall, now full of people, but he has disappeared from sight. I push through the crowded corridor and make it to the back door of the courthouse without being recognized. There are no cameras here, and only a few people, no sign of Gregory. I make my way across the courthouse drive and down into the parking lot. My hands as I turn the key in the car lock are icy cold. Gregory knows. Did he even suspect before this? I have betrayed him. A conversation from years and years ago flashes in my mind: "What would you do if I were unfaithful?" I asked him. I was being playful—it was early in our marriage. We had been at a cocktail party and I was teasing him about a woman who spent the evening flirting with him. "I'd leave you," he answered. He wasn't kidding.

Will he? Leave me now? Do I want a life without him, alone with the girls, here? And what of Demetrius? I'm not sure he saw Gregory that brief moment in the doorway. He feels such guilt about what happened those years ago—does he agonize about what he and I have done to Gregory now?

Gregory is in the parlor when I get back. He doesn't answer when I come in through the kitchen and call his name. He waits silently for me to find him, sitting on Phoebe's Victorian settee, the only formal piece of furniture in the only formal room in the house. It's cold in here, on the north side, much colder than in the kitchen. I sit down in the antique rocker opposite him, Phoebe's chair. It faces the window, looking out through the fading daylight at the locusts, torn and split by the hurricane. Above them on top of the hill looms Phoebe's rock.

For once Gregory is looking straight at me. "Well, Anna, I see why you acted so strange all last summer. Tell me I'm wrong. You and the handyman?"

"Demetrius. He has a name. Does it upset you, Gregory, that he's not our kind?" I'm going on the offensive—I can hear the sarcasm in my voice. I've borrowed a phrase from Gregory's aunt, his father's sister. They're a class-conscious family, the Dylans. Dover, St. Paul's, Harvard, how could they not be?

Gregory ignores my remark. "Unbelievable. You've blind-sided me. I never thought I'd have to question—you're my wife, for God's sake. You belong to me."

The words make me bristle with anger. "Belong? What century are we living in? I'm your property—is that what you mean?"

"You know what I mean. I trusted you. And I haven't been screwing around, though believe you me, I've had offers. Explain to me, Anna, exactly what's been going on here. Is this some sort of menopausal sexual fling?"

Menopausal: That's a nasty crack, an oblique way of saying I ought to act my age. As if we ever outgrow our need for love, or our heedless delight when it finds us. "It wasn't like that at all," I say. "He didn't come on to me. We're friends. He's been there, all summer. He's been kind to Dorothea and Lesley."

"And so you said thank you by screwing him? Tell me, where did these sordid little trysts take place? Does Lesley know?" The word *screw* jars, coming from Gregory. He's said it twice. He hardly ever swears, never uses vulgar language, at least in my hearing; it's part of his good breeding. I can see his knee vibrating. He's forcing himself to sit there facing me, when what he really wants is to get up, escape into the hall or storm outside, smash something.

"No, Lesley doesn't know," I say. It feels so odd, explaining, analyzing what at the time happened with no reference to motives or consequences. It's like being back at the trial in the witness box. The words feel fake, like those wooden columns in front of the courthouse. "It didn't start until late in the summer."

"Where? Here?"

"Not here in the house."

"Thank God for small favors. Where, then?"

"At his house. And over at West Marsh." I leave out the other times, the two nights up there on the hill by the rock. I can look out through the dusk and just make out where we spread the quilt.

"In the bog house? The same goddamned place where those boys took our girls? Do you realize what the defense lawyers could have done with that? Or the press? Like mother, like daughter, they'd say. Jesus Christ, Anna, what were you thinking? You had to be insane."

"I didn't know last summer that our girls were going to be raped."

"Maybe if you'd been home paying attention, they wouldn't have been."

That's a low blow. I sit there without replying. There doesn't seem to be anything to say. He's right. Perhaps I was, am, insane, or perhaps I was like a starving person who comes upon a feast. Not insane, but not calculating the cost, either.

Gregory gets up so suddenly he cracks his shin on the coffee table. "Shit," he says. "I hate this place. I've got to get out of here." He strides out into the hallway and up the stairs. I stay where I am, listening to the floorboards creak as he walks back and forth over my head. He must be collecting his things. In not more than five minutes he's back downstairs and out the kitchen door. It takes longer than I expect for the car to start. I'm just about to go out to the porch to see what he's doing when I hear the engine, hear him back out of the driveway a little too fast and drive away, the tires skidding on loose gravel.

I stay there in Phoebe's rocking chair a long time, thinking about what to do. Jeannine doesn't expect us home tonight because we thought the trial would last another day. I should call home, but I can't bring myself to do it. Gregory will tell them about the verdict when he gets there, anyway. I wonder what he'll tell them about me. It's dark now. I have no idea what time it is. My first impulse is to run across the lane to Daphne. She would give me a hug and a glass of wine, and listen while my story tumbled out. But Susan is there, and the new baby. We wouldn't be able to talk. I could ask her over here, but more than anything I want to call Demetrius. I have no idea what he thinks after all these months. Remembering him holding me, that brief moment at the courthouse, I know my feelings for him haven't changed, but what about his? Did he see the look on Gregory's face? He could be fearful for me or himself. A man who finds out his wife's been unfaithful is capable of anything. Does Demetrius imagine Gregory coming after him with a gun? But he knows Gregory. How well do I know him? I sit there staring at the black windows. They reveal nothing but my own reflection.

Finally my stiff body and the cold drive me back out into the kitchen. The clock says after nine. I've had nothing to eat since lunchtime. I fetch a can of vegetable soup from the cupboard, rummage through the drawer for an opener, crank open the soup and heat it up on the stove. It warms me a little, but the house is still freezing. I need to go to bed or start a fire. I decide to go out to the garage for some dry wood. A wind has risen and the early spring air feels damp and raw. I'm startled to find the garage door ajar. When I turn on the light, the bright red of the kayak seems to leap at me. Did Gregory come in here before he left? If so, he would have seen it, still sitting where it's been all winter. Then wouldn't he have come back into the house to ask if I knew about it? I'm grateful that didn't happen. I wouldn't be able to lie, and he would have one more secret to blame me for.

I carry an armload of wood back to the kitchen, conscious that Demetrius is the one who stacked it there in the garage weeks ago. Demetrius, always there when I need him, taking care, of me, the girls. A habit formed from his years of looking after Phoebe, and before that, Marte, his wife. Once I'm back inside the house, the exhaustion of the long day hits and I decide to go to bed. Maybe things will look clearer in the morning.

Upstairs I get ready for bed, quickly changing into my nightgown in the cold master bedroom, wondering whether Gregory and I will ever sleep there again. All I know is I don't want to be in that bed now. I slip on my bathrobe, pick up the extra quilt at the foot of the bed, and make my way down the dark hall to Phoebe's little room. It's no warmer in here, but the small space feels cosier. Even so I can't sleep. I lie there with the image of Gregory at the courthouse in my mind. And I'm worried about the girls, wondering what Lesley will think about the verdict. Hendricks won't be away for long, and the others not at all. I'm grateful that Jake's family has sold the house. At least he won't be a threat. We won't have to think about him just down the beach, over there on Lighthouse Lane, or pass his truck driving down 6A.

Then my thoughts turn back to Gregory, his presumption that I am a piece of property he has legal claim to. That cold interview in the parlor, like a deposition. He never asked, never said anything about love. Do I love him? Did I ever? Yes, once long ago, passionately. But that passion was never answered. All those years of making excuses for his distance, his lack of desire, trying to supply the heat for both of us. And does Gregory love me now? Did he ever? Or did he just want what a wife provides—a home, children? "You're a good mother," he always said when I asked about love. It's been a long time since I've even asked. It's his pride that is wounded now. Having all this happen here, where Gregory never wanted us to be. "I hate this place," he said tonight, before he went upstairs to pack. Here where he spent those first awful summers after his mother died, where his father banished him because he couldn't cope, where—oh, the irony of it—he was raped. No one to protect him. Not Phoebe, not Dennis, not Demetrius. And now Demetrius feels he has failed again, failed to protect my daughters, though he is the one who saved them from the worst that could happen. But Gregory, still living with that buried helpless rage he felt at fifteen, can never see Demetrius that way. Not now. Not now that he has stolen his wife.

I lie there going over it all for what seems like hours, alone on Phoebe's narrow little cot. After a long time I doze fitfully, only to be startled awake by a strange sound, soft, from out in the hall, something brushing against the floor. An animal, maybe, but it doesn't have the familiar skittering sound of mice across the attic. And it's not overhead; it's near, in the hall. Could Gregory have come back, or could it be Demetrius? But it's not a man's step, not my husband's, not the sound of shoes. The bed is finally warm and I'm loath to throw back the covers, but I know I'll never sleep until I look. I pull on my robe and step barefoot out into the freezing hall. There's no one there, nothing, no sound. But now that I'm fully awake I know I'll never go back to sleep, and I know what I want to do.

I make my way down the hall to the master bedroom, dress quickly in my flannel shirt, jeans, and a warm sweater, and head downstairs and out through the porch door to my car. I want to see Demetrius, and now there is no reason not to. I have just started the car when I remember something. I leave the engine idling while I run back to the house, up two flights of stairs, and across to the far end of the attic. It takes a minute to remember how to open the lock and find the secret spring. I pull out the envelope and put it in the pocket of my jacket. In five minutes I'm driving slowly down the lane and turning left, on my way to the little house on the marsh.

At first I assume that Demetrius is asleep, but after five minutes of knocking I can't raise him. It's not until then that I notice that the truck is gone. Could he be at West Marsh, now, in the middle of the night? Is it possible that he's spending the night there? It seems unlikely that he'd be misting the vines. It's the wrong time of year, and though it's cold, it's not cold enough for a frost. Or has he gone away somewhere, to get away from all the publicity of the trial? Maybe reporters have been pestering him. Maybe he's gone to his nephews in West Barnstable or his father's relatives over in Wareham. Now that I'm here, now that I'm committed to seeing him I feel overwhelmed with frustration. It's worth a look at West

Marsh; it's not very far. And so I drive the short distance to the bog. I've forgotten my watch and I have no idea what time it is. It must be very late—there is no one on the road.

They're visible from a quarter mile away, reflected against the pre-dawn haze, the flashing lights of a police car, the beams of headlights. Fire trucks, three of them, and an assortment of strange cars and trucks have been pulled up and parked every which way on the track across the bog. Then I see the column of smoke. Six or seven men are standing motionless in front of it, and beyond them, below the smoke, a heap of red embers and blackened beams where the bog house used to be. My heart lurches until I see that one of the men is Demetruis—I can tell by the shape of his shoulders. Relief floods over me and my eyes fill with tears. I call his name, and he turns and walks slowly toward me, a black silhouette backlit by the devastation behind him. I can't see his face.

"Is that you, Anna? What are you doing here?" he asks. His voice sounds weary and his clothes reek of smoke. "How did you know? I thought you'd be back in Needham by now."

"No, I'm leaving in the morning. We planned to stay, but then Gregory left. He saw us together. At the courthouse. We had words."

"You all right?" Even now thinking of me and not himself.

"I'm okay, but I couldn't sleep, and I wanted to talk to you. And so I came out looking for you. Over at your house, and then here. I didn't expect this."

"I didn't either." Demetrius stands there a few feet away from me, his face still in shadow, and tells me his story: A neighbor saw the smoke about midnight and called him and the fire department. The fire was set, they're pretty sure; there's a smell of gasoline everywhere. One of the boys, possibly, or one of their friends angry about Demetrius's testimony.

I ask him what was in the bog house, and he says not too much, tools and equipment and things like his waders, but everything was pretty old. His biggest regret is losing Dennis's trimmer because it's one of a kind, Dennis's invention, one of the last ties to the old man. I remember the day he showed it to me, an odd-looking machine on a bicycle wheel. Demetrius thinks he can remember how to build a similar one, but he liked having the original. After he runs out of things to say about the fire there is a pause. He's still standing a little distance from me. "You sure you're all right?" he asks again. "Gregory didn't . . .?"

"No. He was angry, but anger just makes him more calm. He's a lawyer, remember."

"I don't think you should be here, Anna. If he comes back and finds you not home, won't he assume—?"

"He won't come back."

"Even so, I think you should leave."

His words crush me. What do they mean? "I guess you're right," I say. "You're all right, aren't you? You didn't go inside or inhale smoke or anything?"

"No, I'm not so foolish. By the time I got here it was about burned down."

"I'm just glad you're all right. I'll call you soon—if you want."

"Anna?" Demetrius steps forward and puts his arms around me. The smell of smoke is overwhelming. It will cling to my jacket for a long time. His embrace is brief; I can already feel him letting go. I hold on to him for a moment. Over his shoulder I see the last wisps of smoke rising from the ruined timbers.

Back at the house I realize that trying to sleep any more would be futile. I sit at Phoebe's battered kitchen table drinking tea, thinking about the bog house. I wonder how old it was—was it there when Phoebe and Dennis bought the place? It must have been. I don't remember any mention in the journals about them building it. So many things happened there. The picnic lunch, making love, all ruined now. Sandwiched in between two rapes, a generation apart. I climb back upstairs and sit on Phoebe's bed, imagining the nights she must have lain awake thinking about her lost daughter. Then I remember the envelope, still in my jacket pocket, the picture I was going to give to Demetrius, forgotten in my shock at seeing the fire. I stand up and step over to Phoebe's old desk, pick up the copy of John Donne's poems that has been lying there since last summer, and leaf through the pages. I know the one I want. Donne knew them well, these feelings—regret and loss and sadness. "*I am every dead thing*," he wrote. "*I am re-begot / Of absence, darkness, death; things which are not.*"

I am too tired and shocked and numb to cry. Despite myself I climb back under the covers in my clothes and sleep fitfully, a few hours at least, waking again at first light to the sound of something in the hall. Nothing to worry about, I decide, an animal in the walls, maybe. Or Phoebe's ghost. I doze a little more and wake just at six. I must go home and finish what I've started.

I leave as soon as I can pack the car, taking 495 to avoid the morning crush on the Southeast Expressway. I stop halfway for coffee and a bagel and still am home before nine. Jeannine is just finishing Dorothea's breakfast. She doesn't ask me why I didn't come home last night, which makes me wonder what Gregory's explanation was. Gregory has left and is flying back to Washington, she says. Lesley is at school. The trial is on the front page of the *Globe*, and she's dreading being the center of attention again but didn't even ask to stay home. Considering everything she seems okay.

We work together on Dorothea's morning routine. Halfway through I remember it's trash day, and hurry to empty the waste baskets and kitchen bin and carry everything out to the garage before the truck arrives. I'm about to dump one of the plastic bags when I notice the odor. I pull a crumpled paper bag out of the bin and open it to find Gregory's good black gloves, smelling of gasoline.

Confessions

They pried loose rocks the size of houses from their native ledges.

I GO BACK INTO the house and pull an empty coffee can out from under the kitchen sink, one I've been saving for cleaning paint brushes. Not that I've had time in the past five years to paint anything. I used to like to refinish things, before. Back in the garage I stuff the gloves inside the can. They just fit. Supple, good quality leather, a present from Dorothea last Christmas, picked out by Lesley and me. I set the can in plain sight, on the high shelf over the workbench where we keep the paint thinner and insecticides. Then I go back into the house and straight upstairs without stopping in the kitchen or even speaking to Jeannine, who glances at me, puzzled. In the bathroom I turn the water on full and scrub my hands for a long time, but nothing seems to make the smell go away.

All of this happens automatically, without conscious thought, but now I have to decide what to do. I have a day and a half—Gregory is due home Friday night. It seems impossible to believe. If it's true, if Gregory—but I know it's true. What have I done to him? How could he lose control like that, this man who values integrity above all virtues, who knows—firsthand—the fruits of violence. Maybe anyone is capable of anything. Some nasty little corner of my mind is pleased. He's given me a weapon, something to bargain with. For what? For Phoebe's house, for my freedom? Is that what I want? I'm in no condition to know. If I threatened and he called my bluff, would I be willing to destroy him? I lie awake most of Thursday night mulling it all over in my mind. Can I really blame Gregory for lashing out when I—what did he call it—blind-sided him? Arson, a felony. The only thing I'm sure of is I can tell no one. Except Gregory. But how?

Jeannine cooks a special supper Friday night and stays and eats with us, even though she is supposed to have the whole weekend off. She's made all of Lesley's favorites: homemade lasagna, a Caesar salad, ice cream and fresh strawberries for dessert. Strawberries, the first of the season, trucked north from Florida or somewhere else far south of here. A sign of spring.

Spring, to be followed by summer and its inevitable decisions. Jeannine is relaxed and bubbly. "Time to celebrate," she says, wheeling Dorothea up to the table and giving her a squeeze from behind. She's been different lately, happier, more demonstrative. And it's had an effect on Dorothea, who slowly, day by day, seems to be letting go of her fear. "That old trial is all over," Jeannine goes on. "Now things will get back to normal."

Normal? Will things ever be normal? Just then Gregory arrives from the airport, adding to the irony.

I spend another sleepless night lying stiffly beside Gregory, thinking how strange it is that we can live with another person for years, scrupulously avoiding the most crucial issues. With my parents it was sex, and later my father's cancer, a word no one in my family dared say. With Gregory and me it's any overt display of anger. Maybe any emotion, even joy, taken to extreme. Here in this bedroom where we have slept and made love together all these years—I could just as well be closed in with a stranger.

Sometime early Saturday morning I decide what I'm going to do. I confront Gregory while we are still in bed. I sit up, prop a pillow between my back and the headboard, and look over at him, sleeping on his back and lightly snoring. "I found your gloves," I say. It's unfair, starting in when he's not even awake. But I need all the leverage I can get.

We used to read the Sunday paper propped up in bed together, years ago, before the children, back when life was simple. I would go downstairs and make coffee and bring the mugs up and climb back in beside him. Sometimes we'd make love, laughing at the noise of the paper crinkling. I loved those companionable times, but when the children came they ended. The sex changed too, once I had turned into a mother.

"Gloves?" Gregory says, coming awake.

"Your black ones. In the garage. In the trash. I could smell the gas, so I looked in the bag." There, it's said.

Greg responds, finally. "Anna, I can't explain. I was just so angry. That place—I had to do something. I got the lawn mower gas out of the shed and then just drove around for a couple of hours. But I still did it. I don't know why. I couldn't stop myself." He sits there unmoving, looking bleakly ahead.

"Because you're human like the rest of us, maybe?" It comes out sounding sarcastic, though that's the last thing I intend. He's been more honest about himself than I can ever remember. He's always been so sure about what to do. Now he doesn't seem sure about anything. I feel warmer toward him than I have in a long time.

"Will you tell Demetrius?" Gregory asks softly after another long silence.

"No, but I think—I think you should. You owe him that. It's his livelihood, the bog."

"Anna, I can't. I should compensate him, though. I've been thinking, we could tell him it's money from Phoebe's estate, that she would want us to."

"No." The firmness in my own voice takes me by surprise. "Demetrius heard the will. He was there. No more lies. We've had enough of those. You've got to tell him."

"He'll bring charges, Anna. Do you realize what that would mean?"

"Of course I do. It's all I've thought about for the past two days. But I'm not sure he will. I'll go with you; we'll tell him together. I don't think he'd want to ruin you when it would only hurt me."

"No, Anna." Gregory turns his back to me and sits on the edge of the bed. His hair is tousled from sleep; it makes him look almost boyish. I notice it's getting a little thin on top. He's about to get up, go into the bathroom, shave, put on his clothes. His armor. I have to play my trump card now.

"Will you tell Demetrius, or shall I?" I ask him. He stares at me, surprised.

"Wait a minute, Anna. We need to think hard about this."

"I have thought about it. I'm not going to lie for you." I feel a core of stubbornness forming inside me, like a steel rod. It's an unfamiliar feeling, but satisfying. I am not afraid of what Gregory will do or say, or even what he might think. Right now he's looking at me as if I were a stranger, as maybe I am. "I don't think you could live with keeping this a secret," I add.

"Who would stay with the girls?" So he's considering it, at least. I'm amazed he doesn't put up more resistance. Part of him must want this encounter.

"I'll call Jeannine and see if she can come—we'd be back before supper."

Jeannine agrees, as long as we're back by six. She has a date, she says shyly. I call Demetrius at eight o'clock to say that Gregory and I want to meet with him. I persuade Gregory to let me be the one to call—I don't want Demetrius to feel threatened. It's an uncomfortable conversation with Gregory right there listening. I have to hide my emotions and sound businesslike. "What's this about? He's not bringing a gun, is he?" Demetrius asks, half-facetiously.

"Nothing like that; it's not about that," I say, trying to keep my voice level. Not about us, I mean. Later, in the car, I imagine he will think we are letting him go; that would make sense. He'll wonder why I said to meet at West Marsh. I want us to be there, not on Kettle Lane. It's Demetrius's turf, the place where he's landlord, not hired help. And more than that, Gregory needs to see what he's done, and confront whatever demons are there. I think back over the years we've been married, and even before, that day he refused to come along when Uncle Dennis took me on a tour of the bog. I'm not sure he's ever been back, not since that long-ago summer when he was fifteen.

By ten o'clock we are on our way to the Cape. I keep wondering if we'll ever make this trip again. We ride together in silence, both of us conscious of the uncertainty, the momentousness of what we're about to do. I think back to that other day just over a year ago when we drove back after Phoebe's funeral, my excitement. It was the day we learned about the house.

We arrive at West Marsh before noon to find Demetrius already there, waiting in his truck, which he's parked over by the shed, away from the blackened rectangle marking the outline of the ruined bog house. Lord knows what he's thinking. By the time we pull up behind him he's out of the truck and standing there facing us with his hands clasped in front of him, looking deferential, like an employee. Gregory gets out of the car and faces him. They do not shake hands. I pause a moment before opening the car door to look at them there together, the two men I have loved. How different they are! Gregory taller, more imposing, even in a windbreaker and corduroy pants. Demetrius older, more weathered. He's wearing jeans and his blue-black navy sweater over a plaid flannel shirt. Both of them physically calm, that's what they have in common, though I can sense the tension beneath the surface. The moment is fraught—with what? With danger? Under the civilized pleasantries they are two male animals sizing each other up.

They talk for a few minutes about the cranberry market, which was disastrous last season, with a crop surplus and a steep drop in prices. Then Gregory launches in. "I set the fire," he says, gesturing in the direction of the bog house without looking at it. "I don't want some kid accused. Of course I'll pay the reconstruction cost."

"So," says Demetrius. He looks at me quizzically. He thought this conversation would be about us. Of course it is, in a way.

"I don't expect you to understand," Gregory says.

"I think I can," Demetrius replies, glancing over toward the bog house, or where it used to be. "If I'd been here . . ."

There is a silence, which I feel obligated to fill. "But you did come, you were here. If Lesley . . ." I can't finish the sentence. Maybe Demetrius meant the other time, before. I look beseechingly at him, no longer caring what Gregory thinks.

But Greg is looking at Demetrius, not me. Whatever is going on is just between them. "It's up to you what you want to do," Gregory says.

"The police are still on it."

"Do they have any evidence?"

"Not that they've said. I know a couple folks in the Department."

"You can't very well call them off the case, can you? But if they don't come up with anything, then . . ."

"Don't s'pose I'll do anything," Demetrius answers, almost under his breath.

I hear Gregory's little gasp of relief. He should say thank you but he doesn't. Instead he reaches out, offering the handshake he withheld when we arrived, and Demetrius takes his hand after a moment's hesitation. I suppose the two consider it a deal, a matter of honor. Then Gregory turns, and for the first time, looks behind him at the charred wreckage of the bog house. "I'll send a check, for the building," he says.

"Not needed," Demetrius says, withdrawing his hand and turning back toward his truck without looking in my direction. Gregory takes my elbow and steers me toward the car. No one says goodbye. When we get back onto 6A I look at the dashboard clock. The whole encounter has lasted less than ten minutes.

We stop for lobster rolls at a deli in Sandwich. I walk in first and choose one of the booths so we'll be able to talk. "It doesn't sound as if he'll want to prosecute," I say.

"You think he means that? We took him by surprise. He could change his mind."

"I don't think so," I answer. The waitress arrives to take our order, and when she leaves, I can't think of anything else to say. Such a brief confrontation. What must be going through Gregory's mind, looking at Demetrius, knowing we've been together? There's no way I can make him understand. It angers me, his assumption of superiority, all to do with externals, with economics and education and class. The same snobbery that drove Phoebe out of Boston—did Uncle Dennis bridle under it, the disdain of her relatives? And what of the Dylans and Gregory's mother?

And what must Demetrius be thinking? The strangeness of our driving all the way to the Cape to tell him face to face. And my peculiar role in it, present but inarticulate. The supportive wife. Will he expect me to call, to reassure, explain? The sudden way Demetrius turned away from us and left, just after Gregory mentioned the money. Of course. He's insulted. It feels like a payoff. If he accepts the money, his act of forgiveness will mean nothing.

The numbness lasts until Monday morning. Somehow I get through the weekend, making up a story for Jeannine about why our sudden trip to the Cape, something to do with Aunt Phoebe's estate, I say. Gregory listens to me lie. How casual I've become about the truth, since last August. Jeannine barely hears me anyway; she's excited about her date. She's done something to her hair, streaked it or frosted it in the front, that flatters her pale complexion. She makes a quick getaway soon after we arrive.

We order pizza for supper and disperse soon afterwards, Gregory to his little den to work on his brief, Lesley upstairs to finish a writing project for school. I settle Dorothea and watch an inane romantic movie on television and find myself in tears. By midday on Sunday Gregory is gone, back to Washington. We have no more discussions about Demetrius or our visit to West Marsh.

On Monday the pain hits. It's ironic, I think, since I've barely spoken to Demetrius for months. All day he stays on my mind while I try to imagine how he might interpret my behavior on Saturday. I must have come across as the loyal wife, determined to stand by her husband's side now that he needs her. What did Daphne say that time last summer, about relationships, that they were all about power? I have more power now that Greg has committed a crime and I have, presumably, forgiven him. He's lost the moral high ground and become a sinner like the rest of us. When Demetrius agreed not to press charges, did he see it as a favor for me, or compensation for Gregory's suffering all those years ago? Or was he, in his quiet understated way, displaying his power?

An Ordinary Miracle

. . . rivulets of leftover tidal waters channel their way
back to the sea.

DAPHNE HITS THE print button with a satisfied sigh. Three pages, and still not a peep from Sophie. Modest progress, but she's set modest goals for herself these days, given the circumstances. She gets up and crosses to the door of the deck, gently slides it open, and steps outside. Still a bite in the air, but she can feel the heat of the sun, almost like a warm hand on her back. Mid-May already, with all of late spring and summer stretching ahead. She moves quietly over to the carriage, carefully positioned to keep the sun off the baby's face, and looks down at her granddaughter, still sound asleep. Amazing, the perfect skin, the long eyelashes, the pretty mouth pursed and just barely moving in a dream of nursing, the first sign that hunger will soon wake her up. Funny how the rules change. Babies now are put to bed on their backs. When Susan was this age that was thought to be dangerous. Sophie has a bald spot from sleeping on her back, where the fine brown birth hair has worn away. But a haze of new hair, lighter, blonde or even reddish, is just beginning to be visible. She'll be fair like Susan, like Daniel's family, though her eyes are very dark blue and beginning to look cloudy, will probably turn brown. Sophie—Sophia. Not a name belonging to anyone she knows, Susan said when Daphne asked about it. It's a wish for her: It means *wisdom*. Daphne likes the name. Part of a tradition anyway, that old New England habit of naming babies for the virtues we hope they'll possess. *Sophia*: Wisdom: knowledge put to use.

Two more months and she'll be gone, not just to Boston, but all the way back to San Francisco. After dreading the disruption, now Daphne wonders how she'll survive without Sophie. Not that Susan doesn't drive her to distraction sometimes, the way she fills up the house with her clothes, her clutter, her insistent voice breaking in when Daphne's trying to concentrate on her writing, her opinions, her infernal way of turning every discussion into an angry argument. Motherhood has changed her, nevertheless. Daphne was surprised at how placid Susan was, those last uncomfortable weeks of late pregnancy. Now Daphne marvels at Susan's fierceness, a lioness tireless in her vigilance. After she gave up on the idea of practicing law in Boston—the raw winter weather and a couple of disappointing interviews had a lot to do with that, Daphne thinks—Susan negotiated a six-month maternity leave from her old firm even though she was no longer employed there. They really wanted her back. She'll bring the baby along with her to work for a while, she claims, because she plans to nurse for a year. Daphne smiles. A four-month-old in the office is one thing; a crawling baby is something else. But Susan will have to figure that out for herself.

Sophie's eyelids flicker; she sighs, settles into sleep for a few moments, then opens her eyes, squinting in the bright outdoor light. Big eyes, widely spaced on her face. She doesn't look like Susan, or Daphne's memory of Susan at that age. Sophie must favor her father, whoever he is. Does Susan's decision to go back have anything to do with him? Will he ever know Sophie is his child? Will she ever know him?

"Hey, Sophie," Daphne says gently. She's rewarded with a crooked smile. Surely one of Nature's master strokes, that smile, coming so early in life, long before a baby even knows where her own body ends and the world begins. We're bonded for life, Daphne thinks, no matter what coast she lives on. She reaches down and picks Sophie up, carefully supporting her head while she props her on her shoulder, a soft little package wrapped in yellow flannel. Susan believes tight bundling makes a baby feel secure. Daphne steps back into the house and heads for the refrigerator, where Susan has left a bottle of expressed milk. She's gone up to Cohasset to visit a college friend, but she'll be home before the next feeding. In the meantime it's a treat for Daphne to have Sophie to herself. She must feed and bathe her and find some festive little outfit to show her off to Anna, who arrived on the lane this morning and can't wait to see the baby. Her first visit since the trial. They'll both have a lot to say.

Anna arrives not fifteen minutes after Daphne calls her, Dorothea in tow. They're down for a couple of days, just the two of them, to give Jeannine a break so she can study for final exams. Lesley has school, but Jeannine will be there to get her off in the mornings and take care of dinner. Gregory is back in Washington, something to do with that case he was working on last summer, which has dragged on and on and which he's involved with again now that the trial is over.

Daphne has just finished bathing the baby and is changing her when she hears Anna at the door. "We're back here. Come on through," Daphne calls.

Anna wheels Dorothea into Daphne's little bedroom and right up to the bed, where Daphne has set up a changing station with a flannel pad, an enormous stack of disposable diapers, and a basket containing baby wipes, a tube of cream, tiny nail clippers, and a soft little hairbrush. Sophie is lying naked on the bed smiling up at them. "She's grown!" Anna says. "What's it been, two months? She looks twice as big. You know, they look just like pink frogs at this stage."

Daphne laughs. "You're right. It's the legs, angling out the way they do." She takes Sophie's hands and pulls her up to a sitting position. Her head bobs. "Hey Dorrie, this is Sophie. What do you think?" Dorrie's eyes widen and she leans forward in her chair, reaching out toward the baby with her good arm. Daphne sits down on the bed and sets Sophie on her lap where Dorrie can just touch her arm with her fingers. "What do you think? Soft, isn't she? Look, Anna!" Dorothea smiles her crooked smile, and Sophie, whether by accident or design, smiles crookedly back.

Anna and Daphne spend the afternoon happily passing Sophie back and forth between them while they eat the subs Anna has brought for lunch and catch up on everything that has happened. It's been nearly seven months since they've had time for a real visit, undistracted by the stresses of the trial. Daphne has a lot to ask Anna, but first Anna insists on hearing everything about the baby and Susan. Daphne describes Susan's arrival in early December. "She looked big as a house and acted like someone I've never seen, so calm and maternal. I think she was overdosed on estrogen. And then she went two and a half weeks overdue. I would have been climbing the walls, but she was incredibly blasé about it." Daphne lays Sophie across her knees and jiggles her gently up and down. Sophie is making faint complaining noises and squirming uncomfortably, plagued by some vague baby distress.

"She's not the only one," Anna laughs. "Look at you. One would think you'd had twelve kids the way you handle her."

"It's like riding a bicycle, as they say," Daphne answers, chuckling and shifting Sophie back up onto her shoulder. "I thought I would be terrified, but I wasn't, not even the first day. I got to room in with Susan the night after Sophie was born. Just us and the baby, so different from the way it used to be, with the babies all sealed off in the nursery. Isn't she something? Such a miracle."

"Yes," Anna says. "An ordinary miracle. So much joy. It seems like anything is possible." She looks across the room to where Dorothea is happily swaying to the music on her Walkman, the *Goldberg Variations* Daphne has found again for her.

"I think she'll settle now. I'll just put her down in her crib," Daphne says, standing up. Sophie has relaxed and grown heavy on her shoulder. Dear weight. She can feel her eyes filling as she crosses the room. The things we can't foresee, when—oh God—the things we remember to ᐧ fear are bad enough. Moving thousands of miles away across the country. War, earthquake, random violence. Love turned to disaster. Growing up without a father. When she comes back to sit down in her wing chair, she can see tears in Anna's eyes as well.

"Okay, no more baby talk. Dare I ask how the writing's going?" Anna says. She's pulled a tissue out of her pocket and is making some pretense of blowing her nose.

"Hey, I forgot to tell you. I've sold my new book. I've got an advance. It's going pretty well, considering the mayhem around here. I'm getting in a couple of hours a day, sometimes three or four."

"You mean that novel you were working on last summer?"

"No, this is the new one. I guess we haven't talked about it. It's been germinating in there for months, though. I used it as a distraction when I didn't want to buckle down and finish my rewrites. Starting is so much more appealing than finishing, don't you think? Now, voilá, I've got a contract and I'm still correcting galleys on the last one. God help me."

"That's wonderful! Congratulations."

"I don't even like to think about how much my reputation had to do with it. I'm just grateful. And it's coming, just flowing out, so far at least. It feels good."

"Can you talk about it?"

"Not yet. But when you come back this summer I'll give you a draft to read. I think you'll be interested."

They talk about the trial. Daphne feels outraged that two of the boys got off scot-free, and it surprises her that Anna is not more angry about it. "It wouldn't make up for anything," Anna says. "I really believe Jake wasn't the one that thought it up. He's an angry kid, but he's weak. A follower. I met his mother, you know, last fall. I went over there to talk about the kayak, about returning it. She struck me as frightened. I think the father has a temper."

"You talked to her?"

"Yes. I wanted to meet her, to see what kind of a family it was. Those two boys—Phil so sweet and gentle, and Jake so—"

"Out of control?"

"Yes, that's it. He had no way of saying no. How would jail teach him anything about that?"

This isn't what we should be spending our time on, Daphne thinks. The thought of those boys makes her seethe with anger. "The girls—are they over it, do you think?" she asks. "Dorothea seems like her old self."

"She is, pretty much, at least when she's on familiar territory. And I can take her out now, places like the grocery, and here. But situations still scare her, and people—young boys with loud voices mostly, anybody strange who gets too close."

Daphne glances over at Dorothea, who's humming a little, still into the music, looking perfectly relaxed. "She seems just like last summer to me," she says. "And what about Lesley?"

Anna strokes Haephestus, who has crossed the room and jumped into her lap. Daphne smiles at him, lovely big cat, so territorial. Anna's sitting in his chair. "It's been easier for Lesley in a way because she doesn't remember. I don't think it seems real to her. She was fascinated by the trial, read every word in the *Globe*, and got mad at us because we wouldn't let her sit in the courtroom. She handled her testimony very well. I was proud of her. But it's been as if it all happened to somebody else. The trouble's been with the kids at school, all the publicity. You know how eighth graders can be. There have been some nasty remarks."

"Ah yes, eighth grade," says Daphne. "The pits."

"For a long time she just came home every day. Now she's spending some time with friends, but there's still the notoriety. In March the trial was all over the papers and on TV, and that dredged it all up again. She hates being quizzed about it all the time."

Daphne remembers Lesley last summer, how sensitive she was, how hurt over the business with Paul. "Have you thought about another school?" she asks.

"We decided last fall she should apply to private school," Anna says in reply. "She's a really good student and she's never been really challenged. We've just heard she's gotten into Oakley."

"Boarding school?"

"No, no, though that's exactly what Gregory wanted to do—he wanted her to try for St. Paul's. But I wouldn't hear of it. She's too young. He got sent away at fourteen and I don't think he ever recovered. Oakley is a compromise—it's top notch, but it's just across the town line. She can be a day student. And it's all girls."

"How does Lesley feel about it?"

"She grumbles a little, but I think she's more excited than she wants to show. The art program is wonderful, and she met one of the science teachers at the interview who has her intrigued. Sometimes she talks about medicine. She's really bright, you know."

"You don't have to tell me, Anna. I knew that the day I met her. And talented. She draws like a pro already."

"Daphne, I'm not sure I've ever thanked you for befriending Lesley last summer. Giving her that sketchbook. It did a lot for her self-confidence."

Daphne feels a little nudge of guilt, remembering. "I didn't do much for her once Paul entered the picture, if you remember."

"Lesley's forgotten about that. She still talks about going sailing with you. I'm hoping you'll spend some time with her this summer."

"Oh Anna, you really are coming back? I've been hoping, but I've been afraid to ask. I thought maybe you were getting the house ready to sell, and I so want you here this summer. I'm going to need someone to vent to, once Susan and Sophie leave."

"Well, I've had experience at patching you back together, if you remember," says Anna, laughing. Then her face changes; she looks thoughtful and sad. "You'll have some patching to do as well."

"What does Lesley say about coming back?"

"Not much. She has just assumed we will. In spite of everything she seems to feel at home here. Even last fall, with Gregory insisting we had to sell the house, she told him she wants to come back. God knows I want to! Am I crazy, Daphne?"

No, Anna, not crazy, Daphne wants to say. You're my friend! I need you here. But she can't say that now. She looks over at Anna, who has gently put Haephestus on the floor, stood up and crossed the room to straighten out Dorothea in her chair. Dorothea flinches when Anna first touches her, but then opens her eyes and relaxes again. She must have dozed off. The tape has run out, so Anna ejects it, turns it over, and presses the *play* button before coming back to sit down. Daphne looks up at her, amazed as always at the matter-of-fact way Anna does it, spends her days, all day every day, providing whatever Dorothea needs. But then she herself is that way with Sophie these days. Maybe she and Anna are not all that different. "And how does Gregory feel about the house now?" she asks.

Anna sighs and rubs Haephestus, who has jumped back up into her lap. "I don't think he'll fight it any more. He's staying in Washington for the time being. I'm not sure what he's going to do now, about the house or the marriage, for that matter."

"Meaning?"

"Meaning he knows. He says he's tired of fighting."

"About the house, or about you?"

"Both, I think. The irony is we never fought. We just avoided. Now he knows about Demetrius. He saw us together at the courthouse, after the trial."

"What?"

"We were kissing. Demetrius was just comforting me."

"Oh, God."

"We had a confrontation afterwards, over at the house, but since then he hasn't said a word. I think he could go on forever and never even discuss it."

Avoidance—that weapon of emotional cowards, Daphne thinks. She can see what will happen with Gregory—he'll retreat and wait, leaving the decision to Anna, who'll agonize over it and take on all the guilt. There's something cold about Gregory, a passive cruelty that seems to crush Anna, to negate all her warmth. Daphne's seen the way Gregory refuses to look Anna in the eye. What must it be like to live for twenty years with someone who never looks you square in the face? It's as though he doesn't know she's there. Or wishes she weren't. Anna is still cuddling Haephestus, looking apologetic, as if she shouldn't be occupying his chair. Doesn't she ever claim anything for herself?

"Did I tell you we went to therapy all winter? Lesley, too."

"Doesn't sound as though it helped much."

"It helped Lesley. I don't think it did much for us. The whole issue of Demetrius never got out in the open. I told Dr. Bradley about him at one of my individual sessions, but he wanted us to look at the marriage, what's happened between us, without what he calls 'the complicating issue of an affair.' But now Gregory knows about it anyway."

"So what did you talk about, besides the elephant in the room?"

"Well, Lesley was there a lot of the time. The whole way I got Gregory to agree was to persuade him it was for her. What she's been feeling, ever since Dorothea. That way he didn't have to focus on himself. And we made some progress. Gregory's started spending more time with Lesley and being less critical. And she's changed with me, Daphne, and with her sister, though I think some of it is just growing up."

"I'm so glad to hear that. I couldn't bear for her to be damaged, to not get over ..."

Damaged too, she nearly said.

"There's no guarantee she isn't. But I'm hopeful. Dr. B. is, too."

Poor Anna. So much to deal with all at once. At least she's been seeing a therapist. Pray he's a good one. "So—the marriage. Is there hope for it?" Even as Daphne asks the question, she's conscious of what she wants the answer to be.

"I still don't know," Anna says thoughtfully. "Gregory's given up on the therapy sessions, but he says he wants to stay married. 'Let's not rock the boat at this late date,' is how he puts it."

She sighs. "I've blamed him for everything for so long. I've been angry for years and just wouldn't let myself feel it. Blamed him for the way our lives turned out. Demetrius saw that—once he said I'd given my anger to Lesley."

"Oh, Anna."

"The funny thing is I'm not upset. Guilty and regretful, yes, and really worried about how Lesley's going to react. But on the whole, relieved. Glad not to be lying."

"Have you separated?"

Just then the noise of something falling on the floor makes them both turn their heads. The Walkman has slipped off of Dorothea's head, and she has sagged sideways in her chair trying to reach it with her good hand. She is making strange, rhythmic sounds, disturbingly loud. Anna is beside her in a flash, straightening her out, replacing the earphones, finding the music. It takes a long time to quiet her.

Amazingly, she remembers Daphne's question. "We're still in the same house, but I've moved into the guest room. He's had an offer from the firm down there. I think he might take it. It might be the best thing, for all of us."

"He's avoiding, isn't he? Did you ever think, Anna, that maybe that's how Gregory survived, back when he was a kid? Losing his mother, and then what you say happened to him here—"

"He learned it from his father. Now that I know it all, I understand him better. But still, living in the same house and never connecting—I can't do it any more. It's as if I've spent twenty years pushing against a weight, and now all at once it's given way."

"What about Demetrius?"

Anna pauses. "I haven't talked to him since the week of the trial. Part of the deal with the therapy was I wouldn't contact him. God, I don't know. I feel that things between us are impossible now." Anna lifts Haephestus and sets him against her shoulder as she strokes his back. Like a baby, Daphne thinks. Is she trying to calm him, or herself?

"I keep thinking about him and Phoebe, and Camilla. There's been so much damage. Now three generations of damage. I don't know how he's dealt with any of it."

"Then he doesn't know you know about Camilla."

"No. I went to see him, to tell him, after the trial, but that was the night of the fire. It was such a shock—I never told him."

Anna is near tears, Daphne can tell. "I just don't see how things could work out for us. I've tried so hard all winter to put him out of my mind, but it hasn't worked. Maybe I don't deserve him. And Lord knows what he's feeling now. Maybe I'm destined to live alone."

"Hardly alone."

"True. But you know what I mean."

Daphne knows what she means. Alone with Dorothea once Lesley has grown up and left home, with the burden of care there forever, growing older, worrying about the future. But how different would things be with Gregory? Other than financial support, what has he provided? Is it possible that in a few years, when Lesley goes off to college, she could have Anna here on the lane, just across the way, that they could spend late afternoons out on the deck together, sharing the sunset and a bottle of wine?

"I know," Daphne says. "But don't you want to know where things are with Demetrius? At the very least you need to talk. Go see him. Now, today. I'll keep Dorothea for you."

"Oh Daphne, no."

"Why not?"

"What about the baby?"

"She sleeps at least a couple of hours this time of day. And Susan will be home soon. We'll manage just fine. Just go."

"Daphne . . ."

"Go. Now, before you have time to think about it." Daphne looks up at the clock on the mantel. Quarter past three. Susan will be home any minute, and then Anna will feel like she's imposing. "Come on. I'll get your coat. Don't worry about Dorothea; I'll take care of her. Maybe I'll broaden her musical tastes a little—I've got a tape I took off the radio the other day and am dying to listen to—an old recording of the Dave Brubeck quartet."

It works. Anna protests, but Daphne finally gets her out the door. Ten minutes later she hears the car drive past the house, heading for 6A. It's not gone five minutes when Daphne hears Sophie cry, and right on cue, her daughter Susan turning into the driveway.

Ashes

Unchecked winds . . . diluted the rich soils with sand,
dried them out, blew them away.

SEEKING OUT DEMETRIUS is probably madness. I'm breaking my word to Dr. Bradley. On the other hand, Gregory has stopped going to the therapy sessions. He claims it's because he's too busy with the Washington case. He feels he's done what he agreed to, which was to examine his relationship with Lesley. Things are a little better between them these days, when he's here, when she sees him, which is seldom. As for us, nothing has changed since that terrible night of the fire. Mostly he's not here. When he is, the atmosphere is glacial.

Daphne is right; it's better not to think. Just go, and so I do. Back to the house just long enough to retrieve Camilla's picture and the little envelope with the lock of hair. Demetrius will most likely be at West Marsh—this is a busy season. There's ditch clearing to be done, and weeding, and a section where he told me last summer he planned to set out new plants. I know the way, can make the turns without reading the signs. Still, it's a shock when I get there and see the sun shining down on what I last viewed by the lurid beams of headlights two months ago. The bog house is gone, nothing but a black square of ashes and charred timbers.

At first I don't think he's here, but then I see the truck, and then him, over by the pump house near the open shed. He looks up, hesitates, waves. I drive up and stop, get out of the car. It's getting late in the day and the air feels chilly. He looks wary.

"I see the buggy's still here," I say. I have to start somewhere.

"Yup," Demetrius says. "No way to replace that. Genuine Model A. Some collector came and looked at it back in the fall—offered me a bundle for it."

"I'm sorry about the bog house," I say.

"I'm over it. Better it's gone. Too much happened there." He's right, too much just in the past year. Lord knows what other secrets it held, from those other years. Phoebe, probably. Maybe Camilla began there.

Thinking of her makes me remember why I'm here, but Demetrius is still talking about the fire, something about rebuilding.

". . . cousins. Lumber coming end of the week."

"So you'll rebuild?"

"It won't take long. Hardest part was coming up with the cash. The family helped. A nephew in construction I've been helping out. I got a good price. We'll have a barn raising. Bog raising." Demetrius smiles faintly at his own joke.

I'll have to start right in—it's getting late. "I brought you something," I say, "something I found in Phoebe's attic last fall. I thought you might want it. Do you have time to sit in the car a minute?" The air is turning cold, or at least I'm feeling chilled.

Demetrius gives me a puzzled look but follows me back to the car. We get in, one to a side, and I take the envelope out of my pocketbook and hand it to him. He pulls out the picture. He sits there perfectly still, not moving, not saying anything, not even looking as if he's breathing. I don't dare break the silence. Finally he turns and looks at me. His eyes are shiny with tears.

"So. Did Phoebe?"

"No. I found it in the attic, in an old lap desk, with some letters from an old friend."

"That one from Alabama?"

"Yes, Selena. She wrote about Dennis destroying all the pictures. I wondered why there were never any around the house. And then I looked at the picture, her eyes, and there it was."

"Oh, Anna, it's been so long since I've thought about that time."

"Was I wrong to give it to you?"

"This is for me?"

"Yes. And I won't tell anyone. Daphne knows. Phoebe told her before she died, but no one in the family knows, and there's no point now."

"No, no point."

"Did Marte know?"

"I don't think she did. She was housebound by then, and Phoebe never took Cammie over to see her. Marte asked after her a couple times, but we put her off—she might have guessed. I worried Dennis might tell her after Cammie died, but he didn't."

"Dennis was never cruel."

"No, never was. Not on purpose anyway. We were the cruel ones, thinking no one would get hurt."

"Like you and me?"

"There are always other people, aren't there?" Demetrius looks down again at the photograph, then slips it back into its envelope and puts it in the pocket of his flannel shirt. I don't tell him about other smaller envelope that's inside, the lock of hair. He'll find that later. I look at his hair, a little whiter now than it was last summer, the curls at the back of his neck I always wanted to touch. Want to touch now.

I turn to face him, but he keeps looking straight ahead through the windshield at the space where the bog house used to be. "How did you survive, you and Phoebe?" I ask.

Demetrius sighs. "I wasn't sure we would. Phoebe was so guilty Camilla got sick. They had the vaccine by then, you see. They were just starting to give it to everybody. Another year, a few months even, and she would have been all right."

"What did she do, Phoebe?"

"She wouldn't see me. Dennis was crazy for a while after Cammie died, drunk all the time. I ran West Marsh and stayed away. Then one day, about six months later it was, February or March, she called me. She needed help with a tree limb that had come down on top of the garage. Dennis was sick in bed then and I went in to see him. Offered me a beer—can you figure? He said something—can't remember what—about the way things used to be. And things went back more or less the way they'd been, except Phoebe and I weren't . . ."

"But you stayed friends! All of you. How did you do that?" I try to imagine Gregory and Demetrius talking, drinking beer, now, after everything. It would never happen. Of course it had never happened before.

"Don't know. Maybe because we were friends first."

"Did you and Phoebe ever . . . ?"

"Never."

"Not even after Marte died?"

"We'd made a pact. She wouldn't leave Dennis. He was sick a long time, you know."

"And her penance was to take care of him?"

"Ah, Anna, it wasn't like that. Not at all. She didn't think that way, like it was a sacrifice. She loved him."

Not like me, I'm thinking. I'm doing the same thing, taking care of somebody helpless, but resenting it most of the time. And resenting Gregory for not being there for me. Was that what Demetrius was for me, a way to escape the relentlessness of every day with Dorothea? Both

Demetrius and Phoebe had someone they had to take care of, someone they loved. "And when Dennis died?" I go on. I feel guilty, digging at their past this way, but I want to know. I need a blueprint for what's ahead. "After he died, couldn't it have been possible?"

"By then we were a habit. We were good friends. We didn't want to upset that. Can you see the families if they found out, hers and mine too? Too much upheaval. They'd think Phoebe had gone demented and I was after the house." That's just what Gregory did think after Phoebe's funeral, I remember, that Demetrius wanted the house. And what I thought, that day I found out about him and Phoebe.

Demetrius turns and looks at me. It's the first time he's smiled. "Don't feel sorry for us, Anna. It wasn't all tragic. We had lots of time together. We talked every day. We loved each other. The hardest thing was when she died, I had no one to tell."

"I saw you cry, the day of the funeral. It touched me that you were the only one. Is that how it's going to be for us, one of us crying at a funeral with no one to tell?"

"That would be you, Anna, not me. I'm an old man. I'm the wrong age for you. I was the wrong age for Phoebe."

"When did that ever matter?"

We talk a few more minutes, about my girls, about West Marsh, about the house and the stumps in the yard. Eventually Demetrius rests his hand against the side of my head for a moment, turns away, and gets out of the car.

I drive back to Kettle Lane and collect Dorothea from Daphne's house. Susan is there and they are in the middle of cooking supper, so I don't stay. In answer to Daphne's mute question I tell her I'm all right, things are all right.

Later that night I lie in Phoebe's little bed musing about the past, Phoebe's and Demetrius's past. Now we are part of the past, too. What will happen between us? Nothing, for now. But Lesley will grow up, and soon Gregory and I will probably be living apart. Maybe I'll end up here, on the lane, alone, growing older, caring for Dorothea. So many sad things have happened in this house, but the house itself doesn't feel sad to me, not like our Needham house, with Gregory's family orientals, the silent piano, the wide front hall made for welcoming guests we never have. I draw my cold feet up into the warm part of the bed and curl into a ball. I'm tired of thinking. But all the while I can feel where Demetrius laid his warm hand against my face.

I spend another day and a half on Phoebe's attic. With Dorothea here I can't stay upstairs, so I haul down boxes of papers and sit at the kitchen table sorting through them. Gradually the throwaway pile grows: old bills, West Marsh receipts from twenty, thirty, forty years ago. I keep the handwritten ledgers; perhaps Demetrius will want them, or some local historical society. An idiosyncratic collection of magazine and newspaper clippings, most unsorted, slows me down, as I can't resist the temptation to read every one and try to figure out why Phoebe wanted to save it. But late in the afternoon I grow impatient. I start a fire in the cold parlor and feed papers to it, watching the remnants of Phoebe's life curl and blacken and turn to smoke. It's a ritual of sorts. I wheel Dorothea in and station her facing the fire. She likes to watch the flames rising and dying back and sits there swaying happily, humming to some secret rhythm in her mind.

A Visit

When the ice reached a temporary or final stopping place
. . . meltwaters were particularly lively.

THE EYES GIVE her away in spite of all the years that have passed, bright and mischievous, set slightly aslant on her face above apple cheeks, like a cat's. But the dark curly bob in the faded snapshot on Phoebe's mantel has turned pure white, a soft cloud framing her face. She's shorter than I imagined, grown plump with age, but she approaches the little crowd of us waiting at the security barrier with a lively brisk walk. I call her name, *Selena*, and she comes right over to me, her face lighting up with an impish smile.

"I thought that was you," she says. "You might not know Phoebe sent me your wedding picture. I have shoe boxes full of old snapshots someday I'll put in albums and I hunted it up. It was the good Lord's grace I was able to find it." Her voice has the soothing blurry vowels of her native Alabama, and something else, a musical lilt I remember from our conversations on the phone. A young voice. Her face looks young, too, full of animation and high color, though up close I can see that her skin is covered with a network of tiny lines, like a piece of tissue paper that has been crumpled and then smoothed out. I'm amazed that she would know me from a picture taken twenty years ago, but then I recognized her, didn't I? Maybe Phoebe is here at the airport as well, having a hand in it.

I intended to write to her last fall when I realized I had never notified her about Phoebe's death, but after a few days of trying to frame the words, I ended up calling her instead. She was shocked but most gracious, anxious to keep me from feeling guilty. They had last communicated at Christmas, she said, and then she had not written again, so not hearing from Phoebe hadn't worried her. There had been other long silences over the years. She asked about the house—she knew Phoebe planned to leave it to Dorothea—and was relieved that we hadn't sold it. Her husband was very ill, she said, so she would not have been able to come to the funeral anyway. That was why she hadn't responded to my note, as well. Then two weeks ago she called out of the blue. Her husband had died in early spring. She was flying north in mid-June to visit an old college friend in Cambridge and would like to pay her respects to Phoebe. Would I be at the Cape and available to take her to the cemetery?

Of course I would. Meeting Selena face to face would be almost like having Phoebe back, someone who knew her as a girl, who corresponded with her all those years. I offer to meet her plane at Logan and drive her to Cummaquid. She of course must stay with me at the house, I say. It would assuage my guilt over not letting her know when Phoebe died. By mid-June Jeannine's exams will be over; she will be available to look after the girls. Selena and I could stay overnight, and I could drive her back to her friend's in Cambridge the next day. It takes a little persuasion, but she finally agrees. After we hang up, I realize she probably hasn't been to visit since just after Camilla died, back in the early fifties when the Cape was still mostly rural and the trains still stopped at all the little village stations. Yet the friendship survived. Selena wants to be here one more time, to square the real place with the imaginary one she has carried in her head all these years. I can understand that.

I call Daphne, who of course wants to meet her as well, now that she's started on the new novel, Phoebe's story. "I'll take you out to dinner," she offers. "And would you like the house gotten ready? I know someone—she helped out when Sophie was born, Brazilian, a nurse, really, but she's not licensed yet and she's looking for any kind of work right now. She's got two daughters. They could clean the place in a couple of hours."

It's a wonderful idea. It hadn't occurred to me that Selena might be a good deal more fastidious than Phoebe. She's a Southerner, after all. What did she call the Cape in that note she sent with the lap desk, way back when Phoebe and Dennis got married? *The Wilds*. And she's probably thin-blooded. She'll freeze in that drafty house if it's cold and windy. I'll put her downstairs in Dorothea's room, and carry the quilt down from the master bedroom and bring an extra eiderdown from home, a set of our guest towels to replace Phoebe's worn and mismatched ones. And hire the three energetic women to clean the house, though I know from experience that no amount of dusting and vacuuming will make it look spotless or even tidy.

SELENA IS AMAZED at the swift trip from the airport to the Cape. The traffic has not reached summer levels this early in June, and we cross the Sagamore bridge in an easy hour and a half. I turn off the Mid-Cape highway and drive through the picturesque old town of Sandwich. Selena has never seen it before. She's entranced by the old houses, the perennial gardens backed by ancient stone walls. As we start to pass the mill pond in the middle of the village she begs to stop for a moment. "Ducks!" she cries, getting out of the car, as excited as any child. On the way down to the pond we stop in at the old grist mill, where she buys a small bag of cracked corn for the birds and a cloth sack of corn meal for us. "I'll make you spoon bread for breakfast," she says. "Ever had spoon bread?"

"Oh yes," I say, laughing. "My father was from Knoxville. I love it. With lots of butter."

Flocks of ducks and geese swiftly gather as soon as they discover we are offering something to eat. When the supply of corn is gone we settle ourselves on a bench for a few minutes, enjoying the warmth of the sun. I'm no longer worried about impressing Selena. Maybe it's all the references to her in Phoebe's journals, but she feels like someone I've known a long time. I resist the temptation to ask questions about Phoebe; I'll save those for the dinner with Daphne. I ask Selena about herself instead. She surprises me—why do I always assume that her generation of women were all housewives, living circumscribed, conventional lives?

She tells me about her first husband, who died in the war, leaving her with two little boys, and how she moved back in with her mother and took graduate courses, working six years as a teaching assistant while she got her Ph.D. in history and then spending two years fruitlessly looking for a job until she learned to sign her application letters with her middle name. "It's Randolph, luckily," she says without rancor. "It wasn't at all unusual back then to just toss all the letters from women in the circular file. People still thought female professors couldn't possibly be mothers. It was odd enough for us to be married. The irony is I got hired by my own alma mater right there in Birmingham. And there I stayed, and there I met John. He taught physics. He spent our first date explaining Heisenberg's uncertainty principle to me. We never did run out of things to say. I miss that about him, the running conversation."

Funny; Phoebe used the same words to describe her marriage to Dennis. I glance over at Selena and smile, happy for her happy marriage, and envious. That's what Phoebe and Dennis had as well, despite the drinking, the failures, the losses—that running conversation. It's what I wanted, but Greg and I never managed. One of the things, anyway.

We continue through Sandwich and onto the old King's Highway along the north side. This part of the Cape, at least, looks pretty much the way it always did. We stop at Crow farm for fresh eggs and some potted geraniums for the cemetery, then at the Tavern in Barnstable for a late lunch. I run into the village general store for a bottle of wine and a few more supplies for breakfast. It's midafternoon by time we arrive at Kettle Lane. I'm grateful for the pretty weather. Despite the bite in the air there's a deep blue sky and brilliant sunshine.

As we turn into the driveway, Selena sighs. "It's the same," she says. "Oh my, you've kept up the garden!" And with that she lets herself out of the car and heads out back, where the perennials, I have to admit, are putting on a good show even though they haven't been weeded since last August. The early daylilies are all in bloom, along with Phoebe's white bleeding heart and mounds of blue geraniums along the front. Selena bends down for a moment to pick one of the small yellow daylilies and raises it to her nose. "Oh, yes," she says. "So much sweeter than the showy ones that come later in the summer." She sounds just like Phoebe. Have they picked up each other's habits of speech, writing to each other all those years?

"Now I've one more place to see before we go inside," she continues, turning and heading up the hill towards the big rock. I trail after her, wondering if she's planning to climb up on top the way Phoebe did the first day I met her. But she just pauses at its base, looking up, then leans her face against it, her cheek against the stone. "It's warm," she says, "warm as a living body."

"It holds the heat from the sun," I say. "I come up here to sit sometimes on sunny cool days to get out of the wind. Did you ever climb up?"

"No, I was just here the once, after Camilla died, but Phoebe mentioned it so often I feel as if I've spent time here. Even now, it's as if her spirit is here."

I put my hand out and touch the rough granite. It is indeed warm, surprisingly so. Even though the air today feels cold, the sun is at its strongest this time of year. Next week is the summer solstice. We let a little space of silence pass, neither one wanting to intrude on the other's thoughts.

"Gracious, you must wonder why I'm out here wandering around the yard," Selena says at last. "It's just that I don't want to go inside and find her not there."

"Oh, she's there all right," I say. "I don't tell this to everybody, but I think I hear her in the house sometimes, at night, walking in the upstairs hall. She had these fuzzy slippers, lambskin moccasins. My daughter Lesley thinks she hears her too."

"I wouldn't put it past her," Selena says, looking up at me with a sly smile. Then her face turns thoughtful again. "Are you too tired to pay her a visit?" she asks.

"No, I was going to suggest it, the afternoon's so pretty." I'm amused that she would be worrying about me being tired when she's thirty years older. Where does she get her energy? She reminds me of Phoebe, her determination to keep moving. I can imagine the two of them all those years ago at Smith, dashing here and there on their bicycles with their hair flying, not wanting to miss anything.

I carry in our bags and settle Selena in the downstairs bedroom, lay out the fresh towels and the eiderdown from home. The upstairs quilt looks charming on the bed, and there's a jar of white rugosa roses on the table next to it. The house looks and smells clean after being closed up all those weeks. I say a little prayer of thanks for Daphne and her Brazilian work crew.

We take a half hour to settle in before driving to the cemetery. It's only about a mile away, down Mary Dunn's road. It embarrasses me to think that I haven't been there since that day a year ago when Daphne and I walked over to inspect Phoebe's name carved on the plain granite stone she shares with Dennis. The Turnstones arranged that.

Today we go in the car. I bring along a trowel and a bucket of water for the three geranium plants Selena has picked out, a bright coral-red. "Phoebe always hated pink," she said as we looked over the selection back at the farm stand. It takes me awhile to dig through the tough sod to set in the plants. I should have brought a spade, not a trowel. And some clippers to cut back the grass growing at the base of the stone. I'll come back later with some mulch and make a proper planting bed so the flowers won't get lopped off by whoever mows the grass.

While I'm working, Selena wanders back and forth, reading inscriptions. "Quite a flock of Turnstones," she says, smiling at her own remark. "More than Phoebe needed, most likely."

"She didn't like Dennis's family?"

"More that they didn't like her. They didn't approve of her, being from Boston and all that, and with a fancy education. There are all sorts of snobberies, aren't there?"

"How well did you know Dennis?" I ask, thinking how Phoebe's family must have looked down on him.

"I was at their wedding. The Gardeners were even more disapproving than his family, but he won them over. They respected his intelligence. He was clever and funny, and he and Phoebe were so very much in love—everybody could see that. So much laughter when they were together. They had the same sense of irony, a whimsical take on the world, and I think they both felt like misfits in their own families."

"Maybe that's what drew them together. I always wondered."

"Could be. They had a way of making fun of themselves that I don't think they ever lost, even later, when things got bad. As if life were a cosmic joke, and the only possible response was to laugh at it." Her remark gives me pause. Could I ever regard what life has dealt me and my daughters as a cosmic joke?

I have finally managed to dig three holes for the geraniums. I pick up the bucket and pour water into each one, then set the plants and tamp the dirt in around them. The ground is discouragingly hard and dry. I'll have to remember to come over with water until they get established, even though I've never seen the sense in spending time tending graves. My Tennessee grandmother loved visiting the cemetery, now that I remember. She'd sit down on Grandpa's grave on Sunday afternoons and talk to him. Maybe it's a Southern thing. I promise myself I'll take better care of Phoebe's grave, in honor of Selena.

"It's lovely here," Selena says. "It suits her." We stand there together for a while, each with her own thoughts. I'm grateful not to have to make conversation. If I am missing Phoebe, think what Selena must be feeling. All those years of friendship going back to the thirties. Even though they hardly saw each other, the friendship sustained them. They must have written letters back and forth, lots of them. People wrote letters in those days; long distance calls were reserved for momentous events like births and deaths. Old friends are wonderful, I think, standing there next to this lively old lady I have only just met, yet feel akin to. They sustain us through space and time in ways we can't imagine when we are young and a limitless future stretches ahead of us. As we grow older, it's the past that seems more real. And so we treasure those who shared it and know our secrets. Even if they are far away, even gone altogether, we can still keep them with us, the running conversation in our heads, the laughter getting us through.

AFTER AN HOUR to rest and change, we walk across the lane for drinks on Daphne's deck. I introduce them with an odd mixture of feelings, conscious that Selena can offer Daphne a chance to see a different Phoebe, the young girl we can only glimpse in the early pages of her journal. At the same time I'm envious of the two of them. They had the years to spend with Phoebe that I never had.

Daphne greets us at the door with Sophie in her arms, proud to show off her granddaughter. It amuses me no end. Susan appears briefly and then disappears into the bedroom with the baby, leaving us on the deck to talk. Daphne and Selena trade amusing stories about their old friend. I sit between them, wishing I had more reminiscences to share.

Daphne takes us to dinner at the old inn in Cummaquid. She's arranged for us to sit by the window where we have a magnificent view of the harbor. It's a barn-like old place, especially this early in the season when less than half the tables are occupied, but the food is good and the service is unobtrusive.

"How did Phoebe and Dennis meet?" I ask.

"They met here, on the Cape," Selena says. Phoebe was staying with her great aunt in Falmouth. I still remember how she described her—a quirky old dowager with a great mausoleum of a place out by the lighthouse. Dennis was working at a boatyard, fixing engines, and he rescued Phoebe and her friends one night when they got stranded out on an island somewhere."

"One of the Elizabeths, I bet," Daphne interjects.

"The great aunt invited him to dinner to thank him—though Phoebe probably talked her into it. The aunt hated social pretentiousness too—I think Phoebe took after her. Anyway, he came to that huge house, furnished in early Teddy Roosevelt style Phoebe always said, and when the maid brought in the finger bowls he picked up a spoon and took a taste. Phoebe and the aunt nearly exploded trying not to laugh. 'I was led astray by the lemon slice,' Dennis said, and then they all laughed together, and that was the start of things. It got to be one of those little family phrases. Whenever either of them did something embarrassing they'd say it and end up in fits of laughter."

"It still seems an unlikely match," I say.

"Oh my, yes. Opposition on both sides. The only one rooting for them was the great aunt. What was her name? Florence? Frances? I wish I could remember."

The waitress approaches to take our orders. Daphne and I indulge in the lobster special. Selena passes on the lobster, saying they look like enormous crawdads to her, and opts for duck with a cranberry glaze. We all order a cup of the locally famous clam chowder to start.

"This calls for champagne," Daphne says.

How lovely this is, I think, as the wine steward pops the cork for us and fills our glasses. Thanks be to Phoebe, who brought us all together. It's comforting to think that on some lovely June evening far in the future, my friends might gather to enjoy delicious food and good company in my memory. Perhaps when we are gone we don't disappear entirely. "A toast," I say, looking at the empty fourth chair and out the window beyond it, where a great pile of cumulus clouds is beginning to turn rosy in the setting sun. "To Phoebe," I say. And as if we all had the same thought, we raise our glasses to the empty chair and repeat, "To Phoebe."

In the lull between the chowder and the main course Daphne brings up the subject of her novel. I know she is nervous about it because she made me promise not to mention it ahead of time. People have odd reactions about turning someone's life into fiction, she said. And it isn't just that. Daphne doesn't want to offend Selena because she wants her help. Selena knows a side of Phoebe no one else knows.

Daphne pours us all another glass of champagne before launching in. She starts by telling Selena about how she stole the journals out of the house the day of the funeral, and how Phoebe wanted both of us to read them. "Now you must read them, too," she says to Selena. "When I read her words I could hear her voice, clear as day. I guess that was when I got the idea of putting her in a book."

"A biography?" Selena asks. "Her life was hardly a series of adventures."

"No, I mean fiction. Not what happened in her life, but her, her sensibility. And her voice, the sound of it, which I miss."

"I miss it too. It was in her letters. So her secrets will stay secret?"

"Oh, yes. I'll think of other secrets."

"Well, I suppose that's what novelists do, isn't it?"

"All the time. The characters are imaginary, but that isn't to say they aren't patched together from all sorts of snippets—a daughter's hair, a friend's gestures, an overheard snatch of conversation, all pieced together. We hope what we end up with feels real. My characters seem more real to me than the people in my life when I'm writing. And every bit as unpredictable. I never know what they're going to do next."

We are interrupted by the arrival of our main courses. I regard my lobster with amazement. It's been split and cracked apart and carefully reassembled so that every morsel is accessible without a struggle. I squeeze a lemon wedge over a chunk of claw meat and taste it happily. A rare luxury, rich enough without gilding it with butter.

"Selena, you're the one who knows Phoebe best," Daphne goes on. I would love to hear any stories you would be willing to share."

"Oh, I could tell you stories," Selena says with her impish smile.

It's AFTER TEN by the time we get back to the lane. We're too full of champagne and good food to stay up any later, but before I go to bed I gather the pile of Phoebe's journals and carry them downstairs to Selena. "Here," I say. "If anybody deserves to read these, it's you." I give her a quick hug and leave her alone with her old friend.

The Maze

*Nothing . . . is more graceful than the curves of the creeks
through which the tidal waters enter and depart.*

L ESLEY SETTLES HERSELF into the kayak and shoves away from the
shore with the edge of her paddle, gently and steadily so she won't
mar the finish, the way Phil showed her last summer. She loves the paddle
because it's not one of those plastic ones. It's real wood, its streaky grain
showing under the thick spar varnish. The two halves of the handle click
together with a metal sleeve and a button that compresses, then springs
out in one of three positions. A beautiful thing. She'd like to work in
wood, learn to carve. Maybe in art class at her new school. Art will be fun
there, even if nothing else is. At least she knows two girls already, Emily
who was in fifth grade with her, and Sally from up the street who's older
but she's known her forever.

One more hour before high tide, just enough time to make it down
to the far end of the harbor. She's getting good at paddling, and when she
goes with the current she can really fly along and not get tired. It took
a few days to remember how to do it right. She had to keep reminding
herself to keep her arms straight and turn with each stroke. Lead with the
shoulder, like Phil taught her last summer. Awkward at first until her body
got the hang of it again, but now she feels like she can paddle forever. August already. It's weird to get here so late in the summer, with the season
half over. But she wouldn't have given up the trip out West for anything.

This is the longest paddle she's tried so far, something she's wanted
to do since Mom showed her the old map she found in the attic, a
nautical chart of the whole harbor. It's hanging in her room now, in a
frame with glass because it's an antique. You can tell from the way the
ink is faded and the paper is yellowish around the edges. It has the date,
1861, and neat little lines and squares showing all the roads and lot lines
that were here then. What's really weird is how the shape of Sandy Neck
has changed. It was much thicker on the end back then, shorter and
stubbier, like a fist with the thumb sticking out. Demetrius says it gets
longer and skinnier every year, and he should know because he's lived

where he can see it since Aunt Phoebe and Uncle Dennis were still alive, and even before that.

What got her about the map, though, was that when you've paddled and paddled down to what you thought was the end you were really only halfway. There were miles of green marshes with zillions of creeks wandering through and straight ditches dug who knows how long ago. She wants to paddle up one of the creeks, the big one on the Sandy Neck side, and see how far she can go.

She had to tell Mom about it because she'd be gone a long time. After some begging and pleading, Mom was okay about it but made her take a big water bottle and lunch and bug spray and even a whistle to blow in case she got into trouble. Funny to think she would have been scared to go into the marsh by herself last summer. Not now, not when she's been hiking in the Cascades and rigging bear bags to keep grizzlies from getting into the food. For Pete's sake, if she got stuck she could just wade ashore and walk out over the marsh to Sandy Neck beach, couldn't she? But Mom knew somebody, one of the neighbors, who told a story about a man who went duck hunting years ago and never came back. They looked for weeks and they never found the body. Of course that was December. He probably died of hypothermia, something she learned about while she was hiking in the high country. It would be something, wouldn't it, if she paddled around a corner somewhere way up one of the creeks and found a human skull? The thought makes her feel shivery. But she won't get lost. She remembers what Demetrius told her: If you don't know which way to turn, just drift. Let the current lead you out. Funny thought. The kayak will know the way home.

It would be more fun if Phil were here. It's hard not to think about him when she's out paddling in his own kayak. So amazing, the second day she was here and Mom sent her out to the garage and there it was, with the note and everything. Mom said it had been there since Phil's family moved away last fall. Lesley would like to write and thank him but she doesn't know his address. He never gave it to her, and she can't even remember the name of the town. Mom probably knows it but pretends she doesn't. She doesn't want to have to think about that family any more now that things are over. So unfair. Phil never did anything wrong. But Lesley doesn't think about him all the time the way she did last year, just when she's out paddling like they used to do together.

She did paddle up the second creek one time to take a look at his house. A new family's living there now, with little kids. There's a swing set in the yard. It doesn't even look like Phil's house any more. They've built a big wing on one side and a huge deck all across the back facing the creek. Phil wouldn't like it, but then he'll probably never get to see it. It's spooky to think he kissed her. First kiss. She can't even remember now what it was like.

Up ahead is what looks like a house sitting in the middle of the bay. Lesley knows what it is because she and Daphne saw it one day last summer when they sailed down to this end of the harbor. It's for the shellfish farmers, a place for them to keep their stuff. There are clam and oyster farms here, places that belong to different people. They use seed clams, another word to make it sound like farming, as if you could farm the ocean, mark off part of it and say it's yours. It takes much longer than she thought to paddle up to the house. It looks funny, sitting on a raft with two outboard motors on the back, a thing like a lookout tower on the top. Is there a steering wheel up there? She'd like to get onto the raft and peek in, but she can't figure out how to get out of the kayak and there's nothing to tie up with. That would be something, if the kayak drifted away and she got marooned on this raft. She'd have to wait five or six hours, until low tide. By then someone would have spotted the empty kayak and Mom would hear about it and think Lesley was dead. She settles for circling around to get a good look. She startles a few birds, too small for seagulls, terns probably, but they fly back as soon as she's a few yards away. They think it's their territory.

It's still a long way over to the edge of the marsh. The biggest creek is at the end of the harbor near Sandy Neck. Scorton Creek, it's called. She saw the name on the map. It starts out pretty straight and wide, wide enough to sail the Beetle Cat in, a little way at least. Ahead of her she can see the high dunes on Sandy Neck, and beyond them a blue sky over the hidden waters of Cape Cod bay. That's where she went that night with Phil and Jake and Ken and those girls whose names she forgot. The place where the kiss happened. She decides not to think about that—she looks around where she is instead. The tide looks like it has just turned. There's not any current that she can see, but the stems of the tall grasses and the muddy creek banks have a narrow border marking the upper limit of the tide. It's not more than an inch wide, but it will fall fast. She tries to calculate: six hours, ten or eleven feet. Close to two feet an hour. She'll have to keep an eye on that mark so she won't get stranded.

She comes to what looks like a fork and stays to the left, paddling around a big grassy island. Then she sees a group of strange-looking birds, four of them, picking away at the mud bank under their feet. Black and white, too big to be plovers, with amazing thick orange beaks that look like carrots. Oystercatchers. She saw some once last summer with Phil. Phil again. At least he taught her a lot about birds.

The creek takes another sharp turn to the left, facing her into the sun for a long stretch until another turn makes her double back the other way. Even now, at high tide when the creek is full, Lesley is amazed at how closed in she feels. The grasses bordering the creek are three feet over her head, some of them waving fluffy plumes much taller than that. Another corner and the creek narrows down considerably. She could never turn around here, not unless she came to a place where the water pools. More turns, more forks. Every time she chooses to go left. That will make it easier to find her way out. Or will it?

Finally she comes to a place that's so narrow she's afraid she might get stuck. The coarse grasses on one side have been flattened out. She's just nosing the front of her kayak around the next corner when a great noise of splashing and flapping of wings startles her. Ducks, she's not sure what kind except they're not mallards, take off in a flurry of panic. They must nest here. How big would the babies be, this time of year? Big enough to fly?

It doesn't make sense to go any further. She checks the tide mark along the edge of the creek. More than a foot, maybe fifteen inches. She needs to think about turning back, except where can she turn? She might have to paddle out backwards, at least for a while. First, though, she'll take a lunch break. She ships her paddle and lets the kayak wedge itself gently up against the bank. Now that she's stopped she can see there is a current. She feels around for the dry bag down near her feet, hauls it up and opens it, pulls out her big water bottle and a sandwich. Turkey and Swiss on sourdough bread with lettuce, no mayonnaise. Mom didn't forget what she likes while she was gone. The warmish water feels good going down and the sandwich tastes wonderful. She's hungry.

If she were still out West she would have made this sandwich herself, along with enough for seventeen other people. Amazing what she can do now. Figure out a food budget and supplies for eighteen people for three days. Her team would plan the menus, descend on a supermarket out on the highway somewhere. The people in the stores all know the Jacksons, their leaders, because they've been running these trips for years. "Here comes the plague of locusts," one of the store managers said. But then he gave them a good discount and threw in some bruised peaches for free. Then she and her partners—they always did KP duty in teams of four—had to bag everything and divide it up for everyone to carry. Then the cooking and washing up. Amazing that mothers all over the country do it all the time, except most of them aren't cooking for eighteen. Not something she'd want to do every day. The best part is once you've done it, you can coast until it's your turn again.

So much fun, backpacking. She must write to Tiffany tonight. Amazing to find a friend who does art and is really good at it. They've already talked about applying to the same college so they can be roommates. The whole trip so much fun, at least after the first horrible week of rain and blisters and finding out to her surprise that she missed home. She loved sleeping outside, waking in the night and seeing a million more stars overhead than were ever visible in Massachusetts. And the feeling of growing strong, even the ache in her muscles after the days of hiking, learning about rocks and little things like lichen she had never noticed before. Even all the work of KP duty made her feel proud and capable. Knowing she'd made it, that she could survive.

Coming home was weird in lots of ways. Even sleeping in a bed felt strange. One night she took her sleeping bag out to the back yard and lay down on the grass. Too buggy, though, and too much light from all the street lights and cars going by and people's houses.

The really different thing was that Dad was gone, staying down in Washington nearly all the time now. He was gone for a lot of the winter, but he usually came home on weekends. Now he's not coming home. It didn't surprise her too much, after some of the stuff that went on in family therapy. One thing she found out was that some of the feelings she had about her parents were right. They were always so polite to each other. Every other married couple she knew had fights, sometimes even when she was over at their houses. And most of them got silly and joked around with each other sometimes. Her parents were more like robots. And now Dad's gone. She asked her mother if they were going to get a divorce, and Mom didn't get upset and deny it. She just said she didn't know. Lesley doesn't know how her mother feels about it, or even how she feels about it herself. Here on the Cape she doesn't think about him too much, because he was never here much anyway. It's as if she's made a decision not to feel anything until she knows for sure what's going to happen.

The other really weird thing was how relieved she was to see Dorrie. Dorrie almost killed by those boys last fall, and her fault. What if she'd died? There was a dream that kept waking her up while she was away, that

Dorrie had some horrible injury they hadn't found, had started bleeding inside where no one could see and died. She'd come home from out West and Dorrie wouldn't be there, or Jeannine, or her wheel chair or any of her special stuff. Mom would say she hadn't told her because she didn't want to spoil her summer. She'd wake in the middle of the night from the dream and believe it, and be so scared until the next time they came in off the trail and she could call home. "How's Dorrie?" she'd ask her mother, trying to sound casual when her heart was in her throat. But now she's home and Dorrie's fine, almost back to normal, Mom says, except every now and then when she cringes and cries. She wears her Walkman all the time. Funny old Dorrie. Her big sister.

She does feel more grown up. Mom noticed it at the airport. People treat her differently now. Sometimes they even listen to what she has to say. Living with other people around all summer, never being alone, having to get along. If there was one thing the Jacksons couldn't stand, it was a sulk.

The other thing that's happened is she got her period, finally, the week after she got home. Mom hugged her and got teary-eyed and said it's official, she's a woman. Then she took her to lunch at the Thai restaurant in town. Lesley can't imagine having to cope with the mess, every month until she's old. But she didn't feel yucky or have cramps or anything. It's not that big a deal.

Lesley feels relaxed and sleepy, tipped back in her seat, her legs pulled up and extending out over the top of the kayak in the sunshine. Precariously balanced, but the sun feels good on her legs, and as long as she doesn't move, doesn't let herself go out of balance, she'll be all right. Enclosed in this narrow watery place, nothing to see but waving grasses, the blue August sky overhead. No one knows where she is. She could get stuck in here like that missing man, alone where no one could find her.

She thinks about going to see Dr. Bradley with Mom and Dad all last winter, how he kept saying to her over and over, "It's up to you how you want to feel about it." Weird to have her parents all hovering and guilty when she was the one who did the stupid thing. And they're so worried, still, that she's damaged, when she can't even remember anything scary except Jake's hands on her arms when she was trying to wheel Dorrie outside. Even all the awful things people said at school, the trial on TV and all the stories, it was like something she read about, that happened to someone else. The trip out West was to get her away, teach her self-confidence. Well, it worked. And now she's here inside a maze of creeks at

the far end of the harbor. Should she feel trapped, helpless, lost? Or safe
and satisfied, having made it to the very place she's been wanting to go?
"It's up to me," she says out loud to herself.

Lesley sits up and rearranges herself, leaning a little so she can fit her
leg back inside the kayak. All at once she feels it tip under her. She can't
free her leg to brace herself, and the next thing she knows she's in the
water and the kayak is over on its side. She's surprised when she gets her
feet under her at how deep the creek is, above her waist. The boat rights
itself once she's free of it. Not too much water inside, thank goodness. She
feels her feet sinking into the soft mud. Don't let me get sucked under,
she prays wildly, until she feels firmer ground under her feet. The mud is
up somewhere around her ankles. She grabs for the paddle and her water
bottle that have spilled out. It takes her several minutes to get back aboard,
but she finally heaves herself up and scrambles inside, her feet coated with
smelly mud. It takes a long time to stop shaking. But she's not going to
end up disappearing into the marsh, turning into a gruesome story.

The tide has dropped a good two feet. She's got to get going—she
needs to work her way out of the maze of turns while she still can. The only
thing to do is paddle backwards. She's just getting the hang of it when she
finds a spot wide enough so she can maneuver herself around by paddling
backwards and forwards between the banks until the kayak finally points
downstream. There's no way she can remember all the turns she took.
Everything looks the same, with no landmarks she can recognize. The
water is lower now. She seems to be gliding down a long twisting corridor.
But the current is there, pulling her along ever so gently. She only needs
the paddle to fend off the muddy banks when she comes to a turn. The
tide will lead her out, and if she wants to, she can float all the way home.

The Wolf Tree

. . . tradition tells of once-rich forests of oak and pine.

JANUARY 18: Awakened this morning by one of those strange vivid
dreams that stay around all day and yet dissolve once we try to
translate them into words. As always, a peculiar mix of people, times,
and places. D was in it, and I, traveling somewhere we've never been
together—so maddening how the dream recedes as I try to pin it
down! Up-country Vermont. I was there, long ago once, in college,
for a wedding, wasn't it? We were driving up a long hill, young and
laughing as always, full of anticipation as if it were *our* wedding—not
the solemn one at Trinity, but outdoors, the way we imagined we'd
like it to be when we first decided. D's old Ford truck from the war
days, struggling up and over the crest of the hill, and then the whole
valley before us, sugar maples brilliant orange and red, we were almost
there, just in time . . . the anticipation woke me.

All day D on my mind—the young one, from that dream,
before the disillusionments and losses. I was too patient, I suppose—
enabling, they call it these days, but back then there wasn't a word
for that. Staying home during the war broke his spirit, I think, and
wanting to live up to my family's expectations—though not mine!
I was happy a long while. Then all those years trying and failing to
conceive, and then those brief years of betrayal, joy, loss . . . D found it
in his heart to forgive, and we all went on. But in the dream none of
it had happened yet, we were driving over the ridge into a glorious fall
day—I can still see the reds and yellows, maples and birches against
the green of the pines as I write this—and down below, our friends
waiting, something wonderful about to happen.

January 27: The tremendous high storm tides have scoured everything
clean and piled what look like bales of salt hay halfway up the sea
wall in front of Common Fields. Walked past a black and white bird
washed up—puzzled me and sent me to Peterson's, not a loon but a
murre. Sea bird. Rarely seen here unless blown in by gales. Brought

home a gnarled piece of driftwood, cedar from Sandy Neck. The beach after a storm always yields dead things, and beautiful things. Sometimes they are the same things.

February 2: So stiff this morning but determined to walk it off—I will not give in to the nagging of these old bones! Decided against my usual circuit around the marsh—instead walked the other way to Bone Hill where the Audubon has opened a new preserve with trails across the fields and down toward the bay. A smallish tract but nicely various with pasture, marsh, woods, and a little round pond just up from the shore. Remembered the day early in our marriage when D took me to this same property (owned then by one of his many friends or cousins, names lost to time). That was summer, though, and years ago—I recall lawns around the house, daylilies and shrubs. All grown up now and gone wild. And I remembered the stand of white pines—rare now on the Cape and so large it's a wonder they've weathered the years and storms, standing only a few hundred yards from the shore as they do. The ground beneath stays clear of bramble and bull briar, the inviting carpet of needles a soft cushion for picnics and naps. As I remember, we indulged in both—still newlyweds that long-ago afternoon.

White pines elegant with their straight trunks and lovely soft needles in their packets of five—the trunks and branches of these thick and sturdy, overtopping the neighboring scrub oaks. The enormous one we encountered at the edge of the grove—a huge trunk branching out low into five or six limbs, each one bending out and then up like so many thick fingers forming a hand, and above, a shrubby thicket of smaller branches crowding against each other, the whole thing dwarfing the other pines. Nothing elegant about it but powerful. Wolf tree, D called it. Lost its leader when it was young, he said, broke off in a storm most likely, but put out all those vigorous branches to compensate—many trunks now instead of one. Lumbermen cull them because they don't make good boards and steal space from other, straighter trees.

The trail goes right by it and I was glad to greet my old friend. Gnarled and awkward but still very much alive—all those thick graceless trunks pushing up toward the light without regard for original design. Then again, whose life goes according to plan? Our parents hand us one set of blueprints and we devise another. In the end neither has much resemblance to the house we find ourselves inhabiting.

I have been dipping into Phoebe's journals again now that I am going to part with them, at least for a while. It's strange how Phoebe's mind returned to her early days with Dennis in those last few entries, looking back on her life—could she have had a premonition? I'm reminded of what her friend Selena said, that morning back in June when we sat at Phoebe's old kitchen table in our nightgowns and robes, warming ourselves with cups of tea. "I love this," Selena said, "sitting where she sat every morning. Now I'll be able to see her in my mind's eye, in her proper setting."

"Not the setting her mother envisioned for her, I imagine," I said, thinking about the way Selena had described the Gardeners the night before.

"The right setting for Phoebe in any case," Selena replied. "She loved this place. It nourished her imagination. Some people have no inner lives, so they keep trying to fill themselves up with things, or accomplishments, or social status. Phoebe never needed any of that."

I sat across the table from her, thinking about my own mother, my own upbringing and the messages I had internalized. What did I use to fill myself up? That life I built with Gregory, successful according to all the usual measures, marriage to an Ivy League lawyer from a good family, handsome and successful, the charming old house in a comfortable suburb, and of course my obsession with Dorothea's talent, the way I organized my life around it, to the neglect of Lesley, Gregory, myself. Used it to fulfill myself. *Fulfill*, a funny word. To fill up the empty places. Isn't that the loss I've been grieving about most, these past six years? The center of my life, gone. I'll have to find something else to give it meaning now. Is this the gift Phoebe mentioned in her letter about the house?

Selena had more to say about Phoebe. "Some people are born in the wrong place, or into the wrong family, or at least they feel that way."

"Don't all children have a fantasy sometimes that they were adopted," I said, "that there are other, more suitable parents out there somewhere? I know I did."

"Well, yes, I suppose, but most of them outgrow it, don't you think? But some people truly seem to be misfits. If they're lucky, they find where they belong. Phoebe did." Then Selena sighed, and gazed into her empty teacup as if she might be trying to read the future. "I, on the other hand, always thought I wanted to get away, and found out I was in the right place all along."

It wasn't until we were in Cambridge saying goodbye that Selena mentioned the journals. She had stayed up most of the night reading them. "You can't know how grateful I am," she said, her eyes swimming with tears. "I want to return the favor. You know, I have every letter Phoebe ever wrote to me. I want you and Daphne to read them. They'll fill in some of the empty spaces."

THIS EVENING I'M returning the journals to Daphne, who's been working all summer on her new novel that has a character based on Phoebe. It's set here during the forties. But when she is through with them, they will come back to this house. They belong here. I want them for Lesley. I see Phoebe in my daughter, her naturalist's eye, her love of solitude and ocean and wild weather. I looked out just now and saw her gazing at the harbor, up on Phoebe's rock. She has made it her own.

It's hard to believe another summer is over, or that it's been a year since that terrible night. I have been folding and packing clothes and linens all day. We'll drive home this evening and Lesley will go to an orientation session at Oakley tomorrow afternoon. Classes start Thursday. As always I think of fall as the real start of the year, so much of my life organized around school schedules, first my own and then the children's. The bright warm weather has held, not like last year when the hurricane seared the landscape and brought an abrupt end to everything. But the sunlight is losing its strength, the days are noticeably shorter, and the first tinges of red are starting to show around the edges of ponds.

I have had few real conversations with Demetrius, though he shows up regularly to mow the grass and work away at cutting up the enormous pile of downed branches from the hurricane last summer. I drove once past West Marsh, but I didn't stop. The new bog house is up, looking raw and too big. In just a few months the brazen color of the cedar shakes will weather and blend into the landscape. Demetrius and I are awkward around each other. The longing is still there, but everything that has happened hangs between us. Still, I feel comforted having him around. And Lesley likes it when he's here. She keeps him company sometimes when he's out back splitting wood, and they talk easily, about fishing, about his uncle the rum runner, about the Cape when he was a boy.

After the year-long trauma I feel as if I have my girls back, more or less. Lesley came home from her backpacking trip looking and acting years older. I'm grateful I didn't insist that the Petersens take back the kayak. She's spent hours in it, out exploring the harbor. And Dorothea is her old self most of the time, the sudden stiffening and fits of terror now few and far between. They happen most often around strangers, men and boys, loud music leaking from passing cars, people approaching her suddenly or getting too close. She remembers, that's clear, and probably always will. But it is no longer the center of her consciousness.

Jeannine has not been here this summer, though she will live with us one more school year, her senior year, before she goes out into the world who knows where. She is in love with a senior from Boston College. It's made her bloom. Even her pale complexion seems rosier.

Her replacement this summer is Natalia, the Brazilian woman who helped Susan after her baby was born, a registered nurse in her own country who is reduced to doing home care until she can get certified in Massachusetts. A voluble, warm-hearted woman of endless energy, she shows up every morning at eight to help out with Dorothea. In exchange she's trying to talk me into working at the Literacy Center in Hyannis. When she found out I had taught ESL classes all those years ago, she was relentless. "Come and live here, Anna. Bring my Dorrie back for good and teach English." In the end I drove over to Hyannis one day and sat in on her class. Yes, they are desperate for teachers, and someone with experience would be welcome. They provide all the training and materials. The classes are mostly in the late afternoons and evenings because the students all have jobs. It doesn't pay much, but it's exciting to think about, a possible future path to take.

Not now, of course. Lesley has five more years of school, though she may end up wanting to board at Oakley her junior and senior years. Gregory is already pushing that idea, since he couldn't persuade her to consider St. Paul's. Only three years more and she may be gone.

Where will I be in three years? In Needham, with Gregory? The possibility seems less and less likely. The marriage already feels over, although neither of us has brought up the subject. Gregory is gone now, in Washington ninety per cent of the time. I think there is a woman there, but I avoid facing my feelings about that. Most of the time it's a relief to have him away. At least the question of the Cape house is settled. Gregory has never said why he capitulated, but I think it has to do with the gloves I found in the trash. Or maybe he sees it the way I do, as a place for me to go. Still, we hang on, the words *separation* and *divorce* not yet part of our vocabulary, though we sleep separately and talk about nothing except family logistics. What I expected would be a terrible rending has been nothing of the kind. We have simply fallen apart, gradually, silently, like an abandoned house decaying slowly away. One thing I know: living in Needham, with Gregory gone and Lesley off at boarding school and then college would be impossible. Our friends' lives are organized for couples. Better a clean break from that world.

What I do have, thanks to Phoebe and this shabby house I have grown to love, is a possible vision for the future. For six years now I've been afraid to think ahead. Now I can imagine ten years from now, Lesley out of college and on her own, Dorothea here with me still, but room for a life. My life. Teaching people like Natalia, perhaps, work that matters, work I know how to do. Living to the rhythms of the tides, the seasons. And Demetrius? Ten years from now he will be in his seventies. A vigorous old man. Not so old. We could be friends, maybe lovers still. Daphne still here, just across the lane. And others I haven't met. Enough to make a life.

The Kettle Pond

*The Pleistocene has ended, but have the Ice Ages? We
cannot be sure.*

Pᴀᴄᴋɪɴɢ ᴛʜᴇ ᴄᴀʀ takes longer than I thought it would, and I have
to drive into Yarmouth Port to get a pizza for the girls. It's almost
six o'clock before I get over to Daphne's. I hate the thought of leaving
her behind. We've seen a lot of each other since Susan and Sophie flew
back to San Francisco at the end of July. She misses them more than she
thought she would. She fetches us each a glass of wine and leads me out
onto the deck. The air feels damp and cool, washed clean by the rain. The
trees are still dripping a little but the sky is nearly clear, a chilly pale blue,
the color of September, of fall coming. The sun is low, shining in our eyes
through the trunks of the locusts. It is setting earlier these days—summer
is almost over. Once again I am struck by how perfectly round the pond
looks. It is barely riffled by a breeze we can't feel, nearly still, mysterious,
full of light.

"This is such a magical place," I say, looking down at the silvery water.
"To think it was a block of ice once. One of the things I love about living
on the Cape is feeling the past all the time, not just Phoebe and the house
but the long ago past, before any of us."

"Yes, it's like living in a village in Asia Minor and having an
archeologist tell you that somewhere under your foundation is Troy."

"Or hitting something with a shovel in your pasture and finding a
skeleton with a pot on its head. It changes your perspective! What I've
been doing, over there in Phoebe's house—it's a sort of archaeology."

"Reconstructing her?"

"Yes. I so wish we hadn't wasted the chance to be friends. We took to
each other right away, and then never saw each other more than once or
twice. It makes me sad. I keep feeling she wants to tell me something. If I
were superstitious I'd say she's there sometimes. I keep thinking I hear her
coming down the hall—remember those funny woolly slippers she wore,
that swishing sound they made?"

"You think you hear Phoebe's ghost?"

"I don't know. Lesley tells me she hears her, and nobody's more matter-of-fact than Lesley. Could we both be imagining things?" I look over at Daphne, who is gazing out over the pond. I think again about how lovely it must be to have this view in front of her every day, what an inspiration.

"Our rational minds miss a lot, that's one thing I've come to believe," Daphne says.

She chuckles and pulls her sweater around her shoulders. It's growing cool. "I don't believe in ghosts, but I do believe dead people speak to us," she says. "They're like our dreams. I read somewhere that all the characters in them are aspects of ourselves. Maybe once people are dead we turn them into dream images, into whoever we need them to be." She pauses to take a sip of wine. "Or maybe people we would like to be ourselves. Am I making any sense?"

"Oh, yes, yes you are," I say, filled with gratitude for the chance to have conversations like this, full of speculation, stretching the mind. For years I didn't think at all, too busy with the physical demands of getting through the day. My mind flashes back to the first afternoon I was here, nearly a year and a half ago.

"You make me think about my mother," I go on. "She was a stiff woman, so wrapped up in appearances, not ever one for heart-to-heart talks. But she had all these little sayings—folk wisdom that I think maybe she heard from her mother. I never got along with her while she was alive, but now that she's gone she keeps popping into my mind as a sort of commentator. I keep hearing her little mottoes and proverbs, but the pressure, the disapproval I always felt around her—that's all gone." I add, "Do you think Phoebe thinks she has unfinished business? That we need her? Isn't that why ghosts hang around?"

"The important thing is what you think."

I take a sip of my wine, remembering the night of the fire when I thought I heard Phoebe in the hall. She woke me, and I ended up looking for Demetrius. "I know she's always fascinated me—maybe because she never seemed to care what people thought. She was oblivious to all those little social rules we all turn ourselves inside out trying to follow."

"Well, she was the victim of those rules, or would have been if she'd been the kind of person who cared about them. Her family wrote her off when she married Dennis and moved away from their precious Boston. In those days living on the Cape year round was like being in Siberia. And Dennis's family snubbed her precisely because she was from Boston, because they assumed she looked down on them. And Dennis—well you knew how he was. You don't have to contend with anything like that."

"No, I don't. I have to contend with Dorothea."

"I guess we all have something we have to contend with."

I look over at Daphne, remembering my first impression of her the day of Phoebe's funeral and how wrong I was, Daphne living here on her own, escaping from her past, and now missing the daughter she lost and got back and lost again. The granddaughter she never expected, now thousands of miles away. "Well," I say, "one thing Phoebe gave us is each other."

"She's the connection, isn't she? Remember the time I told you I thought she was a witch?"

"It's funny, the three of us. We've all lived here and gotten entwined in each other's lives. And yet we're so different."

"You're right there. I'm so turned inward, living here by myself with nobody to be responsible for except the cats. Spinning webs. You called me a spider once, remember? It's a selfish sort of life."

There was a time when I saw Daphne as selfish, but now the word makes me angry. "No, it isn't selfish. Don't you think what you write has any value? Your gift is words, putting into words what the rest of us feel and have no language for. That novel you wrote about growing up—I remember reading it and feeling how much grief there is at the end of childhood, all the loss we feel, for those illusions we have when we're little, that our parents are invincible, that the world is there to yield whatever we want, that we'll always be safe. I never realized until I read your book that children have to grieve over losing all that."

"What's lovely thing to say," Daphne says, smiling at me. "You can always win me over complimenting my writing. I'm such a cynic. I don't trust people. You do. You complained once about being innocent. But that innocence is wonderful. People respond to it, it makes them hopeful. I'm so territorial. I throw up walls so I won't be invaded. I'm lonely sometimes, yes, but in my heart of hearts I know I was meant to live by myself. But you—"

"—were meant to live with other people?"

"Yes, you were. You take care of people. You're good at it, and people know it. You give people what they need, instinctively. It's not an effort for you. You don't make people think they owe you something back. Remember the day I broke up with Paul, and you came over and made me lunch and rubbed my back?"

I nodded.

"The tears in my ears afternoon?" Daphne laughs. How amazed I was to see her in such a state. What insanity love leads us to sometimes, I think, how narrow the line between comedy and tragedy.

"You'd have done the same for me," I say.

"No, I wouldn't. Not in the same way, at least. I wouldn't know how. I wouldn't have caught on that you were desperate. But you caught on and were over here in a flash. You're a caretaker."

"I'd say it's more I got forced into it," I say, thinking about the girls back at the house, the need to get on the road soon.

"It's what you're in the world to do. You know, I believe Phoebe—I think she arranged for us to be friends. She knew we'd learn things from each other, that you need to be a little more like me, to fight harder to make a space for yourself, and I need to be more like you, willing to take time, to give, to care—"

"Willing? Willing? What does willing have to do with it? What else can I do?" My voice has gone shrill; I burst into tears.

Daphne reaches across and puts her hand over mine and pats it. It's an awkward gesture; she's not the kind of person who touches easily. "Easy, easy. Sure, you got a bad deal. It must be overwhelming sometimes. Of course you want some freedom, some time for yourself. But what would you do if you had it? You'd find someone else to take care of, I bet. You know what I think? If Dorothea hadn't happened, you'd have invented her."

The outrageousness of what Daphne has said stuns me, but I know there is at least a little truth in it. What would my life have been like if that medical disaster hadn't happened? That year Dorrie was twelve—I had just begun working part-time in the high school library. I liked it, loved being there with the students coming and going, the air buzzing with their energy, their humor. I liked helping them find what they were looking for, easing them past their confusion, making them believe in their own competence, using my ESL training to tutor two Vietnamese girls in English. I had even considered starting on a graduate degree. It had been years since I'd thought about that, until Natalia started prodding me. Years of despair and hope and grueling physical work. The lawsuit, Greg's stony anger, having to live the nightmare all over again. But then, finally, there was enough money. We could have hired someone full time to stay with Dorothea. I could have gone to school, I could have worked if that was what I wanted to do. Could have, and didn't. Was it what I wanted to do? Is it what I want now? If Dorothea didn't exist, if, God forbid, she'd been killed by those boys, what would I do with my life? The concept forms in my mind like a vast open space, like being alone out on the bay with the tide out, beautiful but empty, nothing, no one around me. Would I feel afraid? Or free?

"You're not the only one with someone to take care of," Daphne is saying. "There are lots of Dorotheas around—most of them just aren't so easy to spot. Think of Phoebe."

Yes, Phoebe. I've thought of little else since I arrived in Cumma-quid—the Phoebe of the journals, growing old and lame but still out there in the garden and down on the bay glorying in the world around her, joyful—"I do think of Phoebe," I say. "She was happy, in spite of what everybody thought. She didn't rage against what she was dealt. How did she do it?"

"Phoebe lived in her mind. She had this wonderful imagination, this intense inner life. And she had a gift for happiness, I think. It was a talent, like perfect pitch—it was hard for her to realize everyone doesn't have it. She said to me once, when she walked out on the flats with me one morning after Dennis died, one of those blue days in late September. 'You know,' she said, 'it's so glorious. I used to come out here and forget all about Dennis. I'd forget to be miserable for him.'"

"A talent for happiness. That's it. That's what I want to learn from her."

Daphne smiles at me. "I don't know if it's something we can learn. I think we all go through life in a habitual frame of mind, happy or miserable or somewhere in between. What happens to us doesn't have a lot to do with it. And anyway, I think you do have it. How in God's name could you have survived the past five years without it?"

"And you, are you like Phoebe? Do you forget to be miserable?"

"Ah. I'm the other way around. I got rid of everything I thought was making me unhappy. I cleared it all out, things, people, everything that would get in the way of my work. There's nothing here I have to tend to, except the cats. But sometimes I forget to be happy. It's a terrible thing I've done, getting rid of all my scapegoats. Because if I still can't do it, if I fail, I have no excuses."

"Do you think that's what Dorothea is?"

"What do you mean?"

"My excuse? I used to think to myself—back before the operation, when Dorothea was whole and it was dawning on us how talented she was, how gifted, really, that she was my ace in the hole, that no matter what else I did in my life I had given this wonderful child to the world, somebody who'd bring music—it justified my life. Then all that was gone."

I'm surprised to feel tears spring into my eyes. The loss hits me again, the way it does, unexpectedly, over and over. But I need to go on, to say what's forming in my mind. "Maybe she's still my ace in the hole. Greg accuses me of being obsessive about her, of being attached to her like a new mother to her baby, and it's true. Maybe I've kept on using her to justify my life, telling myself no one can meet her needs the way I do."

"Ace in the hole, interesting phrase," Daphne says with the suggestion of a smile. "Dennis was Phoebe's ace in the hole, you know. He was her excuse. He freed her from all sorts of obligations she didn't want to take on in the first place, that she moved all the way down here from Boston to get away from."

"We thought of her as trapped, and she thought of herself as free. You know, Phoebe said a funny thing about Dorothea in that letter she left for me: 'She has gifts for you yet,' she wrote. I didn't know what she meant then, but now I think I do."

We sit on the deck for a while, both of us conscious that it is time to say goodbye, neither of us wanting to be the one to say it. The sun has disappeared behind the underbrush on the far side of the pond. A chill rises from the water, making me remember that once thousands of years ago it was frozen solid, a chunk of glacial ice. As the air darkens, the pond seems to gather more light into itself until I begin to imagine it not as water at all but as a piece of sky, the way Thoreau saw Walden as a lower heaven. How many times did Phoebe sit here like this with Daphne, watching the day and the summer drain away? And how many times will I get to sit here again?

It's growing late, and chilly. Lesley will be wondering where I am, and we have a long drive home. But I don't want to leave, because once I do summer will be over. "Summer is over on the Fourth of July," my mother used to say. But it isn't, not as long as we are here together watching the night coming down, the pond below us not ready to yield to it yet, holding on to the light.

Acknowledgments

Fɪʀꜱᴛ ᴀɴᴅ ꜰᴏʀᴇᴍᴏꜱᴛ, my gratitude goes to Sena Naslund, *sine qua non*, whose wise advice, encouragement, and enthusiasm for this project have sustained me from the very beginning in ways I can never repay.

To Barbara Blau Chamberlain, whose beautifully written geology book *These Fragile Outposts* provided me with a title and symbolic framework for *The Ice Margin*.

To Hepzibah Roskelley, Carla Topper, Bob Finch, and Leslie Daniels for providing useful insights on various versions of the novel; to the By the Sea Book Club of Ormond Beach, Florida, for their support and generous hospitality, and to Bob Keane for providing careful editorial notes and a male perspective.

To my student Philip Field for helpful advice on police and court procedures.

To the Cape Cod Museum of Natural History for its professional-quality training in the history, geology, and wildlife of Cape Cod; and for its interest and support in promoting *The Ice Margin*.

To the faculty and staff at the Spalding University brief-residency MFA in Writing Program for providing the nourishing atmosphere of a community of writers, most especially Bob Finch, Julie Brickman, Jody Lisberger, and Dianne Aprile.

To everyone at Fleur-de-Lis Press who collaborated to turn *The Ice Margin* from a digital typescript to a book, especially Karen Mann for her patience, her guidance through the complexities of the publishing process, her meticulous editing, and her eagle eye for spotting chronological discrepancies. And to Jonathan Weinert, for beautifully capturing the spirit of the novel in his book design.

To Virginia and John Heyburn and their children, who have taught me everything I know about confronting misfortune with courage, humor, and grace.

And with gratitude for the love and support of my children: Kate, Lisle, Laura, and Clay; my "in-law" sons and daughters Mark, Rebekah, Davey, and Lisa; my late father, Louis Frank Woodruff, who took a small girl walking on the beach and taught her how to see what was there; and Ann, Virginia, and Roscoe, the joys of my life, who walk on the beach with me.

The Fleur-de-Lis Press is named to celebrate the life
of Flora Lee Sims Jeter
(1901–1990)